AN EYE FOR GLORY

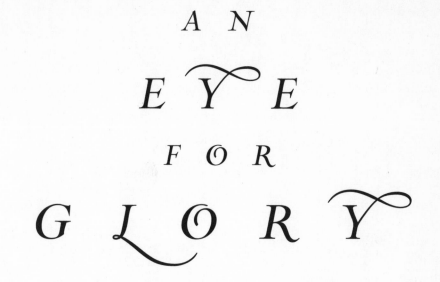

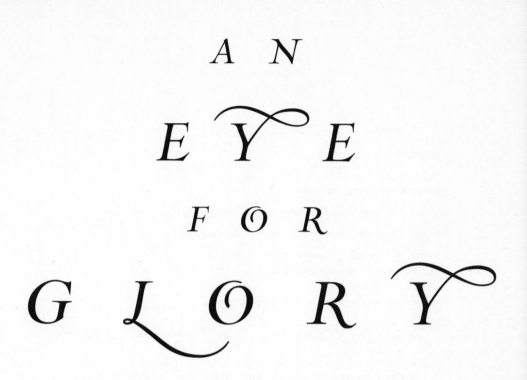

AN EYE FOR GLORY

The Civil War Chronicles *of a* Citizen Soldier

KARL A. BACON

ZONDERVAN.com/
AUTHORTRACKER
follow your favorite authors

ZONDERVAN

An Eye for Glory
Copyright © 2011 by Karl Bacon

This title is also available as a Zondervan ebook. Visit www.zondervan.com/ebooks.

This title is also available in a Zondervan audio edition. Visit www.zondervan.fm.

Requests for information should be addressed to:

Zondervan, *Grand Rapids, Michigan 49530*

Library of Congress Cataloging-in-Publication Data

Bacon, Karl A.
    An eye for glory : the Civil War chronicles of a citizen soldier / Karl A. Bacon.
        p.   cm.
    ISBN 978-0-310-32202-3
    1. United States—History—Civil War, 1861-1865—Fiction. 2. Soldiers—United
States—Fiction. I. Title.
PS3602.A3532E94   2011
813'.6--dc22   2010044402

All quotations from the Bible are from the King James Version.

Any Internet addresses (websites, blogs, etc.) and telephone numbers printed in this book are offered as a resource. They are not intended in any way to be or imply an endorsement by Zondervan, nor does Zondervan vouch for the content of these sites and numbers for the life of this book.

Cover design: James Hall
Cover illustration: iStockphoto®
Edited by Sue Brower, Dave Lambert, and Bob Hudson
Interior design: Beth Shagene
Interior illustrations: Ruth Pettis

Printed in the United States of America

11 12 13 14 15 16 /DCI/ 23 22 21 20 19 18 17 16 15 14 13 12 11 10 9 8 7 6 5 4 3 2 1

The citizen soldier:
fearless in battle
industrious in peace

INSCRIPTION, CIVIL WAR MONUMENT,
NAUGATUCK, CONNECTICUT

For which cause we faint not;
but though our outward man perish,
yet the inward man is renewed day by day.
For our light affliction, which is but for a moment,
worketh for us a far more exceeding and eternal weight of glory;
While we look not at the things which are seen,
but at the things which are not seen:
for the things which are seen are temporal;
but the things which are not seen are eternal.

2 CORINTHIANS 4:16–18

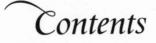

Contents

Acknowledgments

FOR ALL MY HELPERS ALONG THE WAY, FROM ADELE AT THE start to Julia at the end, and for the love and support of my wife, Jackie, throughout, I give thanks and praise to the One who has supplied my every need.

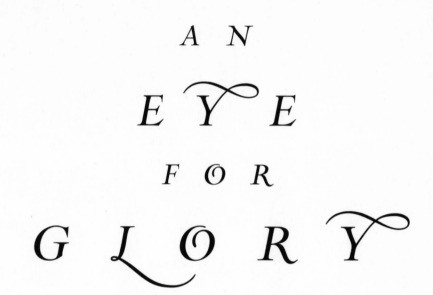

AN

EYE

FOR

GLORY

August, 1882

To My Dear Children—Sarah, Edward, and James,

You may be wondering why, at this time in my earthly pilgrimage, some twenty years since my enlistment in the Union Army, I should pen such a manuscript as this. You have asked me countless times to tell of my experiences during the Great War of Rebellion. Until this writing I have always answered with but small morsels of the story, and I never satisfied your appetite with a full and true accounting of what occurred, perhaps because I was not inclined to recount the many dark and painful memories. So many good friends, brothers in arms and in the faith, were lost, and I still mourn each one. That I survived the war, and returned to the bosom of my family, can only be attributed to the abundant mercy and grace of our Almighty Father, for I deserved no such mercy, no such grace.

The recent death of your mother, my dearest Jessie Anne, has once again caused me to consider the brevity of my own earthly existence. Although I am not yet an old man, at least so far as I think of it, I do not know when I shall be called to put off this earthly tent and receive my eternal inheritance; then who shall write of these things? You are older now—Sarah has married, Edward shall shortly marry, and James has but one year of school remaining—so it seems prudent to set down on paper these remembrances of the war before the memories fade forever.

A soldier's life is filled with long stretches of interminable boredom in camp or on the march, broken only by short periods of confusion and terror in battle. Throughout the war, I kept a series of journals in which I recorded my experiences. As I filled each journal with notes and musings, I posted it home and your mother sent me a new one. The writing of these journals and letters helped me immeasurably, during both pleasant days and not, to pass the time in a more fruitful manner. She also preserved every letter I ever wrote to her and I kept most of her letters to me. These have served well to refresh my memory. I have included several of those letters, either in part or in their entirety, so that you might better understand how we were sustained throughout those long years. However, the more personal contents of these correspondences shall forever remain between your mother and me.

No man could wish to have three finer children. When I think that not only do you not harbor any ill will toward me, but that your love for me has remained steadfast and undiminished through all these years, I can only marvel at God's goodness. Your mother was certainly the primary instrument of this goodness, since for such a long time, I had little to do with your rearing and did little deserving of your affection.

And so I write to you, Sarah, Edward, and James, and to your children after you, not as excuse or explanation of my actions, but rather as confession, for surely I was granted a most profound and gracious forgiveness, by yourselves, by your dear mother, and by God, for which I am sincerely thankful.

May these words also serve as a memorial, not of me and of what I did, but of the fallen, those noble men who fought "with firmness in the right, as God gave us to see the right."

With sincerest affection
I remain your loving father,

Michael Gabriel Palmer

CHAPTER 1

Over the Mountain

Why art thou cast down, O my soul?
and why art thou disquieted within me?
PSALM 42:11

GENERAL RENO'S CORPSE WAS THE FIRST I SAW DURING THE war. As the hour approached midnight on Sunday, September 14th, 1862, the thoroughly winded green recruits, among which I was proud to be numbered, crested South Mountain at Turner's Gap. The march from Frederick, Maryland, had been long and hot, with few breaks for coffee and rations. When, during the course of the afternoon, the men heard the din of fighting erupt, and when they saw battle smoke enshroud the long ridge ahead of them, each untested man looked about at his mates. He saw jaws clenched, faces drawn, skin pallid, and eyes wide with fear and uncertainty, countenances that mirrored his own.

With nightfall the battle clamor ebbed, then stopped altogether as the men toiled up the mountain toward the gap. All were eager to end the day with a hot cup of coffee and a peaceful night's sleep.

An ambulance was parked in the grass next to the road. A mule hitched to the front of it stamped nervously as we passed. At the rear of the ambulance a single torch of pitch blazed and a lone soldier stood guard, head low to his chest, stoop shouldered. He stirred at our approach, raising his head slowly, as if with great effort.

"What unit you boys with?"

"Fourteenth Connecticut Volunteer Infantry of French's Division," someone answered.

The sentinel stood with his back to the torchlight, his black slouch hat pulled low, casting his visage deeply in the shadow of the half moon. He appeared a faceless phantom, breathing and moving as one of the living, but when he spoke, his voice was hollow and lifeless.

"Did you hear about General Reno?" He waved at the ambulance behind him.

No one said a word.

"Major General Jesse Lee Reno—a great patriot, a soldier's soldier, a true fighting man, not like some of these other dandies we have. We loved him like a father." The man spat at the ground. "Now he's dead." The man shook an upraised fist at the darkness to the south. "My general. He's dead and I wouldn't believe it unless I'd seen it myself. We'd already whipped those devils, but they just shot him down as they turned to run." The man lowered his head to his chest again, his voice a murmur. "He died with the setting of the sun."

Still none of us had any words for him. Our feet began to shuffle forward, leaving the sentinel to resume his mournful vigil.

"The night will be long and dark," he called to anyone within earshot. "What will become of us now?"

A few minutes later we came upon a large field. Gasps of horror arose from the column as spectral shadows flitted from place to place about the starlit meadow. But as our eyes adjusted, the shadowy figures turned out to be some of our own troops. There had been a great and bloody fight upon that mountain and our boys had won it, but there had been many casualties, both Union and Confederate. Burial details worked by torchlight on both sides of the road, moving from one black heap to another, checking for any signs of life before tagging the body for interment. The bodies of our Federal comrades would be the first to be retrieved. If time and will allowed it, the enemy dead would also be buried, albeit in cursory fashion. Otherwise, their corpses would be left to the elements and their rotting flesh would see yet another battle, this time between the birds of the air or the beasts of the field which would carry off the choicest parts.

The regiment was ordered off the road to camp for the night in this field of death. We moved slowly among the corpses,

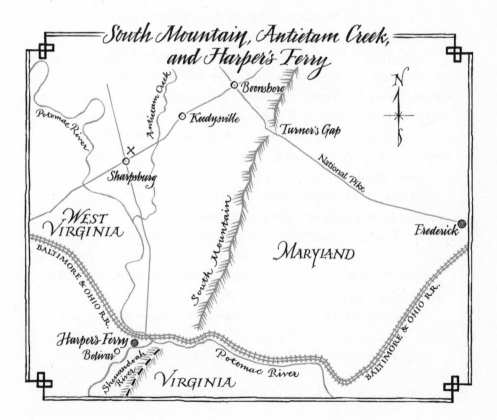

carefully trying not to stumble over them in the darkness or tread on any flailed appendage. Some of the men were fortunate to find enough room to spread out their rubber blankets and build campfires, but for most, the stiffening, bloating corpses of the enemy dead had to be moved aside and even stacked one upon the other to clear sufficient space. It was the first time I had seen dead bodies like that. I had been to several memorial services in our church, but the body of the deceased was always someone known to us, possibly a loved one, and the body was always laid out carefully in a simple coffin, making it easy for the viewer to imagine the person asleep rather than dead. But in that field, the pale moonlight revealed the bodies of those pitiable soldiers to be grotesquely contorted in every imaginable way, a terrible testament to the agonies suffered in the last moments of their struggles with death.

"Michael?" John Robinson, my closest and dearest friend since childhood, was by my side, as he had been during the last seven days of hard marching from Fort Ethan Allen. "Could you ever have imagined this just six weeks ago?"

"No, I never . . . I thought . . . I don't know what I thought it would be like. War means killing, but this is so . . . terrible."

John and I roamed the field in search of an unspoiled place.

"Here, this looks all right," John said. "It's soft and grassy and the closest body is a few yards away."

We began to unroll our rubber blankets. "Nobody forced us into this," John said. "We volunteered. We talked about it over and over." John paused for a response, but I offered none. "Are we still agreed that it's God's will for us to be here?"

"Yes, you heard me say it. Reverend Preston was most convincing about the evils of slavery."

"Easy to say in church on Sunday. But what about here and now?"

"I know, John. Death is suddenly so close—I'm face-to-face

with it. I can reach out and touch it, feel it reaching out to touch me."

"Unless we crawl under a rock, staring death in the face is something we'll have to get used to. That will be my prayer tonight, that God will calm and steady me."

Perhaps the worst was the smell of the freshly dead. The sickly sweet odor of blood spilled upon the ground and the more powerful stench of bodies blown apart with their entrails cast to the four winds combined in a reeking aroma that, perhaps even more than sight, spoke sickening volumes of the gore all around. As I lay on my blanket, I could look only upward at the heavenly host above me, or I could close my eyes tightly shut against the hideous specter of those bodies, but I could not shut out the smell. I turned over, face downward to the earth, and tried to will myself to sleep. I buried my face in the crook of my elbow, hoping the odors of earth and grass and India rubber would crowd out the sickening odor of death. At last, I remembered the words of the psalmist and repeated them over and over until they grew into a drumbeat for my troubled heart, *Thou shalt not be afraid for the terror by night . . . Thou shalt not be afraid for the terror by night . . . Thou shalt not be afraid for the terror by night. . .*

CHAPTER 2

Daily Bread

Wisdom is better than weapons of war.
ECCLESIASTES 9:18

I AWOKE TO WARM SUNLIGHT FILTERING THROUGH MY EYELIDS.
My first thought was that I should turn out and get moving,
but the idea of rising only to find the horrible scene of the previous night fully exposed to the light of day kept me prone upon
my blanket, eyes tightly closed.

Someone's boot tapped the side of mine—once, twice, three
times. "Rise and shine, Palmer, rise and shine. You don't want
to waste this bloody fine day abed, do you?"

When Sergeant Needham spoke, new recruits like me listened. His voice was actually quite pleasing, for he spoke with a
decidedly British accent, and his words were confident and sure.
Sergeant Needham commanded immediate obedience.

"Yes, Sarge," I answered, opening my eyes just enough to
see him standing over me. "I mean, no, Sarge ... I think."

"Robinson's got the fire going and the bloody coffee is almost
ready. Adams and Whitting have gone off to find some clean
water, should be back within the hour. Mind if I throw my meat
into your pan this morning?"

"No, Sarge."

Sergeant Needham was known as an "old soldier," not in reference to his age, for he had certainly not yet reached his fortieth year, but rather as a concise and complimentary expression of the value of a man who had met the foe on the battlefield and learned the hard lessons of earlier campaigns. From the day Company C had mustered in at Camp Foote in Hartford, Needham had insisted that we call him "Sarge, just Sarge." Sarge had a full head of bushy hair the color of fine beach sand. Bushy eyebrows framed his piercing gray eyes, and an equally bushy moustache hid his upper lip. He had surely once been handsome, when his youthful face was smooth and unmarked. Now his regular features were deeply lined by weather and war, a visible testament to the hardness of the man. Of less than average height—closer to five feet than to six, and quite thin, not more than one hundred and thirty pounds—Sarge's confident manner and wealth of battlefield wisdom caused one to disregard his diminutive size and rather consider him a man to be reckoned with. He had a habit of saying "bloody this" or "bloody that," as in "You lads don't know bloody nothing, but you're bloody well gonna learn." Yet I never heard him take the Lord's name in vain, nor did any other curse escape his lips in my hearing, as was so common among his peers.

"Good morning, Michael." John's tall frame was hunched over the campfire; his voice was bright and cheery. "Did you sleep well?"

I stood and stretched. "No, not very." In fact, not at all.

I gazed about the field. The burial details had worked through the night. All the bodies of the slain had been removed; only traces remained of the recent carnage.

"It'll be our turn soon, lads," said Sarge, as if he could read my thoughts. "The Rebs have already taken Harper's Ferry, so they'll probably make a stand up near Hagerstown. First we march—another day ought to do it. Then we fight, and if I

24

read the signs correctly, it'll be a bloody great fight—tomorrow maybe, or Wednesday."

"Coffee's ready," John said. Sarge and I waited eagerly as John poured the hot brew from the blackened coffee tin into three tin coffee cups.

"I see you boys have learned well," said Sarge, lifting his cup and savoring the aroma. "Smells great. It's a small thing, really, but a soldier needs a bloody good cup of coffee whenever he can get one. And you're keeping your coffee and sugar together?"

"Yes, Sarge," John and I answered in unison. "We'll never have one without the other." Sarge laughed as we recited his own words back to him in our best, though admittedly poor, imitations of his British accent.

John poured the last of the water in his canteen into the coffee tin and set the can on the ground before us. "That's for the pork."

Each man reached into his own haversack, took out a slab of salt pork, and held it under his nose to see if it would curl his nose hairs. Approved for consumption, the pork was tossed into the tin can to soak some of the salt out of it. John got a small skillet from his pack and, after a few minutes, transferred the slabs of pork from the tin can to the skillet.

The wisdom of an old soldier can never be valued too highly. Whenever Sarge happened by our campfire, which had been twice since leaving Fort Ethan Allen in Arlington, he always imparted some lesson or other he had learned while soldiering. "Are you and Adams friends?" he asked this time.

"Acquaintances rather than friends. I see him at the store and about town. I really don't know him well. He says he got into this because life at home was too boring."

"He's a bloody muscular young fellow, though," said Sarge. "Looks about twice your size, Palmer, but not an inch taller. He knows next to nothing about what he's gotten himself into, but he's tough. He'll likely become a fine soldier. But I am a bit concerned about Whitting."

"Harry told me he joined up because he didn't want people to think poorly of him," John said. "He didn't want to enlist but thought everyone expected him to."

"When we left for Camp Foote," I added, "his mother cried and cried and wouldn't let go of Harry at the train station. It was as if she was seeing her son for the last time."

"Well," said Sarge, "Mrs. Whitting may have been right. Her boy drills bloody well, but he seems weak in both body and spirit. He's pale and he has nervous eyes, so I don't quite know what to expect from him. Keep an eye on him. I will too, but I fear his experience of this war will be bloody short."

"What's it like, Sarge?" The question had been tormenting me all night.

Needham looked at me, puzzled.

"Battle, I mean. What's it like when the firing starts in earnest?"

"Rough, very rough," he said. "You'll know shortly. The bloody Rebs fight hard. They think they're independent from the United States. That makes us foreign invaders, so they're fighting to defend their homeland. Their officers are first-rate and the men fight well. Sometimes we've had to attack the Rebs in their defenses, and more of our boys are killed than theirs. It's the price we have to pay."

"Were you afraid?" I asked.

"Always. You will be too—every man is, though he may not admit it. And the fear will be there no matter what you do. It's like a shadow that follows me wherever I go. I've learned to expect it and deal with it so I control it rather than letting it control me, but if any man tells you he's not afraid, run away as fast and far as you can. It will be more perilous to be in his company than to be with a hundred bloody cowards."

"So how *do* you deal with it?" I asked.

Sarge paused for a moment, watching keenly as John stirred and flipped the sizzling pork. "How old are you, Palmer?"

"Thirty-four now, Sarge. My birthday was two days after we arrived at Camp Foote."

"Robinson?"

"Thirty-six, Sarge."

"I knew you two were older than most of the other fellows. Married?"

We both nodded. "Yes, Sarge."

"Children?"

"Three, Sarge, two sons and a daughter," John said. "Michael has one of each. What about you, Sarge?"

"Five beautiful children," Sarge answered, proudly holding up the five fingers of his right hand. "But two died just after they were born." His eyes clouded for a moment, then brightened. "My childhood sweetheart's family lived next to my family on Trentham Street in Birmingham. Still do. We married as soon as our parents would agree to it, almost fifteen years ago. I worked years in a bloody shoe factory and dreamed of coming to America. But the babies arrived every other year, as if on a schedule, and any plans for coming here had to be put off. I finally came over on a steamship out of Liverpool in April of fifty-eight. A family friend lived in Waterbury. He took me in and I was able to send for my family six months later."

"So you've only been in America for four years?" I asked.

"Yes."

"And you're fighting in this war?"

"Sure."

"You didn't have to."

"Maybe not. The Union Jack is very dear to me, but Old Glory is my flag now. America is my bloody country, so her wars are my wars."

"Leaving home was most difficult for us too, Sarge," I said quietly. "We've been gone just five weeks, but already I miss my wife terribly . . . and my children too."

At the fire John nodded his agreement.

"Aye, that's the rub, Palmer, and you older fellows know it far better than these bloody young ones. You long to be with your lifelong companion just as she longs for you. For me, it's a deep and keen ache for which there is no balm. *Bittersweet* is the word I use for it. The pain is always there along with the fear, but it's what helps me do what must be done."

"What do you mean?" John asked.

"I would like nothing better than to be done with this war and go home, but I know the best thing I can do for my wife and children is what I'm doing now, fighting the bloody Rebs so my family can live in a united and free nation. I expect it'll be the same for you, and I wish I could say the ache will heal, but it'll only worsen with the passage of time. The only remedy is victory—or perhaps, if God wills it, the final muster call."

John and I looked blankly at Sarge, not understanding his meaning.

"Death," he whispered. "Death is the final muster call."

For several seconds Sarge gazed into the flames. Then his eyes fixed on John. "Are we frying the hardtack today?"

"Yes, Sarge, just like you told us," John said, "and this pork has some good fat."

Sarge nodded. "You can crumble the crackers into your coffee too. They'll soak up the coffee and get nice and soft. I haven't seen any bloody weevils in the crackers yet."

"Weevils?" I asked.

"Bugs. Sometimes the crackers get infested, so always check your coffee before you drink it. If there are any weevils, the boiling will kill them and the bloody buggers will float to the top. Won't hurt you to eat one, but the coffee is better without."

The pork now cooked, John speared each slab with a fork and placed it on one of our tin plates. Each man anted up two hardtack crackers and John set to work over the fire again.

"You asked me how I deal with fear, Palmer. I'll speak only another word or two about it, and then I'll say no more. Why does a bullet strike one man and not another?"

"The hand of God," John replied.

"Right you are. If you believe as I do that the Almighty controls these things, then it's best to leave matters of life and death in His hands. Am I afraid to die? I've thought much about this, and I think that I'm not so much afraid of death because I know what my end will be. But the uncertainty of the circumstances—if it's in the next days or weeks, or if I'll suffer much or little—that's what troubles me. And I'm afraid of leaving my wife widowed and my children fatherless."

A minute or two passed, the only sound around our fire the crackle of hard crackers in a pan of hot pork fat.

Sarge cleared his throat. "I've written a letter to help me be prepared, whenever that time might be—a pocket letter."

"Pocket letter?" I asked.

"To my wife. Some veterans call it a death letter, but I like my name better. Nobody knows his time, so a few days ago I wrote a letter to my wife. I keep it in the breast pocket of my jacket, right here." Sarge gently tapped the spot with his hand. "A lot of veteran soldiers carry them. The letter will be sent to my wife only if I'm killed. Captain Carpenter knows about it. I think every man would be best served by doing the same.

"At Bull Run, when the air was bloody thick with hot lead and the whole world seemed to be ending around us, I knew the next moment might be my last on this bloody earth, and I took comfort from having that letter in my pocket. I knew that whatever happened to me, I had left nothing unsaid to my dear wife that should have been said, and at least she would have that simple letter as a remembrance."

"You were at Bull Run, Sarge?" John said.

"I was. I volunteered for three months with the First Connecticut right after Sumter."

"You did your duty, Sarge," John said. "You didn't have to reenlist."

"No, probably not. I went home after my three months thinking the bloody war would end soon, but this summer, when President Lincoln called for three hundred thousand more men, I thought he was calling me back. Slavery's a bad business, and we have to whip those bloody Rebs and put an end to it. If we don't save this country, it'll be torn apart and all is lost." When Sarge put it like that, it seemed a simple thing to press onward toward victory, but I knew it was not.

"Breakfast is served," John announced as he deftly flipped two now golden-brown hardtack crackers onto each plate. "Spoons or fingers?"

"We from the old country always use our best silver," Sarge spoke with unabashed pride, "but no manners are expected from revolutionists such as you." John and I doubled up with laughter.

"Around our fire we always give thanks and ask God's blessing on our food," John told Sarge when we had recovered sufficiently.

"I would be pleased to do so," Sarge said, and when his prayer was done, the three of us ate our plain and meager fare with gladness.

CHAPTER 3

Through the Valley

Even we ourselves groan within ourselves,
waiting for the adoption,
to wit, the redemption of our body.
ROMANS 8:23

A S NOON APPROACHED, THOSE OF US IN FRENCH'S DIVISION
entered the small town of Boonsboro at the base of the
northern slope of South Mountain. The column turned left onto
the Sharpsburg Road, and it was soon clear to all that the entire
Army of the Potomac was coming together. Battle was sure to
follow, and as we neared Keedysville later in the day, occasional
blasts of artillery fire rumbled across the low farm country.

Darkness fell as we began to march through the vast
encampment of the army. Tens of thousands of soldiers lined
either side of the road, gathered around thousands of campfires.
Familiar and reassuring were the aromas of fire and coffee and
fried meat, and our empty bellies awoke once again. After about
a mile we were ordered off the road into a large field to the left.
A line of tall trees silhouetted against the dark night sky marked
the bank of a nearby creek. Its gently flowing waters meandered
back and forth, generally from north to south, deep and slow in
many places, yet quite fordable at others.

"That's Antietam Creek," Sarge told the company. "Just across are plenty of bloody Rebs. Stay on your guard and don't make yourself too bloody visible."

The brigade laid out its camp by regiment and company. Then we foraged for wood and water at the creek, careful not to attract the attention of the enemy. We cooked our supper of more hardtack, salt pork, and coffee, and then turned in for the night.

⟨≈⟩⟨≈⟩

The quiet of the dawn was shattered by a Rebel shell cleaving the misty air as it passed overhead with a noise akin to that of a piece of fine cloth suddenly being rent in two. As far as I could tell, it did no damage other than awaken our weary camp. The Rebs continued to fire shells over us as we tried to cook breakfast, which only angered most of the men. The quickest and surest manner of putting a soldier in a foul temper is to keep him from his breakfast. Our artillery answered back, and the infantry spent most of the day hugging the ground.

Across the Sharpsburg Road from our camp was a large brick house that General McClellan was using as his headquarters. About noon, during a lull in the cannonading, the general strode onto the porch and peered across the creek toward the Rebel lines for a few minutes. Then he descended the steps and began to walk among the men.

To my surprise, the general in command of the Army of the Potomac appeared quite young, perhaps my own age. He was not a large man, but he carried himself with an air of refinement and nobility that commanded respect and deference from all around him. He was also a handsome man with a finely featured, almost boyish face, clean-shaven except for a thick, dark moustache.

General McClellan crossed the road and strode among the

men of the Fourteenth and the other two regiments of the brigade. He motioned all to gather around.

"I am told you men are new to this army. Well, that is good, very good, since we need every man, but I wish to say a few words to you."

The general paused as if seeking our permission to continue.

"This is our soil," he told us. "The enemy has come north to pay us a visit, and we must show them that they are not welcome here."

Three thousand Yankee voices yelled in approval.

"We are over here and they are over there, and as the enemy does not seem inclined to leave, we must force them to retreat back across the Potomac. Nothing less than the survival of our nation is at stake here, so there will be a battle tomorrow."

The men listened quietly now.

"Tonight, get what rest you can. It will not be easy to drive Bobby Lee back across the Potomac, but that is our duty and we must do it. If we do not, then our cause is lost. Your brothers here," the general opened his arms wide to encompass the entire army, "have pledged to do their duty to its fullest extent, and they expect the same from you. Your nation needs your best efforts now, and I know that when the history of this day is written, your names will be remembered with honor and reverence for your sacrifice on this field of battle."

A great cheer went up again from all who heard the general's words. Several men began to chant, "Little Mac! Little Mac! Little Mac!" and the chant was taken up by the entire throng.

The problem was that the Rebels also heard the cheering and opened up with their artillery again. Some of these shells fell nearby, killing a few and wounding several others. General McClellan, visibly shaken, returned to the shelter of the Pry house in a rush, and we didn't see him again until the fighting was done.

When silence finally settled upon the valley of the Antietam that evening, Chaplain Stevens held a special religious service for the regiment. He made his way toward the center of our bivouac and urged the men to gather around him. Eager soldiers edged closer so that not a word would fall to the ground unheard. The chaplain stood, Bible in hand, and delivered a message that was short and sharp, with penetrating simplicity and clarity.

"There have already been many desperate and bloody battles in this war," he began. "You know the names of those places, places forever inscribed in the history of this nation, places forever hallowed by the blood of those who fell there. Tomorrow, it is certain that the name of Antietam Creek will be added to that hallowed history.

"This will be your first fight. It is certain that some of you will not live to see the sun set tomorrow. I do not say this to grieve you or to scare you, but rather to have you think soberly about the state of your immortal soul. Do not think that because you are young and brave that death will pass you by. Do not think that it will be the fellow next to you that falls rather than you. None of us knows the time or the hour. Only God knows these things. Therefore, listen to the words of the Lord Jesus from the Gospel of John: 'Thomas saith unto him, Lord, we know not whither thou goest; and how can we know the way? Jesus saith unto him, I am the way, the truth, and the life: no man cometh unto the Father, but by me.'

"These are precious words of promise, blessed words of assurance. The Lord challenged His disciples to believe in Him as the only way, the only road to God the Father. Look into your own heart and see the sin that is at home within you. The Lord Jesus Christ died to cleanse you of that sin; He arose on the third day victorious over sin and death and hell. He will not turn away

anyone who turns to Him with a sincere heart. I plead with you
to believe in Him as your only salvation, and I pray for your
deliverance, soul and body, into the presence of God above."

Amens echoed throughout the ranks, as did several huzzahs,
but most of the men stood silent and motionless, heads bared and
bowed, hands clasped before or behind, intent on hearing every
precious word. My own eyes stung and brimmed with tears.

"Consider this," the chaplain continued, "no matter how terrible it is for you on the field of battle tomorrow, the terrors of
hell will be infinitely worse. Be assured of this, God will be on
this battlefield tomorrow with you, working out His will and
purposes, but God does not dwell in the place of eternal torment
reserved for unrepentant and unbelieving sinners.

"No matter how peaceful your life was before, or how pleasant you think it will be when this war is done and you have
returned in safety to the bosom of your families, the bliss of
heaven will be infinitely greater. The words of the Savior guaran-
tee those who trust in Him a room in His Father's house forever.

"Think on this as well. Your present sorrows, no matter how
deeply they oppress you, shall pass. Indeed, your present joys, no
matter how rich and fulfilling you find them, shall pass as well.
Instead, you have been extended the richest of all invitations, an
invitation guaranteed by the promise of the Lord Jesus, an invitation to a life of eternal blessing, eternal security, and eternal
peace in the very house of the living and true God. Find your
hope in this and fix your hearts eternally upon it."

Then the chaplain offered prayer on behalf of the regiment
and dismissed us with a benediction. There was no talk in the
ranks as the men returned to their chosen places, for the message
had sobered all who heard it. I poured myself one last cup of coffee and sat down on my rubber blanket.

I saw that I was not alone in my desire to be my own companion, to be content to engage in conversation within myself.

Throughout the camp many a soldier could be seen on his knees or taking solace and assurance from the blessed words of Scripture, perhaps quietly probing his soul with questions both high and deep as I was doing that night. Would I be among the sheep or the goats? Would God above, the one I called Father, receive me as a son or cast me out of His presence forever? Would I be clothed in the glorious white robes of the Revelation saints or would I be condemned to an eternity of weeping and gnashing of teeth?

In the end I could only echo back to myself the words of the apostle Paul that Reverend Preston had so ably preached upon the Sabbath prior to my leaving for the army, *For I am persuaded, that neither death, nor life, nor angels, nor principalities, nor powers, nor things present, nor things to come, nor height, nor depth, nor any other creature, shall be able to separate us from the love of God, which is in Christ Jesus our Lord.* These words I had confessed openly and trusted all my lifelong. Did I trust them now? Would I trust them tomorrow when hot lead filled the air around me?

At last I took my Bible from my pocket, unfastened the clasp, and opened it. My intent was to read again that eighth chapter of Romans, but when I opened the clasp, the photograph of Jessie Anne, Sarah, and little Edward fell out upon my lap. I picked up the photograph and gazed upon the faces of my family for what, I realized, might be the last time. I pressed their image to my lips as the tears rolled freely down my cheeks.

CHAPTER 4

Wife of My Youth

And the LORD God said,
It is not good that the man should be alone;
I will make him an help meet for him.
GENESIS 2:18

N O, MICHAEL, YOU WILL NOT GO!" JESSIE ANNE'S DARK EYES burned brighter than flames consuming seasoned hickory. "You *will not* leave me and Sarah and little Ed. How could you think such a thing? What will become of us?" Her words remained frozen in the summer air as she stormed up the stairs.

The steps creaked softly as I followed slowly and deliberately. I paused at the door of the candlelit room. Jessie Anne lay on the bed, her face buried in the down pillow. "Are we not enough for you?" she said.

I inched my way toward my beloved. Slowly and quietly I began to plead my case. "Three hundred thousand, Jessie Anne. President Lincoln needs three hundred thousand more men."

No weeping, just heavy breathing and silence.

I fought to maintain a steady, gentle tone. "I listened to Reverend Preston. I know he's right and so do you, Jessie Anne. You've told me yourself that America must be done with slavery. Do you want our children living under that dark cloud?"

More silence, but at least her breathing had slowed some.

"This is something I must do, Jessie Anne. When I heard Colonel Morris speak tonight, I thought he was speaking only to me. John said the same."

"I should have told you not to go to the rally." Finally, a response, sharp as a finely honed knife edge, but a response nonetheless.

"But I knew what I had to do before the rally. Because, my dear, and I hope you will understand this, I believe God has laid it upon my heart to enlist."

Jessie Anne raised her head slowly and looked at me with red, weepy eyes.

"No, I didn't hear a voice from heaven or anything like that, Jessie Anne, but I do believe in the rightness of the cause, and I believe I must be willing to do my part. Why should I remain at home while someone else bears the burden? John feels the same."

"John, *always* John. Must you *always* do what he does?" The weight of bitterness in her words surprised me.

"How can you say that, Jessie Anne? We've been like brothers since we were children. I could not love him more if he really was my brother."

"But have you two *brothers* thought about what will become of us?" She buried her face in the pillow again.

"Yes, we have." I sat down on the bed next to Jessie Anne and laid my hand lightly upon her back. "The Robinsons should be all right. Mr. Tuttle told John he will continue to pay Abby one-half of John's wages for as long as John is in the army if John agreed to return to his position as master wheelwright after the war. With the bounty payments and John's army salary, the Robinson family should not be in want.

"As for us, it was only two years ago that my father signed the store over to me. He has agreed to manage the store as he is able, but of course, I think you should help out too, and my mother can help around the house—if you let her. I know how well you run this house and you take such joy and pride in it, but Mama can help with the kids, and cook meals and tidy up."

Jessie Anne raised herself once again. She turned over, rested her head upon my knee, and looked into my eyes. "And what if you are killed?"

"Only God knows if I will live or die. But I do believe this is His will for me and that I must obey Him—*we* must obey Him—and He will watch over us."

Jessie Anne closed her eyes while I ran my fingers lightly through her hair. "Go away, Michael," my beloved whispered after several minutes. "I'm going to have a long, long cry and you should not see me like that."

⋞⋟

My mother told me that the first time I saw Jessie Anne Morton was shortly after her birth, when her father and mother presented her for baptism, although I have no memory of it. The earliest recollections I have are of a skinny girl with long dark hair, at times sitting in the pew next to her parents, at others running squealing about the churchyard chasing other children or being chased by them. But the first real notice I took of her was on a Sunday morning in 1849, when I was twenty-one years old. The railroad was nearing completion and my own eyes were being opened to the many new prospects the world had to offer a young man. As Jessie Anne and I happened to pass each other at the door of the church, my head turned. Who was that? Oh yes, wasn't that the Morton girl?

To be truthful, several other young ladies had caught my eye in the preceding months, and I had even expressed mild interest in one or two of them, but Jessie Anne was different. As an unseen caterpillar changes into an exquisite butterfly that captures our gaze on a summer afternoon, so the scrawny, awkward child had been transformed overnight into a graceful young woman. If one looked at her closely, as so often I found myself doing, one saw a pleasantly attractive and faintly exotic face, fair but not pale skin, a nose that was just a bit shorter and wider than most of direct European ancestry, and dark brown eyes that were ever so slightly almond shaped, and one might conclude that there was, quite possibly, an Indian or two hidden among her progenitors. As I later learned, a great-grandmother on her father's side had been Mohegan.

I set out to win the heart of this young lass. Jessie Anne was certainly much too young for marriage, and I had no idea if she had taken any notice of me, so I contrived ways to cause our paths to cross. I greeted her by name at church nearly every Sunday and tried to sit close to her at social events. Whenever the Mortons appeared at the store with Jessie Anne in tow, it was I who waited on them. If the Mortons needed goods delivered to their farm, it was I who drove the wagon the two miles out and back, and whether in blustery cold or blazing heat, the smile never left my face.

In the spring of 1853, shortly after Jessie Anne's seventeenth birthday, I determined to make my intentions known. On a cool and cloudy Saturday afternoon, I donned my best woolen jacket and a new felt hat. With a quick "I'll return for dinner" to my mother, I was out the door to the stable to saddle our mare, Becky. This time a tight frown replaced my usual smile as I steeled my nerve and rehearsed again and again what I should say.

"Hello, Michael," Mrs. Morton said warmly as she opened the door. "What brings you all the way out here today?"

"I was wondering if I might speak with Jessie Anne for just a moment."

"Of course," Mrs. Morton said with a faint smile. "Come in. She's upstairs. I'll call her."

Mrs. Morton showed me into the parlor and called up the stairs for her daughter, "Jessie Anne, Michael Palmer is here to see you." With a final glance back at me, Mrs. Morton disappeared in the direction of the kitchen.

I sat down on the settee, hat in one hand and the fingers of the other drumming nervously on the armrest. I closed my eyes and listened for footsteps upon the stairs, which were several long minutes in coming. I was on my feet before Jessie Anne rounded the corner, a whirl of rustling petticoats and dark flowing tresses. She took a few steps into the parlor and stopped to look at me, her hands clasped demurely in front of her.

"Mr. Palmer, how nice it is to see you." Her voice was light and playful.

"Miss Morton . . . ." My throat was like that of a cat choking on a ball of fur; my lips seemed stuck together with horsehide glue. I half turned and placed my hat on the settee. Then I swallowed once, hard.

"Yes, Mr. Palmer?"

"I . . . I would like to call on you."

"Call on me, Mr. Palmer? Whatever for?" She was not making this easy for me. I shuffled forward a few feet, thinking that what I wished to say to her need not be trumpeted throughout the house.

"Well, I was hoping that I might come to see you from time to time, Miss Morton, to court you."

Jessie Anne looked at me in doe-eyed wonder for several long seconds. My heart turned over with fear that her answer might not be the one I desired.

"Why, Mr. Palmer," she said, looking down at her hands. "How is it that you, a gentleman so well established and with such fine prospects, should pay any attention to a simple country girl like me?" She raised her head and looked me squarely in the eye. "I should think there are a dozen girls more suitable."

41

Her words seemed innocent, delivered without any hint of malevolence or scorn. Still, events were not transpiring the way I had rehearsed them. I took a long, deep breath and lifted up a silent prayer, *Let my words be true and Your will be done.*

"No, Jessie Anne," I said gently, "there is no one more suitable." I stepped slowly forward, allowing her brightly shining eyes to draw me, and when I took her hands in mine, Jessie Anne made no effort to withdraw them. "I have waited four long years to be here today. I dared not declare myself sooner because of your tender age. I hoped and prayed all the while that you would not pledge yourself to another. I ask only that you allow me to prove myself worthy of your affections and that I might win your heart as you did mine long ago."

There. It was said. It was done. I had stated my position clearly. There could be no mistaking my intentions. We stood motionless for a time, her soft, feminine hands in my hard, sweaty ones. I searched for a twinkle in her eyes or the slightest trace of a smile, but Jessie Anne was not revealing what her response might be.

"Well, then," she finally whispered, leaning in toward me to bring her lips up to my ear, "I suppose I must start calling you Michael." It took a moment or two until the full import of her words made me the happiest man on the face of the earth. "Come," Jessie Anne said taking my hand in hers, now all awhirl again and beaming with happiness, "let's tell Mama and Papa."

As Jessie Anne allowed later, the victory had actually been won before that Saturday afternoon. "I always thought you were an admirable man of fine reputation and tolerable appearance, if a bit older. But what would you have thought of me if I had accepted immediately? I wanted you to wriggle a little, to see how determined you were, and how true your devotion was."

The day after Jessie Anne received her diploma from Union School we met with her father and I asked for her hand in marriage. Jessie Anne and I never doubted that Mr. Morton would grant his permission and his blessing, for by that time, it was obvious to all that our two souls were being knit together. Still, we wished to show proper respect and follow the dictates of centuries-old tradition. The following spring, on Saturday, the twenty-eighth day of April 1855, with John Robinson standing by my side, Jessie Anne and I were married. She had just turned nineteen years of age in February and I would be twenty-seven in August.

⋖≋⋗

Sunday night, the night before John and I were to travel to the enlistment office in Waterbury, I tossed and turned in my bed, drifting in and out of troubled sleep. I finally rose, paced about the room for a time, and paused at the front window, which overlooks the river. Another time, I could have envisioned two young boys playing in the cool, shallow water, but now sweat and tears poured down my face. Imaginary shells burst in my head and bullets tore at my flesh. I saw myself dying horribly a hundred different ways in battle, my wife a widow, my children fatherless. What if I ran? What if I turned tail and fled from the enemy in panicked fear for my life? Would that be even worse than death?

Jessie Anne came up quietly from behind and gently slipped her arms around me. "This morning at church a few of the ladies asked me, 'How could Michael go off and leave his wife and children, let alone the store?' Tell me again why this must be so."

I turned to her and cupped her lovely face in my hands. Indeed, how could I leave her and Sarah and little Ed and go off to war? "I know there are many reasons why I should remain here. And I'm certainly no youth full of daring and vigor, eager for a glorious adventure. Jessie Anne, please do not think I'm in any way unhappy with you or our life together. I don't think I could be more comfortable or content. But for a long time I have sensed a deep restlessness—I think of it as an itch that I cannot scratch."

Jessie Anne gazed intently into my eyes. "You're saying you need to go off to war to scratch an itch?"

"No, my dear, I believe there is some other duty that God is calling me to do at this time in my life. For seven years you have been 'bone of my bones and flesh of my flesh,' and I could not love you any more than I do at this moment. You must never think that I'm enlisting because I want to leave you. In fact, I wish only to remain here, but I *must* go."

We held each other in silence for several long minutes. "Do you still feel that God has called you to this?" Jessie Anne whispered.

I thought for a moment, wanting to be sure of my answer. "Yes, I do. I truly do, and even as I say it, my heart aches at the thought of being without you, my love. I sometimes think I am abandoning you and the children, and I may not return at all. You need to prepare for that."

"How can I ever prepare for that? Since our wedding day we've been apart only a few times, and then just for a day or two when you've gone to Hartford or New York. My heart will break when you leave me, and it will mend again when I receive a letter from you. It will break again when I read of a dreadful battle in the newspaper. How can I prepare for any of that? I can only tell you that I love you with all my heart. When you are gone, more than half of me will be gone as well."

I cradled her head against my chest. My nightshirt became damp, yet I could only hold her more closely.

Finally, Jessie Anne raised her head and looked at me. There was nothing but love and compassion in her gaze. Her words were clear and firm. "Then if it is His will for you to go, then it is also His will for us to remain and trust His providence and protection. We must rest and hope in that. And if, in God's providence, you are taken from us, then let His will be done and I pray only that I shall be able to bear it. Then I'll have to take pleasure in seeing you in the faces of our children."

What a marvelous woman, truly a gift from God above. Two evenings before her tears had been abundant, but when her weeping ceased, Jessie Anne steeled herself, and from that point forward, stood resolute with me. What had formerly been my decision was now our decision.

We kissed tenderly and returned to the comfort of our bed. I squeezed my eyes shut, covered my face with my hands, and prayed desperately to my Father in Heaven for the wisdom of Solomon, the courage of David, and the strength of Samson. Above all, I prayed for peace of mind and spirit. Then, exhausted, I slept.

CHAPTER 5

Answering the Call

Every purpose is established by counsel:
and with good advice make war.
PROVERBS 20:18

ARE THINGS ALL RIGHT AT HOME?" I HAD HALF EXPECTED
John's question since I had said hardly a word since meeting him at Doc Innes's office. The physical examinations were hastily done and cursory at best, and John and I were pronounced fit for duty. Now we sat on opposite sides of the aisle aboard the 8:28 train for Waterbury.

"It's been very hard for Jessie Anne, but she now accepts what must be. No, John, that's not quite right. She has more than accepted it; her resolve and encouragement amaze me. It's just that now I'm feeling the weight of what we're about to do."

John nodded. "Abby had known I was thinking about it for some time, so she was not completely surprised when I told her. She has accepted it as well, but reluctantly."

The train stopped in Union City. One or two passengers got off, several more got on. John moved across the aisle and sat beside me to make room. "There is still time to change your mind," he said quietly, so no one else would hear.

"As I've said, I must go. You've heard me say it more than

once, I can either tolerate the sin of slavery or do my best to abolish it."

"Yes, I've heard you. I was just making sure you hadn't changed your mind. But do you think you can kill a man?"

"How can I answer that, John? Maybe we'll never see the Rebels. Maybe the war will end soon and we'll never have to fight. What a question. I can tell you this—I'm no cold-blooded killer. But how can we know for sure until we have to do it?"

⋘⋙

At the office of the Justice of the Peace, there was a sign in front: Recruiting Office Here. The sign touted the reputation of Colonel Morris, listed available enlistment bounties, and promised the recruit Opportunities for Travel and Possible Promotion.

A sergeant was seated at a large table in the front corner of the office. The justice sat at a desk in another office off to the right.

"Good morning. Please be seated. I'm Sergeant Hawley of the Fourteenth Connecticut Volunteers. What are your names?"

"Hello, sir. I'm Michael Palmer," I said.

"I'm John Robinson, sir."

"Are you both enlisting?"

"Yes, sir."

"Save the 'sirs' for the officers. Call me Sergeant. How old are you?"

"Thirty-three, Sergeant, thirty-four on the thirteenth of August," I said.

"I'm thirty-six, Sergeant," John said.

Hawley nodded and gave a slight grunt. "You boys certainly won't need your parents to sign for you. Are you from Waterbury too?"

"No, Sergeant," John replied, "we're from Naugatuck."

Sergeant Hawley told us about the bounties being offered

to new recruits. While the Federal and state bounties were only about thirty dollars each, the town of Naugatuck offered an additional bounty of three hundred dollars. That money would surely benefit our families.

"Do you have a doctor's certificate?" Hawley asked.

John and I gave him the papers from Doc Innes, and then we filled out and signed three copies of the yellow enlistment form. The first two copies were for the army; the third was for our wives to take to Naugatuck officials to register for the bounty payments. Then the sergeant summoned the justice. The justice told us to raise our right hands and repeat the oath of enlistment after him: "I, Michael Gabriel Palmer, do solemnly swear that I will support the Constitution of the United States. I, Michael Gabriel Palmer, do solemnly swear to bear true allegiance to the United States of America and to serve them honestly and faithfully against all their enemies or opposers whatsoever, and to observe and obey the orders of the President of the United States of America, and the orders of the officers appointed over me."

⋐⋙⋇⋘⋑

On Sunday the tenth, I went to church as usual with my family. It was well known that John and I were leaving for the army the next day, and Reverend Preston preached an especially fine sermon that Sunday for our benefit. He preached on a text from Romans 8: "For I am persuaded, that neither death, nor life, nor angels, nor principalities, nor powers, nor things present, nor things to come, nor height, nor depth, nor any other creature, shall be able to separate us from the love of God, which is in Christ Jesus our Lord."

John's family sat two pews in front. His big arms were wrapped around his two sons, William to the right and Jonathan to the left. Abby hugged their daughter, Eliza, close while she dabbed regularly at her eyes with a white kerchief. To the side were my parents, with heads lowered, shedding their tears as privately as they could in that public setting. It seemed that only Jessie Anne remained stolid, staring with fixed gaze at what I could not tell. She was determined to do her weeping in private, "For the sake of the children," she said.

Reverend Preston closed his sermon with words I have never forgotten. "Death is but our entrance into glory, so fix your eyes on that glory and do not waver. Do not fear the death of your mortal body, for whether the days that remain for you on this earth be many or few, your body must die anyway. Fear the devil and flee from his ways, because if you give him a foothold, he is able to kill both your body and your soul. May God in His mercy give you courage and strength, and may He keep you safe from all harm, so that you may return to your families, and to this church, in the due course of His Providence. Go with God and with our blessing. Amen."

◆◆◆

That Sunday night, after our family returned as usual from the evening service, we quietly said our good-byes. My parents were there too, as were Jessie Anne's. Each of my loved ones, from the oldest to the youngest, even little Edward, offered a prayer for my safe return or read a passage from Scripture. Then we sang a hymn. Afterward, a number of needed and cherished gifts were presented to me. Sarah gave me two quill pens and a small bottle of dried ink, Edward a packet of paper and envelopes for writing letters, and Jessie Anne the first of my journals and a small sewing and shaving kit wrapped in a piece of plaid cloth. My mother gave me a small canvas satchel, and my father presented me with a hunting knife and a small Bible covered in black leather with a strap to keep it closed. I opened to the front leaves that are common to many Bibles for the purpose of writing inscriptions and for recording family historical information. *Michael G. Palmer*

14th Conn. Vol. Rgt. Thy word is a lamp unto my feet, and a light unto my path—Ps. 119:105 was written in my father's hand.

I looked at my father. His eyes were bright and moist. "Don't worry about the store," he said. "Mama says it's good for me to be active again, and Jessie Anne has learned to manage things quite well. We'll do just fine—just come home safe, Son."

I mixed a small amount of the ink powder with water and turned to the next plate. Taking up one of my new quills, I wrote the following:

> *Married: Jessie Anne Morton, 28 Apr. 1855*
> *Born: Sarah Anne, 13 Mar. 1856 Bap: 3 Aug. 1856*
> *Born: David Michael, 17 Nov. 1857 Bap: 13 Dec. 1857*
> *Died: 14 Jan. 1858*
> *Born: Edward Philip, 24 Apr. 1860 Bap: 20 May 1860*

I blew on the page to dry the ink, and then Jessie Anne gave me one last gift, a precious photograph of a mother and two children. Edward was perched on Jessie Anne's knee while Sarah stood by her mother's right shoulder. Without my knowledge, they had gone to the photographer's shop the week previous to sit for the camera. Jessie Anne and the children were all finely attired as if going to church. How was such a secret kept? I placed the photograph inside the front cover of the Bible and latched it closed.

Finally, we all hugged and kissed each other and sang another hymn. There were tears of sadness for our coming separation, but also smiles and laughter as we shared fond memories of days long ago.

But it was not so much "Farewell" as it was "Until we meet again."

CHAPTER 6

The Hour of Trial

A sound of battle is in the land,
and of great destruction.
JEREMIAH 50:22

HAD I THE OCCASION TO VISIT THE LAND ALONG THE ANTIE-
tam at any other time, I would have been very much
attracted by the simplicity and beauty of the place. From South
Mountain at the south and east, the land rolled gently in a procession of low hills and shallow valleys to the Potomac River
at the north and west. It was an abundant and fertile land, well
watered by meandering, gently flowing streams, a land that for
two hundred years or more had been cultivated by generation
after generation of simple hardworking folk with their hands
always at the plow or in the earth, laboring to reap a bountiful
harvest.

It was a land of fields—fields of tall, green corn planted in
regular straight rows, fields of vegetables, fields of golden wheat
or sweet alfalfa, and fields of emerald grass dotted all over with
wildflowers for the grazing of dairy cattle. It was a land of
orchards, apple, crab apple, pear, and peach, the fruit even then
hanging heavily on the bough, ready for harvest. It was a land
where the oak and the maple and the beech lined the banks of the

streams and where tracts of deep woods formed natural boundaries between one farm and the next. It was a land of homesteads, of barns and springhouses and root cellars and sturdy, well-kept, and whitewashed farmhouses, all connected one to another, and to the markets in town, by a series of well-worn country lanes cut deeply into the earth by countless wagons heaped high with produce. It was a land that sang the blessings of God's Providence, a land that yielded an abundance of the fine life-sustaining things given from His hand, a land ripe for harvest.

Yet on that day, September 17th, 1862, the produce would not come to harvest. The crops would be cut down before their time as would many of the men now occupying the land. Earth and field, livestock and humankind would know devastation and corruption beyond all imagining.

At about nine o'clock that Wednesday morning, when the men of the Fourteenth Connecticut marched into a forested area known as the East Woods, that corruption was well under way. Just beyond the woods lay the Miller cornfield, where General Hooker's men had fought for about three hours already that morning. The fighting had been sustained and brutal, going back and forth across that field as first one side, then the other, gained the upper hand. Hundreds of men lost their lives, and thousands more, those fortunate enough to have been preserved, huddled in the East Woods in small squads, the broken remnants of the brigades and regiments that had carried out the earlier assaults. But even the woods were being devastated by solid shot and exploding shell as Confederate artillery attempted to inflict as much damage as possible upon the men seeking shelter under the canopy.

The walking wounded streamed back through our lines, and I read our future in their eyes. The time had come. This was what I had enlisted for, what Jessie Anne had seen through her tears, and what I perhaps had not seen clearly enough. I had been in the army just five weeks, I had fired my rifle only a few times, and I had not yet seen the enemy face-to-face on the field of battle. Sarge was right. Tighter than my own skin was the fear that enveloped me.

I cowered behind a tree for protection. Shells burst in the trees overhead, pelting the men below with hot metal fragments and splinters of wood. Several men fell to the ground with bright red gashes on heads or shoulders or limbs, the regiment's first battlefield casualties. A man could be killed just as readily with shards of wood as with hot iron or lead.

General French rode furiously through the woods. "On your feet! Line of battle!" he screamed.

Colonel Perkins ran up and down our line. "Fourteenth, form up! Line of battle! Fix bayonets!"

The men came cautiously out from cover. Three thousand bayonets clanked home upon three thousand rifle barrels. The three regiments of the Second Brigade formed in lines that were nearly straight, in spite of the many trees. The brigade pivoted southward, the 108th New York in the front line, the 130th Pennsylvania in the middle, and the Fourteenth Connecticut at the rear.

Sergeant Needham's voice rang out. "When it gets hot, lads, I'll be right behind you. Just listen to me. Think about your loading and firing, loading and firing. Don't let fear master you. Just load, aim, and fire, men, and you'll do bloody fine."

The band struck up a chorus of "Yankee Doodle," and the Second Brigade began to march southward out of the East Woods. The 108th New York cleared the tree line and filed off to the left, the 130th Pennsylvania continued straight on, filling the center of the line, and the Fourteenth executed a precise right sidestepping movement that brought us up on the right of the Pennsylvania boys. We must have been a beautiful sight, three thousand men, all newly uniformed in dark blue coats and light blue trousers, our lines smartly dressed and our regimental ensigns flying high.

It seemed a hundred heavy guns opened up at once, trying to blast us off the face of the earth. Every tendon, every sinew was taut. There arose deep within me, from my bones and from my bowels, a yearning to turn around and go back to the woods, to endure the shelling there rather than advance across that field. Was this the time? Was my death at hand? Would the next few minutes or hours leave Jessie Anne a widow and my children orphans? I strained within myself to attend to my marching all the more, because the marching forced me to concentrate on the commands of the screaming officers, rather than on the danger flying all around me.

"Steady, men, steady," Sarge said, his voice high-pitched and piercing.

General Weber's brigade was a hundred yards or so to our front. A fine sight they were too, as they advanced in nearly perfect order. We followed Weber's men down into a glen past one farm, then a second, and on up through a cornfield toward the Rebel line at a sunken country lane. A shell exploded in Weber's ranks, then another and another. One man was struck directly; he simply was no more. A few men were thrown a dozen or more feet into the air like little blue rag dolls only to flop back to the ground and lie motionless. Several more fell kicking and writhing in obvious pain. Still others, less seriously struck, hopped about on one foot or the other, or clutched an arm or put a hand to a bleeding face. Weber's men closed ranks and continued onward in a slow, deadly advance.

Shot and shell screamed all around us. With each burst, heads ducked and bobbed, some even dove to the ground. Again my heart fainted within me, and I yearned to turn aside to the farm buildings for shelter.

"Steady, men, steady. It'll not be long now."

Sarge remained stolid and upright as he led the company forward, and I resolved to do the same. His lips quivered slightly, with fear I thought at first, but the movement was too rhythmical. Sarge had said he was always afraid when the shooting started, but I was sure he would never quiver with fear. I believe he was praying, for what I know not, but at such a time as was upon us, there was no shortage of things to pray for.

The slope up to the enemy line at the sunken road was bisected by a second wagon lane. The 130th Pennsylvania and the Fourteenth Connecticut advanced along the western side of this lane while the 108th New York advanced along the eastern side, but the New York regiment slowed its pace and halted just below the crest of the hill, safely out of sight of the enemy, and they did not move until the fighting was done.

The Pennsylvania and Connecticut boys continued up the slope and entered a cornfield. Much of the corn had been broken down by Weber's men, some of whom lay dead or dying among the stalks. We stepped around them or over them and pressed onward. Wounded men staggered back through our line, at times being aided by one or two "concerned" friends. There was a low fence at the end of the cornfield, which marked its boundary with a mown hayfield. Across this grassy field we saw what we were up against.

The land before us sloped downward for about a hundred yards, ending at a sunken lane with a strongly fortified fence. Sunlight gleamed off hundreds of Confederate bayonets, but little else could be seen of them as they lay in wait to kill as many of us as they could. Their officers walked back and forth behind the lines of riflemen, looking in our direction and barking orders.

The First Delaware, in front of the Fourteenth, and the Fifth Maryland, in front of the 130th Pennsylvania, began to advance into the hayfield toward the sunken road. They marched in perfect step, shoulder to shoulder, down the gentle slope, drawing ever nearer to the Rebel guns. Their colors flew high in the breeze, leading the straight line of blue toward the enemy. Sixty yards ... fifty yards ... forty yards. The line stopped about twenty-five yards from the sunken road.

A Confederate officer brandished his saber high in the air. "Fire!"

As if triggered by a single hand, a sheet of lead and flame leaped toward the men in blue. A second distinct sound, almost in the same instant, carried up that slope to my ears, the dull thud of hundreds of Rebel bullets simultaneously striking home in Federal flesh. Red blood misted the air. Almost all the color-bearers were shot down, the colors fell to the earth, and nearly half of the men went down as well. Some were blown over backward by the force of the volley, dead before they hit the ground. Others spun around, their arms flailing in a kind of grotesque pirouette, then pitching face downward into the dirt, never to move again. Many more were left writhing in agony in the red Maryland earth, staining it redder still with their life's blood.

I looked at the men on either side of me. John Robinson was just to my left, Jim Adams and Harry Whitting to the right. Fear was etched on the faces of my brothers, as I knew it was on mine. Wide eyes blinked again and again, breathing was quick and shallow, sweat dripped from chins and cap brims.

"Steady, men, steady," Sarge called out.

Battle smoke drifted up the slope toward us. Gray, shadowy figures appeared moving toward us. Men began to fire sporadically through the smoke. I fingered the trigger of my Springfield; it bucked painfully against my shoulder.

"Cease fire! Cease fire!" Captain Carpenter screamed. "The Delaware boys are falling back! Cease fire!" The order was repeated up and down the line until the firing ceased. As the shadowy figures neared, it became clear to all that they wore dark blue coats and light blue trousers.

"Run for your lives, boys! It's murder out there!" the survivors cried as they raced through our line. Some of our boys heeded that advice and started for the rear with them. I reloaded my rifle and huddled close to the ground.

"Fourteenth! On your feet!" Colonel Perkins shouted. Then he gave the order I had both wished for and dreaded: "Men of the Fourteenth Connecticut, to the front!"

A great cheer went up as our regimental colors were raised in the center of the line. The Stars and Stripes, with the words "14th REGT CONN VOLS" embroidered in gold across the middle red stripe, and the field of blue adorned with a bald eagle with wings spread wide surrounded by thirty-three stars, flew proudly next to our regimental flag. This flag was of deepest royal blue, fringed all around with gold tassels, and again, our majestic national bird was embroidered with wings spread, this time atop the state seal of Connecticut with its trinity of twisted grapevines, and with the name of our regiment proudly stitched beneath the seal. Some of the fleeing Delaware and Maryland boys about-faced and fell into line under our colors.

"Forward, march!" We jumped over the low fence in front and began to advance in line abreast with the 130th Pennsylvania down the slope toward the enemy, elbow to elbow, each man feeling the presence of the man on either side. As soon as we started to advance, the Rebels increased the urgency of their fire. Bullets flew all about. Several struck the earth in front of me, throwing up small plumes of dirt. One spent ball struck my left foot a glancing blow, surprising me more than hurting me. Another passed cleanly between my legs, causing a slight abrasion on my trouser leg. Still another plucked at my cartridge case. Others were not as fortunate. Up and down our line, men fell as they were struck and either died where they fell, or tried to hobble off to the rear.

About seventy-five yards from the sunken road, Colonel Perkins ordered us to stop. We fired a powerful volley into the line of smoke that marked the sunken road.

"Lie down!" echoed up and down the line. "Fire at will!" Companies A and B began to deliver a rapid fire with their Sharps breech-loading rifles. The rest of us with Springfields tried frantically to reload.

"Settle down, boys," Sarge's shrill voice cried out. "Just do your work. Load, aim, and fire. Load, aim, and fire. On my command." Sarge scurried up and down our line at a low crouch, calling out the reload commands loud enough for all in our company to hear. Then we aimed as a single man and fired, again at his command. We did it again, and again, and again, until we were caught up in our deadly work to the exclusion of all else.

"Company C, fire at will," Sarge ordered after a few minutes. I didn't need to hear Sarge calling the cadence anymore, for my body was going through the drill without thought, almost as if it was a natural thing for me. Sarge kept moving up and down the line, crouching low and encouraging all of the riflemen in his charge. Once again, Sarge had been right. I was afraid but not overly so, just load, aim, and fire; just load, aim, and fire. I was aware of nothing but working my Springfield.

After several more shots, a bullet whizzed passed my left ear, so close that I felt the air part with its passage. My stomach turned and bile rose in my throat at the closeness of it. I froze. Listen for Sarge, I thought, just listen for his voice and obey. I tried and tried to listen for those familiar words of encouragement and instruction amid the din of battle, but he had fallen silent. I looked up and down the line. Here and there a dead man lay motionless; gaps in the line evidenced the many wounded that were even now seeking safety, but there was no sign of Sarge. Then I looked directly behind me, and there he was, flat on his back, face to the sky, about five yards away. I crawled over to him and saw the red-black bullet hole in his left temple. His clear gray eyes stared sightlessly at the hot sun above, the fire forever gone.

"John, they got Sarge," I shouted.

John pointed to the empty place beside him. "Come on back, Michael."

"But Sarge is dead! What should we do?"

"I'm just going to do what Sarge told me to do. You should do the same."

John went about loading his rifle again while I remained next to Sarge. Should I find someone and tell them? Should I return to the fight? Should I head for the rear? Many others already had, especially on the right end of the regiment.

"What's your name, Private?" a voice yelled above the roar of battle.

I looked up and came face-to-face with Captain Carpenter, crouched low, his pistol leveled at my forehead.

"Sir, Palmer, sir."

"You're not thinking about quitting on us, are you, Palmer?"

"Sir?"

"Well, Palmer, if I have to inform your family of your death, would you like them to know that you died facing the enemy or running away from them? Look at the Sharps boys! Look at the rest of Company C." I looked right and left. "Company C is still holding. So are the Sharps boys and the Pennsylvania boys."

"Sir, Sergeant Needham is—he's dead, sir."

"I know that, Private. It's a great shame. Now get back to it, Palmer."

I did as I was ordered and returned to my place beside John. I reloaded and fired again and again, sighting through tear-filled eyes, oblivious to all else save the desire to see one of my bullets strike home to avenge Sarge. But before any such satisfaction could be had, General Kimball's brigade came up to relieve us and our fight was done.

The Rebels had treated us severely and I had behaved badly. The regiment had done some good work, and it did seem that the firing from that section of the road had slackened some. The men of the Fourteenth fell back up the slope, being careful to provide assistance for all their wounded brothers, so that all of the still living would make it off that field. Over the low fence and back through the trampled corn we went, moving swiftly toward the safety that lay over the brow of the hill.

CHAPTER 7

Fall of the Mighty

The LORD killeth, and maketh alive:
he bringeth down to the grave, and bringeth up.
1 SAMUEL 2:6

THE FARMSTEAD IN THE SHALLOW GLEN HAD ALREADY BEEN converted into a field hospital. Hundreds of Federal wounded lay about the grounds. Warm water from my canteen refreshed my parched throat but did nothing to improve my spirits. The carnage of war was inescapable. My ears ached with the cries of the afflicted, and my eyes burned at the appalling scene as my senses once again assaulted me with the ghastly human toll being exacted this day.

We spent only a few minutes at the farm before being ordered forward to prevent the enemy from advancing down the lane that led from the sunken road to this sheltered farm. We ran a few hundred yards up the lane and sat behind a rock wall, thankful to be shielded from most of the danger, and even more thankful to move even a short distance away from that dreadful hospital. The respite allowed us a brief rest, a more few swallows of water, and an opportunity to regain a measure of the composure and morale we needed to function as a disciplined unit once again.

Captain Carpenter chose this opportunity to address the

men of Company C. "I am proud of the way you handled your-selves this morning. You have been tested and bloodied, but now you know the business of battle." He pointed at the cornfield atop the rise behind him. "You all know that Sergeant Needham was killed up on that hill. He was a great soldier, and he will be missed. I am promoting Sergeant Holt to the rank of first ser-geant. Obey his orders as you did Sergeant Needham's, and you will do well. That is all."

"Sir, yes, sir!" we all answered.

A great cheer went up from the men in the road. "The Irish! The Irish!" A long straight line of blue-clad troops marched in step through a freshly plowed field, toward the brow of the hill to the east of the lane. "It's the Irish! They'll whip them Rebs!"

Indeed, their brilliant green banner waved lazily in the gen-tle breeze. Their general rode proudly at the front, leading them into the fight, facing the flying perils of lead and iron along with his men. The brigade crested the hill and marched with both bayonets and faces fixed toward the sunken road. For well over half an hour the sounds of fighting waxed and waned as the Irish made repeated attempts to take the Rebel position. They stood their ground in the open field and poured as much lead as they were able into the Rebels, but to no avail.

The brave Irish finally gave way to fresh troops coming up behind them. These men had an easier go of it, mostly because the Irish, even as they were being cut down, had done their duty and killed many of the enemy. Finally the Rebels started to aban-don the sunken road, first by ones or twos and then by dozens, to head toward the rear. A short time later the Stars and Stripes was lifted above the sunken road and a mighty hurrah arose from the entire Federal line.

"Form by companies!" Colonel Perkins ordered the regiment out from behind the wall and into the lane. "Forward at the double-quick!"

A shell screamed down the lane. Those toward the front of the column dove for the ground, but those farther down the line were not as fortunate. The shell exploded amid the boys of Company D, and when the smoke cleared, three more of our friends lay dead, one with his head blown entirely off. Several men retched by the side of the road. My own stomach turned heavily at the sudden and sickening manner in which death had visited us.

Once order was restored, we marched through the large field of soft earth to the east of the lane, once again toward the sunken road. When we crested the hill, we chose our steps with care so as not to tread on any of the hundreds of Union dead. Most of them had *SNY* belt buckles and regimental numbers on their caps — *69* or *63* or *88* — remnants of the Irish Brigade. Ambulance attendants moved here and there among the hundreds of wounded, ministering what aid and comfort they could. Other men were engaged in private struggles for survival, hobbling or crawling toward the rear, one agonizing yard at a time.

The Fourteenth was assigned to support Colonel Brooke's brigade of General Richardson's division. While they pursued the Rebels into a large cornfield south of the sunken lane, we were to guard a battery of artillery being maneuvered into position along the north side of the sunken lane.

The carnage in the lane was dreadful. Confederate dead lay in twisted heaps, covering the lane from side to side for hundreds of yards, sometimes two or three deep. Here and there, the dark blue of a Union corpse lay in stark contrast to the drab grays and tans of the dead Rebels. Already, Federal burial details were at work clearing paths across the lane. They recovered the dead in blue for burial and made gruesome piles of the rest.

We deployed around Battery K, First U.S. Artillery, to protect it from Rebel counterattack. We lay down and hugged the earth just behind the guns as they began to throw shells into the cornfield beyond the sunken road. The guns bucked and nearly leaped off the ground each time they were fired. I covered my ears with my hands to dampen the noise and tried to glue my body to the earth, which tried its best to shake me loose with every blast.

A general galloped frantically up the hill behind us, waving his hat furiously and screaming incomprehensibly. He rode straight through our line, causing several men to dive to one side or the other to keep from getting trampled. The general pulled his steed up next to the officer in charge of the guns.

"Captain Graham," the general yelled, "those scoundrels are trying to move by our right flank. See? Over there." The general waved his hat at some shadowy figures moving through a stand of trees. "They're trying to get into that swale behind us. Move your guns over there immediately and drive them off."

"Yes, sir, General Richardson." The captain saluted and immediately issued the necessary orders. Since the guns needed to be moved only a short distance to the right, it was much quicker to use men to move the guns rather than the usual teams of horses, and as it was the duty of our regiment to support and protect the battery, it fell to us to help the gun crews manhandle the big guns over to their new positions under the watchful eye of General Richardson.

"That's fine, Captain," he said when he was satisfied. "Now give them canister until they leave." At that moment a shell exploded over the battery. The general clutched his left shoulder, swayed slowly in the saddle, and fell heavily to the ground between two of the guns. Several of the gunners clustered around him, but the general waved them back to their guns. "Make it hot for them, Captain Graham," the general ordered. Then he lay back on the earth.

The battery gunners produced a stretcher. Four men were chosen from the ranks, and the general was borne off toward the hospital at the farmstead down in the glen. Several weeks later we learned that General Richardson died of his wound. No one was safe, not even a major general.

"The regiment is now attached to the first division," Captain Carpenter told us, "and the division is now under the command of General Hancock. We have been placed in line between his first and second brigades. The brigade just to our left, the one we're supporting, is Meagher's Irish Brigade. We are ordered to hold here against any attack until relieved. Now, stay down and try not to draw fire."

We remained where we were, prone in the dirt of that plowed field, not moving a muscle for fear of drawing fire. Afternoon gave way to a beautiful evening with the last rays of a dying blood-red sun beaming through a layer of clouds off to the west. The shelling continued until darkness finally ended that long, hot day of bloodletting. When it was fully dark, an eerie hush fell over the field, broken only by occasional shots traded by the pickets and the cries of the wounded lying stranded between the lines. Believing it was safe to move, I took a long drink from my canteen and ate a couple of crackers and a few bites of salt pork. Then I lay back in the place I had spent the last several hours and soon fell into exhausted sleep.

About midnight, I awakened to the touch of raindrops upon my face. The cries of the wounded continued, but they were fewer in number. Some were haunting howls of pain and desperation that could be heard over some distance. Others were low, deep groans of resigned agony, which I knew were much nearer at hand. As the intensity of the rain increased, the sound of its falling muted all but the most piercing wails. I turned my face heavenward and opened my eyes, allowing the heaven-sent droplets to cleanse my sight and wash the filth of the day of battle from my face.

Then I prayed. I realized to my shame that it was the first

time since Fort Ethan Allen, so long ago, that I had really prayed. I lifted my spirit to God and prayed for my family, thanking God for my deliverance that day. I prayed for Sergeant Needham's family, that God would comfort them in their sorrow and meet their every need in abundance. And I prayed that God would calm and soothe my already war-weary soul.

Then I began to weep over all that I had seen and heard and known that day—the dread, the horror, the gore, the fear. I wept for Sarge and for the young men from Company D I had seen killed in the lane, and for the thousands of others now dead, so many lost in a single long day. Sarge's family would grieve his loss, and I knew it could have as easily been Jessie Anne and Sarah and Edward grieving for me. I opened my eyes wide and stared heavenward as raindrops fell heavily from the blackness above. The rain merged with my tears and spilled off my face into the same red earth that had so freely drunk of the blood of so many good men that day.

How long, O God, how long?

CHAPTER 8

Requiem

He will swallow up death in victory;
and the Lord GOD will wipe away tears from off all faces.
ISAIAH 25:8

THE ARTILLERY OPENED UP AT BREAK OF DAWN. IT SEEMED AT first as if the fighting would resume in earnest, but the cannonading lacked both intensity and longevity. The energies of both armies had been spent in the rampant slaughter of the preceding day. Now and again, fighting flared up at one point or other along the line, but it subsided quickly. Sometime after noon, the shelling and musketry ceased altogether. A short time later a rider came up from the rear bearing the news that a twelve-hour cease-fire had been agreed upon to tend to the wounded and bury the dead.

In the field where the boys from Connecticut lay, the nighttime rain had turned the furrows of freshly turned earth to little muddy sloughs. As the clouds disappeared and the sun began to dry us, our new uniforms looked new no longer. In fact, the caked mud made us look more Confederate butternut than Union blue.

Sergeant Holt approached. "Palmer."

"Yes, Sergeant?"

"You said Sarge was killed near you?"

My head drooped low between my shoulders. "Yes, Sergeant."

"Think you can find him?"

"Yes, Sergeant Holt. I believe I know exactly where he is."

Sergeant Holt chose John and four other men from the company. Our small squad set off in silence across the battlefield.

The powerful stench of rotting flesh assaulted my nostrils as carrion birds feasted upon untold hundreds of dead soldiers. I closed my mouth and held a kerchief to my nose, thus reducing the stench to a tolerable level, but nothing could shield me from it entirely. Here, a corporal had died where he fell facedown, the fingers of his right hand frozen about his rifle, the fingers of his left hand clutching the earth, as if trying to hold on. There, a captain was sitting against a fencepost, appearing to be asleep, until one approached and saw the dried, bloody hole in the middle of his chest. Had the captain managed to sit down there before he expired or had some caring companion placed him there? And this boyish private here, with his leg blown off at mid-thigh, the blackened stain around him showed how he had bled to death. His contorted features evidenced the agony of his passing; his mouth gaped wide at me in a grotesque, silent scream. Some of the bodies could not even be recognized as human remains; they were just blackened heaps on the ground adorned with a soldier's accoutrements. In addition to the human carnage, there were mutilated horses, blasted caissons, cratered earth, and splintered trees—corruption of man, beast, and nature itself. I recalled the haunting words of the preacher just two days before, *Hell will be infinitely worse.*

Sarge was already swollen almost beyond recognition by the hot sun, but I knew him immediately by his bushy sand-colored hair and moustache. Still, we checked for the *14* on his cap just to make sure. John fell to his knees beside Sarge. With deliberate care John unfastened the top four buttons of Sarge's jacket, slipped a hand inside and retrieved Sarge's pocket letter.

"I'll take that," said Sergeant Holt. His gruff manner disturbed the solemnity of the occasion. "Captain Carpenter will see to it."

We lifted Sarge onto a blanket and carried him to the rear. Orderlies directed us to an area being used as a burial ground. We laid Sarge gently in the wide, shallow trench and watched as the burial detail spaded dark red earth over him. A small wooden cross was stabbed into the ground at the head of his grave. I took the knife my father had given me and carved "1st Sgt. John Needham, 14th Conn. Vol." on it. The men removed their caps and John offered a short prayer.

And when he had finished, he quoted, "Greater love hath no man than this, that a man lay down his life for his friends."

⋘∞⋙

Sunday, September 21, 1862
Camp of the 14th Conn. Rgt. Vol. Inf.
Near Sharpsburg, Maryland

My Dearest Jessie Anne,

By now you surely have read newspaper accounts of the great battle fought near this place. I assure you that while the 14th was heavily engaged, the Lord preserved me without so much as a scratch. John was also preserved unharmed and proved he is the finer soldier. A hearty dinner was prepared for us on Friday and another today, so I have had plenty to eat for now.

The enemy was drawn up behind their barriers, with their backs to the Potomac. We advanced generally against their front, and after much severe fighting, the enemy was thrown back and have retreated south of the Potomac. Regrettably, 21 men of the regiment were killed and 88 wounded. 1st Sgt. Needham was among those killed. Sarge was a good man. He commanded respect for his knowledge and leadership. If I am a soldier now, it is because he made me a soldier. Sarge was a sincere Christian, I believe, and I cannot fathom a divine purpose in taking this saint from us. His friendly manner and skillful teaching will be missed by all. Pray the Almighty for this man's grieving family.

This morning a memorial service was conducted under a stand of trees by Chaplain Stevens. It was a somber occasion. The band played a prelude of several hymns; never have they played better or more fervently. Chaplain Stevens gave a prayer of invocation and read several Scripture passages. Then he preached on the first eight verses of Isaiah 40. The chaplain spoke of the suddenly empty places where friends had been a few short days ago, like grass that is here today and is tomorrow cut down. How sharp these words now sound in my ears, "All flesh is grass."

After the sermon, Colonel Perkins read the names of our twenty-one dead in a high-pitched, strident voice, as a gentle breeze stirred the leaves of the trees over our heads. The service ended with the singing of the hymn "Abide with Me." The band played in perfect harmony, and the chorus of several hundred soldier voices rose high into the arching trees and was carried heavenward. I sang from memory, as you and I have many times before. The words came to my lips without thinking, but the words of the fourth verse stuck in my throat. How could I sing "I fear no foe" when indeed fear had held me in its grasp all during the fight? I have shed bitter tears; I have felt death's sting.

Yesterday, General McClellan and General French inspected the brigade. They pranced back and forth atop their steeds and made flowery speeches. They proclaimed the fight a great victory — then they rode away. The mood of the men does not speak of victory, and many wonder if, in the not too distant future, we will have to do the thing all over again, since the enemy has escaped and we are pursuing them. In spite of all I have known from childhood, I fear the only victor in the recent battle was the grave. Pray the Almighty for the promised triumph, that this war may swiftly and victoriously end, and that I may return to you and the children.

Lest you think me entirely without hope, John's unfailing friendship strengthens me each day. He is as ever a sturdy oak. He never wavered when we were under fire and even now, after a few short weeks, he shows a leadership uncommon among others in the company or even the regiment. Has it truly been little more than a month since we left home? Pray the Almighty for John and that beloved family.

On Monday, we will march away from here. Our destination will probably be near Harper's Ferry. I will write again once we have encamped. Words fail, but tears do not, when I think of you and the children. How I miss you all and long for you. Kiss Sarah and little Edward for me and assure them of their father's (and their Father's) love. Please pray the Almighty that He will continue to guard me and that I might know more of His tender mercies.

> With much love and deepest affection,
> I am your loving husband,
>
> *Michael*

CHAPTER 9

The Dark Times

The sword is without, and the pestilence and the famine within:
he that is in the field shall die with the sword;
and he that is in the city, famine and pestilence shall devour him.
EZEKIEL 7:15

O N MONDAY THE TWENTY-SECOND DAY OF SEPTEMBER, THE men of the Fourteenth Connecticut broke camp at first light and formed in columns of four abreast at the head of the mile-long column that comprised General French's division. We moved out in silent respect for the comrades we were leaving behind. Words were few, only brief whispered remarks, as the living passed soberly through the place where so many had fallen. In the mists of the dawn, we marched up the Smoketown Road and turned left onto the Hagerstown Pike. A small, white, spire-less church stood near the intersection, the meetinghouse of a small sect known as the Dunkers. This simple house of worship, now despoiled with its many scars and holes, bore silent testimony to the human storm that had enveloped it.

The pike led through the town of Sharpsburg. There were no crowds lining the streets to cheer our victory; the few town folk we did encounter were simply trying to put their lives back in order after the recent devastation. No bunting adorned the

simple homes, the two or three churches we passed, the meetinghouse, or the small library. Indeed the only display of any
kind was a lone Union flag hanging slack in the still morning
air next to a second-floor window of a grayish-white house near
the town center. The flag was tattered and torn and very dirty.
The red, white, and blue of her stars and stripes were stained
with several mottled shades of brown and gray. Surely this flag
had waved proudly in the breeze when the Confederate army
entered the town, and surely she had been thrown angrily down
and dragged through the mud. Perhaps she had even been kicked
and beaten or run through with saber or bayonet. And yet she
flew once more, wounded and soiled to be sure, but unbroken
and unbowed, just like the army that defended her. I stared and
stared at the simple beauty of that flag as my steps drew me
closer, until a slight movement at the window caught my eye—
an old, white wrinkled face, of a man or a woman I knew not
which, faintly but clearly illumined by the light of the new day.
A frail, trembling hand rose slowly beside the face and gave a
feeble wave. I tipped my cap in return.

We left the town behind and the day began to brighten. The
warm September sun warmed our spirits once more. The way
ahead had been scouted and was clear of the enemy. It was our
lot simply to march, and as the lead regiment in the column, the
Fourteenth was able to set the mood of the march. The band
struck up marching music to help us on our way.

"Sergeant Holt, when we get to Harper's Ferry, do you think
we'll have to fight again?" Every head within earshot swiveled
toward Jim Adams, the questioner, then to the sergeant, who
was marching alongside.

"Nah, I don't think so. If the Rebs are still there, our big
guns will just blast them to kingdom come."

"So what's going to happen to us now, Sergeant Holt?" John
asked.

"Don't know exactly," Holt answered. "Just have to wait until we get there."

Like King Saul of old, Holt was a large man, taller than every other man in the regiment, the sort of man you would much rather fight with than against. However, he possessed neither the acute intellect nor the pleasant disposition of Sergeant Needham, and to us he would always be Sergeant Holt, never Sarge.

We reached the Potomac at about two o'clock that afternoon. Harper's Ferry lay just across the river, and it should have been a simple matter to march across the railroad bridge. But the bridge had been destroyed and burned by the Confederates, and the only path into Harper's Ferry was through the rapid currents of the Potomac itself. Mr. McCarthy, the leader of the band, ordered his players to step off to the side of the road to let the regiment pass. They struck up a happy tune as the men of the Fourteenth started to wade across.

Captain Carpenter approached the bandmaster as Company C started down the bank into the river. "Mr. McCarthy, this brass band of yours is pretty fair, but just how good are you?"

"What do you mean, Captain?"

"How about a little wager, Mr. McCarthy? Ten dollars maybe?"

"All right," said Mr. McCarthy, his arms never missing a beat as he conducted the band. "What's the wager?"

"I'll wager that the boys in your band cannot keep playing all the way across the river. If any one of them stops playing his instrument for any reason from this side to the other, I win. Agreed?"

Mr. McCarthy laughed. "I'll take that wager, Captain. My boys will show you and all the rest of these men the stuff they're made of, . . . sir."

The water was only about waist deep, but the current was

swift and footing on the rocky bottom was tenuous. The regiment splashed its way merrily across, the river's cool flow refreshing and exhilarating. As each of the ten companies climbed the opposite bank, the men sought out vantage points from which they could view the crossing's finale.

The band members carefully made their way down the opposite bank into the waters of the Potomac. Thousands of eyes looked on intently; thousands of ears strained to catch every note. With every passing moment we expected one or more of the players to slip and fall. But Mr. McCarthy handled his charges wonderfully. He worked his way slowly across the river, feeling his way carefully step by step, and allowing each member of the band to do the same. On they came, foot by hesitant foot, fighting the buffeting current, fighting at once to maintain their tune and their balance, and slowly but surely nearing the hooting and hollering of the crowd that lined the bank to welcome them.

And then it happened.

"Look there, look at that fellow," someone said.

"Which one?"

"The third one, with the cornet—he almost went in." Indeed the young musician did seem to be struggling. The pitch of his horn had increased a tone or two and had begun to waver so that he was suddenly out of tune with the rest of the band.

"He's probably dancing like crazy on those slippery rocks."

"Yeah, tryin' to do the underwater double-quick."

"There he goes." The cornet player's tenuous hold on the river bottom was reduced to none at all, and he was quickly swept a few feet downstream.

Yet the man played on.

"He's going under." Waist-deep water was suddenly chest deep; then it was up to his neck. The man inclined his instrument upward and ceased fingering the keys while he fought to keep the river out of his horn. One more step forward and the man went completely under but for the very top of his head and the bell of his horn.

Yet the man played on, albeit in monotone.

"He's coming back up." Everyone began to cheer, at first hopefully and then lustily, as the soggy cornet player, with footing regained, slowly began to ascend in a gradual resurrection from the abyss. His head emerged, and his gasp for breath was clearly heard from the bank of the river. The man inched his way forward, rising little by little, recovering the tune and playing on to the great delight of us all, although with a somewhat damp timbre to his music.

When he finally reached the riverbank, the soaked cornet player, Charlie Merrills by name, was lifted clear of the water by a host of helping hands with much cheering and backslapping. I doubt that Captain Carpenter was ever happier to lose a wager.

The refreshing respite ended and reality closed around us once again. We marched past the armory made famous by the abolitionist John Brown. He and his small band of followers had seized it in hopes of arming an uprising of slaves, but after a few days, John Brown and his cronies had been captured and hanged for treason. Our route led us through the center of town, then steeply uphill for another two miles to Bolivar Heights. Our assignment was to occupy the breastworks on the heights and guard against any possible Rebel attack, but as we soon discovered, the breastworks were not vacant. They were already occupied by dozens of Union men, albeit dead ones, who had been killed in the fighting the week before when the town fell to the Rebels. Animals had savaged some of the corpses and all had decayed rapidly in the heat and humidity. The bodies were quickly moved outside the works and buried. The earth was turned over where the corpses had lain, and the Fourteenth Connecticut Volunteers set up camp within the breastworks.

And there we remained until the end of October. As the shorter autumn days gave way to chilly and even frosty nights, we lacked the things we needed most, clean clothes, warm woolen blankets, and tents for shelter. The army had forced us to leave our knapsacks at Fort Ethan Allen when we marched for Maryland, so we had only what clothes we were wearing at the time and our rubber blankets, which served as our only protection against the weather.

We lived in squalor. The drinking water was poor, and the unvarying diet of hardtack and salt pork might fill a soldier's belly, but it was hardly sufficient to keep him hale and hardy. Nearly everyone became sick with colds or fevers, and some fell ill with pneumonia. To a man, the regiment weakened by the day. Dysentery and diarrhea were epidemic. Some in our ranks fell to more deadly illnesses like malaria and typhus. As for myself, in addition to regular bouts of diarrhea, I came down with a bad cold just a few days after crossing the river. I became weak and feverish and was plagued with a coarse, hacking cough that at times seemed about to tear me asunder. The next morning, immediately after roll call, I reported for sick call.

"What's the matter with you, Private?" Doc Rockwell asked.

"I have a bad cough and a cold." I coughed two or three times as proof. Doc Rockwell thumped my chest and my back. He put a hand on my forehead for a second or two to check for fever.

"You do have a cold, but you're not that bad," Doc Rockwell said. "You don't need to go to a hospital." He reached into a cupboard, removed the lid from a small jar, and dispensed a large brown pill into his open hand. "Here," he said, holding the pill out to me, "take this."

I popped the pill into my mouth just as I noticed something like a cruel grin on the Doc's face. "Swallow it," he ordered.

My eyes went wide and I looked for a place to spit the horrid thing out.

"Swallow it, Private!"

I can attest that this pill was indeed a cure-all, since at Bolivar I reported for sick call only the one time. The next day, though no better, I passed on sick call and reported for duty as usual and tried to stay as warm and dry as possible.

Nineteen enlisted members of our regiment died at Bolivar, the same number as were killed at Antietam. Additional scores spent long weeks in hospitals; some recovered sufficiently to return to the ranks, but many were so weakened that they were sent home on medical discharges. These numbers were multiplied throughout all the other units at Bolivar. A worthless, needless waste of good men could have been easily avoided if the army had seen fit to give us proper shelter, warm clothing, and nourishing food. Merely the arrival of our knapsacks would have improved our lot immeasurably.

"Remember the Dark Ages?" John asked one evening as the four soldiers from Naugatuck warmed themselves before a blazing fire. "The plague and the Black Death?"

"Sure, we read about it at Union School," said Jim Adams.

"This place reminds me of that time," John said.

"You mean because no one was safe?" I asked. "And no one knew why people were dying or how to prevent it? All of us have been sick, even Jim."

"And every morning carts went around collecting the corpses," Jim said. " 'Bring out your dead,' the drivers called, 'bring out your dead.' "

Harry's eyes darted from one face to the other. "It's ... it's not that bad, is it?"

"Isn't it, Harry?" John said. "During the Black Death, many people ceased to care whether they lived or died. 'Eat, drink, and be merry for tomorrow we die' were the words they lived by."

"I think you're overstating it, John," Jim said.

"But I see this same attitude in many of the men," said John. "Do you keep a close eye on your money, Jim?"

"Sure, everybody does since we came here," Jim said. "There are thieves in this camp."

"Why so?" John asked.

"Because they have no money."

"Right you are, Jim, and why is that? Because they've wagered it away or wasted it on whiskey—rogues of the worst sort. Now they steal from men like us who carefully save their funds."

"So we are just sitting around waiting to die," I said. "On the battlefield there is honor, but here in camp, like this?"

"Michael." John's usually gentle voice was suddenly sharp and direct. "You know better. Just a short time ago you spoke of the will of God for your life. What has changed? Are you now just waiting to die?"

A weak shrug was all the response I could muster.

"That is a dark and hopeless place to be in, Michael," John said. "But for the grace of God, you or I might be one of those thieving rogues. I prefer to look for God's hand at work in all circumstances."

"So how is God working here at Bolivar?" I asked. Both Jim and Harry turned expectantly toward John.

"When I feel weak and downcast, I often turn to God for strength, and He lifts me up. But when I feel strong and content, it's all too easy for me to see God's blessings as my own successes. Self-pity and despair must not control me. I must believe in the eternal will of a holy, just, and merciful God. I must count on His love for me and stand on His promise, 'I will never leave thee, nor forsake thee.' Perhaps this is what God is teaching this army."

❦

Our spirits were soon raised by the arrival of a wagonload of new half-shelter tents, new woolen blankets, and new knapsacks. John and I teamed up as did Jim and Harry. I laid out John's half-shelter and my own upon the ground and buttoned the two halves together. While I was doing this, John fixed the bayonets to our two Springfield rifles, stuck them into the ground at either end of the tent, and tied a length of rope between the trigger guards. Then we draped the shelter tent over the rope to form the peak. The corners of the tent were held in place by sticks driven into the earth. Lastly, we laid our rubber blankets on the ground inside the tent.

That evening John and I sat before the campfire reading our Bibles, as was often our custom when other duties allowed it. John began to chuckle.

"What's so funny?" I asked.

"I've been reading through Luke, and I just read the verse in which Jesus says, 'Foxes have holes, and birds of the air have nests; but the Son of man hath not where to lay his head.' It just struck me as funny, that for the last month we lived like our Lord with nowhere to lay our heads. The Lord's timing is incredible, that I should read those words tonight when we finally do have a place to lay our heads."

I nodded slowly, still not seeing the humor in it. When we closed our Bibles to pray, John said, "Michael, the Lord told us, 'Take therefore no thought for the morrow: for the morrow shall take thought for the things of itself.' Think of the many simple blessings we see every day — food, shelter, clothing, fire, basic necessities all, but what of friendship, the birds of the air, the beauty of this land all around us, the love of our families? Give thanks tonight for each and also thank God for giving you His only Son. Only in Him is there lasting peace and hope."

I wrapped myself tightly in my new woolen blanket and slid under the cover of our new shelter tent. I knew John was right, and my prayer ended in restful sleep, but in the morning I awoke thoroughly chilled once again. Another gloomy day lay ahead.

CHAPTER 10

Bugs and the Band

And he hath put a new song in my mouth,
even praise unto our God.

PSALM 40:3

IT WAS DURING MANUAL-OF-ARMS DRILL ONE MORNING AT BOLI-var that my compatriots and I were schooled in another form of warfare. As we formed into squads to start the drill, it soon became impossible to maintain order in the ranks as first one, then another, and another of the men began to fret and fidget. Fidgeting gave way to furtive scratching, such as using the toe of one shoe to scratch the opposite ankle, as we tried to conceal our movements from the watchful eye of Captain Carpenter. But soon all semblance of secrecy was gone, and each man scratched busily not only at his ankles, but also at his wrists, armpits, belt-lines, and nether regions.

"Cooties!" Captain Carpenter spat with disgust. "You all have cooties! Sergeant Holt, deal with these men!" The captain stalked off in the direction of his tent.

"Cooties?" a score of voices asked in unison.

"Yeah! Bugs! Graybacks! *Lice!*" Sergeant Holt was refer-ring to the insidious little parasite known as the body louse, but they were generally called by the names suggested by Sergeant Holt—or other names not fit to mention.

"What should we do, Sergeant Holt?" I asked.

"I'll show you. You others gather round, 'cause I'm only going through this once. Where are you itching?"

"My legs, my armpits, my back, my—"

"Okay, okay, just one place—your leg. Roll up your trouser leg." I rolled it up to my knee. "Where's it itch worst?"

"Right here," I said, indicating a place on the inside on my left knee.

"Look for a small reddish bump there. See it? Feel it?"

"Yes, Sergeant Holt." I ran the tip of my finger over the spot.

"That's a cootie!" Sergeant Holt laughed a fiendish laugh. "It's under your skin where it's nice and warm, and it's eating away at your flesh." Sergeant Holt was the only one laughing. Sarge would have been sympathetic to our affliction. He would have forewarned us. How dearly I missed the man.

"How do I get rid of it, Sergeant Holt?"

"You need something sharp, like a small knife."

"A sewing needle?"

"Sure," Sergeant Holt responded. "It'll hurt like the dickens, but just dig the little devil out and squish him between your fingers. Now, go get 'em, men!"

I reached into my pocket for the small sewing kit Jessie Anne had given me, wondering how she would have reacted had she witnessed the purpose for which it was first employed. I clenched my teeth against the pain, forced the needle under the telltale bump, and pried the cootie out. The pest was about a tenth of an inch long, but occasionally I found them up to twice that length. He had a small head and six crooked legs that he used to attach himself to his host—*me!* The louse popped most satisfyingly as my fingers squeezed the life out of him. I went in search of another, dug him out, and popped him. In half an hour I had found and killed a dozen of these vermin and quickly realized that, were I to engage in this pastime constantly, I could never defeat the enemy that way.

Doc Rockwell told us that the only real cure was to bathe often and well with strong soap, something a body is reluctant to do during pleasant weather, but especially so during the cold winter months. Our clothing could not just be washed in a stream; it had to be boiled for fifteen minutes to assure the elimination of this scourge. Bedding and outerwear also had to be boiled, and we had to take special care when we were near a dead or dying person. These little pests seemed to know when their host was sinking away and they would jump ship, as it were, to the nearest warm body. Yet even with the strictest regimen of bathing and boiling and wariness, it was never more than a few weeks before the cooties came back for another visit and battle commenced again.

⋘∼⋙

It should not be thought that all of the time at Bolivar was spent in melancholy, with our only activities being drill, fatigue duty, guard duty, foraging and cooking, the exercises of religion, or digging for cooties. There were some especially memorable times that lifted our spirits and knit the men together in an unspoken bond of brotherhood. There was laughter aplenty, regular letters and news from home, and every evening there was music. The music would often start simply with a single man sitting at his campfire after supper slowly strumming his banjo or bowing his fiddle, and whether his tune was a mournful lament over a lost love or a lively Scottish reel, a few friends would gather round, one or two members of the band might join in, and others would soon draw close.

I was always eager to join in when the singing started. At first these army songs were new to me, but I learned them quickly.

Having learned in my childhood the many hymns of the faith, and having sung them continually ever since, these campfire songs came very naturally to me. Songs about life in the army, army food, national leaders, patriotism, loves left at home, and friends lost on the field of battle, written by George Root, Walter Kittredge, H. T. Merrill, and others, stirred the spirits of the men, and the singing of these soldiers' songs became the usual manner in which I chose to end each day at Bolivar.

"Play the 'Battle Cry of Freedom,'" a voice might ask, or "How about 'Tenting on the Old Camp Ground'?" Then we might sing the new "Battle Hymn of the Republic" and follow it with the northern version of "Maryland, My Maryland," since we were just across the river from her. If the mood was light, "The Army Bean" song might be next along with "Hard Crackers" and its many hilarious verses of both official and unofficial authorship.

Discordant voices joined together, softly at first as each man sought his place in the chorus, then more firmly and even boisterously as they became more secure with the words and the tune and with their singing brothers. My warm baritone must have stood out from the mix, for sometimes, when the men had tired of the singing in general, or perhaps of their own singing in particular, a voice or two might be heard during a pause, "Palmer ... Michael Palmer ... give us a song." At first, I modestly tried to put off these requests, but the one or two voices bred others; firm but gentle hands propelled me forward into the full glow of the firelight.

And so I began to sing for the troops, nervously at first, but bright, fire-filled eyes looked to me and calmed me. I sang "Take Your Gun and Go, John," a song that was dear to my heart, because it told the story of a wife telling her husband that she would tend to the farm and the children as he went off to war:

Don't stop a moment to think, *John*;
   Our country calls, then go.
Don't fear for me nor the children, *John*,
   I'll care for them, you know!
Leave the corn upon the stalk, *John*,
   The fruit upon the tree,
And all our little stores, *John*,
   Yes, leave them all to me.

This scene was repeated for several nights, but soon the men became dissatisfied with a single song from me. I understood that whenever the men wanted me to sing for them at the end of the day just before the final roll call, that they wanted to hear the soft, reflective, and often mournful tunes that brought to mind deeply etched memories they could cherish in silence as the words rolled over them. And so I added several more songs to my repertoire: "Brother, Tell Me of the Battle," "Our Comrade Has Fallen," "The Vacant Chair," "Mother Would Comfort Me," and "Weeping, Sad and Lonely." Indeed, I preferred these somber, heartbreaking songs above all others, for they suited my general disposition, and I had no difficulty evoking the sorrowful mood required. I usually sang from memory with my eyes closed, thinking only of the story being told, for I knew that should I open my eyes and gaze upon the faces of the men gathered around, the firelight would doubtless reveal many a tear-streaked cheek.

One bright, sunny day during early October, as John and I sat about our campfire enjoying our midday coffee, a member of our regimental band sidled over and sat down with us. It was the notorious cornet player Charlie Merrills. He appeared very young, perhaps still in his teens. John offered Charlie a cup of coffee.

"No thank you, Mr. Robinson." Charlie was polite and

respectful when addressing his elders. "I just came over to talk to Mr. Palmer.

"Some of the boys in the band have been talking with Mr. McCarthy," he continued. "We've heard you singing at the campfires and we think you sing very well. You have great warmth and the men respond well to it. We would like you to consider singing with our band."

I nodded a sheepish "Thank you."

"Mr. McCarthy thinks you could do maybe five or six songs, some of the ones you sing now plus a few others. We would have to rehearse of course, but we all think it could be very good. You could be part of our regular Saturday evening concerts if you wish, and you would have the opportunity to perform for the officers as well as the troops."

"I've never done anything like that," I said. "I enjoy singing for the men, I really do, but that's a personal thing between the men and me. I've never sung in front of a crowd of strangers."

"You have a gift and you need to use it," John said. "Your singing has warmed many soldiers around our campfires, but many more have never heard you sing. You should allow them to be blessed by your singing as well. Doesn't that seem right to you?"

"But you've heard the band. They play very well, but also very loudly, too loudly for my one voice." I knew it was my last desperate objection, but I voiced it anyway.

"That's not a problem," said Merrills. "We'll make sure the audience can hear every word. Now, what do you think, Mr. Palmer?"

I heaved a large sigh and nodded my head. "All right."

"Fabulous!" Merrills said, pumping my hand while John clapped me on the back. "I'll tell Mr. McCarthy and he'll see Captain Carpenter about arranging time for you to rehearse with us. This is going to be great!"

And so it was that on the evening of Saturday, the eighteenth of October, I, Michael Gabriel Palmer, debuted in concert with the band of the Fourteenth Connecticut Volunteer Infantry Regiment at a small Methodist church in Bolivar. When every pew was filled, some of the men stood quietly at the back of the church. After the band played several pieces, Mr. McCarthy motioned for me to come forward. I sang just two songs. The first was my favorite "Take Your Gun and Go, John." The audience listened attentively and applauded warmly when the song was done. Then Mr. McCarthy struck up the rousing "Battle Cry of Freedom." As I finished the fourth and last verse, every officer and enlisted man in the place stood up and joined heartily in the chorus:

> The Union forever,
> *Hurrah, boys, Hurrah!*
> Down with the traitor,
> Up with the star;
> While we rally round the flag, boys,
> Rally once again,
> Shouting the battle cry of Freedom!

Their singing done, the hundred or more voices gave way to wild cheering. I bowed stiffly once and returned to my seat. Afterward, several officers shook my hand and expressed their appreciation. Some wished for me to appear with the band at every concert. But any satisfaction was small and short-lived; there would be only one more concert at Bolivar. The army was, after all, an instrument of war, and the war could not be fought and won with band concerts.

CHAPTER 11

Trudge to the Rappahannock

And they shall march every one on his ways,
and they shall not break their ranks.
JOEL 2:7

Michael, get up here and take a look. The entire Confederate Army is down there."

I hastily clambered over a few more large rocks and finally reached John, who stood atop a stony crag overlooking the road through Snicker's Gap, where the men of the Fourteenth had been posted to guard against possible flank attack. It was a crisp, cloudless night, and the view from the ridge appeared endless.

"There must be ten thousand campfires if there's one," I said. "How far away are they?"

"Five miles, at least, maybe ten," John said. "That's the Shenandoah Valley down there. Now, turn around and look back down the road."

A few miles to the east the scene was repeated, perhaps on an even grander scale, with the fires of the Army of the Potomac spreading across the floor of the Loudon Valley.

"It's a glorious sight," I said, "like a tapestry of fiery tongues—but these two armies must come together again."

"And Rebel pickets could be just out of sight down this road with us dead in their sights."

"What's your point, John?"

"Of late you seem to dwell on the darker side of things. I've never seen that in you before."

"Is it so strange?"

"I look at all this," John said, waving his long arms high and wide, "as a gift from God. There is glory before and behind and above and below, but you seem to see it as an omen of doom. Sure, I know, tonight could be my last here on earth—these words might be my last—and thoughts like these are never far off. But I know in whom I believe and I'm prepared to face the final muster out, as Sarge would say."

"But the Rebs could storm up through this gap in the next hour," I said. "How could our single regiment, only a few hundred men, stop thousands of them? Or—"

"Or we might die of pneumonia or typhus or some other disease. My times are in His hand, Michael; so are yours. I will do my duty and leave my end to Him. And I will try always to be prepared, come what may."

⋘⋙

Friday, November 14, 1862
Camp of the 14th Conn. Rgt. Vol. Inf.
Near Warrenton, Virginia

My Dearest Wife Jessie Anne,

Your letter of October 24th I have just received. The last several days have been cold. It snowed lightly for several hours on the 4th when we were some miles north near Upperville and the north wind drove the flakes along almost horizontally. There was naught to do but turn against the blast and shield my reddened, near-frozen face. The army has not seen fit to issue the promised heavy blue greatcoats, so I always wear every piece of clothing I have, and even then I shiver uncontrollably and stamp my feet constantly whenever I am away from the campfire. Your lovely letter has warmed my heart beyond measure and I thank God daily for loved ones at home, because the local folk seem as cold as the weather.

Please forgive the somber words in previous letters. This new soldier was unaware of the tolls this war would exact upon every part of his person. However, please do not think me entirely wretched. John's friendship is as vital as ever—he lifts my spirits daily. The routines of the march and camp occupy my thoughts and my time, but I continue to yearn for you and the children.

I continue in reasonably good health. I do have food sufficient to my need, even though I wish it were more satisfying. Perhaps you might send me some canned fruits and other goodies in sufficient quantity that I might share with John, Jim, and Harry. Also, and I hope it is not too late for this request, I would like to give each of these men a new pair of boots for Christmas. Hickham's are the best, and the warmest. Sizes: John (12), Jim (10), Harry (8), and the usual size 9 for me. Please send all packages in care of Captain Carpenter, Company C, 14th Conn. Rgt. Vol. Inf. It seems that packages addressed to officers always reach their destinations, while those addressed to enlisted men often do not.

Last week Colonel Perkins told us that General Richardson died of the wound he received at Antietam. Our colonel said, "Warriors such as General Richardson are too few and this army will long lament his passing." I think he was right. The only way to finish this thing is to fight and fight hard. The men are willing—they just need a leader like Joshua, strong and very courageous.

As you will have read in the newspaper long before this letter arrives, General McClellan has been relieved of command by the President. The entire army stood and cheered with unrestrained vigor as General McClellan, perched tall and erect astride his prancing horse, passed slowly in review throughout the entire assembled army. Then he merely rode away, and I expect we'll never see him again. Our new commander is General Burnside, and I do not know of one man in our regiment who is pleased with this change. It is now known that General Burnside was very slow to commit his corps to the fighting along Antietam Creek when decisive action could have turned the tide of battle heavily in our favor. Most judge him as a man lacking three qualities most necessary to a commanding general, a great military intellect, courage under adverse circumstances, and the ability to inspire others to greatness. Many think he will only lead us into disaster.

We have received orders to prepare to march tomorrow at daybreak. Our destination is near Fredericksburg, but I do not know how many days this move may take or what we shall do when we arrive there. Because of the lateness of the season, battle is unlikely. We will probably just build huts and go into quarters for the winter. I do not know when I shall have an opportunity to write to you again, but until then,

I remain your most devoted husband,

Michael

⊲⋛⋖⊳

The army finally issued winter greatcoats on Monday the seventeenth at Falmouth, a town on the north side of the Rappahannock River opposite Fredericksburg. We marched the next day in a heavy, soaking rain, to Belle Plain, a landing on the Potomac River, where supply ships docked, some down from Washington, others up from the Chesapeake Bay.

Our duty at the landing was not to guard it, as we had been

told by our officers, but to serve as laborers to unload the cargo from the ships. Working in shifts, night and day, seven days a week, we labored alongside a gang of escaped slaves who were pressed into service in return for food and shelter tents. The men grunted and cursed under the heavy loads of cases of hardtack, sacks of grain, barrels of salt pork, and boxes of ammunition. Sweat soaked our clothing and chilled us to the bone equally as much as the constant rain did. Already weakened from poor food, hard marching, and exposure to the weather, nearly every man in the regiment fell ill during the stay at Belle Plain. Harry Whitting's health worsened immediately, and he was unfit for duty at Belle Plain after the first day or two. The strength of our regiment dropped daily as the poor living conditions once again proved a more severe trial than any battle.

⋖⊱∝⊰⋗

Thanksgiving morning Captain Carpenter ordered Company C to turn out for a special assignment.

"Men," he said, "we have been detailed to procure Thanksgiving dinner for the regiment. You will assist the officers in every way to make this happen. Do you understand?"

"Sir, yes, sir," we all yelled enthusiastically, for the thought of better food made all of our prospects instantly brighter and merrier. The weather was pleasantly clear and mild, the best we had had in over a week, and there would be none of the backbreaking tedium this day.

"We will leave immediately and return this afternoon," our captain said. "Take nothing except your muskets and cartridge boxes. We will cross the river to pay a visit to a few farms where we should find all we need in short order. Those of you of high moral character," he added, looking in John's direction, "might think that we intend to steal from those people, but I assure you this is not the case. The federal government fully intends to compensate these people for their support of the Union cause. We are taking a wagon full of things to trade — soap, coffee, and so on — and each officer carries Federal claim certificates that may be tendered in exchange for the goods we obtain. The secessionists need only to present these certificates to the proper authorities to receive appropriate payment. I expect that each of you will behave in a manner that will be a credit to the regiment. Do you understand?"

"Sir, yes, sir!"

Our column of about forty officers and men, with three wagons in the rear, boarded a steam barge, crossed to the other side of the Potomac, and invaded the eastern shore in a spirited fashion with high hopes for the success of our mission.

Things went downhill from there. Apparently, Captain Carpenter had received no clear indication where these flourishing Rebel farms were, so we scouted about the countryside until a suitably prosperous looking farmstead was found. To say that the farmer and his kin were not happy to see us, both because we were "Yankee scalawags" and because we had disturbed them mid-feast is, of course, an understatement. After the officers negotiated the "purchase" price, the downcast farmer was asked where the next farm was. He gestured vociferously and gave very detailed directions, but of course whatever directions he gave were wrong, and the search for that next farm would begin anew. This scene played out several times that day, but slowly the wagons filled and our anticipation rose as we looked forward to the good eating we would enjoy back at camp.

I can only assume the barge pilot was unfamiliar with that part of the Potomac, for merely a hundred yards offshore, the barge, with its cargo of jubilant and hungry soldiers and the wherewithal for a sumptuous feast, grounded fast upon a sandbar. The pilot apologized profusely for his error, but there was nothing to do but remain on that barge overnight with no warm clothing or blankets to shelter us from the cold night air. The next morning, a steamboat put out from the opposite shore and towed the barge into deeper water.

Colonel Perkins, kept informed of the procurement party's progress, or lack thereof, proclaimed the observance of Thanksgiving would continue through Friday. Upon Company C's triumphant arrival at camp, we found a kitchen already prepared, fires blazing, and volunteer butchers and cooks waiting. Sacks of large onions and slabs of bacon were turned into a deliciously fatty and salty hot soup. Bushels of sweet potatoes were boiled and mashed and served with sweet, creamy butter. Sacks of cornmeal were baked into muffins and topped with fresh clover honey. Dozens of chickens were slaughtered, plucked, and roasted over the open fires and divided among the men. Several smoke-cured Virginia hams, by reputation the best on the continent, were sliced and served cold. But the crowning achievement of our little foray across the river was a large hog ready for slaughter. After splitting the carcass into several pieces, each piece was run through with a spit and roasted. Dozens of soldiers stood around the fires grinning widely, their faces sooty and their eyes teary with the smoke of the sizzling pork fat that dripped in a steady stream onto the hot embers. Each one eagerly took his turn at the spit, rotating the meat over the flames and relishing the anticipation of that first bite.

Albeit a day late, it was with great joy and genuine gratitude that the men of the Fourteenth enjoyed a Thanksgiving feast second to none. For the first time in several weeks, all went to sleep that night with full and contented bellies.

⋐᯾⋑

General Burnside was all threat and bluster when he appeared at the landing a few days later. Several large ships had arrived overnight with a cargo of pontoon boats.

"Quickly, boys, quickly—every hour is critical! Those boats must be taken to the Rappahannock without delay!" One by one the pontoon boats were unloaded and lashed to carts waiting on the landing. "Go get another one, step lively now!"

The general's constant chatter from atop his mount quickly became tiresome, as there were only so many men at the docks and each man could only do so much before being completely exhausted.

John, usually one of the last to complain, finally could take no more. "Michael," he said, "I'm almost done in."

"As am I, and every other man."

"I'm praying that something will take that man with the magnificent facial fur away from here so we can rest a spell."

And something did take General Burnside away. Teams of horses and mules were necessary to draw the carts onto which the boats were lashed. But there were not nearly enough teams and soon, work slowed to a standstill.

"Captain Taylor," General Burnside screamed at one of his aides, "where's Butterfield? Tell him to send us every horse and mule he can find by noon today or I'll bust him down to second lieutenant! Take them from the artillery, from the quartermasters, and from anywhere else he can. I must have these boats at the river now!" The general rode off in the direction of Falmouth, still casting invectives and curses at the wind in his face.

"Winter quarters will have to wait," John said. "We're in for another fight."

"I've thought so for some time," I said. "All the arms and supplies and back-breaking labor without letup—now, there's no doubt about it. War in winter—another happy thought."

John just turned and glared at me.

We finally broke camp at Belle Plain on Saturday, December 6th, slogging back to Falmouth through more rain and cold and mud. Colonel Morris had fallen ill, and command of the brigade fell to another less suited, Colonel Palmer (no relation of mine) of the 108th New York, who had held his regiment out of the fighting at Antietam while the Fourteenth and the 130th Pennsylvania marched forward and did their duty. Morale was already very low from the return of the poor weather, but at this news our hearts grew heavier still.

At Falmouth the men of the Fourteenth camped under a stand of pine trees. It was snowing, and the trees provided partial shelter from the snow and a soft carpet of pine needles underfoot. John and I, and Jim Adams working without his tent-mate, threw up our tents and tried to sleep. By the next morning, there was a foot of snow on the ground and no way to build any camp-fires. The weather cleared after the snow, and the day was spent drying out, cleaning up, and foraging for firewood. By the light of day, we took down our tents, set them up properly, and somehow, mercifully, managed to light our cooking fire that evening. Coffee was just beginning to boil when Harry Whitting walked up. He sat down heavily on a log and tried to warm himself.

"Welcome home, Harry!" I said, slapping him on the shoulder. Harry coughed several times, hoarse and deep. "I'm sorry, Harry. Have some coffee." Harry, always of slight build, now appeared frail and gaunt.

"We've been told to start building a hut," Jim told Harry, "and we were thinking about building a larger hut for four men rather than for two." Harry nodded slowly.

"It'll only be a little more work," said John, "and each man will have his own bunk."

"We already share our possessions and camp duties," I said. "And after the hut is done, we only have to cut firewood for one hut. What do you think, Harry?"

Harry again nodded slowly.

"How about you, Jim?"

"I'm all for it," Jim replied, "and besides, if each man has his own bunk, I figure each man will keep his cooties to himself."

We all heaved with laugher, even Harry, whose face finally brightened enough to reveal the narrow but noticeable space between his two front upper teeth. But his laughter ended in another fit of coughing.

"How do we start?" Jim asked.

"We start by digging," John said. "A lot of digging."

Our four shelter tent halves would form the roof of our hut. We laid out the shelter tents and drove sticks into the ground to mark the corners. Our hut would be about eight feet wide by ten feet long with an inside area of about six feet by eight feet,

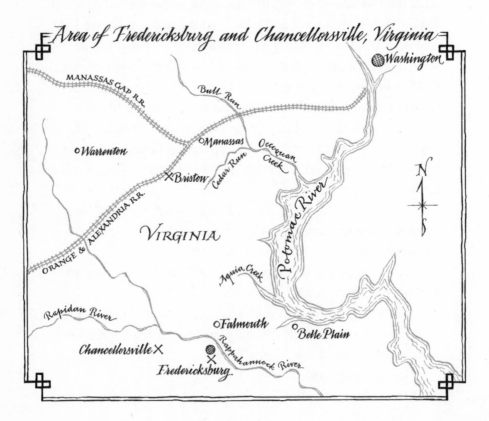

Area of Fredericksburg and Chancellorsville, Virginia

perhaps a little more depending upon the diameter of the logs we used.

It was dirty, nasty, toilsome work that occupied all of the hours we were not required to drill or do picket duty. Jim managed to borrow a spade from another regiment near our camp, so one man dug with the spade while another dug at the earth with his bayonet and another used the cooking pot for scooping. Harry tried to lend a hand when he could, but mostly he was just too weak for the heavy labor. By Wednesday afternoon the digging was done, and we were looking forward to getting out of the mud and into the construction of our hut.

However, that construction would have to wait. There was a war to fight.

CHAPTER 12

A Carol
for Caroline Street

Glory to God in the highest,
and on earth peace,
good will toward men!
LUKE 2:14

*T*HIS IS MADNESS!" JIM ADAMS PACED WHILE MOST OF THE MEN sat quietly awaiting orders, trying to enjoy what was left of the late-afternoon sunshine. "Sheer madness. It's useless and everyone knows it."

The river crossing into the city of Fredericksburg on the morning of Friday, December 12th, had been, for us, without opposition or injury. That price had been paid by others. We were ordered to occupy a street that ran along the bank of the river in plain view of the pontoon bridge that had granted us safe and dry access to the city. Throughout the day the leather-soled feet of columns of infantry, the shod hooves of horses and mules, and the iron-bound wheels of trains of wagons echoed hollowly as they tramped, clopped, and clanked across the wooden decking of the bridge into the city.

As if to punctuate Jim's vehement words, a shell screamed

overhead and exploded in the river just a few yards from the bridge, showering man and beast alike with icy water. A team of dray horses near mid-span reared on their hind legs and bellowed wildly into the cold air. The driver fought for control as the team strained against the harnesses that bound them to the heavy wagon. The very thing the beasts wished to be free of was the only thing that kept them from dashing headlong into the depths of the river.

"Useless," cried Jim to anyone who would pay him heed, "utterly useless. Burnside must be the only one that doesn't see it."

John beckoned to Jim. "Come have some coffee."

Jim shook his head in disgust and spat in the street, then came slowly to the fire.

"Jim, it may indeed be madness, as you say," said John, "but what can we do about it? We're soldiers under orders. It's our duty."

Jim turned on John. "Duty? Duty to go blindly forward and be killed, just because some general who's safely on the other side of the river says so? Every man in this army knows what's going to happen tomorrow. All that time we were at Belle Plain, Old Bobby Lee was preparing a warm reception for us. It's a trap, and we're walking right into it. We have no chance for success."

Harry shifted uncomfortably where he sat, but said nothing.

"I've heard that talk too," I said. "They're ready and waiting. Some even say the Rebs are begging us to march out and fight." I hesitated for a moment, wanting to be sure that the words I was about to utter I truly believed. "When the order comes down, I have resolved to do my duty and let God determine the outcome."

"God — He's nowhere in this army." Once again Jim spat in the street.

"You're wrong, Jim," John said. "He's all around us working out His purposes."

Jim ignored John's words. "So, Michael, you'll obey orders tomorrow, whatever they are, even if it kills you?"

I was taken aback by Jim's bluntness. I looked at John and held his steady gaze.

"Even so," I finally said, "even so." But even as those words escaped my lips, I shuddered at the implication of them. Were my words an expression of a sincere, childlike trust in my Heavenly Father? Or did they give voice to resignation, indifference, and acceptance of a fate yet to be determined?

⋈

Later that afternoon the three hundred and fifty men of the Fourteenth Connecticut, along with the rest of the brigade, were ordered away from the river into the next street parallel to the river, Caroline Street. Tens of thousands of Federal soldiers, now transient citizens of the city, occupied the substantial brick and wooden houses of the city folk, as well as the public buildings that, until a few days before, had been the exclusive realm of the Southern gentry of Fredericksburg. Most of the citizens had fled, preferring to wait out the impending storm behind the lines of Lee's army rather than remain in their homes to face the invading Vandal horde of Yankees.

Several dwellings in the city had been set ablaze by the shelling; Confederate or Federal, it would matter not when the owner finally returned to the smoldering ruin. Clouds of gray smoke hung lazily over the city. When the wind came from the direction of the river, I could sit quietly and breathe in fresh, clean air. But when the wind changed, it was all I could do to draw a breath. My eyes burned and teared; acrid smoke filled my lungs. I gasped and coughed and finally buried my face in the folds of my greatcoat, using the thick cloth to filter the smoke from the air.

"Hey, nutmeggers," a sergeant from the 108th New York yelled from a few houses up the street. "We're building fires in the cellars here for coffee. You boys should do the same." The army had been ordered not to build any fires for fear that the Rebel gunners would see them, but a soldier could be an extremely inventive character, especially when it comes to coffee.

"Let's go," yelled Sergeant Holt. He waved us toward a large house that appeared deserted. It was a fine and stately brick structure that had no doubt housed a fine and stately family before the tide of war had driven them out. "Find a way to the cellar. Take some wood, slats from that picket fence will do. Furniture will burn too—lots of wood in a house like this."

With great bravado Holt led the way in this domestic assault and in no time at all, smoke began drifting upward from the chimney. Knowing it would be a long night, John and I waited until the initial rush passed. We went around to the rear of the house and down a short flight of stone steps into the cellar. The cellar was divided into two main sections, a storage room, the shelves of which had been picked clean to prevent the foodstuffs from falling into our hands, I assumed, and a kitchen area with a fireplace for cooking during the hot summer months. Harry Whitting stood quietly next to the fireplace, warming himself and savoring his coffee.

"Hi, Michael. Hi, John." Harry tried to give us his gaptoothed grin, but his eyes told another tale; he was obviously unwell. "The men have been using the fire hooks or one of these long spoons to hold their cups over the fire."

"Thanks, Harry," John replied. "How are you feeling?"

"Not well. I still feel so weak, and I find breathing difficult. The smoke makes it worse."

"I'm sorry," said John. "Perhaps a warm and dry place to sleep tonight will do you good."

Harry shrugged. "Jim and Charlie Merrills came through a while ago. I think they're upstairs looking around."

Once John and I had our own cups of steaming coffee, we

climbed a narrow, twisting stairway to another kitchen, bigger and better equipped than the summer kitchen below. How the enticing aroma of a juicy roast beef or turkey, freshly baked bread and pies, or a pan full of sizzling bacon must have filled the entire house, reaching into every room, causing every empty stomach to growl in eager anticipation of the fine meal being prepared.

A doorway led to the dining room. Late afternoon sunlight slanted in through three windows and reflected brightly off polished hardwood floors. Still-life paintings, sketches, water colors, and portraits adorned the walls, personal remembrances of past and present generations, like those seen in many a home, even mine.

"I wonder if these were done by family members and who the people are in the portraits?" I said.

"Can you make out any of the signatures?" John asked.

"A few, but who knows who this family is?"

John ran his hand lightly over the top of the large rectangular dining table that occupied the center of the room. "This furniture is of the finest quality, Michael." Ten chairs stood in perfect order around the table, one at each end, four along each side.

"Must be a large family," I said.

"And look at this hutch cabinet," John continued. "It probably held the family's heirloom china and silverware. They must have taken it with them. This is surely the biggest hutch I've ever seen, almost the length of the table. See that grain? It's oak, like the table. The color and grain are so similar, maybe both pieces were made from the wood of a single tree."

I ran my hand over the smooth top of the table as John had. I tried to find the correct word to describe what I felt in the tips of my fingers. "It's so ... soft."

"That's the wax. You see how deep it looks?" I nodded,

seeing a dim reflection of myself in its depths. "That kind of finish can only be obtained through hours and hours of hand rubbing. I hope this family is able to enjoy these things for many years after we've gone."

The sound of someone playing a piano drew me away from the table and into the next room, the parlor. Several of our men, including Jim Adams, were taking their ease on the soft, plush furniture in this room that included four upholstered cushioned chairs and a long velvet-covered settee. One entire wall was covered with bookcases that seemed to hold every book ever printed. In the far wall was a pair of doors entirely made of panes of glass, like windows from floor to ceiling that opened to allow passage outside to a well-tended garden behind the house. But the room's main attraction was the American cherry-wood grand piano that stood just inside the windowed doors.

"Hello, Michael and John." Charlie Merrill's familiar eyes peered at us over the music brace atop the piano.

"You play the piano as well, Charlie?" His talents continued to impress me.

"Yes, and I find it much more interesting than the cornet. In my opinion the piano is the most perfect of instruments. But it's rather difficult to march with a piano strapped to my back." We all laughed heartily.

"And Michael, this is an excellent piano," Charlie added. "See this?" He pointed at an emblem above the keyboard. "William Knabe and Company, Baltimore, Maryland. She's a finely built instrument about fifteen years old. Her tone can be full and rich or dainty and delicate, and the action of the keys is clean and crisp, not sluggish like some less costly pianos. And look at the cabinetry. It's the best I've seen, first rate in every way."

"It is fine work," said John.

Charlie resumed his playing, softly and tenderly, as if savoring every nuance of tone that he drew from the piano. The tune he played was sweetly lyrical but unfamiliar.

"What are you playing?" I asked Charlie.

"A Christmas carol. I heard it for the first time only two or three years ago, but it's now one of my favorites. It's called 'It Came Upon the Midnight Clear.' Do you like it?"

"It's lovely."

"I was thinking that when we get back to camp, we should prepare a Christmas concert for the men. Listen to the words as I sing."

And so Charlie sang for us in his simple, unadulterated tenor.

> It came upon the midnight clear,
> That glorious song of old,
> From angels bending near the earth
> To touch their harps of gold:
> "Peace on the earth, good will to men,
> From heav'n's all-gracious King."
> The world in solemn stillness lay,
> To hear the angels sing.

"That's a good Christmas carol for a soldier," said John.

"There are more verses, but I only know the first," Charlie said.

"The music complements the words nicely," I said. "I'm sure the other verses will be just as pleasing."

"May God grant that we may all see Christmas," said John.

Sergeant Holt appeared in the doorway. "All of you men, on your feet. These houses are for officers only. You can still use the cellar for coffee, but stay outside otherwise."

The lounging men groaned, mumbled "Yes, Sergeant," and trudged out into the dark night.

John and I wrapped up in our blankets and found some comfort by leaning against a tree in front of the house. Everyone else settled down to try to sleep.

"John, I meant what I said—about doing my duty, whatever happens."

"I know you did."

"This is going to be tough. Tougher than Antietam, I think. At least there, the Rebs didn't have a hill behind them for their guns. When we were in the cellar boiling our coffee, I heard that their infantry's dug in behind a rock wall at the bottom of that hill."

"Many of us will probably not see sunset tomorrow," John said. "Let's not stand next to each other in the line—one shell could get us both, and that would be very sad for both families. Here, I wrote my pocket letter." John drew a sealed envelope from his breast pocket. "You know what to do with it. If you ever see them again, give them my love and tell them that I know we shall see each other again in glory."

"I will, John, and here is mine. I wrote it a month ago at Warrenton."

The words of that letter had not come easily. In fact, it was the most difficult thing I had ever written, because much of what was in my heart I could find no words for, and the words that I finally did write never seemed quite satisfactory. I kept that letter with me throughout the war. I rewrote it several times as the paper became old and worn, changing the date and location as circumstances dictated, since I never knew when I might have need of it.

Camp of the 14th Conn. Rgt. Vol. Inf.
Fredericksburg, Virginia
Saturday, December 13, 1862

My Dearest Wife Jessie Anne,

If you receive this letter, then you will know that I have been killed in battle and that I now delight in the nearer presence of our Lord and Savior and the eternal reward of blessed Sabbath rest. By now you have read in the newspaper of a great battle at this place. I am sure that our men at arms have done their duty and inflicted great harm on the enemy.

You must be assured of my love for you and for our children. Yet despite the depth of my love, it in no way compares to the love our Heavenly Father has for you. I commend you, Jessie Anne, and Sarah and Edward into His care. Throw all of your grief and pain and burdens upon Him, and He will satisfy your every need.

We spoke of my wishes for you and the children before I left for the army, but I think I should affirm them for you once again. I wish only that you would remain faithful to your Christian faith and in the training up of our children in that faith. Continue to teach Sarah and Edward the eternal things of His Word as we did when I was with you, and as you have done in the months since. You know that our Savior has always been faithful, "an ever present help in time of need." Rely fully upon His help, allow the church and Pastor Preston to extend a merciful hand, and pray without ceasing to the Almighty for strength and wisdom.

My darling, you are a young and beautiful woman, intelligent and gracious and of good humor, so do not endlessly grieve for me. In spite of the despair that may now hold you, your life can be full and joyous once again. If it pleases you to do so, and according to

His Most Gracious Providence, it would be good for you to take another husband. Do not let past sentiment for me hinder you from marrying a man who will be both a fine husband and father.

Please give Sarah and Edward a hug and a kiss from their loving father.

Until we meet before His glorious throne,
I remain your most devoted and adoring husband,

Michael G. Palmer

→ CHAPTER 13 ←

Plain of the Dead

My breath is corrupt, my days are extinct,
the graves are ready for me.
JOB 17:1

FOG LAY OVER THE CITY LIKE A DEATH SHROUD, SHIELDING US completely from view of the enemy. About nine o'clock, "Fall in!" echoed up and down the street. Groans and curses filled the air as the men slowly rose, rolled and tied their blankets, and shuffled into some semblance of an orderly line. We marched down Caroline Street a short distance, turned right for one city block, then turned left onto Princess Anne Street, one of the main thoroughfares in Fredericksburg. A halt was called near a church.

As the morning wore on, the fog began to lift. With the improving visibility, Rebel gunners opened up on us with shells from the low hills that surrounded Fredericksburg to the west and south. A shell was a hollow metal sphere with a small hole for a fuse through one side. The shell was packed full of black powder and bits of metal called shrapnel. When the shell was fired over a target, namely our marching lines of blue infantry, the fuse exploded the shell and the shrapnel and shell fragments are sprayed over a wide area.

Whenever a shell struck the façade of a brick building, men in the street below were pelted with a hail of dislodged bricks in addition to bits of hot metal. One such shell hit high on the wall of a three-story building. Several soldiers standing directly beneath ran into the street to avoid the falling bricks. A second shell caromed off a nearby building and fell into the middle of the street, where it exploded. All of the men who had run into the street were either killed instantly or grievously wounded.

Colonel Perkins rode forward. "Men of the Fourteenth," he began, "General French's division has been chosen to lead the assault against the Confederate position." Mumbled words passed up and down through the ranks as the import of these words hit home with the men. "We will attack in three lines of battle, General Kimball's brigade first, then Colonel Andrews's brigade, and then our brigade under Colonel Palmer. Behind us, other divisions will follow to carry on the assault. The task ahead is formidable. The danger is great; I'll not hide that from you. But we must do our duty. You will acquit yourselves well this day, and Connecticut's defense of the Union will long be remembered. May God bless us all. Prepare to march."

The Rebels knew how to use their shells to great effect. From the heights outside the city, their cannon were positioned in line with the cross streets so that, about noon, when Kimball's and Andrews's brigades began to march up Princess Anne Street, they were exposed to flanking fire from these guns. The Rebels started sending shells down the cross streets as fast as they could. Several shells exploded in the marching ranks, killing or maiming dozens of men before they exited the city onto the field of battle beyond.

When our turn came to move out we had learned how to deal with this threat at the cross streets. At every intersection, our officers stopped at the head of the column and waited until the tail end of the Andrews brigade cleared the intersection.

With no visible targets, the Rebels slowed their rate of fire. Then we dashed, one company at a time, across the intersection. We played this deadly game several times as we worked our way, block by block, down Princess Anne Street to the end of town near the train depot, but the injuries sustained by our brigade were few and minor and no one was killed.

We were resting between two cross streets, in what we considered relative safety, when a shell exploded about ten yards away. I saw it explode and tried to turn my back to it, but a small fragment struck the outer part of my left thigh. Bright red blood stained my bright blue trousers. I howled in pain.

"Michael, hold still a minute." John's steady voice calmed me. I howled again when he gripped the metal bit and pulled. "There, not so bad. I have a few bandages that I made, just in case. Would you like to go to the hospital? You have been wounded."

"No, John," I said, gritting my teeth as he tied the bandage, "I don't need the hospital for this little scratch." Yet I sensed another question behind his words. "That would make me a shirk, in my own eyes, if in no one else's," I added.

At the end of Princess Anne Street, Kimball's and Andrews's brigades had turned the corner and were advancing upon the Rebel position. Artillery fire swelled to a roar, now that the enemy had a clear view of the Union advance, and as our batteries responded in kind. Our officers dismounted and sent their horses to the rear. Colonel Perkins screamed a series of orders above the din that were echoed up and down the line by the company officers.

"Fourteenth, prime muskets!"

"Fourteenth, fix bayonets!"

"Fourteenth, double-quick — march!"

At a quick trot we left the protection of the city and moved out onto the tracks of the Richmond, Fredericksburg & Potomac

Railroad. Just past the depot we came under direct shelling from the Rebel guns. A short distance farther a drainage canal several feet deep cut directly across our route. There were only three places to cross this canal, one of which was a damaged railroad bridge, and the enemy had guns aimed at all three. Timing was crucial. We tried to time our crossings immediately after the detonation of a shell, with the knowledge that at least that gun could not fire again until it was reloaded, but we still lost several men there.

We ran down into a swale and came upon a rock wall that was becoming a gathering place for the wounded of Kimball's and Andrews's brigades. Beyond the rock wall, the ground rose steeply for a short distance, then more gradually for about three hundred yards to the base of the hill where the Rebels were. The men in gray had taken cover behind another rock wall that bordered a sunken wagon road at the base of the hill. Kimball's brigade was just starting to advance up the gradual slope while Andrews's men were taking cover along the steeper slope.

The Confederate artillery was particularly concentrated upon that area of gently rising land that led to the base of the hill and the sunken road. They had carefully planned their fields of fire, meticulously placed every gun, and aimed each gun for maximum effect. As Kimball's line began to advance, the Confederate guns spewed flame and smoke as they opened on our men with canister, a round that functioned like a giant shotgun shell. Wide gaps were ripped in the long blue line as several men in a row were struck down. To their credit, Kimball's men closed ranks and continued forward, crouching low and rushing ever faster, until they were about a hundred yards from the wall at the sunken road. Then the Rebels rose from behind the wall. A sheet of flame erupted and fully half of Kimball's men went down. The remainder returned fire, but as the Rebels had a stout rock wall in front of them, Kimball's men did little damage. They were quickly driven back down the slope in disarray to find whatever shelter they could.

Then it was Andrews's turn. As they started forward, we moved forward to the position they had occupied. The dreadful scene was repeated. There was a loud, hearty cheer and then a desperate rush up the slope toward the Rebels against the blast of shell and canister. A tremendous volley of Confederate and Union muskets split the air. The Union line wavered for a moment, then collapsed altogether. The survivors ran frantically, limping and stumbling down the slope toward cover.

"Don't go, boys, it's murder," they cried as they passed through our line. "That's what it is. It's murder up there. Don't go. You don't stand a chance."

Then we were up and moving forward, dressing our lines, shells coming at us from the front, from the left, and from the right.

Colonel Perkins was at our front, "All right, boys, at the double-quick ... *CHARGE!*"

And charge we did. With our eyes fixed on our leader instead of the enemy, we charged with Colonel Perkins up that slope, as had those before us. The dead and wounded of Kimball's and Andrews's brigades lay all around. We stumbled over some and jumped over others, but we pressed on toward the enemy.

Suddenly our line wavered and almost stopped altogether.

Our colonel had been shot.

He clutched at his throat and fell to his knees. Several men fell out to help him to the rear. Captain Davis, of Company I, ran to the front with the color-bearers. "Fourteenth!" he called out above the clamor, "on the colors! Forward!"

Men fell wounded and dying, but we pressed onward, elbow to elbow with the barrels of our muskets pointing skyward, each pace bringing us closer to the Rebels. Bullets flew at us thick as a swarm of mad bees. Several times I felt a puff of air as a bullet passed close by my face. Jessie Anne would surely become a widow this day.

We advanced about as far as the previous two brigades to a rail fence that afforded the only sparse cover on that part of the field. Then the Rebels' bucking rifles hurled a sheet of flame and thousands of bullets at us. Men fell where they were, shot through the chest, in the head, or in the stomach. Others were hit in legs or arms or feet. I felt several bullets pluck at my clothing and one punched a hole in my haversack. One bullet bounced off something, perhaps the earth in front of me or a fencepost or another soldier, and hit me squarely on the right shin. My leg buckled and I fell heavily to the earth. Another bullet creased my right wrist, though I did not realize it until much later.

As Kimball's and Andrews's men had done, the brigade quickly gave way and started to withdraw down the slope. "Every man for himself," was the cry. I started to struggle to my feet, and as I did so, I saw that Harry Whitting, who had been standing next to me in line, was also down. He cried in pain and clutched his left ankle with both hands; blood oozed from between his clasped fingers.

"Harry, we have to go, we have to go now! The brigade is falling back. Let's go!" I used my rifle like a crutch to stand up; then I helped Harry to stand on his good leg. Bullets continued to fly around us, but thankfully, most of the hostile fire was directed at those of our number still firing at them. Through much pleading and urging, I helped Harry stagger back about fifty yards, but he could go no farther.

"Harry," I shouted, "over to the right, about thirty more feet, is a place we can rest." It was a small depression in the earth that would offer some protection from the leaden hail that continued to fly past us.

"Lie down, Harry, with your head uphill toward the enemy. Turn over! I need your blanket roll." Every move drew groans of agony from Harry. I untied Harry's blanket roll and placed it above his head to serve as added protection from enemy bullets. Then I did the same with my roll.

Harry was in a desperate way. He would have to be seen by a surgeon soon if there was to be any prospect for his survival. How could we make it three hundred yards back to the safety of the swale when Harry could barely do fifty? I saw several of the wounded trying to limp or crawl to safety. One by one they were finished off with a shot in the back.

Where was John? I could use his help now. And where were the rest of the boys? Some with the Sharps rifles were kneeling behind the meager cover of the fence, still trying to hold the ground they had gained, but after several shots, they too joined the rest of the brigade, bobbing and weaving for the rear.

The pain in my shin made me forget about my shrapnel wound. I gingerly pulled up the leg of my trousers and saw a large bluish welt, but little blood. I flexed my leg and ankle several times to make sure they were usable. Apparently, there was no serious damage, but sharp-eyed Rebels sent several shots kicking up the dirt nearby.

I looked around cautiously. There was a small house about fifty yards to the left. The rear of this house was screened from the sight of the enemy, and many of our boys were taking shelter there. I could probably have dashed for the shelter of that house and lived, but I would have to leave Harry behind. I remained where I was, one motionless body on an open plain of the dead and dying. I looked up at the sun; it had hardly moved. Harry and I were trapped until nightfall.

The firing of the Rebels had diminished as our brigade melted away. Now it grew louder again. I lifted my head slowly and peered down the slope. Another line of Union troops had begun their advance. Shells ripped holes in their ranks and others were struck with musket balls. On and on they came, drawing ever nearer to where Harry and I were lying.

I clutched at the coats of those passing close by. "Go back, boys!" I cried. "Go back! You can't take that wall. You'll be killed. Go back!"

But the men continued to fall and the line went forward up to the rail fence, just as our line had a few minutes before. There was a deafening crash of blue and gray musketry, and many more of our boys fell to the earth. In a few minutes, for that was all human endurance could withstand, this brigade too tumbled and stumbled rearward past where Harry and I lay.

Father in heaven, I prayed, *please stop this madness and show me how to take Harry to safety.* Jim Adams had been right, and where was Jim in all of this?

Yet another blue line came up the slope in another vain attempt to overrun the wall and the hill beyond. The brilliant green battle flag of the Irish Brigade fluttered proudly in the breeze, then fell to the ground as the color-bearer was shot down. Another soldier picked up the flag, but the moment he raised it, he was struck by several bullets at once. Others took up the precious standard and were similarly struck. The Irish came abreast of me and pressed the advance forward against the firing of the Rebels from their place of security. As the Lord Jesus had set His face toward Jerusalem, toward the certainty of His own death, so the face of each man appeared chiseled in stone. Each man leaned rigidly forward against both the slope and the leaden fury fired at him, much as one would lean forward against a gale.

"Lads! They've killed me!" a large man directly in front of me cried as he sank to his knees. He swayed once to the left as if he was about to fall completely over, then, with supreme effort, he righted himself.

"I am done," he said, lifting his eyes toward heaven. A second shot drove him over backward. His body came to rest just above the small depression where Harry and I lay. He turned his face toward me. A slow trickle of blood escaped his lips. It ran down the side of his face, over the lobe of his ear, to the back of his neck where it formed a small red rivulet that inched its way toward me. I looked into the man's dimming eyes as the last of his breath left him; the flow of blood ceased. The rivulet stopped and was soon swallowed by the thirsty earth.

After a few minutes, I grabbed the shoulder of the man's greatcoat and tugged at his corpse. At first I could not move him, but I pulled and pulled, and inch by inch was finally able to position him to our best advantage. Then I turned the man's face, his eyes wide and unseeing, away from me, toward the enemy in the sunken road. The dead man was now a shield from the deadly balls of the enemy and I thanked God for this protection.

The Irish advanced farther than any other brigade that day, to within fifty yards of the rock wall. After courageously firing several volleys at the Rebels, they were forced to retire as well, leaving half their number behind, dead or wounded.

The slaughter continued unabated as brigade after brigade of the Second Corps fought their way toward that wall and then fell back, leaving an appropriately large and bloody sacrifice before it. The bloodletting did not diminish that day until the merciful setting of the sun. Thank God for the shortness of daylight in December. How many more would have fallen had the battle taken place in June?

As night fell, I continued my motionless vigil, looking always for the opportunity to get Harry off that field. Under the half moonlight, here and there a shadowy figure would struggle to his feet. After a few furtive, limping steps a shot would ring out, and the man would fall. There was no way Harry and I could survive if we tried to escape, so there was nothing to do but remain where we were until the Rebels either lost interest or fell asleep.

"It's broken," Harry whispered through teeth clenched against the pain. "It has to be broken. I can't move it at all."

I examined Harry's foot as well as I could in the darkness. I probed gently with my fingertips—Harry groaned in agony. The cold had slowed the bleeding from Harry's ankle to a trickle. The bullet had torn away the ankle bone on the inside of his left foot. Harry's war was done, since the surgeon would certainly amputate the mangled foot. I winced at the thought of it.

Harry fell into a fitful sleep. Still weak from his sickness at Belle Plain, he probably should not have been judged fit for duty. He would soon die without medical attention. I lay silently on my back under my woolen blanket, staring up at the moon and the stars.

It must never be thought that the field of battle falls silent once the fighting stops, for when the guns cease firing and the last echoes die, the wailing cries of the thousands of wounded arise in a pitiable chorus of woe. A short distance away I heard the rasping liquid breathing of a man who had probably been shot in the upper chest or throat. The whimpering sighs and guttural groans of those in the throes of deepest distress formed the chords of the ostinato, while from every direction individual voices called out their solo pleas, praying for help, hoping for deliverance.

"Help me ... please help me ..."

"I can't feel anything ... just cold ..."

"Hail Mary, full of grace, blessed art thou ..."

"I am so sorry, Mother ..."

"A sip of water ... anyone ... anyone ..."

"Father, forgive this dying sinner ..."

"Your Josh will not be home again ..."

"Don't leave me, friend ..."

"For thine is the kingdom, and the power, and the glory ..."

Then, from somewhere behind that dreadful rock wall, perhaps atop the frowning hill that had loomed over us all day, and carried between the lines upon a light breeze on that cold night, I heard the mournful strains of a violin as some soldier in gray or butternut bowed his own musical requiem out over that plain. The tune I did not know, but the sentiment that soldier conveyed was exceedingly somber and too familiar. So many had died, and more would die before the dawn.

I wrapped myself up tightly within the folds of my great-coat and allowed the darkness of the night to draw me into its embrace. It was a friend now—killing was a daytime avocation.

CHAPTER 14

The Endless Night

The heavens declare the glory of God;
and the firmament sheweth his handywork.
PSALM 19:1

I SHOOK HARRY GENTLY. HIS ONLY RESPONSE WAS A SOFT, DEEP groan. I leaned over close to his ear. "Harry, come on — wake up." Sleep was a good thing for him, but now was not the time. I shook him again.

Harry coughed several times.

"Shhh, they might hear us," I said. "Only been a few scattered shots in the last hour, just one or two along this part of the line. They might be asleep. Some clouds are moving in; the moon is nearly hidden. If we're going, it has to be now."

I checked Harry's ankle, and even with only the dim illumination of the moon and stars, it did not look good. There was hardly any bleeding; the cold had certainly helped staunch the flow. The shredded remnants of his sock were stiff and crusty, stained black now instead of white. I tried to probe beneath the sock, but my slightest touch was agony to Harry.

"Leave it alone, Michael," Harry gasped. "You're trying to help, but you can't do anything for me."

"All right, Harry, but I have to protect it. Take off your belt."

I took Harry's woolen blanket and folded it several times into a thick pad while Harry tugged his leather belt from his waist. Then I rolled up my own blanket and removed my belt as well.

"Harry, clench my belt in your teeth. This is going to hurt plenty, but only for a little while. Ready?" Harry nodded as he bit down. As smoothly and gently as possible, I lifted Harry's leg and slid my blanket roll underneath his calf. His breathing became fast and shallow, but he made no other sound. Then I wrapped Harry's folded blanket around his injured foot, looped his belt twice around the blanket, and secured it with the buckle. It was the best I could do.

I gave Harry a few minutes to recover. His jaw relaxed, releasing its grip on my belt. "Look, Harry, I'm cinching my belt around my ankle. I'll lead the way and you hold it. If you let go, I'll know you're in trouble. Let's go."

I helped Harry turn himself to the left, toward the house I had noticed earlier. The house was no farther from the Rebels than our current position, but if we could make it to that house, it and the other small outbuildings would serve to screen our movement farther down the slope away from the enemy line.

I flexed my right leg several times and found it painful but serviceable; my left thigh throbbed dully. I slowly raised my head to get the lay of the land. The house was about fifty yards away and many, many bodies lay in between.

I started to inch my way forward. Through the tugs at my ankle, I could tell Harry was moving too. We slid ourselves slowly along between the corpses of our fallen brothers, hugging the earth, never daring to rise above the shielding presence of the dead. Rarely did we progress directly toward the refuge we sought. Instead, we had to slide right, then left, then right again as we weaved our way between the frozen bodies, taking great care to never show a silhouette to the enemy. A few times our path was blocked entirely by the dead. Harry rested while

I cautiously looked for a way around the obstruction. Then, we went forward again.

Harry never let go of the belt. He clung tenaciously to it until, yard by yard, we neared the shelter of the house. I led Harry toward the rear of the house, away from the Rebel line.

"Who's that?" a voice rasped out of the darkness.

"Fourteenth Connecticut," I answered quickly.

"Tenth New York. Hi, Yank."

"Hi, Yank. My friend Harry here's been shot bad in the ankle."

"All right, get back here where it's safe."

"Harry must get to a hospital soon or he'll die."

"There's seven of us here that's still alive, all from different units. Two are pretty bad; the rest should make it okay. Just about to skedaddle, when I heard you. Didn't know if maybe you were a couple of Rebs trying to sneak up on us."

All eyes scanned the night sky. A large cloud began to pass in front of the moon.

"It's now or never," Tenth New York said. "We're going to carry you off this field, Harry. Connecticut, you get under Harry's right arm, I'll be under his left. Harry, you hang on tight, 'cause we might not come back for you if we drop you." Tenth New York chuckled at his own wit. "Let's go."

In twos and threes, our little band started out from the shelter of the house. We moved down the slope, weaving back and forth as we found our way among the dead and dying. I thank God above for sending those clouds, and I thank the Rebels for holding their fire or for being asleep, because all nine men made it safely down the slope to the rock wall near the railroad. We rested there for several minutes and planned our next move.

"What's your name, Tenth New York?" I asked.

"Pat MacMullin," he answered.

"Mine is Michael Palmer, and I'm pleased to make your

acquaintance, Pat." I extended my hand to him; he grasped it firmly. "This is Harry Whitting, and I could not have brought him back here without your help. I can't thank you enough."

"Don't worry about it. I wasn't hit at all. When our unit got into it, most of us just fired once and then hit the dirt. I was lucky enough to make it behind that house before the Rebs got me in their sights. I was just waiting for the night to darken some."

"Thanks all the same."

It was only about a hundred yards to the railroad trestle that led across the canal to the relative security of the city streets beyond. Back on our feet, our small band hobbled the distance to the bridge. The engineers had replaced the planks all the way across and we passed over with ease.

Oil lamps glowed eerily along both sides of Princess Anne Street. Long columns of troops lay about the streets, as we had the night before, waiting for their turn to be thrown into the fighting that was sure to be renewed at first light. I prayed they would be spared. Others, like us, stragglers fresh from the field, walked to and fro in search of the scattered remnants of their units.

It was a simple thing to find a hospital. Many houses had been appropriated for this purpose, and many a grand dining table was pressed into service as a surgeon's table. I thought of the house on Caroline Street. The sighs and groans and screams of the grievously injured once again filled the air, as did the stench of blood and death. I considered these men blessed since they no longer faced the danger of further injury on the battle-field, and nurses moved among the men spreading good cheer, offering comfort, and serving hot coffee.

MacMullin and I approached one of these hospitals, hoping to find treatment for our friends and relief from our burdens. A weary nurse stopped us as we started up the steps.

"What corps are you from?" she asked.

"Second Corps, Third Division, ma'am," I replied.

"Oh no, this hospital is Sixth Corps. So is the next one there," she added, pointing at the large building next door. "He must go to your division's hospital."

"Where is that, ma'am?"

"Second Corps is down next to the river, I think, past the pontoon bridge. Turn right at the next street. At the river, turn left. The hospitals are down a ways, maybe half a mile."

"Thank you, ma'am. Can you spare a stretcher for Harry here?"

"Oh no," said the nurse, "ours are filled with our own wounded. I'm sorry, but I can't help you."

At that, Pat and I turned around and started to carry Harry farther down the street. Both of my wounds throbbed due to the exertions of the last hour, and we still needed to go about as far as we had already come from the field of battle. Strength for the task ahead was gone, and we had to stop for rest before we had gone a hundred paces. Harry groaned as we gently set him down.

Pat and I went into a nearby house, looking for anything we might use to help Harry. The house already held a good number of soldiers, a mix of officers and enlisted men. One or more weary men were already employing every piece of furniture that could be laid upon, sat upon, or leaned against.

"Hey, Palmer," whispered Pat as he moved over to the passage from the dining room to the kitchen, "let's use a door."

"A door?" I asked.

"Yeah, a door. It's the right length; it's flat. Let's just bust the hinges out of the door frame and take it." And so we did, amid the cries of protest from several whose slumber we disturbed with our door wrenching. We carried the door outside and laid Harry upon it.

"Unh ... unh ... unh ... unh," Harry moaned with nearly every step. The door certainly made it easier for Pat and me, but it was tougher on Harry, and we could not stop.

At the river we turned left. After passing a few more cross streets, I finally spotted some familiar faces lit by the dim halos of several small campfires. Pat and I had stumbled upon the remnants of my Fourteenth Regiment. We set Harry down and I found Sergeant Holt.

"Sergeant, Private Palmer reporting for duty. I have Harry Whitting with me, and he's badly wounded. This man, Pat Mac-Mullin from the Tenth New York, helped me get Harry off the field."

"Thanks, MacMullin," said Holt. "Want some coffee?"

"Sure, Sergeant," said Pat. "Thanks."

"We'll take care of Whitting. Blake, Chatfield, Hill, Thompson." Four men got wearily to their feet. "Take Whitting here to the division hospital. Just down the street here about two hundred yards, white house, white fence." They picked Harry up and started off, four sharing the work that Pat and I had done until then.

We drained our coffee cups.

"Pat, thanks again for helping Harry and me tonight. I hope God repays your kindness by seeing you safely home." We shook hands warmly, and Pat went off to find his unit while I turned to follow Harry to the hospital.

The scene at the hospital would make the stoutest heart faint. The large house was reserved for the treatment of officers. Smoke rose from three chimneys; it must have been pleasantly warm inside. I assumed this was where Colonel Perkins had been taken.

All of the wounded enlisted men remained outside in the cold, lying about the yard, waiting for a surgeon to see them. Most had no covering against the cold other than their own clothing. There were a few large trees in the yard, and between two of them, almost screened from the casual observer, I noticed two long tables under the glow of several smoking oil lamps. A surgeon was busily at work at each table, trying to save as many men as possible. I now knew what "sawbones" meant.

A plump gray-haired nurse met us at the gate. "His name is Harold Whitting, ma'am," I told her. The nurse wrote Harry's name on a sheet of paper as I spelled it.

"What regiment?"

"Fourteenth Connecticut, ma'am, Second Brigade, Third Division."

"What's his injury?"

"He was shot in the left ankle, ma'am, sometime after noon today."

"You mean yesterday. It's now Sunday morning, about 3 o'clock."

"Yes, ma'am."

"You boys bring him inside the gate and find a place for him." We found a spot large enough and the four bearers lowered Harry to the ground. "And take that door with you when you leave."

"Thanks, boys," Harry said weakly with a slight wave of his hand. The four helpers took their leave. "Thank you too, Michael."

"I hope a doctor sees you soon, Harry," I told him, gripping his hand in both of mine.

The nurse marked Harry's location in the yard on her paper. "Young man," she told me, "you can't stay here. A surgeon will see him when he can. You should return to your unit. I have many others to look after."

I walked back to the regiment and sat down wearily before a campfire. After another cup of coffee and a few hard crackers, I began to feel somewhat better. I wrapped myself in my woolen blanket and lay down to get some sleep. It didn't take long. I had time for one thought before I lost consciousness: *Where is John?*

⋘⋙

Moments later, or so it seemed, I awoke to warm sunshine filtering through my closed eyelids. I stirred and opened my eyes to a steaming cup of coffee. I looked up and saw John smiling down at me.

"Michael, it's so good to see you. I thought I would have to mail that letter to Jessie Anne."

"Likewise," I said, sitting up stiffly. Both legs hurt, but the right one especially so. "I lost you in the fight; it was so confusing. I couldn't see what happened to you or Jim."

"We made it out all right. Jim should be along shortly. He saw some of the boys in the Twenty-seventh Connecticut a few streets over and went with them to see if they could find a friend of his in their unit. Are you all right?"

"Yes, nothing major. They added a big lump on my shin from a spent bullet. But Harry's bad." I told John every detail, including the help of the good fellow from New York. "Harry will lose his foot," I said. "I left him at the hospital down the street at about three o'clock this morning."

"You did well, my friend. No one could have asked more. They amputated Harry's leg this morning about six inches above the ankle. It's a shame, but it had to be done. He'll be sent home if his wound heals."

"I hope so," I said, sipping the hot coffee. "What about you and Jim? How did you make it through? And how do you know about Harry?"

John poured himself a cup of coffee and sat next to me. "After that first blast up by that wooden fence, most of us just dropped to the ground. Staying put would mean a quick death, so we started back as soon as we got the order." John sipped his

134

coffee several times before continuing. "We didn't turn and run. We faced the enemy so that we could see when they rose up to shoot. Then we dropped again. We backed off about a hundred yards like that, but some of the boys still got hit. Then the next line came up, and when they passed us, most of the fire was concentrated on them, so we ran for the rear."

"Thank God you and Jim are safe. I was anxious when I didn't see you with the regiment last night."

John drank more of his coffee. "I made it back to the city just after dark and the wounded were coming in by the hundreds. I helped one man to our hospital, and the nurse asked me to stay and help. It was horrible. There aren't enough nurses to assist the surgeons, so I helped a surgeon from the First Brigade. I just did whatever he told me to do and tried not to think about the blood and the pain and the sadness of it all, hoping I was doing some small good for these men."

John's eyes were narrow, moist with threatening tears, fixed on the flames before him. "I helped move an injured soldier onto the operating table," he said, "and I learned how to administer a quick dose of chloroform to render him unconscious. Sometimes I held an oil lamp for the surgeon and sometimes I helped hold the injured man down."

John took another sip of coffee. He dabbed at his eyes with his shirtsleeve. "I learned to anticipate which tool the surgeon would need—the knife or the saw. I witnessed so many amputations I could probably perform one myself. The white apron they gave me was soon red with blood, and each time the surgeon was done, I helped move the poor man onto a stretcher so he could be born away by two other helpers. Then I swabbed off the table, threw out the severed limb, and prepared to do it all over again. I don't know how many soldiers came through that room, but I was there for about sixteen hours. It was a dreadful experience that I shall try to forget."

I could only shake my head in sympathy and drink my coffee. John went on to tell me about Colonel Perkins. He had suffered an ugly and serious neck wound, but it appeared that he would survive. The colonel would need to convalesce for quite some time.

"As I was leaving," John said, "a nurse saw the *14* on my cap and told me there were dozens of our men out in the yard, so I went to check on them. That's when I saw Harry. One of the other surgeons had taken his foot off, and he was still in a bad way. Lying out in the open like that, in the cold air, on the frozen ground, I do not think he will survive long enough to be sent home."

"That can't be—Harry can't die." The trembling of my own voice surprised me. "I didn't leave him. I stayed with him. I did my duty." I hugged myself tightly with my own arms.

"You did," John said, laying a gentle hand on my shoulder. Then he closed his eyes and bowed his head. With a warm fire before and the icy Rappahannock behind, John prayed for Harry's recovery, for God's mercy upon him, and that Harry would even now in his hour of distress know the saving grace of God in Christ. John prayed for the regiment and for the army, and he prayed for safety for ourselves and comfort for our families. Then we took our Bibles out of our pockets and began to read, and thus we passed another Sabbath day in the Army of the Potomac.

The two armies continued to face each other as day passed into night, with neither commanding general willing either to withdraw or renew the conflict. Thousands would spend another long night on the field of battle in the private struggle to hold onto life. But in the heavens above, for those with living eyes to behold it, there appeared a glorious sight that could stir even the most jaded of sin-sick souls. At first faintly, then more manifestly, the northern sky began to glow with the streaked and shimmering radiance of the northern lights. Green and red hues with traces of white mingled together in a curtain of color as if stirred by a gentle breeze, performing a slow and beautiful dance in the cold night sky. It was indeed marvelous how our Creator had made Himself known to those who, even in the midst of scenes of fear and blood and agony and death, were able to see His handiwork. When all human words and comforts failed to soothe the hearts and souls of men in torment, the Almighty spoke to all those who knew Him that night—*Lo, I am with you always, even unto the end of the world.*

CHAPTER 15

Tears in the Yuletide

A voice was heard in Ramah,
lamentation, and bitter weeping;
Rachel weeping for her children
refused to be comforted for her children,
because they were not.
JEREMIAH 31:15

Saturday, December 20, 1862
Camp of the 14th Conn. Rgt. Vol. Inf.
Near Falmouth, Virginia

Dearest Jessie Anne,

Though tired and dispirited, I am warm and dry in winter quarters. We crossed over the river on Friday the 12th and spent the night in the streets of Fredericksburg. At noon on Saturday a grand assault was made upon the enemy's line. Suffice it to say, we were repulsed with great losses in men dead and wounded. Details of this disaster I leave you to read elsewhere — I choose not to expend time or ink on them. John and Jim came through the fight unharmed, as did I, but Harry Whitting was wounded in the foot. The serious nature of the wound caused the surgeon to remove the foot to spare his life. Although John thinks Harry may

not recover, I think he must. If God is just and merciful, I believe
He will honor efforts made by myself and others to help Harry in
his time of need. Please do not speak of this to Mrs. Whitting, for
it would only cause her to fret.

We turned our backs to the enemy and returned to this side
of the river Monday night in silence and under cover of darkness.
Every soldier knows the bitter pill of defeat. Doubts grow within
each of us about his own fitness for the work at hand, the justness
of his cause, and the skill of his commanding officers. Perhaps
worst of all, every man now sees his own pitiful condition as if it
were brightest noonday.

The business of building our winter hut began immediately
upon our return, and the three days of hard labor trained our
attentions upon the building rather than the recent disaster. Since
Harry's war is done, a fourth man was required who was willing to
pitch his lot in with us. Such a man is Charlie Merrills, the cornet
player I wrote about. Together we formed an efficient team. John
was the master designer and Jim the tireless axeman. John planned
and measured each cut and each notch and Jim swung the axe
from dawn until dusk. Charlie and I helped John and Jim place the
logs one atop the other in several courses around the perimeter of
the excavation. Every log fit snugly in its place and Charlie filled
the narrow gaps between with red Virginia mud to keep the wind
out and the warmth in. He also kept the fire blazing and the coffee
boiling so we never had lack of it.

I also served as master procurer. An acquaintance named
Pat MacMullin vouched for me with the quartermaster of the
10th New York, and I was able to borrow a heavy felling axe. I
purchased nails and rope from the sutler's tent. Nails were forty
cents per pound. I told Mr. Morgan we charge eight cents at the
store and that forty was akin to thievery in my book, but he would
not lower his price.

We fashioned a door and a small table from cracker boxes, of which there seems to be an endless supply. We also use cracker boxes for stools. Jim Adams split a large three-foot-long log in two using the axe and some wooden wedges he made. Then he set each of the two split halves atop a pair of short logs for support. Now we have a six-foot bench outside where four men can sit comfortably and sun themselves.

You will think our hut very small, only six feet by eight feet on the inside, but it is warm and cozy most of the time. A small fireplace is cut into the center of the left-hand wall. The fireplace is built of logs like the rest of the hut, but it is entirely and thickly covered with dried mud to prevent a conflagration. The table and four stools are set before the fireplace and the floor is entirely "carpeted" with pine boughs.

The roof is the most vulnerable part of the structure. Today's cold and wind have buffeted the four half-shelters mercilessly. Twice already corners have come loose and we have jumped up to tie them down before the roof is carried completely away. Except for a little light snow last night, the weather has been cold and fair for several days, but this cannot last, and all four of us expect to be busy with roof mending and leak plugging when the heavens do finally open upon us.

I have just received word from Captain Carpenter's aide that a wooden crate has arrived for me, so I will close this letter and post it to you when I go to collect the crate. Captain Carpenter was also wounded during the recent unpleasantness across the river, but all expect him to return to duty within a week or two, at most. Tomorrow, there will be a memorial service; Chaplain Stevens will preach. Next week the 14th will begin a regular schedule of picketing along the river a few miles west of here — four days in camp for every day on watch. It is not dangerous duty, but we must always be on guard.

Dearest, you and the children must know that in spite of all I have endured, and may yet be called to endure, you are ever in my heart. There is never a moment in any day when you are far from me. Indeed, my heart aches at the thought of being separated this Christmas season. Please know that my current circumstances are as pleasant as I have had in the army. I have no complaint other than that I hope and pray our generals will go forward with great skill and firm resolve to finally put an end to this war. Pray the Prince of Peace that this might be so. I wish you, my dearest, and Sarah and little Ed a blessed Christmas, although this will not reach you in the few days that remain, along with fondest wishes for the New Year about to commence, that 1863 will see an end to this war and a Palmer family once more united.

Until then, I remain your most devoted husband,

Michael

❖~❖

I hurried off to Captain Carpenter's headquarters. The crate was indeed the expected one from Jessie Anne, and with some difficulty I carried it back to the hut. When I was alone, I pried open the lid. Atop all else was a letter, which I stuffed in my pocket. I quickly checked all of the crate's contents, then pounded the lid shut once again and slid it under my bunk. Then I went outside and sat on Jim's sturdy bench to read the letter.

Sunday, November 30, 1862

Beloved Husband Michael,

As I sit down this Sabbath's eve to write this letter, I do so with kerchief in hand and the mind not to have need of it before I finish. There is no overly sad news, nor am I in a hopelessly gloomy state, but I do miss you deeply every day. I long to see your face around the house, and feel the surprise of those words you often whisper in my ear at odd moments. Besides, I have much to say to you that I can say to no other. I miss particularly our quiet evening times after the children are tucked in their beds. How I would love to hear you read a great book to me once again, and to think that you will soon receive this box, and look lovingly upon the contents, causes me to wish I was packaged along with them. (It seems I have used the kerchief already and pray I have not caused you to need one.)

Other than the usual colds in the head and coughs, we are all in good health. Mother was ill a few weeks ago with the ague. She was abed for three days, but then was up and about and is now fully restored. Mama Palmer continues to help me at home, as I wrote in my last letter, and on Sunday afternoons Papa Palmer has begun to teach Sarah the catechism.

Papa has also taken charge of all affairs at the store. He hired my cousin Donald on as a laborer. Donald gets the goods from the depot and unloads them at the store. He drives the wagon out for deliveries, stocks the shelves, and even sweeps the floor—a true Godsend.

While Sarah is at school, I take little Ed with me to the store. He's such an active little boy, and curious about everything. He loves to talk to every customer, except Mrs. Frost, and is eager to show off his ever-growing vocabulary. Often, it's all I can do to keep little Ed from mischief. When Sarah arrives from school, he loves to chase her around the store, but she's much too quick for him, as I was at her age. Soon she lets him catch her and then it's all hugs and kisses. When the little man tires, he curls up and takes a nap on a little bed I made from a wooden crate and placed behind the store's counter. Every day I see something of you in him and it cheers me.

Sarah is your daughter through and through. Mama showed her how to set the table for dinner, so now Sarah does it every evening and she always sets your place at the head of the table.

She never lets anyone sit in your chair, not your father or mine, not even Reverend Preston when he visits. She tells everyone, "That's Papa's place. When he comes home, he'll be really hungry." (There, I've used the kerchief again.)

Christmas is almost upon us and I dread the thought of this joyous, sacred season without you. I read last week that the army might start granting furloughs when it goes into quarters for the winter. Do you know anything of this? You know my wish to see you. I have also heard that some wives are permitted to visit their husbands, but I do not see the possibility of this. So I pray that the army will go into quarters for the winter so that you, my husband, might have a warmer, more comfortable dwelling, and possibly obtain a furlough. The thought of you each night sleeping on the cold hard ground, when my bed is so soft and warm, chills me as well.

Sarah asked me to write this: "Tell Papa not to worry about us. We're doing well, but please hurry home, because I want to read a story I wrote for you. Merry Christmas, Papa." She also helped me with the shortbread cookies, so excited she was to do something for you. And little Ed says, "I lub you, Papa. Merry Chrithmath." Mother says I had the same trouble with *S*'s when I was little.

As you can see I was able to send the four pairs of boots you asked for, as well as a number of foodstuffs and confections to brighten your holiday, plenty to share with John and Jim and Harry. Abby and I talk every few days and share the news we receive from your letters. I pray for you often every day. Your perils are so great and so many that I can only imagine them in part, whereas my difficulties are so minor in comparison, mere inconveniences and annoyances. My constant prayer is that our Heavenly Father will place you under His mighty hand and outstretched arm to protect and defend you from all harm. You must always remember that you are a son of the Almighty God and trust in His unchanging and unfailing love for you.

With sincerest love and affection I, along with Sarah and Edward, wish you a Merry Christmas. I count it a blessing every day that you are my husband, perhaps even more so now in your absence. You are God's gift to me, second only to His only begotten Son. With dearest wishes for your daily welfare, with a sincere hope and desire for your safe return to me, and with deepest affection for you, my darling husband,

> I am, as always, your loving
> and devoted wife and friend,
>
> *Jessie Anne*

(Yes, the kerchief is well-watered now, but I assure you, my dear, more from joy than sorrow.)

❦

Before the war I had always looked forward to the Christmas season with joy and gladness. Remembering afresh the great love of Our Heavenly Father in sending His Son into this sin-wearied world to save sinners had always colored our celebrations with such an eternal purpose that all of our temporal trials and concerns were for a short time swept aside. Countless blessed hours were spent in singing dozens of familiar nativity hymns in our homes, at church, and up and down the streets of the town, in retelling the wondrous story of the blessed birth and in times of sweet fellowship with family and friends during these yuletides past.

But there was little yuletide cheer on the Federal side of the Rappahannock. Sunday the 21st was declared throughout the Army of the Potomac a day of Sabbath rest and remembrance for our fallen comrades. It was a sunny, blustery day, a day for remaining indoors beside a blazing fire. Light snow had fallen overnight, less than an inch, but enough to lay a thin blanket of whitest white upon the ground, the trees, and our log huts. At noon, all officers and enlisted men were called to assemble in front of Chaplain Stevens's tent for a special memorial service for our regiment. It was pitiful to see how few we now were.

"Three months ago, after the Battle of Antietam Creek," began Chaplain Stevens, "I spoke to you of the shortness of life. At that time I preached from the prophet Isaiah, of how the life of a man is like the grass in the field. It is lively and green; then it is cut down. The next day it is withered and dead. I stand before you today a witness to this truth. While I did not bear arms during the recent fighting, I did follow behind the lines of the advance so as to be ready to give solace or condolence when needed. I saw as you did how the men fell in rows like grass before the grim reaper's scythe. Did you see how the Irish stood to the last? I saw and was terrified, or as Nehemiah said, 'I was very sore afraid.' That ghastly image of death and dying and immeasurable suffering is indelibly etched in the depths of my mind and will remain with me until I rest in the grave."

Pine trees nearby stirred and swayed in the frigid northerly wind. Swirls of tiny snow crystals drifted down upon the men, their icy touch finding the back of the neck of any man who had not turned up the broad collar of his greatcoat. Chaplain Stevens appeared to notice neither the swirling snow nor the fidgeting of the men.

"I was overwhelmed by the horror of it," he continued. "I was powerless to do what I knew I ought to do. Fear and dread overcame me and held me in their power for a time. But then most mercifully I was overcome by something else, something exceedingly simple and glorious that I will now share with you. It can be summarized in one short statement from Scripture, simple words I have known from my youth and repeated often, words from the book of Revelation, heralded throughout the heavens by an angel of the Lord: 'Fear God and give Him the glory.'

"I say that I was overcome for indeed the transformation within me was as instantaneous as it was powerful. No longer was I gripped by fear, no longer was I helpless and trembling. I knew in that moment that God's hand was at work in all that stormed about me, that He was accomplishing His purposes in that moment and so I asked a very simple question, a question that to me now seems obvious and necessary, but in that moment could only have been prompted by the Holy Ghost Himself. 'What would You have me do, Lord?'

"My thoughts were fixed on these words from Mark's gospel, 'For whosoever will save his life shall lose it; but whosoever shall lose his life for my sake and the gospel's, the same shall save it.'

"Immediately I set about in search of the most grievously wounded, those wretched men most near unto death, and I began to speak the words of life to them. After some hours of this, I found that in the comforting of others I was being comforted. In praying with the dying as their lives slipped away, I discovered that my spirit was being renewed within me. The goodness and faithfulness of my Heavenly Father was confirmed to me over and over again so that at the end of my ministrations, when indeed I could not have gone further, I was filled with the nearness of His presence and fullness of His peace and, yes, I dare to say it, I was filled with His joy."

⋘⋙

That evening, John, Jim, Charlie, and I enjoyed the warmth and comfort of our new dwelling. A fire blazed in the fireplace, and most of the smoke went up the chimney, a fact that I considered a major success.

I retrieved a square metal box, tied with a bright red ribbon, from under my bunk. I opened the lid and held the box under my nose for a long moment, allowing the familiar home-sweet-home aroma to fill me. "Shortbread cookies," I said, "Jessie Anne and Sarah made them. I thought we should eat them now," I said, "as they're as fresh as they're ever going to be."

That Sabbath evening, the four of us sat upon cracker box stools, drinking coffee and pleasuring in the munching of those deliciously sweet cookies. We talked about our lives before we were soldiers and shared news of loved ones at home.

There was a sharp knock on the door. Since I was seated closest, I rose, opened the door, and was greeted with the fire-lit face of our chaplain.

"Chaplain Stevens, how good it is to see you, sir. Come in and warm yourself. There are still a few shortbread cookies from home." I offered the box to him.

"No, thank you, Mr. Palmer." Chaplain Stevens always called the enlisted men "Mr." He nodded his greeting to each of the others in turn. "Mr. Robinson, Mr. Merrills, of course from the band, and Mr. Adams, is it?"

"Yes, sir," Jim said.

"As our numbers have become fewer," the chaplain said, "it has become easier for me to remember your names. Friends, this is not a social visit. I was just given some sad news. Your friend Harry Whitting has died."

"When, sir?" asked Jim.

"Early this morning."

"We have not heard anything about Harry since we left Fredericksburg," John said. "Do you know anything, sir?"

"I understand that Harry was taken by horse cart over to the landing at Belle Plain we are all so familiar with, then by steamship to a hospital in Alexandria. He probably did not succumb to his wound but to a resulting infection. They say he was fevered and not in his right mind at the end. Maybe he should have stayed here in Falmouth. I know he was your friend, and I'm sorry to bring you this sad news. Let us pray together for God's mercy upon Harry's family and the men of the regiment."

From that day forth we rarely mentioned Harry Whitting, and never again did we speak of his death, but for me the matter weighed most heavily. I had seen to my duty to Harry personally. I had not left it to another and no obligation went unattended to. Yet in the end in mattered not—the boy still died. My noblest efforts had been in vain.

⋘⋙

For the Army of the Potomac, Christmas came and went almost without recognition. The band did not assemble. I was not asked to sing, nor was I at all displeased about it, for of all men I felt particularly unblessed and the thought of my blessing the men by singing the carols of my youth seemed most hypocritical. Perhaps others felt the same, for I heard no singing in the streets of the camp, and except for a lone cornet player, who for almost an hour on Christmas Eve stood outside our hut playing those blessed hymns of the nativity, the lovely tunes were not heard at all.

On Christmas Day the army saw fit to issue a special ration of beef and a couple of onions per man. John, Jim, Charlie, and I took our meat and onion rations and, along with some crumbled hard crackers, made a more than passable lobscouse. Jim surprised us when he produced a fistful of salt and added it to the pot. "I've been saving a little here and a little there for a special occasion," he explained, "and I guess Christmas is special enough." After it had simmered about two hours, our hunger got the better of us and we devoured the stew with great relish.

After dinner I slid my crate from under my bunk and pried open the lid. "We sell Hickham's outdoor boots at the Palmer

General Store, and in my opinion, they are the best a man can have." The three men looked down at their feet. Red socks had started to show through the sides of the boots of John and Jim, and Charlie's boots were in only slightly better condition.

"John, here is your pair, size twelve, and yours, Jim, size ten. And Charlie, I ordered a pair for Harry, size eight. Can you use them?"

"I can try," Charlie said. "They'll be a little tight, but I might be able to stretch them." And he did. Over the next few weeks, he wore his new Hickham's a little longer each day until he could slide them on and off quite comfortably.

It was John's usual practice, after the evening meal, to tamp fresh tobacco into his cherry-wood pipe and have a smoke. This night was no exception. For him, it was one of those calming, individual pleasures that added to one's sense of contentment and was easily afforded by any poor foot soldier. Several times I had commented that I would like to take up smoking, but I had never gone so far as to purchase the necessary pipe and tobacco from the sutler, probably because I wished to support the sutler's usurious habits as rarely as possible.

John walked over to his greatcoat, hanging on a nail by the door. He reached into the deep pocket and returned to the table carrying two small plainly wrapped packages tied with string. He placed one in front of me, the other in front of Jim. "Merry Christmas, Michael and Jim." A few seconds later the paper lay in shreds and Jim and I each held up a new pipe made of hickory wood and a pouch of smoking tobacco.

"A local farmer made them," John said, "and he was eager to sell when he saw that I carried real dollars instead of Confederate scrip."

"Thank you, John!" Jim fairly shouted with glee.

"Yes, thank you, John," I said. "How do I light it?"

"Just remember child, mother, father," John said.

My look told him I thought army rations had finally driven him mad.

"No, no, it's easy," he said. "Fill the bowl with tobacco. Good. Now press it down very gently, as if a child like little Ed was doing it. Good. Now, fill it a second time and press it down like a woman would, like Jessie Anne. Fill the bowl once more and press it down hard the way you, the father, would."

I lit a match, drew in the first of the aromatic smoke, and immediately started to cough. "Slowly at first, Michael," John said, slapping me on the back, "until you get used to it."

"And you, Charlie, would you like one as well?" John asked. "You've been with us only a few days, so I know nothing of your thoughts on the matter, but if you do, I will get one for you."

"No, I don't think so," Charlie replied. "I've never taken to it."

Then Jim opened the small crate he had received from his mother. "I sent for this stuff from home," he said quietly, shy now that the moment of revelation was at hand. "I wanted enough for all four of us to share, but with Harry gone ... and now with Charlie ..."

"Go ahead, Jim, show us," I said.

The crate was filled with culinary delights the likes of which had only been the stuff of whimsical musings for the last several months. There was a sack of onions, a jar of dill pickles, several tins of canned fruit, a box of chocolate confections, four cans of condensed milk (a boon for the enjoyment of our coffee), a small wheel of cheese, a fruit cake, and the crowning item, a smoked ham wrapped tightly so as to retain all of its savory goodness. For the next week or two, we would eat very well. After that the memories would remain.

"I don't have much to offer," Charlie said, producing another small sack. "I bought these six potatoes, but they should go very well with that ham."

The day after Christmas was spent on picket duty, so we

151

planned our feast for the twenty-seventh. And such a feast it was. The ham was devoured so that only the bone remained, and Jim had the honor of gnawing at the last savory bits. The potatoes and onions were boiled together and quickly consumed as well. And when our bellies were full, we took to nibbling at the cheese and the chocolates and pieces of the fruitcake. Then we sat and smoked our pipes peacefully.

A cold rain fell during the night of December 31st. The roof leaked in places, but not severely. We retired early, for we would be up at first light for picket duty. The others fell quickly asleep, but I tossed and turned in my bunk. No place or position offered comfort. Finally, I rose and sat by the fire. I tamped tobacco into the bowl of my pipe—child, mother, father. Then I sat and smoked and stared into the fire. The flames beckoned, drawing me in. Sarge was there, and Harry too. General Richardson was there, as was the man of the Irish Brigade, along with a host of others I had seen but didn't know. I searched the faces for my own—it was not there. No good was to be found, no lasting significance, no glorious purpose, none of the joy Chaplain Stevens had spoken of, only more longing, more hunger, more suffering, and more death—more of what already was.

CHAPTER 16

General Decline

I sink in deep mire,
where there is no standing:
I am come into deep waters,
where the floods overflow me.
PSALM 69:2

THE SPIRIT OF THE ARMY COULD NOT HAVE BEEN AT A LOWER ebb as the New Year began. We were disheartened, weakened, depleted, wounded, and sick. Before, we had been going forward, chasing the enemy, bringing the war to his hearth. Now we were discouraged and defeated; our cause was reversed; every effort ended in futility. Camp life settled into a tedium of mud and drudgery. Food was always the same—coffee, hardtack, salt pork, and some boiled meat from time to time—unsuitable for maintaining our weakened bodies, let alone for building the reserves of strength the army would need for carrying the fight to the enemy. Sickness was again widespread; almost everyone suffered from diarrhea or scurvy or both. Countless men went into hospitals and never returned. Memorials for the dead were held nearly every day.

Even the landscape reflected the mood of the army. When we had arrived at Falmouth in November, the place had been verdant and well forested. With each passing week, everything green disappeared under the incessant tramp of army feet or fell to the constant chop-chop-chop of army axemen. The expanse of brown and gray expanded farther as the tree line receded in every direction.

Grumbling became our favorite pastime. We grumbled about everything, from rations to the miserable living conditions to the state of our health. Every ache was magnified and every sniffle became a deadly disease. No one had been paid since leaving Hartford so we griped about that too. We also complained about the weather. It was always cold and it snowed or rained often. Mud was always with us. We went on to grumble about General Burnside, President Lincoln, and anyone else in authority; we made disparaging remarks about their character and even sometimes about their kinfolk.

Jim Adams was particularly incensed. "Lincoln should go back to the woods of Kentucky."

"What's the matter?" John asked.

"He freed the slaves the first of the year. It says so right here in the *National Intelligencer.* As far as I'm concerned, the Johnny Rebs can keep their slaves if they just quit the war and come back to the Union. I didn't sign up to die for darkies."

I understood Jim's frustration. Although the principal reason John and I enlisted was to rid the country of the scourge of slavery, many others had joined the army for different reasons, and these men seemed to care little about slavery. When Abraham Lincoln, with a single stroke of his presidential pen, declared all slaves to be free—including the freedom to enlist, if they chose, in the Union army—rumbles of discord echoed throughout our ranks. For many of the men, it was the final straw. They would sooner desert their posts than fight a war for the black man.

During January the regiment had few official duties except

for arms drill and picketing the river. We went out on picket duty every fifth day. Picket duty started at eight o'clock in the morning and lasted twenty-four hours. The regiment usually guarded a portion of the Rappahannock River near Banks Ford, and it was our duty to see that no unsavory Rebel activity occurred along our stretch of the river. We left camp at six o'clock and marched for two hours—west toward Warrenton for a few miles, then south toward the river, where we relieved the departing regiment and deployed. While some of the men patrolled the immediate bank of the river, others occupied dozens of rifle pits some yards farther back.

While John and I were patrolling the advanced picket line early one morning, one of the rifle pits partway up the riverbank attracted my attention.

"See that pit?" I pointed up the slope.

"What about it?"

"We've passed by here three times in the last thirty minutes, and he hasn't moved at all. Maybe he's asleep."

"Or dead," said John, since that option was just as likely.

At first, the pit appeared to be normally occupied, but as we approached, we saw that something was definitely amiss. A vacant soldier's greatcoat had been stuffed with fallen leaves and carefully arranged in the rifle pit. A musket lay across the lip of the pit, propped up with sticks. The armless sleeves of the coat had been carefully draped over the musket to resemble the standard firing position. As a final touch, a cap with the telltale *14* on the top had been placed atop the empty collar, pulled low the way we always did on a cold night with just an eye-slit between the bill and the collar. In the dark of night, if one was passing casually by and cared not to engage the man in conversation, the phantom watchman appeared the model of readiness.

"Let's find Sergeant Holt," John said. "I think this was Warner's pit."

John was correct. The former occupant of that spectral uniform had deserted his post. Warner had probably written a letter to a sympathetic friend or relative or wife at home. "Please purchase with the enclosed funds," he'd have written, "items of civilian clothing and send them along, possibly in separate packages, or along with some other shipment of foodstuffs or other necessaries, to the kind attention of the soldier." Upon receipt, Warner had surely hidden his new civilian clothing at some secret location. Then, at an opportune time, the soldier had reported to his rifle pit, doffed his Union blues and stuffed them to create the phantom rifleman, donned his new garments, and started with impunity northward.

I stood staring down into the rifle pit. In recent weeks I too had entertained tempting notions to depart. I had even hatched a few illusory plans and half-considered schemes to that end, but I never said a word of these things to anyone nor did I ever take one step toward fulfilling them. Certainly the thought of abandoning John was unbearable, but what could I ever have said to Jessie Anne in my defense?

◇≈◇

Another cold January night, again while picketing along the river, John called to me in a low voice, "Michael, you have to see this. There's a Reb across the river. I think he wants to talk to someone."

We edged our way through the brush to the water's edge.

"Hey, Yank," called the Rebel in a nasally twang, waving a small white flag or kerchief. "Y'all sure make a lot of racket. Careful or you'll wake your dead back in Fredericksburg." A low chuckle was distinctly heard across the water.

"What do you want, Johnny?" John called back, hands cupped to his mouth.

"Coffee. Got any coffee?"

"Don't you have any?"

"Nah, Yank, that's one thing Ol' Bobby Lee cain't get much of, and what we do get is more like floor sweepin's than coffee."

"What'll you give for it, Johnnie?"

"I got lots of tobacca, Yank."

"Yeah, Reb, what kind?"

"Virginny, of course. Best smokin' a man can get."

"How much coffee do you want, Reb?"

"How much you got?"

"I don't know," said John, reaching into his haversack to feel for his sack of coffee. "Maybe we can come up with a couple of pounds."

"Yeah, Yank? That'd be all right. I think we can get up maybe four pounds tobacca. Two for one, okay?"

"There will be some sugar mixed with the coffee," I said.

"Yeah? Sugar? Even better—almost never get sugar."

"How do we do this?" asked John.

"You boys are new, ain'tcha? Put your coffee in a sack and tie it up tight. Up river about a hundred yards, there's rapids, fast but not deep. Just go a ways out in the river, and we'll meet ya."

"It'll take some time to get the coffee together," John said.

"We got all night. How much time?"

"About an hour," answered John.

"All right, about an hour."

"John," I whispered, "how are we going to come up with two pounds of coffee when we don't even have one pound between us?"

"Let's find Sergeant Holt. He smokes too. I'm sure he'll know what to do."

Holt's eyes widened when John explained. He did indeed know what to do, and he was already savoring the thought of smoking fine Virginia tobacco. But it had to be done quietly, he said, because talking with the enemy was strictly forbidden.

"Go to every man in Company C," he told John and me. "Ask 'em if they want to trade coffee for tobacco, one handful of coffee for one share of tobacco. Make a list, 'cause I won't stand for no bickering over tobacco."

Most of our men eagerly reached into their haversacks and put in a single handful of coffee, but several, including John and me, contributed two handfuls for a double share. As John collected the coffee in a sack, I noted each man's stake in the deal on a piece of my journal paper. In no time at all, a goodly quantity of coffee had been collected, surely in excess of the required two pounds.

Sergeant Holt supervised the completion of the transaction in the middle of the river that night. I don't know if it was his impressive stature or his consummate skill in parley, but he was able to get another pound of tobacco out of the Reb, and it was of the finest quality indeed, just as the Johnnie had said. Great clouds of aromatic smoke rose about our company's campfires for weeks afterward, and the other men of the company looked upon John and me with a more appreciative glint in their eyes for several weeks.

⋘⋙

Sunday, January 25, 1863
Camp of the 14th Conn. Rgt. Vol. Inf.
Near Falmouth, Virginia

Dearest Jessie Anne,

The boys and I remain in generally fine health while others have suffered more severely. We certainly credit your regular packages, along with those of Mrs. Adams, without which we would not have been able to supplement our rations with such necessaries as canned peas and beans and fruit. The arrival of a box every three weeks works well, and we are able to plan our consumption accordingly. There was some talk of resuming Saturday evening band concerts, but there has been no official word, and now recent events have delayed them once again.

An incident occurred which, if it were not for the entirely pitiable nature of the affair, would otherwise appear quite amusing. Rumors always abound when the army is in camp. The most recent rumor with the greatest credibility was that General McClellan would be recalled to lead us in our next campaign, which should have begun under the sunny warmth of springtime. However, about two weeks ago, more rumors began to fly that the army was going to move against the Rebels. Indeed, orders were given that the army would move out on Tuesday the 20th. Our brigade was detailed to be the rear guard of the grand army column, in case the enemy tried to sneak around behind us to steal our supply wagons.

Captain Bronson, acting commander of the 14th, read the orders from General Burnside. The army was to march west along our side of the river, cross the river at an opportune place, then attack the Rebels at Fredericksburg from the rear. Of course, this was all supposed to be accomplished without those on the other side of the river finding out about it. After reading the orders, Captain Bronson exhorted us to greater effort for our noble cause.

"Three cheers for General Burnside! Hurrah! Hurrah! Hurrah!" he yelled, but almost no one else cheered with him. The commanding general of the recent foray into disaster is not a popular figure among the ranks of the army, so the thought of giving up a cheer of adoring appreciation was, of course, ridiculous.

Each man in the regiment received sixty rounds of cartridges from the quartermaster along with three days' supply of coffee, hardtack, and salt pork. Charlie cooked up our pork rations while John and Jim stripped our hut of its shelter tent roof and I rolled up our rubber and woolen blankets. We packed everything that would fit into our knapsacks.

The Army of the Potomac started to move. We had nothing to do until the entire column had passed, so we walked to the top of a small hill nearby and were afforded an excellent view of the road our troops were using as they headed off to the southwest. Column after column of blue infantry marched below us in an endless tide.

At first, progress was at normal army slow on the hard-frozen roads. Thousands of supply wagons, artillery pieces, and caissons accompanied the columns of infantry. Teams of horses drew hundreds of pontoon boats on wheeled carts. The whole mass of men, beasts, and machinery inched relentlessly forward in fits and starts.

From the top of our little hill, we could also see across to the opposite side of the river. It was clear that the steady tramp of tens of thousands of feet, the sound of countless straining animals, and the rattling of our wheeled pieces had drawn the attention of the enemy. In fact, I saw several distant figures across the way jumping up and down, waving their hats, and signaling others of their ilk to come and see the "secret" movements of our army. Some of the ragamuffins even called over to us with jeering offers of help in rebuilding the pontoon bridges so we could cross over and renew our futile assaults.

Clouds began to move in, just a few in the morning, then more numerous in the afternoon so that, by late in the day, the sky was completely overcast and ominous. By evening it was raining, lightly at first, but then the wind started to howl and the rain came pelting down in slanting, icy sheets. In just minutes, the road became a quagmire, thick and sticky as mashed potatoes that have been in the pot too long. Wagons, artillery pieces and pontoon boats sank into the miry depths, and normal army slow came to a full army halt. All that night and into Wednesday the army hardly moved a step forward, and from our vantage point we continued to stand in the rain, awaiting orders to add our boots to this disaster.

The orders never came. Instead, seeing it was hopeless to go farther, Burnside ordered the army back to camp. We rebuilt the roof over our hut, unpacked everything we had packed the day before, and built a blazing fire in the fireplace. Then we sat smoking our pipes as the rest of the weary and muddied army stumbled and grumbled back in the other direction. It took two full days for that stream of wasted and dispirited souls to finally complete its passage in front of our hut, accompanied all the while by hoots and hollers of derision from the other side of the river. Our brigade was indeed the least pitiable part of that pitiful army, as we never had to endure the full experience of this latest fiasco that is already being called the "Mud March." We were the first to put our huts back in order, the first to dry wet clothing, the first to enjoy hot coffee and hot food, the first to find warmth for both body and spirit.

The army as a whole, and this soldier in particular, is weary of the hardships thrown upon us through the bungling of our generals. Those in high positions seem to have little regard for those below them—basic human decency apparently is not taught in the military academy. There is so little I can do to improve my lot and disposition that I fear I am becoming as gray and dismal as the weather. Please continue to uphold us in your prayers.

I remain your most affectionate husband,

Michael

CHAPTER 17

General Renewal

Whosoever smiteth the Jebusites
first shall be chief and captain.
1 CHRONICLES 11:6

IMMEDIATELY FOLLOWING THE DEBACLE OF THE MUD MARCH, news raced through the Army of the Potomac—Burnside had been sent packing; General Hooker was now in charge. Over the next several weeks, Hooker brought several fundamental changes to the army. Most of these changes were welcomed by the soldiers in the ranks, none more so than the promise that each man would finally receive all wages due him. It was a promise kept, and every man in the Fourteenth received four months' pay along with his Federal enlistment bounty. There were changes in command: Generals Franklin and Sumner were relieved of duty. General Couch still commanded the Second Corps, and General French was still our division commander, but General William Hays was given command of our brigade. For the first time since the Second Brigade was formed, it would be led by a general officer, rather than a colonel, and the Twelfth New Jersey regiment was added to the brigade to increase its strength.

On the third day of February, in the year of Our Lord 1863,

a single wagon entered the camp, its load draped with a large white cloth. Wisps of steam rose carrying a most pleasing aroma to any and all who happened to be nearby. Our appetites had craved this wagon's cargo; our hopes and dreams had been filled with it—fresh bread. Every man in the regiment dropped what he was doing and raced to get his share. The civilian at home cannot imagine what a blessing it was for a soldier to finally hold in his hands a loaf of soft fresh bread, still warm from the oven, after months of hard crackers.

Rations of fresh meat, onions, potatoes, and other vegetables became more frequent. Prospects of better food immediately raised the morale of the entire army; grumbling decreased considerably.

A system of furloughs was instituted. Two enlisted men out of every hundred were given a ten-day leave of absence. This was a stroke of genius because the disposition of every man in the army brightened as he contemplated the prospect, dim though it might be, of a visit to his loved ones. Numbers were drawn for these furloughs and the names of the men of the Fourteenth were entered into a ledger kept by Adjutant Ellis. John drew number 35 and I drew 42, so the prospects of either of us receiving furlough before the start of the spring campaign season were small indeed, but now there was hope.

General Hooker's stock seemed to improve daily in the eyes of all the men—except Charlie, because Hooker ordered all of the bands to disband, claiming they were a waste of men and resources.

Charlie was furious. "Philistine!" he said, his voice shaking. "How can he outlaw music?" But the order stood. Mr. McCarthy resigned and went home; the other band members joined the ranks and took up soldiering. As for me, the order meant little and I remained silent on the matter, for I had little desire to take up singing again.

By the end of February, our regiment nearly doubled in size to about two hundred men fit for duty. Some of the less-seriously wounded, such as Captain Carpenter, returned from convalescent leave. Also, some who had mysteriously disappeared, either just before or during the fighting at Fredericksburg, chose this time to mysteriously reappear. A few of the more serious delinquents were jailed, but most were severely reprimanded and awarded extra fatigue duty, such as chopping firewood, digging sinks, and burying dead horses and mules. A sufficient supply of delinquents meant that those of us who had remained at our posts were relieved of these onerous duties and had more time for relaxation and writing letters and smoking our pipes. It also had the benefit of shortening our wait for furlough, since a regiment with only one hundred men could only send two men at a time whereas a regiment of two hundred could send four.

As the health of the men began to improve, arms drills were carried out every day. Dress parades and inspections were more frequent. We started to look and feel more like an army again, rather than a ragtag mass of homeless wanderers. Every man in the Army of the Potomac was issued a badge that was sewn atop his forage cap. The shape of the badge indicated which army corps the wearer belonged to. For instance, the First Corps badge was in the shape of a circle, the Second Corps a trefoil (similar to a three-leaf clover), the Third Corps a diamond, and so forth. The color of the badge identified our division within the corps— red for the first division, white for the second, and blue for the third. So everyone in our regiment sewed a blue trefoil badge to the top of his cap, because we were in the Third Division of the Second Corps. Every soldier was now instantly identifiable as belonging to this or that division. He began to take pride in his new identity. He warmly greeted others along the way with similar badges as if they were old friends. He paid more attention to his personal appearance, appearing taller and walking with a surer step.

⊲⋛⋗⊳

Saturday, the 14th of March, was the day of the great snowball fight. Adjutant Ellis, a staff officer with the Fourteenth from the start, was soon to be promoted to the rank of major and permanent command of the regiment. Upon seeing a fresh blanket of heavy, wet snow, and having nothing of import scheduled for the day, Adjutant Ellis challenged Colonel Powers, who was also newly in command of the 108th New York, to a snowball fight, not adjutant versus colonel, but regiment versus regiment. Powers readily accepted the challenge, thinking Ellis, an officer of inferior rank, to be an easy mark.

One hour was given to prepare positions for the upcoming fray. Both sides threw up mounds of snow about twenty-five yards apart on the parade ground; the higher the mound, the better the protection from incoming ice bombs. As the agreed-upon time neared, Adjutant Ellis called the regiment together for last-minute orders.

"The rules are simple. This is a fight to the finish; last regiment standing wins. The officers of the Twelfth New Jersey will serve as marshals. If you're hit squarely, you're dead and you will be ordered from the field. Now, I have a plan for this little engagement. You all know how we drill the Sharps rifle companies in pairs? How one man loads both weapons and the other man fires them?"

Ellis looked from side to side as he spoke; attentive heads nodded slowly.

"Work in pairs. One will make snowballs as fast as he can. Pack them well so they do not come apart, and stay low so you do not get killed. The other will be the shooter. Aim carefully and make every shot count."

Happy murmurs broke out as the men grasped the grand strategy.

"Aim at their best shooters first. Kill them and the day is ours. Listen to your officers. They will direct your fire just as they do in real battle. We will reduce their numbers to the point where we can successfully charge and carry their works. When I call 'Fix bayonets!' that will be the signal for everyone to stop throwing and arm themselves with two or three snowballs for the charge. Any questions?"

With a great cheer we took up positions behind our mound of snow. Jim and I were snowball shooters; John was my loader and Charlie was Jim's loader. A revolver was fired into the air at the appointed hour. "Fire at will!" echoed up and down our line and the melee began.

The air was filled with snowballs arcing across the intervening space. Like most of the other men, my first few throws either fell short or went long as I homed in on the correct range, but one by one, my shots started to find their marks. As a young boy, I became very good at throwing rotting apples at tree trunks, a skill that had no particular purpose except that every direct hit was rewarded with a satisfying mushy *thwop*. I developed a technique that began with drawing the apple back behind my right ear in line with the direction of my target. After pausing for just a split second, I brought my arm over and across my body in an overhand motion, releasing my projectile with a flick of the wrist, much as they do in the new game of baseball. This practiced motion practically guaranteed that an apple would fly straight at a tree trunk or that a snowball would fly straight for a man's head. One by one, dead but still cursing participants were ordered off the field by the marshals.

Ellis's strategy had one other advantage. As a shooter, I never had to look away from the enemy to get another snowball. I put my hand down at my side, John put his finished snowball in my waiting hand, and then I raised it and got ready to throw. After completing the throw I just put my hand down for another ball and did it all over again. Although I was exposed to incoming fire all of the time, I could see the shots coming and, if the shot appeared close to ending my day, I could dodge or weave. My eyes never left the target. I watched our opponents across the way and timed my throws with their movements. A New Yorker would throw his snowball, stoop down to make another, and, just as he started to rise up again, I would let loose with mine. Often, my ball struck him before he was able to focus on the instrument of his "death."

Jim Adams was not as fortunate. Several times I saw him out of the side of my eye turning his back on the New Yorkers to receive a snowball from Charlie. "I'm dead!" Jim yelled when he was struck in the hip during the early stages of the fight, and he was forced to stand aside to watch the rest of the engagement. For several minutes, the issue was truly in the balance; we lost as many as the New Yorkers, but we had heard our commander, and the men we were picking off one by one were their better throwers. Gradually, the accuracy of their fire deteriorated.

Half an hour later the outcome was no longer in doubt. Both regiments had started with about two hundred men "fit for duty." We had been reduced to about one hundred; the 108th to about seventy, and many of their survivors were not major threats. They were expending greater and greater effort in throwing their snowballs, many of which fell short of our breastwork of snow. Our shooters were also tiring, and some changed places with their loaders to rest while fresh arms kept up the fire on the New Yorkers. The numbers in the 108th continued to dwindle, while only a few more of our men retired from the field.

"Fix bayonets!" ordered Adjutant Ellis. Wide eyes and bewildered faces appeared over the works across the way. The surviving members of the Fourteenth quickly made their small arsenals of snowballs and waited only a few seconds for the anticipated order.

"CHARGE!"

Up we jumped over our mound of snow, screaming like wild men, racing toward the enemy, weaving this way and that to avoid snowballs fired frantically at us in a last-ditch effort to avoid disaster. We sped across to the enemy's works, holding our fire until we were immediately upon them. To their credit, many of the New Yorkers died in gallant defense of their line, but others started to run for the rear and were shot in the back. No quarter was asked and none given. John and I and several others gave chase as some retreated back toward an encampment of tents and huts along the edge of the parade ground. Running as fast as our legs could carry us, we started in among the first line of huts.

"Yow!" John yelled. I heard rather than saw him crash to the ground behind me. I left the pursuit to my comrades and turned back. John had fallen heavily against the base of a hut much like our own. He quickly struggled back to his feet, but stood hunched over, holding his right hand against his ribs.

"Are you all right, John?" I asked.

"Yeah—I think so." John gasped for breath. "My feet just went out from under me. Hurts something terrible though—maybe broke a rib." After a minute or two John was able to stand erect. He shook his head with a wry laugh. "I'm not a youngster anymore, and I should know better than to go racing off through the snow like that."

The wet snow had soaked him through. The fight was over and the Fourteenth had clearly won a great victory that day. Except for John, injuries were limited to a smattering of black eyes, split lips, and bloodied noses. All would recover. There was celebration all around, and even the men from the 108th New York, after conceding their humbling defeat, joined the celebration. There was a special ration of fresh beef and vegetables that evening, and we retired to our huts to prepare our minor feasts. John painfully removed his clothes and sat shivering by the fire in an effort to warm up. He asked me to look at his back and side to see if I could see anything wrong, but there was no visible wound.

I heard John grunt in pain several times that night as he turned in his bunk. In the morning Doc Rockwell examined John and confirmed that John had probably cracked one or more of his ribs. The surgeon bandaged John's torso and sent him to the hospital for a few days of "observation."

John healed quickly, and while he was able to resume many of his normal duties, he could not engage in any strenuous labor. He was released from the hospital on St. Patrick's Day, a day of great celebration in the Second Corps because of the Irish Brigade and the many Irishmen throughout the corps. It was a beautiful day for such enjoyment, a pledge of the full bloom of spring soon to come. Good food, whiskey, and rum were consumed in abundance. Merriment ruled the day, the noise of which I hoped would carry across the river to the camp of the enemy.

A curious thing happened during those long, trying winter months at Falmouth. The defeated, dispirited, and dejected army was transformed. Constant drilling, better food, changes in command, and a few dollars in our pockets all served to rebuild a quiet confidence in our abilities as men and as soldiers. Morale improved along with our health and spirit; resolve was reborn to see this war to a victorious conclusion.

The Army of the Potomac emerged ready to march. It was spoiling for a fight. It was hungry for victory. And so was I.

CHAPTER 18

A Grand Design

A wise man feareth, and departeth from evil:
but the fool rageth, and is confident.
PROVERBS 14:16

JOHN ROBINSON DIED ON THE 12TH DAY OF APRIL. HIS RIBS HAD healed satisfactorily, but during the last few days of March he came down with a severe cold. Every day seemed to bring with it a new symptom, first a pounding headache, then a fever, and then chills racked his body.

One night during the first few days of April, we were out on picket duty with the rest of the regiment. "Every part of my body aches," he told me; his voice was now raspy and his breathing labored.

"I know you try to avoid sick call, but I don't think this is just another cold, John. You should see Doc again. Go see him as soon as we return to camp."

The next morning Doc Rockwell examined John for a few minutes and ordered him to go immediately to the hospital. I went along to help him if necessary. After a thorough examination, the doctor at the hospital said that John's ribs had healed and that he most likely had pneumonia. John was admitted to the hospital for further rest and treatment.

When not out on picket duty, I visited John as often as possible. Terrible fits of coughing contorted his entire body. How greatly he suffered I will never know, but whenever I approached his bedside, his eyes lit up in joyful greeting. For several days in a row Jim, Charlie, and I went to visit John whenever we could. I concluded each visit with a reading from my Bible and prayer for my beloved friend. No matter which passage I had decided to read, John always requested that I read the first few verses of the fourteenth chapter of the Gospel of John, and I could not help but notice a faint smile on his lips when I read verse 3: *And if I go and prepare a place for you, I will come again, and receive you unto myself; that where I am, there ye may be also.*

On Saturday the 11th I visited John in the evening. John had a different request.

"Read from Job," he said.

"Job?"

"Chapter nineteen. Here, let me find it," he said, reaching out a feeble hand to take the Bible from me. He found the page he wanted; a shaking finger weaved down the page as his eyes followed. "Here," he said, handing the Bible back to me, "verses twenty-five and twenty-six."

" 'For I know that my redeemer liveth, and that he shall stand at the latter day upon the earth: And though after my skin worms destroy this body, yet in my flesh shall I see God.' "

"Those are good words, Michael," John said, "full of promise and full of life. They're words you can live by, Michael, and they're words I can die by."

I could only shake my head against that thought. I took John's hand in my own—we had never touched like that before—and knelt beside his bed. I implored our heavenly Father to spare John and allow him to return to all those who loved him.

John reached under the blanket. "Here is my pocket letter.

Please see that Abby gets it. I love her ... and the children ... so ... so much. Tell her I deeply regret leaving her."

I took my prayers to my bed that night. In the morning I rose early and quietly so as not to disturb Jim and Charlie. I walked to the hospital as soon as it was light enough to see the way, confident that my nightlong supplications had been heard, and that God would certainly accede to my pleas for John and his beloved family—and for myself.

In the heavy gloom of the ward I made my way to John's bedside.

"John?" I shook him several times. "John?" His eyes were fixed and his chest was still. He was gone.

I sagged to the floor in the dark shadows beside John's bed and buried my face in my hands. *Why, God? Why now? Why this way? He was my brother—it was Your will for us to be here, wasn't it? How often he cheered me when I was miserable! And who is there, now that he is gone? His war is ended, but mine goes on. Must I fight alone?* I was powerless to resist the wracking sobs that woe and despair tore from my body and my soul.

Sometime later a pair of ward orderlies appeared and wrapped John's body in a bed linen. I watched through bleary eyes as the orderlies carried John slowly down the length of the ward, through a doorway in a whitewashed wall now brilliantly bathed in the rising springtime sun beaming through the windows.

The only official observance of John's death was Chaplain Stevens's brief remembrance of him in his pastoral prayer during the regular morning service. Afterward I went to regimental headquarters where I asked for and received permission to accompany John's coffin as it, along with one other, was taken by horse-drawn cart to Aquia for transport northward. I remained at the landing until the steamship cast off and sailed up the Potomac, until the last traces of the trail of dark smoke marking its passage had fully disappeared.

Every step of the eight-mile walk back to Falmouth was filled with complaint to the trees that lined both sides of the road and to the cool night air above, but mostly to the ground beneath my feet.

"God in Heaven, I know You plan and do all things for Your own glory, but why did You take John? I could understand if he had been killed in battle. We both understood that from the beginning. But of pneumonia brought on by a silly snowball fight? How can I tell Abby and Jessie Anne what happened? Lord God Almighty! There is no glory in that, merely added grief for Abby and the children and me at the senseless tragedy of it. Did I not pray enough? Have I committed some great sin? Was some great duty left undone? Have I offended You in some way?

⋘⋙

Sunday, April 19, 1863
Camp of the 14th Conn. Rgt. Vol. Inf.
Near Falmouth, Virginia

Dear Jessie Anne,

The second letter enclosed herewith is, as you can see, addressed to Abby. John wrote it shortly before his death. I trust that you will deliver this letter to Abby by your own hand.

A week has passed since that black day, and I am trying to employ myself usefully in the everyday affairs of army life. Four cracker boxes are on their way to you, evidence of such employment. There is one box each for Jim, Charlie, and me, full of things we cannot carry on the march, but may have need of again. Please launder the greatcoats so they will be ready for us when autumn returns.

The fourth box holds John's personal possessions. Please give it to Abby. How deeply Abby and the little ones must grieve. Words cannot express my love and sorrow, yet I have written her a short letter, which is in the box as well. I hope it will be some small comfort for her. I know I need not ask this of you, but please go to visit our dear sister and her children often.

I was allowed to accompany John's coffin to the landing. When I returned to camp, I dealt with John's possessions. Jim and Charlie offered help, but I reckoned this my final service to John. I cleaned and polished John's Springfield rifle. How many hours did we spend doing this chore together? We often engaged in a private competition whenever we had shooting practice. "How many shots did you get off?" or "How many hit the center of the target?" we would ask each other. John usually won the former contest, probably because of his longer arms, and I usually won the latter, perhaps because of my somewhat younger eyes. I lay the gleaming rifle down on John's bunk and added his cartridge box, canteen, haversack, greatcoat, and several other items of army issue. Then I carried the pile across camp to the quartermaster.

Then I folded each item of clothing neatly, even his extra pair of long flannel drawers, and packed them into the aforementioned crate. I polished his muddied Hickham's until they were spotless and shiny. His Bible I packed as I found it, for I knew it contained the well-worn photograph of his family, and I thought it best not to view their images. His smoking pipe I held under my nose for several moments, savoring the sweet aroma of the burnt tobacco and knowing how that smell would forever remind me of him. Only two of John's possessions did I retain — his coffee sack and his tobacco pouch — both of which I thought no one of John's family would desire and that I could make good use of.

All furloughs have been canceled in preparation for the spring campaign. On Wednesday the 15th, we were under orders to march away from this place with eight days' rations. A day's ration is twelve ounces salt pork and one pound hard crackers. With a total ration of twelve ounces of ground coffee and an equal amount of sugar, rations for eight days weigh something over fifteen pounds. You might not think this a great burden, and it was not when first setting out on a march, but hour after hour, the knapsack grows heavier; the straps cut into our shoulders and chafe the skin beneath our clothing.

Jim, Charlie, and I packed everything we would not carry with us. After no little wrestling within myself, I finally determined that I needed to take my blankets and my shelter tent, my mess plate and coffee cup, my writing things, an extra change of drawers, my Bible, the sewing kit you gave me, and whatever clothes I chose to wear at the final moment of departure. In addition to my knapsack and haversack I will carry my Springfield rifle, a cartridge box, and a cap box. Whatever remains will fall into the hands of Rebels, opportunists, and scavengers.

We retired on Tuesday evening in full anticipation of an early march the next morning, but it began to rain sometime after midnight, and no gentle, cleansing and refreshing spring shower was this. Rather, the rain came down steadily and heavily all through the day and into the next night. We hastily lashed our shelter tents upon the roof again and once again sat huddled together before a blazing fire.

The roads were once again impassible, and any speculation that the campaign might begin anytime soon was laughable. Truly our only solace was that the rain had come before the army had moved out.

So here we wait, doing regular duty or parade drill as necessary. It is a difficult thing for an army to wait for battle, for it has been primed and readied like a musket that had been loaded and cocked. Day after day passes without action, and the gleaming spirit of the army, which had been painstakingly polished over the last two months, has begun to lose some of its luster. As powder in a musket, when left too long, becomes damp and useless so that no spark can ignite it, so the fire in the belly of an army spoiling for a fight has begun to cool and fade. There are disputes and fights among the men over pitifully insignificant things, slights more imagined than real. I think an army must fight an enemy or it will fight itself.

As for me, I do not like being idle either, as idleness allows my thinking to drift toward how I dearly wish to be at home or how sharply I miss John. In your latest letter you expressed concern for my welfare, particularly my state of mind. I have concern as well, for I fear I have become the man of Lamentations — "I am the man that hath seen affliction by the rod of his wrath. He hath led me, and brought me into darkness, but not into light. Surely against me is he turned; he turneth his hand against me all the day." Has He set His hand against me? I often feel only the hard back of it, rather than the softer palm. If for some past or ongoing sin, it has not been shown me and I do not know of it. I see only that I must endure this affliction as I see no way of escape.

The comfort of friends like Charlie and Jim is precious to me, but I often think I am now all alone, even though I know that the Almighty attends unto my way without fail. Pray for me that this knowledge will suffice and at last provide comfort. May I again know Him as the Hope of the hopeless. Do what you are able to ease Abby's sorrow and comfort their little ones.

I remain your most affectionate husband,

Michael

⋈

On Saturday the 25th, I was sitting on Jim's bench, reading my Bible and enjoying the warmth of the mid-afternoon sun, when Charlie Merrills approached at a run. "I've just come from Major Ellis. Hooker changed his mind."

"You mean the campaign has been canceled?"

177

"No, no. As of the first of May, the band is going to start up again and I am to lead it."

"That's great, Charlie. I'm happy for you, but now that we're going out in the field there can't be any concerts."

"Perhaps, but now that music is legal again, I intend to see that the band is a credit to the regiment, like it was before."

⊰⊱

The warmer weather of late April had finally dried the roads. No religious services were held the day after my conversation with Charlie as the army prepared to march on Monday. General Hooker's master plan was that the entire Army of the Potomac would swiftly and secretly march out to the west where it would cross the Rappahannock and Rapidan Rivers and assemble ready for battle in the rear of Lee's army.

To everyone's surprise, the plan worked.

The Eleventh Corps, commanded by General Howard and comprised largely of German-speaking immigrants, was new to the army and had seen only limited action as they had been manning the defenses around Washington. No one, not even General Hooker, could say if this new corps would fight well or not. General Hooker sent them marching off to the west, so that they would be positioned as far as possible from the enemy until their worth was known.

As we had done during the Mud March in January, the men of the Fourteenth remained in camp and watched as the rest of the army filed past. The Eleventh Corps marched very well, easily identifiable by the crescent moon badges they sported on their caps. Their route took them only a short distance north of our camp, but they marched almost without a sound. We did not hear them pass by and neither did the Johnnies across the river. The Twelfth Corps under General Slocum and the Fifth Corps under General Meade followed the Eleventh, also without disturbing the peace. Fully half the army now marched west in an effort to outflank General Lee.

Day passed into night and we continued to wait. Tuesday, April 28th, dawned warm with the promise of rain. Still we waited, all the while casting anxious eyes skyward.

The Fourteenth Connecticut Volunteers finally fell into line at about four o'clock in the afternoon, just as a steady but gentle spring rain began to fall. It was not enough to turn the roads into quagmires again, but more than enough to soak us to the skin and thoroughly dampen our already too-heavy knapsacks and blankets. Westward we marched toward Warrenton, then south toward the river, the same route we used whenever we went out for picket duty. After several miles of marching, the gloom of twilight darkened into night and a halt was called. The men dropped in their tracks and camped that night near Bank's Ford. Of course no fires were allowed and therefore no coffee. Rations were eaten cold.

Wednesday dawned cloudy and warm. We broke camp early, without the usual succor of morning coffee. Burdened once again with our heavy packs, we marched to the west, away from the ford, parallel to the northern bank of the Rappahannock. The road was very rough and our bodies strained with every step. In places the road was so poor we were forced to make repairs so that our wagon trains could use the road later without hindrance. Progress was slow, but our officers assured us that we were doing important work and that we were on schedule to meet up with the rest of the army. While we worked with spades and shovels and saws and axes, we were allowed to set our packs aside, exchanging one burden for another. We filled in ruts and sinkholes; we felled trees and used the trunks and limbs and smaller branches to fill in places where muddy streams had washed the roadbed away. Our winter-weakened muscles screamed in protest, but on we went until the daylight failed. Then we slept exhausted beside the road.

Thursday morning we continued alongside the river to a place called United States Ford. The brigade halted just before starting across and General Hays rode to the front to address us.

"Officers and men of the Second Brigade, we are about to cross the Rappahannock River into Rebel territory. I have a dispatch from Major General Thomas J. Hooker, Commanding, United States Army of the Potomac:

" 'To all officers and enlisted men of the United States Army of the Potomac: It is with heartfelt satisfaction the commanding general announces to the army that the operations of the last three days have determined that our enemy must either ingloriously fly or come out from behind his defenses and give us battle on our own ground, where certain destruction awaits him. The operations of the Fifth, Eleventh, and Twelfth Corps have been a succession of splendid achievements.' "

A few men in the ranks greeted this announcement with loud cheering, but most responded with quiet "Humphs!" or resigned shrugs of the shoulders. Another grand design was being played out and we were the pawns on the chessboard. Each man within earshot understood that whatever was about to transpire, the dreadful assaults upon the heights at Fredericksburg would not be repeated. This time, things would be different. Bobby Lee could no longer hide behind a rock wall. But we also understood that our prospects for success rested less in our own skills in battle and more in our officers and their ability, or lack thereof, to lead us to victory. General Hays turned and paraded his horse across the pontoon bridge, then waited on the southern bank while the brigade passed in review before him.

As we marched on into the land of the enemy, thick woods closed in on either side of the road. Trees overhung the road, sometimes completely shutting us off from the bright sky above.

Thick underbrush made it impossible to see more than a few yards into the woods on either side. It was dark and it was warm and it was humid. The air was thick with the strange and pungent odors of deep woods and decay. It was all too easy for me to imagine a fiendish Rebel behind every tree, just waiting for his opportunity to gun me down. I think every man sensed that we were marching into the dark unknown, and no man knew if he would ever march back out.

"What is this place?" someone asked in a hoarse whisper.

"This must be the Wilderness," another answered, equally hoarse. "At least, that's what I've heard they call it around here —so close you can hardly see your hand in front of your face at noontime."

We followed that dark road for about five miles. As the sun sank lower in the sky and nighttime approached, the darkness became almost total. It was all one could do just to follow the steps of the man in front, trusting that the steps of all those who had gone before were sure and true. We finally emerged from the woods and turned off the road into a large clearing near a crossroad. A farmhouse stood on one corner of the crossroad, owned by a man named Bullock.

"Where are we, Sergeant?" I asked Sergeant Morrison. Sergeant Holt had fallen seriously ill during the winter and been granted a medical discharge. Morrison, a man whose capacity to lead I viewed as suspect, had been promoted in Holt's stead.

"Well, Captain said if we just go down this road a little more, we'll hit the turnpike into Fredericksburg about six miles west at a place called Chancellorsville. It's just a little place, just a crossroad and an inn, nothing worth fighting over."

The Inn
at the Crossroad

Our persecutors are swifter than the eagles of the heaven: they pursued us upon the mountains, they laid wait for us in the wilderness.

LAMENTATIONS 4:19

AFTER A PEACEFUL NIGHT, I AWAKENED TO A LANDSCAPE closely shrouded in fog, hued throughout in muted shades of gray. No orders came down, so my companions and I enjoyed a leisurely breakfast and savored the first real coffee we had been allowed since departing the camp at Falmouth. The Second Corps was serving as a reserve force for the rest of the army, ready to march wherever it was needed most when the fighting began in earnest. The day brightened as warm spring sunshine began to penetrate the fog.

"Second Brigade, fall in!" echoed throughout Bullock's field. "Rifles and battle kit only! Leave your packs in the west corner of the field. A guard will be posted." I tucked my Bible inside my jacket pocket and stacked my knapsack along with the others as instructed.

General Hays led the brigade as we marched the short

distance to Chancellorsville. Sergeant Morrison had been precise in his description of the place. The only structure of any consequence was a large brick inn at a crossroad formed by the north-south road from the ford that we were marching on and the Plank Road that ran from the western wilderness east into Fredericksburg. It was called the Plank Road because it was paved all over with wooden planks, so that, while other roads were impassible sloughs during wet weather, as every man in the Army of the Potomac knew well, the Plank Road remained firm, even under the weight of loaded wagons, and travel was eased considerably.

The Chancellor Inn was to the right side of the road on which we marched. Much of the Second Corps milled about preparing for battle. Batteries of artillery were drawn up, placed in position, and dug in. Our brigade moved a short distance off to the left of the road into some woods where we formed a line of battle.

General Hays seemed to be everywhere. He carefully positioned the four regiments of the brigade and supervised the positioning of each of the companies within each regiment so that we might have as strong a defensive position as the terrain would allow. The general made a few final adjustments here and there and then ordered us to build a barricade against the enemy. No sooner had we begun this task, than the rattle of musket fire reached our ears.

Bobby Lee had finally discovered what Joe Hooker was up to. The firing was some distance off, in front and to the right, but it certainly added a sense of urgency to our labors. The men foraged for every piece of fallen timber they could find. Branches, pine boughs, and small logs were stacked to form a low breastwork. The name "breastwork" implies that the barrier should be about chest high, but ours only rose to hip level. On the near side of the barrier, bayonets stabbed at the earth to loosen the soil, and mess plates scooped up the life-saving dirt to fill gaps between the wooden members. Grunts and profanities filled the air, perspiration streamed from every man, but we dared not pause in our preparations until General Hays was satisfied.

The firing toward our front grew louder. Enemy troops marching westward from Fredericksburg under the command of General Stonewall Jackson had found the roads blocked by Federal infantry. Jackson attacked the Twelfth Corps under General Slocum and the Fifth Corps under General Sykes. Hour by hour, the roar of battle waxed and waned as the battle went back and forth, but then the din grew progressively louder as our boys were driven back toward Chancellorsville during the afternoon.

Federal troops continued to flow into Chancellorsville from the north. A perimeter was established around the Chancellor Inn to the east, where we were placed, and to the south and to the west, where the new Eleventh Corps was dug in. Fortifications were thrown up, more artillery was positioned, and a strongly defended line was made ready to receive the Rebel assault that everyone said was imminent. In the unlikely event that disaster befell our army and a route of escape was required, other units guarded the roads back to the river fords to the north.

After sundown the fighting to our front gradually diminished. The Fifth and Twelfth Corps disengaged from the enemy and marched back within the defensive perimeter around Chancellorsville. Our brigade remained in place throughout the night, manning the works and shivering through the chilly night, ever alert for any sign of the Rebels. Relieved by another brigade at dawn, we left our stout breastworks to the new men and marched back to our camp at the farm along with the rest of the Second Corps.

We recovered our knapsacks, built campfires, cooked breakfast, and made coffee. Then we sat and waited for orders. Musketry flared now and again, but there was no heavy fighting, so we remained at the Bullock farm throughout that Saturday. As the sun began to sink into the trees at the edge of Bullock's field, I took out my Bible and began to read from the prophet Daniel.

Suddenly there arose, from some distance away and to our rear, the sound of heavy fighting. We soon discovered the reason there had not been any heavy fighting during the day: Stonewall Jackson had used that time to march 30,000 of his men from our eastern flank all the way around our army to strike the western flank where the untested Eleventh Corps was.

As it turned out, the men of the Eleventh were better at running than fighting. Their officers had done a poor job of positioning them, and the units of the corps were strung out for a couple of miles along the turnpike that ran through the western wilderness. The enemy was known to be miles to the east, east of Chancellorsville where we were, so the men of the Eleventh Corps calmly and peacefully enjoyed their sojourn in the woods, oblivious to their peril. And so, when Jackson's veterans struck the unwary troops of the Eleventh Corps, they were entirely unprepared, and it was no contest. Almost to a man, the corps broke and ran. The few that tried to resist were immediately shot down or quickly captured.

A swarm of men in blue erupted out of the western woods and made haste in our direction. Their officers screamed orders, often with threats and curses, in an effort to restore order. A few of them shot several of the fleeing men in the back with their revolvers. But the tide did not show any sign of slowing. In fact, many of the cursing and threatening officers now joined in the headlong rush for the rear, as Rebel shells and musket balls nipped at their heels. It would take swift and decisive action to check this panicked flight.

"Second Brigade, at the ready!" General Hays screamed as he raced by on his charger. "Stack packs! Load muskets! Fix bayonets! Form line of battle along the eastern tree line and prepare to receive a charge!"

I threw my Bible into my knapsack and, along with every other man in the brigade, rushed across the field. We threw our knapsacks in a large pile and ran where our officers told us, to the edge of the tree line on the eastern side of the crossroad clearing about half a mile north of Chancellorsville. We faced the sound of battle and nervously waited for the Rebels to emerge from the western tree line. Shells from enemy guns arced over the trees and exploded in the field, driving the blue tide along with even greater fury.

Then a small band of courageous fellows stepped out in front of our line in a last-ditch effort to stem the flood of fleeing men that continued to stream through our lines, in places overrunning us as effectively as a determined enemy could. That brave small band was not armed with muskets or pistols, nor were they armed with brilliant oratory to persuade their wayward brethren with force of words. Rather, their weapons were made of brass—trumpets, trombones, euphonium, and tuba, with a pair of drummers trailing behind. Yes indeed, our regimental band, now debuting under the direction of young Charlie Merrills and only about a dozen or so strong in all, marched out between the lines and struck up "The Star Spangled Banner." The band played for about twenty minutes, during which time they never flinched, even though they were showered several times by shell fragments. All who saw it stood in amazement, privileged to witness what was surely one of the most courageous demonstrations of gallantry during the war. Thankfully, none of our players was killed, nor even seriously injured, and when they had finished, each man was welcomed warmly back into the line with claps on the back and many a "well done!"

But, sad to say, the heartening strains of our national anthem had little effect upon the troops of the Eleventh Corps. They continued to flow back through our line by the hundreds and thousands, unstoppable as a flood from a breached dam. I later learned that some ran so far that the Rebels on the eastern side of our army captured them.

"Second Brigade to arms!" cried General Hays. "Form on the road! Columns of four! By company!"

We quickly formed as ordered and started down the road toward Chancellorsville at the double-quick. General Hooker had established his headquarters at the inn. As we passed by, he was on the veranda waving his arms wildly, shouting orders and pointing emphatically at the western forest. Utter chaos swirled about the inn, and here and there, small groups of officers in blue tried valiantly to restore order and mount a defense of the ground. Men cheered us heartily as we pushed past them, but it was like trying to swim upstream against a raging river, since ours was the only column headed toward the enemy.

"Make way!" we cried, "make way!" as we ran down the center of the Plank Road, forcing those in flight to part before us. The Second Corps would save the army while others ran. A quarter of a mile down the narrow tree-shrouded road that led into the Wilderness, the brigade turned to the right and marched into the woods. The Fourteenth Connecticut, leading the column, marched farthest into those dense woods. General Hays came and adjusted our line several times. Then we quickly dug in and built breastworks again, knowing that the Rebels were not far off and could attack at any moment. As we faced the enemy, our regiment was at the right end of the line held by our brigade. No troops, friend or foe, could be seen anywhere farther to the right.

Presently General Hays reappeared. "Major Ellis, I see your boys have put up a fine-looking barricade. There is another brigade in front of you, from Berry's Division of the Third Corps. You will support them. Is this the end of the line?"

"Yes, sir, General, it is," our commander replied.

"That's not good. Send a detail out to the right. There are supposed to be other units out there. See if you can make contact with them. This flank cannot remain exposed like this."

"Yes, sir, at once," answered Major Ellis, as the general turned and rode back down the line. Major Ellis summoned Lieutenant Lucas and gave the young man a few brief orders. A few minutes later, Lieutenant Lucas and a small band of men disappeared into the woods on foot.

Every man within earshot instantly knew the peril he was in, for a line of battle in the midst of dense forest without any protection on the flank was the equivalent of rising up and shouting to the enemy, "Over here! Over here! Here's a good place to attack."

Fighting erupted off to the left somewhere. Shouts went up and down the line. "Are they coming? Are the Rebs coming?"

"No, not yet. The firing is off to the south, probably south of the road."

We remained on edge nonetheless, listening for any sound that might betray the presence of the enemy, the snap of a twig, a sudden flight of birds. After some time, Lieutenant Lucas's squad returned and reported to Major Ellis and to General Hays. The men had not found any other Federals off to the right. The Fourteenth was at the end of the line.

"Lieutenant, ride back to General French's headquarters," ordered General Hays. "Report to him what you have just told me. We need to protect this flank. We need at least two more brigades here, or we're in great peril. Tell him that—those exact words. Ride fast, Lieutenant, ride fast!"

With a crisp "yes, sir" and an even crisper salute, Lieutenant Lucas mounted his horse and galloped away. General Hays, obviously distressed, talked with Major Ellis quietly for some time.

About an hour later, Lieutenant Lucas returned. "General Hays, sir," he began, "Major General French sends his compliments and thanks for your part in stopping the advance of the enemy. He says that you need not worry about the right flank here. He says that he is well aware of the situation and that he will address it personally."

"When can we expect help to arrive?" the general asked.

"He didn't say, sir."

General Hays cursed. "I still don't like it. We need support on that right flank *now*! There must be no delay. Major, I believe the rest of our line is sound enough, and as we are in the most danger here, I will remain with your regiment until such time as the promised help comes up in support or we are attacked elsewhere."

"Very well, General," said Ellis. "Those are Jackson's men over there, aren't they, sir?"

"Yes, I think so, Major. Why do you ask?"

"Well, sir, they say Jackson's a devout Christian man and since tomorrow is Sunday, do you think he'll attack us on the Sabbath?"

"I've known Thomas Jackson since West Point. The fact that tomorrow's Sunday may prompt him to attack. He thinks it's a work of utmost necessity to drive us from Virginia, and whenever there's an opportunity, be it on a Sabbath or any other day, he'll see it as Divine Providence and seize upon it. Jackson will attack and leave the results to his God. Expect a heavy fight as soon as there is light enough to see."

⊰⊱

It began just as General Hays said it would. Jackson's men attacked at dawn. At first, there was just a smattering of shots deep in the woods to our front; then it swelled quickly to a constant rattle, and above the din of battle, a chorus of shouts and screams emanated from the dark forest in front of us. The sound of the firing grew louder in waves, a sure sign that Berry's men were having a tough go of it and were being driven back toward us.

The first men to come into view were indeed Berry's men. They were withdrawing with a fair degree of decorum, walking toward the rear, not running. Most of these men fell back through our line in good order, faces to the enemy, maintaining both their dignity and their possessions, but when they saw our breastwork and how prepared we were for defense, some of Berry's men fell into line beside us.

"The Johnnies are coming," they said, "lots of 'em. Won't be a minute, they'll be here."

"Here they come, boys, get ready!" yelled Sergeant Morrison. We raised our muskets and aimed into the darkness. Several nervous fingers discharged their weapons at nothing; their owners frantically set about the business of reloading. "Hold your fire, men," cried Morrison. "Hold your fire!"

And then the Rebels charged out of the woods in front and also against our right flank. General French had not taken care of our flank as he had promised. We were instead exposed to the full fury of the Rebel onslaught from that quarter as well as from the front. The enemy line came within sight of our works and we delivered a heavy volley. Their line wavered, halted, then surged forward again. The Fourteenth held its ground for a short time, but the savage assault from the front and right decided the issue.

"Fourteenth, fall back," cried Major Ellis. "Look sharp and help the wounded!" We regretted having to leave our breastwork, for with our leaving, the Rebels would be granted instant protection from many of our shots, but we did as ordered and withdrew to a safer place, and we did so in fine order. There was no panic, no running for the rear, and no casting off of burdens. Rather, in spite of the heavy fire, we recovered all of our wounded comrades, over thirty in all, and helped each to safety.

The Sharps companies were magnificent as a rear guard, firing at the Rebels from behind trees and any other available cover whenever the Johnnies tried to pursue us. However, the Sharps boys had not been detailed to look after General Hays, and the Rebels captured him, evidence to all that he was certainly not one to lead from the rear.

Colonel Carroll's First Brigade came forward, made up of several regiments from Indiana, New Jersey, Ohio, and West Virginia. They called us "Yellow Yanks" as we passed through their line, and "Connecticut cowards," and even "Nutmeg no-goods," insults that made my ears burn. Surely the Fourteenth had done all it could under the circumstances, but was my day to be just a few shots followed by hasty retreat? Was my day so soon done, the fight left to others to carry on? Was victory within our grasp—victory I would have no part in or claim to?

I reversed my course and joined Carroll's men. Many brothers of the Fourteenth and some of Berry's men reached similar decisions and also turned to join the counterattack. Many others, including Jim Adams and one of our corporals, continued toward the rear. Some were not seen for several days.

Carroll's men were fighters, a tough lot of men known as "The Granite Brigade." They stopped the Rebel advance in its tracks and started to drive them back. Every time the enemy tried to make a stand, Carroll's men stopped for a few minutes to allow everyone to reload and reorganize. Then they launched a furious charge that forced the Rebels back again. The Johnnies gave ground stubbornly and often we fought them from one tree trunk to the next. Sarge's cadence rang in my ears, and I fell into the routine that I had learned so long ago. Load, aim, fire—load, aim, fire—load, aim, fire.

A shabby man in gray with a black slouch hat cocked to one side stepped from behind a tree and aimed his rifle at me. A puff of smoke, a sharp report, the slap of his bullet striking the tree just inches from my head. I squeezed the trigger of my Springfield. A large red stain blossomed on the man's yellow shirt. "Ah, mother," the man said. Still gripping his rifle with his left hand, his right flew to cover the stain. The man dropped to his knees. Dark red blood seeped between his fingers. He swayed once to the right, then righted himself, then pitched face forward to the ground.

I surged forward with the rest of the men, loading and firing as fast as I could. Soon we came within sight of the breastworks we had abandoned earlier. The Rebels fought us stubbornly from the reverse side but finally gave up and retreated back into the very same woods they had emerged from a couple of hours before.

Colonel Carroll sent forward a strong picket line, but the Rebels had withdrawn farther back into the woods. While the fighting continued loud and hot to the south of the Plank Road off to the left, our front quieted. Carroll's men improved and strengthened the works we had built the previous day. Coffee fires were lit, and we adopted an attitude of comfortable watchfulness.

"You Connecticut boys, why did you run?" The Ohio corporal voiced the accusation of an entire brigade.

"We didn't run," I answered. "At least, not most of us. We were ordered to retreat. We were at the end of the line, and General French didn't cover our flank. That's where the Johnnies hit us. We fell back in good order and brought all of our wounded off with us."

The corporal said, "We're Second Corps, and the Second doesn't run. But a bunch of your boys did run. I saw it, and so did all these men here. Your friends are probably still running now, maybe all the way back to Connecticut."

It seemed that this corporal wanted to engage in more than just an exchange of words, but I would not fall prey to his taunts.

I stuck out my hand. "My name's Palmer, Michael Palmer, from Naugatuck, Connecticut. Pleased to meet you, Corporal." The Ohio man looked blankly at my hand for a second or two before he took it in his own.

"Mills, Teddy Mills," he mumbled, "Fourth Ohio. You do shoot well—I noticed that. Whose brigade you with?"

"Hays, General William Hays, but the Rebs captured him, so I don't know who commands us now."

"You boys had it rough?"

"At first we did. There was no hope of holding against the Johnnies, but it wasn't nearly as bad as Fredericksburg. Say, you men were in Kimball's Brigade? You boys were the first line up to that wall."

Mills's face darkened. "Yeah, we were," he said quietly. "I lost a good friend there."

"Andrews's brigade was the second line, and we were the third—a terrible day for everyone. We lost too many good soldiers. I lost a friend at Fredericksburg too, and my closest friend died at Falmouth, just three weeks ago today." I paused for a few seconds to steady my voice before continuing. "You fellows showed up none too soon today."

"Yeah, our boys have been spoiling for a good fight ever since we were wasted against that wall. We proved our worth today. We whipped them Johnnies today, and we'll whip them tomorrow. All we need is a fair chance, and I reckon that's up to the generals."

CHAPTER 20

A Knock
on the Head

And thou shalt grope at noonday,
as the blind gropeth in darkness,
and thou shalt not prosper in thy ways:
and thou shalt be only oppressed and spoiled evermore,
and no man shall save thee.
DEUTERONOMY 28:29

IT CAME UP THE LINE FROM THE SOUTH, A CHORUS OF HUSHED whispers sweeping toward us like a swarm of angry bees. "Hooker's dead! Killed by a Rebel shell." Each man turned and passed this dreadful news on to the next.

The roar of the cannonading had been constant, and every veteran infantryman could tell that the Federal artillery was not getting the best of it. The firing to the south of our line had gradually shifted eastward, toward the rear of our position, closer and closer to the Chancellorsville crossroad, as our guns withdrew under a heavy Confederate onslaught.

"General Couch must be in command of the whole army now," Teddy Mills said. "I think he's the senior corps commander."

"He is," I said. "Who's got the corps, then? Hancock?"

"Probably—hope it's not French."

"Do you think Couch is the man for the job?" I asked. "Do you think he can command the whole army?"

"Probably not, but who else is there?"

"That's the question. And Lincoln had better find an answer for it if we're ever to win this war. Who is that general of generals who can beat Bobby Lee at his own game?"

A rider galloped up, dismounted, and spoke briefly and excitedly to Colonel Carroll for a few moments, then galloped back the way he had come.

"Men," the colonel called out, "I've just been informed that we're being withdrawn from this advanced position. The army will form a new line back near the Bullock farm where we will prepare to meet the enemy again. These orders have come from General Hooker himself. He has not been killed, only slightly injured, just a knock on the head. He remains in command of this army. Prepare to move out."

"I helped build these works and I fought to take them back from the Rebs," I said to Mills. "We won this ground—and now we're just supposed to walk away and give it all up?"

Yet that is what we did. We simply walked away and left those fine breastworks and that blood-bought ground to the Confederates, not understanding why we were yielding without a fight, but the army never issued explanations along with its orders.

Carroll's brigade withdrew to the northeast, and soon we emerged from the woods into the fields around the Bullock farm. Six corps of Federal infantry, about 70,000 troops in all, were assembling in the vicinity, and pandemonium ruled as units of every type tried to organize and maneuver to their newly assigned positions, all the while dodging the incessant rain of shot and shell from Rebel guns.

Captain Davis of Company I, the ranking officer of the Fourteenth on that part of the field, gathered the forty-odd men of the regiment together. We bade our comrades in Carroll's command a fond farewell and set off to find the rest of the regiment. At the Bullock farm we found, much to our dismay, that our knapsacks were gone, as were the guards who had been posted to watch over them. There was no sign of anyone from our regiment or any indication of where they might be. Captain Davis inquired of some fellows in the Fifth Corps regarding the whereabouts of the Second Corps. They directed us some distance to the east where the Second Corps was taking up its position along the Mineral Springs Road.

We trekked about a mile and a half through untold thousands of men likewise roving in search of their lost comrades and detoured around other untold thousands of men trying to throw up works to establish a defensive perimeter, until we finally were reunited with what remained of the Fourteenth Connecticut. Only about one hundred men, including our number, were present and available for duty. As for our knapsacks, while we were off saving the army from ruin, Rebel skirmishers had overrun the field the previous evening, driven off the guards, and plundered our packs. Once again, we were without shelter tents and blankets and food. At first I was not terribly displeased about losing the days-old food, but the rations in my haversack would not last another day, and there was no prospect of getting more food anytime soon. My writing things were also gone, and I would have to visit the sutler once again and pay his high prices if I was going to continue writing my journal or letters home. But the cruelest blow of all was the realization that the Rebels had also stolen my Bible with the only photograph I had of Jessie Anne and Sarah and Edward. I imagined those rogues looking at that photograph, my photograph, not with love or admiration or respect or even curiosity, but with malevolence, perhaps slurring Jessie Anne's beauty, or worse.

By early afternoon that Sunday much of the fighting had stopped. The artillery of both armies kept up their work, and at times it got quite hot for us, but we moved back into the trees that bordered the road. Later in the afternoon, the shelling diminished greatly and we set about strengthening our line. Many, many trees were felled and dragged to the edge of the tree line, where long lines of stout breastworks were built. The Rebels left us alone, and we worked without stopping throughout the evening, finally falling into exhausted sleep sometime after the midnight hour.

A stalemate developed as both armies sat facing each other, separated by a half mile of ground upon which no man dared tread for fear of being quickly fired upon from both sides. General Hooker seemed content to remain where he was for the time being, and that was all right with us. The fighting on Sunday had been done with two of our six corps of infantry, the Third and the Twelfth, and part of our Second Corps. Now, all six corps were behind stout fortifications. They were rested; their muskets were loaded and ready; the artillery was in place. All waited for the fight to be renewed. The army was prepared for anything the Rebels might attempt. It was as if we were sending up a collective Sabbath's evening prayer: *Lord, let them attack with morning light*, so secure were we in our works and so confident in our ability to hand them a crushing defeat.

But General Lee was not an obliging fellow. Monday morning was actually quite peaceful. Long periods of stillness were broken only by the occasional crackle of musketry from the pickets and a stray shell or two. Wagons were drawn up to our rear; we were issued another three days' rations and enjoyed a leisurely breakfast. The coffee tasted especially fine and fresh that morning.

Captain Davis walked among the regiment and picked out several men to accompany him on a "fishing expedition," as he called it, per order of Major Ellis. He asked Sergeant Hirst from Company D to serve as his sergeant and then called out the names of several others who had joined in the fighting with Carroll's brigade. Captain Davis didn't know my name, but he recognized me.

"Are you in Company C, Private?" he asked as I saluted.

"Sir, yes, sir," I answered.

"What's your name?"

"Sir, Palmer, sir."

"Well, Palmer, you did well yesterday, and I have a job for you. It will mean a lot of marching today, but it will also get you away from here for several hours."

"Sir, yes, sir."

"Do you think you can recognize all of the men from Company C?" Captain Davis asked.

"Sir, we were twenty-three when we crossed the river. I know them all, sir."

"Good. Come with me." Captain Davis led the squad away from the rest of the regiment and explained our mission. "Every regiment has been ordered to send out detachments to round up stragglers and deserters. We will make a circuit around the entire army, looking for able-bodied men from the Fourteenth. We have a lot of ground to cover and our men could be anywhere. Some may have joined up with other units, like some of us did yesterday. Others may have headed back toward the river fords, thinking the army is in full retreat. Those we find will be given a single opportunity to join us and return to the lines. Nothing more than a stern reprimand will be given to those who come willingly. If any man resists, he will be placed under arrest and tried by general court martial for desertion. Understand?"

"Sir, yes, sir."

"Remember, we're looking for your brothers from the Fourteenth Connecticut. They may not have been looking to desert

at all; they may just have become lost and confused in the heat
of battle. Until proven otherwise, we will treat them decently
and fairly."

⬦⬦⬦

The new Federal line was shaped like a large letter *U* with both
arms of the *U* anchored on the Rappahannock to the north and
the curved portion around the Bullock farmstead. The Second
Corps was at the lower part of the eastern or right arm of the *U*.
We started our march by going south through the remainder of
the Second Corps. According to Captain Davis's instructions,
we spread out and searched for our missing comrades, asking
many, especially those gathered behind the lines, if they had
seen any stragglers from the Fourteenth. Around the curved portion at the base of the *U* we passed through Sickle's Third Corps
and entered the lines of Meade's Fifth Corps as we started up the
left arm of the *U*. Meade's line was built along the east bank of a
creek and appeared so strong as to be nearly impregnable. Continuing parallel to the creek, we next came upon Reynolds's First
Corps, whose entrenchments also were stoutly constructed and
stretched to the Rappahannock River. Still having found none of
the men we sought, we turned eastward and followed the bank
of the river until we reached the pontoon bridges at U.S. Ford.

Captain Davis inquired of the engineers at the bridge. They
had seen some men with the telltale blue trefoil and the brass *14*
on their caps crossing to the northern bank on Sunday, but none
today. We about-faced, and Captain Davis led the squad down
the same dark road we had trodden the week before. Clusters
of men had gathered here and there, some making for the ford,
some making coffee, others just sitting beside the road, taking
their ease. Late in the afternoon, we rounded a bend in the road.
Cries went up from our group, as a half dozen of our fellows
were found relaxing under a large oak tree. Sergeant Morrison

and Jim Adams were among them. When challenged by Captain Davis, all six sheepishly stood at attention, took up their arms, and joined us once again. Jim fell in beside me.

"What happened to you, Jim?" I asked.

"Well," he said, with a hint of awkwardness in his voice, "we were told to retreat, and so we did as we were told. We lost track of Major Ellis and the other officers, so we just fell back through the woods until we hit the road; then we followed the road back toward the bridges. Sergeant Morrison figured the army was whipped again and that the best place to rejoin the regiment would be along the road here."

"The best or the safest?" I asked, looking squarely at him.

"Safest too, I guess," was all Jim could mumble.

"Jim, I want to go home. This war killed my best friend and I'm sick of it. I'm sick of living in squalor. I'm sick of eating poor food, and I'm sick of being filthy, and I'm sick of digging cooties, and I'm sick and tired of squatting behind trees to relieve myself. Most of all, I think, I'm sick of retreating rather than fighting. I miss my wife and children—that's an ache that won't go away until I see them again. It would be so easy just to walk away and head north. But I belong here. I signed up for three years or the duration and I mean to hold up my part of the bargain, no matter how bad it gets."

"But the Johnnies were on our flank and we were ordered to retreat," Jim said, "and I was just obeying Sergeant's orders."

"Yes, the Johnnies had our flank, but only one man was killed, and we surely could have given a better account of ourselves. So when Carroll's men came up, I thought, 'Why should these men fight while I sit by and drink coffee? Wasn't it just as much my duty to fight as it was theirs?' So I turned around and joined up with them, as did many of our boys, and together we beat the Rebels back beyond our works where the fight started, and there are now many fewer Rebels to deal with because we did so."

"From your telling of it," Jim said quietly, "our few guns wouldn't have made any difference."

"That's not the point, Jim!" Heads turned at my raised voice. "I dearly wish this war would end, but if we don't stand and fight, it cannot end, or else it will end badly for us. Only by standing and fighting the Rebels tooth and nail can we win so we can return home to our loved ones. This is our fight. We cannot leave it to others. We must stand and do our duty."

We walked in silence for a time. Here and there others of our wayward men were gathered up, sometimes singly or in twos and threes. The squad turned left and followed another road toward the east side of the army. A large logging party was busily at work felling trees, to clear a new road to the bridges at U.S. Ford, they said. Soon we came upon units from Slocum's Twelfth Corps, and farther down the right arm of the defensive *U*, we passed through regiments belonging to Howard's Eleventh Corps. Of all the men in the army, these were easily in the foulest temper, eager to have another chance at the enemy. Heavily accented phrases of fractured English told of the shame they bore as the cause of the army's current distress. They wished for nothing more than to prove their true worth and be accepted into the ranks of the Army of the Potomac.

The sun was sinking behind the western hills as our circuit of the army was completed and we arrived back where we had started in the Second Corps. Our fishing expedition had netted two dozen or more stragglers and, true to his word, Major Ellis restored each man to full duty, after giving each a thorough dressing down in front of the regiment. Supper was cooked in the gathering darkness, and the men settled down to get as much sleep as they could. Tomorrow, the enemy would surely attack, trying to finish the job of throwing us back across the river. But we were ready for them; we would rout them utterly, and then it was on to Richmond to finish this bloody work.

And so it came as a great shock to the entire army the next morning when, instead of receiving orders to prepare for battle, General Hooker ordered a withdrawal to the north side of the Rappahannock. The withdrawal would commence with night-fall and was to be completed by daybreak in order to hide the movements from the Confederates. Heavy fog enshrouded the entire area that morning, and when the fog finally lifted, it gave way to heavy, thick clouds. A high state of vigilance was maintained in case Bobby Lee decided to press an attack, but no attack came. As we settled down to what was to be the last supper of our failed spring campaign, it began to rain heavily. Indeed, this rain was torrential, for within minutes, our entrenchments were turned to mud pits and our campfires to hissing steam.

Night fell and the army remained in place. Hours passed and not one regiment was taken out of line and sent rearward for the bridges. The heavy rain had caused the river to flood beyond its banks. Heroic engineers were forced to extend the length of the pontoon bridges and anchor them upon solid ground, a difficult enough task in the dark of night, but a truly perilous one when bridging a raging torrent.

Things finally started to happen about midnight, but I saw clear as noonday what was happening. General Hooker's knock on the head had cost him his backbone.

One by one, units formed up and marched off to the north. The Fourteenth Connecticut left its stout breastworks at about two o'clock in the morning on Wednesday, May the 6th. Rain continued to pour down as we marched up the new road we had seen the woodsmen cutting on Monday, hewn not for the purpose of communication and supply of a mighty army, but for retreat. How could it be that the Army of the Potomac, bloodied to be sure with thousands more dead and wounded, but with so much energy and will for the fight untapped, should be with-drawn from as strong a defensive position as it had ever known, once again under cover of darkness?

The road was cut straight for the pontoon bridges, but in spite of its straightness, the going was most difficult. Stumps from hundreds of felled trees remained and sent every man time and again tumbling to the ground in the darkness. The road became an avenue of cries and tears. Curses profuse and profane filled that black, rainy night all about me in yet another testament of woe.

The Fourteenth finally arrived at the bridges with knees, elbows, shins, and arms bloodied from countless falls. We crossed over just as the new day began to lighten the black of night to darkest gray. We turned toward the east and marched back the way we had come only eight days before. The march was as silent a one as I had ever known. There was no grumbling, no singing, no jesting, just slogging along in the heavy rain, hour after hour through mud more than ankle deep, until we arrived back at Falmouth about midday.

Jim, Charlie, and I returned to our hut without a roof, where we sat on Jim's bench beside the open door awaiting further orders. We had no greatcoats, for they were well on their way northward, and we had no shelter tents or blankets to wrap up in to ward off the chill, for the Rebels were making good use of them now. There was nothing to do but sit and shiver, soaked to the skin, waiting and praying for the rain to stop, and once again watch the remainder of our mighty army shuffle by.

I took my pipe out of my pocket, one of the few personal things that escaped the clutches of the Johnnies. I held the bowl close to my face under the bill of my cap to shield it from the rain and carefully pressed a fresh load of tobacco into it, just as John had shown me — child, mother, father. Then I struck a match against the heel of my boot.

It had become all too familiar, all too predictable.

But one thing had changed—now I was an instrument of death. I closed my eyes and saw the shabby man dressed in gray with the black slouch hat fall again and again before me. Strangely, I felt little as I watched, no sympathy for the dead man, no compassion for his family, no thankfulness for deliverance, not even mild satisfaction with duty well done.

I just felt ... hollow.

CHAPTER 21

Northward Bound

For my loins are filled with a loathsome disease:
and there is no soundness in my flesh.
I am feeble and sore broken:
I have roared by reason of the disquietness of my heart.
PSALM 38:7–8

*I*T HAD BEEN A WONDERFUL DINNER, THE BEST SINCE I HAD LEFT home. Indeed, I *was* home.

Jessie Anne and Sarah had prepared the sumptuous dinner of roast beef, creamy mashed potatoes, early sweet peas, and freshly baked bread, while Mama watched little Ed and I was upstairs soaking in a hot bath. When dinnertime finally arrived, Jessie Anne sat down next to me instead of at the other end of the table as she usually did, to the great displeasure of little Ed. Several times she reached under the table to caress my hand softly.

Afterward, we went for a stroll along the bank of the river, husband and wife hand in hand, while daughter and son frolicked. How pleasant it was this early June evening with gentle westerly breezes stirring the lush, verdant bloom of late Connecticut springtime. It was warm. It was beautiful. It was tranquil. It was ... oh ... so ... safe.

There was a gentle tap upon my shoulder; a soothing but insistent voice penetrated the veil of half-slumber. "Corporal? We're coming into Philadelphia." I yawned and willed my eyes open, forcing them to focus on the form standing over me. The whitest hair I had ever seen on a man escaped from under a black straight-sided pillbox-style hat. Above its narrow patent leather brim was a shiny, brass pin—the initials *P W & B* in an ornate script above the word *CONDUCTOR* in small block letters. White brows arched above small, round spectacles, a full white moustache drooped lazily from the man's upper lip, partially hiding his mouth.

"You're headed north, right, Corporal?" I stared blankly at the man; my brain had not yet awakened. "Where's home, soldier?"

I finally found my voice. "Naugatuck, Connecticut, sir."

"Sure, the Naugatuck Railroad. I've heard good things about that line. You'll need to change trains to the P and T, Corporal. It leaves at two-thirty."

"P and T?" I asked.

"The Philadelphia and Trenton Line; it goes to Trenton where the New Jersey Railroad takes over. They run express cars all the way to the Jersey City terminal so just stay on that train when you get to Trenton. Should get there about seven o'clock, I think. Then you take the ferry across the Hudson to Manhattan Island."

"Thanks, ... Mr. Tucker." I read the conductor's name from the pin on the breast pocket of his jacket.

"Henry, please, young man."

"Henry it is. Does the P and T train leave from this station?"

"Oh, heavens no," said Henry, "their depot's up in Kensington. Look for an Ames Omnibus on Market Street just outside the station. They make regular runs to the P and T depot. Get you there in plenty of time."

I stretched and looked out the window. In the bright sunshine, I saw that we were rolling up the west side of a river, the Schuylkill, according to Henry. We came into a switching yard, made a slow right-hand turn, and crossed a long bridge over the river into the city proper. A few minutes later the train stopped at the platform. The station clock showed ten past one.

"Let's go, boys," I said, standing up, "we have to go to another train station." I had three companions from the Fourteenth traveling with me, and it was a small but satisfying realization that I was now the ranking member of this little furlough party.

⟨⟫⟩

Yes, I was now a corporal. At Chancellorsville, Corporal Fox went missing for six days and did not reappear until the regiment had returned to camp at Falmouth. He was immediately reduced to the rank of private. Apparently, Captain Davis had given a good report of my actions during the recent campaign to Captain Carpenter, who thereupon summoned me to his tent and informed me of my promotion. I received my new stripes on the first day of June along with an increase in my monthly pay to fifteen dollars.

Several important changes occurred during the days and weeks following our return from Chancellorsville. The Fourteenth moved to a new campground in pinewoods about a mile from the Rappahannock. Upon arrival we found two wagonloads of supplies — new knapsacks, shelter tents, rubber blankets, and woolen blankets — all of the army issue we had lost at Bullock's farm.

The pinewoods was a very fine site for a camp, shaded nearly all day, with a thick carpet of pine needles underfoot and a rippling stream of clear water nearby. Gone was the dreary landscape of the winter camp, with its dust in dry season and its mud in wet. Gone were the ugly log huts made useless as shelter from the weather by the absence of their tent roofs. Gone was the view of the Confederate works around Fredericksburg, a constant reminder of our defeat there. We cleaned and boiled our clothes and bathed in the stream. In a short time our bodies were refreshed, and we settled back into the comfortable life of the soldiers' camp.

Gone also was our brigade commander, General Hays, now a guest of the Confederacy. Colonel Thomas Smyth of the First Delaware Volunteers was promoted to command the brigade. Colonel Smyth had enjoyed the respect of all in the brigade ever since his Delaware boys' courageous display in front of the sunken road at Antietam Creek. So within a few days after our second return from across the river we had brand-new equipment, a new, more peaceful and pleasant campground, and a new leader.

⋗⋙⋘⋖

One day in mid-May, a rider galloped wildly into camp. "Jackson is dead!" he cried, "Stonewall Jackson is dead!" Then he was gone, off to spread the news throughout the rest of the army. It was indeed true. Jackson had mistakenly been shot by his own men. The great Rebel general died about a week later near Fredericksburg. Spirits rose immediately with the realization that we would never again have to face this foxy, indomitable man again in battle.

General Hooker reinstated the furlough system in an effort to boost morale. A bitter irony of this system was that my chances of getting furlough were improved by the misfortunes of others. When a member of the regiment died, John Robinson for example, all those after him on the furlough roster moved up one notch. The wounded still in hospital were displaced by the able-bodied, shirkers were moved to the bottom of the roster, and deserters were removed altogether. As a result, my name rose to eleventh on the list after Chancellorsville, which meant that I would be in the third group of four to be furloughed, if all went according to plan. The time of departure was scheduled for six o'clock p.m. on Thursday, June 4th.

Those were anxious days, the last few of May and the first few of June, as rumors flew that the Rebels were up to something and that the army was getting ready to move. It was also with no little uneasiness that the four shortly-to-be-furloughed comrades awaited the return of the quartet sent home before us. But return they did, and shortly before six o'clock that Thursday evening, we were summoned to Major Ellis's tent.

Adjutant Doten filled out our furlough papers. On each, he wrote a physical description of the furloughed man; then the major signed the paper with a flourish. We accepted the documents with deepest gratitude and a crisp salute, our hands shaking all the while with excited anticipation.

"You are hereby granted ten days furlough to return to Connecticut," the adjutant said. "Present these papers to the provosts whenever they ask for them. A steamship is leaving for Washington from Aquia at nine o'clock this evening and you had best be on it. You will return to camp no later than six o'clock in the evening on Sunday, the fourteenth of June. If you do not report by the appointed time, you will be placed on report as absent without leave and treated as deserters. Do you understand?"

"Sir, yes, sir!" four voices screamed joyfully.

"Enjoy your furloughs, men. Dismissed," Adjutant Doten said, acknowledging our salutes with a quick one of his own.

Pockets had already been stuffed with fresh bread; canteens had already been filled, so the three men and I set off immediately at as fast a pace as we could manage. It was eight miles to the landing, and even though the Aquia Road had been greatly improved since our tour of duty at the landing in November, we knew it would be better than two hours of brisk walking. Scores of other men were heading off for furlough too, and the mood of the men was joyful in the extreme. Many produced bottles of whiskey and freely imbibed of their contents, sometimes with staggering results. Some laughed and joked and told stories of great bravado or harrowing escapes. Others who surely had trouble keeping up on the shortest of marches while on campaign, ran and skipped and frolicked along tirelessly for the entire eight miles. As for me, I chose to remain silent all during that long evening walk, retaining only two thoughts in my mind, the first being my last traversal of this road when I accompanied John's coffin to the landing, and the other of once again seeing Jessie Anne and my dear children. If things went smoothly, I expected to arrive in Naugatuck by noon on Saturday, and my mind fixed fancifully on the many things we would enjoy together during those blessed days at home.

The vessel was a fast river steamer, low and sleek, with twin side-wheels. Besides about two hundred happy soldiers headed home on furlough, several dozen wounded men were carried aboard on stretchers and taken below decks. Sacks of mail and other shipments were laded aboard and stowed. Tired and happy men staked out little claims of space on the open deck, "sleeping quarters" they called them. I found a space in the stern near the wheelhouse and leaned up against the side of the ship. Before long, the gangway was taken up, lines were cast off, and the mighty wheels began to propel the vessel out into the Potomac.

After a pleasant voyage lasting a little more than four hours, the steamer turned into the Anacostia River and docked at the Washington Naval Yard. Provost guards checked each man's papers under the dim light of oil lamps on the wharf. Directions were given to the depot near the Capitol Building. At the station the schedule board on the wall showed that the train to Baltimore was not due to leave until six o'clock, but no rest was to be had that night because revelers paraded through the depot all night, celebrating their temporary freedom.

We reached Baltimore at about seven-thirty in the morning, and our papers were again checked by the provosts. Most of the furloughed men, now much quieter and slower of step after a sleepless night, set off on the one-mile walk across Pratt Street toward President Street Station, the southern terminus of the Philadelphia, Wilmington, and Baltimore Railroad. Most arrived with time to spare, but some, I suspect, did not.

I went directly to the telegraph office. "A dollar for ten words," the agent informed me when I asked the amount of the toll to send a telegram. I gladly paid the man and sent this wire to Jessie Anne, knowing how happy she would be to receive it:

> BE HOME NOON SAT STOP
> 10 DAYS FURLOUGH STOP
> MGP

The train left for Philadelphia at eight-forty. Upon reaching the Susquehanna River at the town of Havre de Grace, the train was carefully loaded aboard a steamship specially built with rails to carry the locomotive and cars. The ship ferried the train across the river, and our rail journey continued on to Wilmington, Delaware, after which I slouched down in my seat. I fell into a sound sleep and beheld ethereal visions of my beloved ones' beautiful faces dancing through my dreams.

⋘⋙

The P & T train departed on schedule, passed through Princeton, New Brunswick, and Elizabeth. It arrived at last at the end of the line, the ferry pier at Jersey City, at about quarter past seven that evening. The ferry had just departed, so we would have to wait forty-five minutes for it to return. I stood gazing

across the Hudson River, at the ferry inching its way across and
the bustling city of New York. I pulled from my pocket Jessie
Anne's latest letter, which I had received the week before. One
paragraph particularly warmed my spirit as I waited:

*Your true brother in the Lord is gone. How sore is the ache in
my heart—yours must be multiplied all the more. Abby was truly
shattered when word came that John had died. Never have I seen
someone I love fall to pieces so quickly and utterly, but I believe she
is mending. Brothers and sisters at church have been wholehearted
in their love for Abby and the children. Many have extended the
hand of Christian charity above and beyond the barest necessities,
loving words and tender embraces have been commonly shared,
and many a sympathetic tear has been shed. There are many
to help that family. For now they will endure. In time they may
flourish once again. My worry is now for you, my beloved, for
there seems no one with whom you might share a tender embrace
or shed a sympathetic tear. Were you here, you know I would do
so, and I pray these few words may be a poor substitute. Come
home to me, my dearest husband. Come home to me in safety
when the Lord wills it.*

How I longed to touch the hand that wrote those words and
to have that hand touch me. Less than a day—the Lord had
willed it—a short river crossing, maybe some sleep at the station
of the New York and New Haven Railroad, aboard the first train
in the morning, a transfer at Bridgeport, and then the pleasant
and familiar ride up the valley, one hundred miles at most. I certainly hoped that Jessie Anne would prepare something special
for lunch, and I so longed for one of her strawberry pies; the ber-
ries should just be in season. But what of Abby? What should I
say to her? What could I say to her?

A cheer went up when the ferry started back across the river.

When it was about halfway across, a commotion from behind caused every head to turn away from the river and the approaching ship. A provost marshal had appeared, along with several guards. Pistols were drawn and at the ready.

"Attention all you men on furlough," he began. "We have just now received this wire from General Butterfield, Adjutant General, Army of the Potomac. 'Per order of Joseph Hooker, General Commanding, Army of the Potomac, as of six o'clock p.m., June 5th, 1863, all furloughs and leaves of absence are hereby immediately rescinded. All officers and enlisted men are ordered to return to their units immediately. Failure to comply with this order will result in swift and sure prosecution for desertion and dereliction of duty.' All of you men must get back on this train and return to Virginia. Present your papers to me as you pass. Return the furlough papers to your commanding officers."

◇≈◈≈◇

The car once again rocked me from side to side, mile after long mile. The iron armrest dug into my side; every bump, every jolt, every joint in the rail sent sharp stabs of pain coursing through my body. I cared not. The furlough was gone. Never would I see my wife and children again. In the next big battle I would surely be killed.

I traveled in silence, wishing not to engage or be engaged in conversation, but to wallow in my own sty of disappointment, despair, and desolation. I stumbled dejectedly back through the same streets and depots I had passed through with such joy just the day before, pausing only once to send Jessie Anne a second telegram with my regrets. Burly provost guards were out by the hundreds, making sure the sullen mobs of disgruntled soldiers boarded the correct southbound trains and, once aboard, that they remained aboard.

215

For what cause had our thousands fallen? What noble calling had dashed young men full of life and promise to pieces, shattered like fine china on stone? Surely the officers in command of our army had failed in their duty. Surely they were guilty of gross negligence. Such repeated and callous disregard for the lives of the men under their charge could have no other explanation. It seemed even murderous—Sergeant Needham, victim of the nerveless McClellan; Harry Whitting, victim of the bungling Burnside; John Robinson, victim of the wine-bibbing and womanizing Hooker.

There stirred within me a profound sensation, the likes of which I had not experienced at any time in my life. It grew within me and spawned a severe and abiding loathing for any and all persons or circumstances that had contributed to my misery. I was powerless when the twin beasts of wrath and malice slowly and silently overcame me during my return to the front. They stole upon me like a thief in the night, but instead of taking something precious from me, they became my dearest friends, faithful and constant bedfellows. Nay, even more, it was as if these twins lived within my skin, taking constant nourishment from the soft tissue of my soul. I neither cursed them nor fought them, but rather, I believe I reveled in this new association.

A fire grew hot deep within me. Upon it a sorcerer's cauldron, glowing red in the flames, boiled over, spewing forth sulfurous gases both putrid and noxious to anyone that happened by.

I wished for mountains of Rebel dead, enough to make Antietam's heaps seem mere molehills, for only in killing these vermin would my travail cease. At least Jackson was dead; now just kill the rest. Kill them all and be done with it.

CHAPTER 22

Northward Bound Again

For innumerable evils have compassed me about:
mine iniquities have taken hold upon me,
so that I am not able to look up.

PSALM 40:12

O N June 11TH, A FEW DAYS AFTER I RETURNED FROM MY CAN-
celed furlough, General Couch resigned his command of
the Second Corps, so thoroughly upset was he with how General
Hooker had mismanaged the Chancellorsville campaign.

The cauldron simmered deep within me. "It's amazing how
easy it is for some people to just walk away when things go
badly," I said to Jim Adams. "Until now I never had any complaint with Couch."

"Granted, Michael. But if he's lost heart for the fight, perhaps we're better off without him."

I shook my head in disgust. "You or I could get shot for
walking away. A general can just ask for other duty."

"To my mind Hancock's an even better general, and I think
he'll be a better corps commander."

"Perhaps," I said. The heat within subsided for a time.

The Army of the Potomac began to move. The Confederates
were marching northward again, possibly to invade Maryland

or Pennsylvania as they had tried to do the previous September. The Second Corps was positioned along the Rappahannock River where it would continue to hold until the last possible moment as the rest of the army started northward. The western end of the Second Corps line near U.S. Ford was the province of the Fourteenth Connecticut Volunteers. For several days we kept sharp eyes on the Rebels to keep them from seeing what our army was doing. We had no idea what Hooker's grand new strategy was, but even if we had known, we could not have had less confidence in it or in the man who had devised it.

Marching orders for the Seconds Corps came down on Monday, June 15th. Well before dawn we silently abandoned our rifle pits along the river and withdrew toward the Warrenton Pike. In the familiar columns of four we marched a short distance back toward Falmouth, but turned off to the left onto a closely wooded road a few miles west of the town. At first this marching was not difficult. The road was firm and the morning was cool, and since ours was the only brigade using the road, we were able to make good time. But the heat began to rise, and with it the humidity, as the sun rose above the trees overspreading the road.

After several miles, we emerged from the woods and came upon the Telegraph Road. It was here that our ordeal truly began. As we turned north toward Stafford Courthouse, the Third Division was the last division of the entire army. Just as the nether end of a cow or a hog is the foulest of places to be, so it is at the tail end of a great army on the march. Nearly one hundred thousand men had tramped up the road during the last several days. Thousands of artillery pieces, caissons, ammunition chests, and endless trains of cartage vehicles, all drawn by teams of heavy draft horses and mules, had toiled along that road. The hard smooth road had been beaten to powder. A yellow-brown cloud settled upon all who passed: the sweating and panting infantryman marching in the grass and brush to the side of the pike, the officer atop his steed bent forward over the pommel in half-sleep, beasts straining against harnesses, and teamsters driving them along with oaths and curses enough to turn the pallid air blue, and then, when voices were shouted hoarse, with whippings.

Men cast off all manner of personal items that weighed even slightly upon them, army issue or not. Each man counted the cost of replacing the thing he thought to throw aside, as well as the added discomfort of doing without, but he invariably found that his present discomfort and weariness far outstripped all else. And so blankets, coats, shelter tents, books, extra clothing, cooking pans, a myriad of small personal items, and even knapsacks were all thrown aside, sometimes with a final mournful look back as when one parts from a dear friend. The soldiers plodded on and on, mile after mile, northward instead of southward, from all appearances an army in full retreat, yet no one called it a retreat.

I fought a sustained battle with myself to retain all that I had begun the march with, thinking somehow that casting it aside would prove my own weakness and unfitness for the work ahead, that it would give others, particularly those in command, the opportunity to point a finger in my direction, "Aha! See old Palmer there? He's done in. We'll not see him in the fight."

The fire within flared anew.

As the rear guard of the army, our duty was ostensibly to protect the army from surprise attack from the rear by Confederate cavalry or infantry, but there were duties that seemed to take precedence over our defensive purpose. Stragglers were prodded forward, sometimes at the point of a bayonet, less because we feared their capture by the Rebels and more because we would not let them shirk their duty. They would be in line alongside us facing the lead and doing their part when the next big battle began. Massive quantities of accoutrements that had been cast aside by the marching multitude that had gone before were heaped into large piles and set ablaze—a great waste of good equipment and another telltale sign of an army in full retreat.

We marched a total of about twenty miles in twelve hours, and when, at about three o'clock that afternoon, we finally came upon Aquia Creek several miles upstream from the landing, what a blessed respite it was. Most of the men jumped fully clothed into the waters of that stream and bathed and splashed and cavorted. Not in a frolicking mood, I just waded into the shallows and swam a few strokes, letting the gently flowing current wash the filth and sweat away. Camp was made on the banks of the creek; a peaceful supper was had in the twilight, and the regiment rotated by companies on picket duty that night.

At three o'clock Tuesday morning, no time was given to fix coffee or breakfast. We marched as soon as we had assembled. We covered the five miles to Dumfries by seven o'clock. A short rest was granted; coffee was immediately boiled and breakfast eaten.

Major Ellis ordered the regiment to gather round. Gone were the days when, if one was standing near the rear of the assembled regiment, one often had difficulty hearing what was said by its commander and would invariably need to ask someone farther forward. Today, Major Ellis's voice had no trouble reaching every ear with clarity. "Men of the Fourteenth Connecticut Volunteers, I have received orders directly from General Hancock. By sundown today he expects every man of the Second Corps to be north of Occoquan Creek. Adjutant Doten tells me it is only ten miles farther up this pike, so it should be easily accomplished."

It was not. That march to Occoquan became a severe trial for the Second Corps, but severest of all for our little regiment. This day the sun burned even hotter than the day before, the air hung heavier with humidity. The Third Division was again at the rear of the long column, but this day, the Fourteenth Connecticut was the last regiment in the division. We were the hindmost end of the entire line of march, followed only by a mounted cavalry screen. Indeed, the word *march* itself is a gross misnomer, for it implies a regular cadence and precision of stride that is entirely lacking when a large army is "on the march." More often than not, this movement could more accurately be described as a long trek when the weather was fine, or sometimes as a pleasant walk when there was no pressing need to meet a schedule. But on this long, hot day, the "march" could only be called a stumble, an endlessly dusty and wearying stumble.

As the sun rose higher in the sky, so did the number of stragglers. Those who could stand on their feet were urged another step forward. Those who could not were loaded into ambulances, and when there were no more ambulances, the Fourteenth was expected to force them back into line with our rifle butts and bayonets, as distasteful a duty as could ever be devised.

The weary man was poked once. "Get along, now," he was told. "Get moving!"

The man would shuffle forward some yards and falter, only to be poked again, over and over again, until an ambulance became available, or some blessed Samaritan offered cool water. Cavalry riders followed closely behind the men of the Fourteenth, driving up our own stragglers. Riders roamed the fields on either side of the road, flushing out any tired and wretched ones found hiding there. Occasionally, a shot rang out if someone tried to flee the encircling net.

With the heat of the afternoon, exhausted men fell out of line to lie down for a rest or a bite to eat in the shade of the trees and shrubs along the road. We were instantly recognized as the rear guard, since we were the only troops carrying muskets with bayonets fixed and cavalry in close support.

"Move on," I would say whenever I approached one of these little bands. "Get up and move on." This always elicited at least profuse grumbling, and several times I was cursed most vehemently to my face. "The horsemen will not be so kind" was my usual response. The men would finally rise of their own accord, shuffle back onto the pike, and resume their plodding northward.

Once I came upon such a group and, predictably, all struggled to their feet breathing every manner of threat and curse— all that is, except one. The men kicked their friend and yelled his name over and over but to no avail. I came up and gave the man a stiff poke with the butt of my rifle, thinking the man was asleep, but this man would never rise again. His heart had failed in the heat of the day, and he had died by the side of the dusty road. But this man was only the first I saw mustered out in such a way. I noted dozens of fresh graves along the way where others had stopped to bury unfortunate comrades who had fallen as they marched, struck down by the sun. Why should men die like this? Could not a halt have been ordered? A half-hour rest and fresh water? It was a murderous profligacy of human lives.

The sorcerer's brew was at full boil.

The sun seemed to stand still that day, as still as it had for Joshua when he fought the Amorites. I put one foot in front of the other, sipped sparingly from my canteen, and toiled northward with the rest of the regiment, poking and prodding others as fatigued as I was, all the while trying to husband my own waning physical resources. My head pounded in the heat, pulsing and throbbing as if the building pressure might explode from within me. Disjointed fragments of song verse rattled around inside my skull, repeating themselves over and over again in a crescendo of maddening, silent cacophony. *We shall linger to caress him while we breathe our evening prayer—better the shot, the blade, the bowl, than the crucifixion of the soul—Farewell mother, you may never press me to your heart again—For we're a-gwine to Washington to fight for Uncle Abe.*

"Just another mile or so" was whispered back down the line,

and finally, at sunset, we stumbled across the short bridge over Occoquan Creek. The regiment moved off the road to camp. I went down to the stream and sat in the cleansing, cooling flow until the gnawing emptiness in my belly forced me to climb out and return to camp. As I lit a fire to start fixing my supper, several men from a Connecticut Artillery regiment came into camp searching for friends among our number. There were handshakes all around, and the men distributed large amounts of food and coffee that they had brought. Their batteries had been stationed in the area around Occoquan since the first of the year, and they had not seen any action, so their uniforms were clean and bright, while ours were faded and dusty. The men of the two regiments talked about home and about the war. Fast friends shared how this or that mutual acquaintance had died or had been wounded in battle or had gone missing. I sat and listened to yet another retelling of these incessant tales of human waste and tragedy, and when I could bear it no longer, I excused myself and retired to a quiet place where I laid out my blanket on the ground. Beaten down as I was from the ordeals of the day, I thought as I lay down that perhaps I would not rise again; perhaps that was even to be preferred. Indeed, that night I slept like the dead.

On Wednesday, we marched again, thirteen more miles to Fairfax Courthouse, but this time the Fourteenth was moved ahead in the order of march, and we were not forced to serve as the last of the rear guard. The heat continued unabated, and I noticed several more dead men, perhaps a dozen, at the roadside as I passed. A day of rest was granted on Thursday; perhaps General Hooker thought we might all drop dead of fatigue and thus accomplish the Rebels' work for them. Clouds rolled in during the afternoon. Heavy evening thundershowers washed us, cooled us, and cleansed the air of the oppressive closeness that had plagued us for days.

We left Fairfax on Friday and marched west to Centreville, a distance of only about seven miles, an easy stroll compared to what we were accustomed. On Saturday, we continued on to the west, toward the Blue Ridge Mountains in the distance. We passed directly through the battlefield at Bull Run and could not help but notice the many scars of the earlier battles—the blasted trees, the exploded caissons, the unburied skeletons of horses and mules picked clean by carrion birds and other vermin, and here and there, the half-buried corpse of one of the fallen.

"Two routs are not enough for Fighting Joe Hooker," I said to Jim. "He's looking to make it three. Nothing good can happen here and he should know it."

The Second Corps camped at Gainesville beside the Orange and Alexandria Railroad for four days. Major Ellis told us the army was in hot pursuit of Lee's army, but the enemy had moved up the west side of the Blue Ridge, occupied Winchester, threatened Harper's Ferry, and had passed by northward, toward southern Pennsylvania.

A large, stinking mess of frustration was stirred into the simmering pot. Why were we doing nothing? How could we be pursuing the enemy while the Second Corps, the best in the army, was in camp? Was this yet another boondoggle or was this yet another skedaddle? Either way, this was not the road to victory.

Finally, on Thursday the 25th, the Second Corps left Gainesville and marched north toward the Potomac. At near midnight on Friday, we crossed over pontoon bridges at Edward's Ferry into Maryland. We had marched a total of about thirty miles in two days. By evening on Sunday the 28th, we were camped between Frederick and Sugarloaf Mountain at Monocacy Junction.

It was at Monocacy that we learned that "Fighting Joe" had no more fight in him. General Hooker resigned entirely from the Army of the Potomac. In his stead, President Lincoln promoted

General George Meade to command the army, a choice that all were fairly pleased with. In addition, the commander of our Third Division, General French, was transferred to command the garrison at Harper's Ferry. The new commander of the Third Division was General Alexander Hays, apparently no relation to our captured former brigade commander.

On Monday, June 29th, the Second Corps marched thirty-four miles to Uniontown under cloudy skies and occasional rain showers, a severe test of our stamina. Dreary, winded men fell out of line for a time but then forced themselves to keep going, evidence that something had changed way down deep in the soul of this army. Perhaps it was the urgency of knowing that the Rebels were taking the war into Union territory that drove us onward. Every man knew that something big was about to happen, and no one wanted to miss out on this next decisive battle. All did their very best to keep going.

This day I truly felt my age. I took several long rests along the way and finally arrived at camp for the night at about three o'clock Tuesday morning, but I never fell back to the prod of the cavalry, and I was by no means the last to arrive; stragglers continued to file into camp well into the daylight hours of the next morning.

❖

Our new corps commander, General Hancock, addressed the assembled corps at its camp outside of Uniontown. "Your endurance has been splendid indeed. The enemy has invaded Pennsylvania and we are closing on them. We will force General Lee to give us battle, and every man of this corps will be at his place in line with his brothers in arms for this decisive fight. We must achieve nothing short of total victory. For now you may rest, but soon, very soon, your very best efforts will be required."

After the general dismissed us, Major Ellis ordered a roll

call. Just 166 officers and enlisted men of the Fourteenth Connecticut Volunteers were counted present and fit for duty. Our once mighty regiment had been reduced in numbers to less than two full companies. But in numbers, we were by no means the most dismal case. At Uniontown, we also met up with the Twenty-seventh Connecticut Volunteers. Much of that regiment had been captured at Chancellorsville and they were now only able to muster seventy-five men of all ranks.

⋄—⋄

July started as hot as June ended. We marched early, before first light, north again, until we reached the road to Taneytown. A short time later we began to hear the muffled thump of artillery firing in the distance ahead of us. The citizens of Taneytown welcomed us warmly, cheering us with gusto, waving Union flags happily, and giving the men whatever sustenance they could afford, a piece of fruit, a hunk of bread, a fresh muffin or biscuit, or a simple, precious cup of cold well water. Spirits rose and hearts were steeled with resolve as we walked on toward Pennsylvania with surer step and quickening pace.

General Hancock galloped by in a clamorous rush. "Reynolds is engaged at Gettysburg! Make time now, boys, you're needed at the front!"

With redoubled effort we marched to within a few miles of Gettysburg by evening. Several soldiers, possibly shirks or maybe just battle weary, and a few wounded men walked slowly southward. There had been a great battle, they all agreed, but each had seen it differently. One said the Rebels had been whipped and were in full retreat. Another swore it was the reverse; it was our boys who had been badly beaten once again. Still another said that both armies had fought all the day long with neither side gaining any real advantage. "It's a stalemate," he said.

Whatever the true result of the day's fighting, we were told to make camp for the night alongside the Taneytown Road. Coffee was made and supper was eaten, and the men turned in for the night with the rumbling echoes of angry guns troubling their ears and stirring the ground beneath them. Within the hour, just after I had fallen asleep, Major Ellis ordered everyone up for picket duty in the woods to the west of the road.

"One thing the army has taught this old soldier very well," I mumbled to Jim Adams, as I felt the heat within flare up once again, "is how to survive without sleep."

CHAPTER 23

Bliss

And Moses said unto the children of Gad
and to the children of Reuben,
Shall your brethren go to war, and shall ye sit here?
NUMBERS 32:6

*I*N THE GRAYING OF THE DAWN OF THURSDAY, JULY 2ND, WITH-out anything resembling rest and without coffee, the boots of the Fourteenth Connecticut once again tramped up the Taney-town road toward Gettysburg. Long columns of artillery, with their attendant caissons and limbers in tow, ruled the center of the road, while troops of infantry from several brigades and divisions fought for space on either side. With the town in sight some units were directed off the road to the right or to the left to take up their positions in the long Union line of battle that was forming.

The Second Brigade marched without stop those last three miles, with the First Delaware in the lead, followed by the Twelfth New Jersey and the 108th New York, with the Four-teenth Connecticut bringing up the rear. Upon entering the town limits of Gettysburg, I noticed a small white house to the left of the road, a dwelling that might have gone completely unno-ticed if not for a flag stirring ever so gently in the early morning air. It was our nation's flag, with thirty-three gold stars upon a field of brilliant blue and four equally brilliant blue tassels along the hoist end. The otherwise simply adorned standard was that of General Meade, the new commander of the Army of the Potomac.

A little farther on we came to a cemetery on a hill that was occupied by General Howard's Eleventh Corps. Many of these men bore witness through blood-stained wrappings to the fierce battle of the day before. The line they now occupied wrapped around the cemetery, following the contours of the hill from left to right until it disappeared down into a shallow vale. Our brigade turned off the road to the left and marched southward a few hundred yards just below the crest of Cemetery Ridge, as it was known, to a grove of trees behind a house belonging to a man by the name of Bryan, where General Hays, our new division commander, established his headquarters. We sat down under the trees and awaited further orders.

The fighting of the previous day had been sustained and brutal. Early in the morning, as the Confederates had tried to push into Gettysburg from the west, they were met by our hard-charging cavalry. The cavalry held Lee's infantry at bay until General Reynolds's First Corps arrived to carry on the fight, and although General Reynolds was killed almost immediately and they were outnumbered, the First Corps fought stubbornly. Howard's Eleventh Corps came up and spread out north of Gettysburg, but as the day wore on, more and more Rebel infantry units arrived to increase the pressure on the two Federal Corps. When the Federals could hold no longer, they fell back through the town to this higher ground just to the south and east, where a new defensive line was planned and engineered by General Hancock.

Across the land in front of us was another low ridge about a mile to the west and thickly occupied by the Confederates.

This was Seminary Ridge, named after a Lutheran seminary that occupied a portion of this ridge to the north. Between the two ridges lay farmland, fields of tall golden grasses and grains, acres of summer harvest ready to be gathered into barns against the winter to come. Across this bountiful land the Emmitsburg Road cut a straight line from northeast to southwest, about two hundred yards in front of our line on Cemetery Ridge and about the same distance from Seminary Ridge at the south. Wooden rail fences lined either side of the road, fences of the kind I had seen along countless miles of country road and lane, the kind we often broke down and used for campfires.

General Caldwell's division of the Second Corps was positioned directly in front of us behind a low stone wall. The wall began at a narrow wagon lane that connected the Bryan farmhouse to the Emmitsburg Road. From the lane the wall ran south, generally parallel to the crest of Cemetery Ridge, for about two hundred yards. Then it turned at a right angle to the west for something less than a hundred yards, where it turned once more at a right angle to the south again. This wall was not carefully constructed, nor was it very high, nor were the stones cleverly fitted together to increase both its longevity and its strength, as were some I had seen in New England. Rather, the wall seemed to be more a demarcation of a property line or perhaps a marking of the limits of acreage set aside for a certain purpose, perhaps a differentiation between crop land and grazing land. It was certainly no true barrier so as to prevent passage of man or horse from one part of the field to the next, although it may have been an effective restriction for the grazing of sheep or cows. Still and all, the wall afforded a good degree of protection to the infantryman, and Caldwell's men set about improving it as best they could. They dug with whatever they had at hand, bayonets, mess plates, and an occasional pick or spade, until they had excavated a shallow trench behind the wall. All of the loose soil and stone was added to the wall. Artillery pieces of the First Rhode Island Light Artillery were drawn up, unlimbered, and carefully positioned at intervals a short distance behind the barrier.

Directly in front of the rock wall, the ground sloped gently downward to the Emmitsburg Road. Across the road, the ground continued to slope gradually downward, and then upward again toward Seminary Ridge. About two-thirds of the way across this shallow depression between the ridges was a farm owned by a man named William Bliss. The Bliss farm buildings consisted of a large barn and a substantial farmhouse. The barn was a two-story structure, sturdily built of stone and brick with wooden

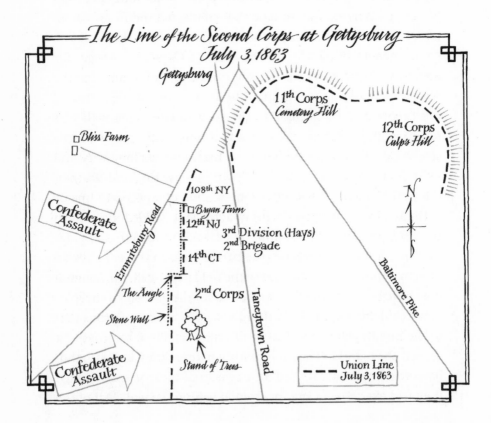

The Line of the Second Corps at Gettysburg
July 3, 1863

gables and a shingled roof; several doors and windows adorned the side of the barn facing the Union line. An orchard of fruit trees to the rear of the structures perfectly completed this pastoral scene.

At first I raged inwardly against the serenity of the scene before me, until I realized that the peace could not last, given the proximity of the opposing armies and the savage character of the fighting the day before. The two armies must yet again lock together in battle, and thousands more would be added to the rolls of the dead. I took my letter to Jessie Anne out of my pocket with the thought of making the customary changes of date and place. I gazed at the letter for a few moments, then out across the field at the opposite ridge. Then I refolded the letter, put it inside the envelope, and slid it back into my pocket. Would I be among the dead at Gettysburg?

No. Not here. Things would be very different this time.

⋘⋙

Late that afternoon peace came to a crashing end. General Sickles's Third Corps advanced to a new position in a peach orchard and wheat field well to the left and front of the Second Corps. The Rebels responded quickly and attacked with strong lines of infantry and several batteries of artillery in support. A fierce battle ensued; the combat was terrible and bloody. The Third Corps fought stubbornly and held their ground for a time, but the Rebels outnumbered them greatly, and our men took heavy losses as they grudgingly, yard by yard, gave up the ground. General Hancock saw this and sent General Caldwell's veteran First Division of about 3,300 men to the aid of the Third Corps in the wheat field. As the four brigades of this division moved out smartly, I caught a glimpse of the flag of our brothers from the Twenty-seventh Connecticut.

When Caldwell's division left the rock wall, General Hancock ordered our division to take its place. Colonel Smyth ordered the Second Brigade to occupy the two-hundred-yard-long portion of the stone wall at the Bryan farm as well as some of the line to the north of the lane to the Emmitsburg Road. Units of the Second Division of the Second Corps under the command of General Gibbon occupied the angle in the rock wall to our left. We were now in the front line with the Rhode Island guns supporting us, and surely we would get into it soon.

The Rhode Island gunners turned their guns to the left and opened fire on the Confederates in the wheat field. I leaned back against the rock wall to watch these fellows fire round after round of solid shot and shell in the afternoon heat. After only a few rounds, all except the officers had stripped off their shirts to work bare-chested in a deadly but finely orchestrated dance about the guns. Each man knew his position and his task; a sergeant barked orders; a corporal with an assistant aimed the gun carefully at the chosen target. Two men worked at the limber, removing the powder charge and the correct ammunition round from the chest and preparing them for use. These were handed over to two more men who carried them forward. The loader first placed the powder charge into the barrel and then the round; another man on the opposite side of the gun rammed them home. The corporal's assistant drove a pick down through a vent hole in the barrel into the powder charge and someone on the opposite side inserted the friction primer with its lanyard attached. All turned away and cupped their ears as the lanyard was pulled. The piece bucked and roared. A highly trained battery like this one from Rhode Island could get off a well-aimed shot every thirty seconds from each gun. Grape and canister did not require the accuracy of shot and shell; they were fired point blank, and each gun could fire up to four shots per minute.

Confederate batteries answered the fire of the Rhode Island

guns and we soon came under heavy bombardment. One man was blown high in the air by a shell; he landed on his head and never rose again. To add to the mayhem, Rebel riflemen came out from their lines and occupied the barn at the Bliss farm. From there the Rebels had a clear view of a large portion of our lines and they started to cut down our artillerymen. One of the Rhode Island boys was shot in the head and fell dead immediately. Several more were wounded by the Rebels in the barn; other members of the battery had to step up and perform double duty in the deadly dance.

General Hays ordered Colonel Smyth to deal with the sharpshooters at the Bliss farm. I fairly leaped for joy at the sudden prospect of seeing some action, but the Twelfth New Jersey was chosen for this assignment. These men left their position along the wall and marched the short distance to Bryan's Lane, which they followed out to the Emmitsburg Road. In the fields across the road they came under heavy fire from the occupants of the barn and from the Rebel pickets in the field; a number of the New Jersey boys went down. A gallant charge routed the Rebels from the barn, and the New Jersey boys were loudly cheered when they returned to our line with nearly one hundred prisoners.

No sooner had the cheering died away than the barn was infested again and the Rebels renewed their deadly game. To my dismay, the 108th New York was sent out and, with some help from the First Delaware, again cleaned out the barn. Once again our men returned to their places in line, and once again, shadowy figures emerged from the tree line across the way and moved toward the barn.

The day ended much as it had begun, with both armies on opposite low ridges glaring at each other. At first Caldwell's men had driven the Confederates backward across the wheat field, but more Rebels were sent into the fight, and Caldwell's division was assailed with renewed fury. So many of our boys in blue fell dead or wounded in the brutal combat that Caldwell's men finally abandoned the wheat field and made their way back to Cemetery Ridge. I counted only about two dozen men still rallying around the colors of the Twenty-seventh Connecticut as they withdrew.

Late in the afternoon, about two miles south of our position, Confederate infantry tried to throw parts of our Fifth Corps off a small rocky knob called Little Round Top. Had they been successful, the Rebels could have placed artillery atop that hill and fired directly down the length of the Federal line. The crackle of musketry waxed each time the Rebels drove up the slopes against unwavering Federal fire and waned as they tumbled back down in defeat. Several times this happened until the Rebels were finally driven back down the slope for good.

The bloodletting of that day had been terrible indeed. For thousands of my brothers in blue, it had been their final day in this world. The only consolation I found was that it seemed an equal number of that ragtag bunch on the opposite ridge had met similar ends. On that day when so many had shed blood, I had not so much as loaded my rifle. I slammed my knapsack up against the wall and tried to find some measure of comfort by lying against it. I stared up at the stars. How I longed to quench the burning in the pit of my stomach. How I longed for the Rebels to cross the field and come up here to this wall that I might deal with them once and for all. But I feared they would not; I feared they would cheat me out of the only antidote so strong as to effectively extinguish the flames of hatred and rage that consumed me from within.

⟨⋇⟩

With sunrise upon Cemetery Ridge, the Rebel sharpshooters in the Bliss barn opened up again, and a few more of the less wary were shot down without warning. General Hays was hopping mad. He screamed at Colonel Smyth to deal with the situation once and for all, and this time, finally and blessedly, the Fourteenth was chosen. Since Company C had not yet served picket duty, we were chosen to lead the assault, along with about forty others. *Good, let's kill some Johnnies.* Captain Moore of Company F was chosen to command our small force, and Lieutenant Seymour of Company I was second in command. Rifles were loaded and capped; bayonets fixed.

Like the regiments of the previous day, we moved out to the north end of the stone wall, then down the lane to the fences at the Emmitsburg Road. Colonel Smyth marched alongside Lieutenant Seymour as far as the road; then the colonel turned back to the safety of our lines.

We sprinted across the road and crouched behind the rails and posts of the fence.

"Listen up, men," Captain Moore shouted. "When I say, 'Charge,' I want all of you to run for that barn as fast as you can. Don't stop for anything; don't shoot at anything, just run for your lives. Run for the wall of the barn, they won't be able to hit you there. Then we'll rush the barn and drive them out. They'll fire on us just as soon as we rise up, and so will the pickets, so do your best not to get hit. Is that clear?"

"*Sir, yes, sir!*" The shooters in the barn already knew we were coming for them, so there was no point in stealth.

"Steady, men, . . . *charge!*"

I ran like I had never run before. It was a good three hundred yards to the barn over open ground, and all the while bullets zipped through the air trying to find me. I dodged this way and that; I never ran more than ten paces in one direction. The first two hundred yards were slightly downhill, but running at a half-crouch with weapon at the ready is never easy. It wasn't long before my lungs burned with the exertion; my chest heaved and I longed to stop to catch my breath, but I knew that to do so would mean certain death. It probably took me about a minute, possibly a little more, to make it to the barn, but make it I did, winded and sweaty, as did most of the other men in the squad. Sadly, several of our men did not, among them Lieutenant Seymour.

As we huddled against the wall of the barn, the Rebels inside found that they could no longer bring their weapons to bear upon us. Captain Moore cautiously peered inside the front door of the barn only to find the scoundrels scurrying out the back door. He fired a couple of shots with his revolver at their fleeting forms. Then we entered the barn.

"Stay away from the doors and windows," he ordered. "They're hiding in the house and the orchard, but they're still shooting at us."

A loud crash rocked the barn as a solid shot struck the western wall. It was just the first shot of a barrage. Rebel gunners fired round after round of shot and shell at the barn. Most struck the walls of stone and brick and did little damage, but one shell came through the roof and exploded inside the loft, killing one of our men and wounding several more.

"All you men," Captain Moore called up the stairs to the loft, "get down here on the double." They didn't need a second invitation. "We're in for it now, boys," Captain Moore shouted above the din, "a few more shots like that last one and we'll be in real trouble. We've been ordered to keep the Johnnies out of this barn, but we can't hold it much longer. It's a death trap, and eventually we'll have to give it up. I've checked out the house where most of their shooters are now. We can probably take it, but we won't be able to hold it either. At least here we're protected; the house won't protect us at all. We must leave this place at once."

No sooner had these words been spoken than the doorway through which we had entered was darkened by the form of Major Ellis. Seeing the straits we were in, he had brought over the remainder of the regiment. They too had lost several men to fire from Rebel pickets and the shooters in the house. Captain Moore explained the difficulties of our situation, and Major Ellis either nodded or shook his head as the details required. The artillery barrage grew in intensity with every passing minute.

"Rider approaching," called out one of our men standing by one of the windows facing the Federal lines. "Look at him go! Is he crazy?"

We all clustered around the various portals, straining to see what the mad horseman was up to. The man reined his horse off to the left, then back to the right, then to the left again as he tried valiantly to evade the hail of fire that was concentrated upon him. As he came nearer, we saw he was an officer; cheers and applause swelled within the barn. By the time the officer reined to a halt next to the doorway, Major Ellis was waiting for him.

"Captain, what news do you have?" Ellis asked.

"Major," the captain shouted, "Colonel Smyth sends his compliments on your taking the objective. The colonel told your Lieutenant Seymour that these buildings should be burned. The colonel wishes you to burn whatever you can of this barn and burn the house to the ground. Then return your regiment to its former position in the line." With a snappy salute, the captain spurred his horse and dashed back across the fields, again swerving this way and that, and again under heavy fire for the entire distance, until he reached our lines safely. I could not help but think that Sarge would have liked that officer.

Our mission was now clear, but first we had to drive the Rebels out of the farmhouse. My company, eleven men in all, was detailed to carry out the assault. As we prepared to rush out into the open space between the buildings, the rest of the men concentrated their fire on the farmhouse and the orchard beyond. After a minute or two of this the Rebels had had enough and were seen leaving the house. We raced from the barn to the house and broke in through the front door. I led a squad to the second floor, taking the steps two at a time. Perhaps I should have crept up the stairs, peering into every corner and searching in every possible hiding place for the rogues, but I knew they had fled.

"Miserable cowards!" I spat on the floor as I rushed into a bedroom at the rear of the house. Through a window I saw the shadowy forms of the lately departed enemy moving swiftly away among the trees of the orchard. I swung the butt of my rifle and smashed the window sash to pieces, then pointed my rifle out the window and sighted down the barrel. A fleeting shape in butternut was nearly at the end of the orchard, about two hundred yards away. I steadied myself and slowly squeezed the trigger. The Springfield bucked and the man dropped. *Good, at least that one won't bother me again.*

We went from room to room gathering anything that would burn—papers, bedding, and straw from mattresses. Then we set fires in every room and went back down the stairs. As we raced back to the barn, smoke billowed from every window of the house, and in a few minutes the entire structure was engulfed in flames. Our men in the barn had already set the hay ablaze and were waiting in the shelter of the east wall for us. Together we ran back toward the Emmitsburg Road as fast as we could, bringing all of our wounded and our single dead comrade along with us. Jim Adams and I came upon Lieutenant Seymour. He had been badly wounded in the leg and was leaning against a fence post.

"Colonel Smyth told me to burn the place to the ground," the lieutenant said, his voice weak and strained.

"Don't worry, lieutenant," I said. "We made it too hot for those devils. They won't be back."

Jim and I helped the lieutenant off the field. The Fourteenth was welcomed back to the line with cheering, both loud and long. The sharpshooters would not plague us again.

The Bliss farm was now a smoldering ruin, but the fire within me burned all the hotter, and the day was not yet half spent.

CHAPTER 24

Dust and Ashes

For which cause we faint not;
but though our outward man perish,
yet the inward man is renewed day by day.
2 CORINTHIANS 4:16

HE REWARDS FOR VICTORY WERE MEAGER INDEED — AND short-lived. The Fourteenth regiment, now reduced to about 125 men of all ranks, was given no duty besides manning its portion of the stone wall. There was a new sense of freedom now that the sharpshooters were gone. Infantryman and artillerist alike relaxed at the wall or in the open ground behind the wall, baking under a hot sun that beat down on us from a cloudless sky. The men dug into their haversacks in search of something to eat.

Across the way, if one looked closely, as I did, there was much shadowy activity under the shielding screen of the trees on the far ridge. Now and again, a team of horses trotted out of the shadows, drawing a single artillery piece into the open field. Throughout the morning, while we had been otherwise engaged at the Bliss farm, the Rebels had been rolling out their guns and lining them up, nearly wheel hub to wheel hub, in a line across the farmland stretching from the south near the peach orchard to a point opposite our position, behind the smoldering ruins of the Bliss house and barn. The men in blue stood and watched the unfolding scene, some in stunned silence and others with exclamations of amazement. I counted over a hundred pieces of artillery, but there were surely more out of my line of sight. My stomach tightened with the growing understanding and apprehension of what was in store. An eerie silence fell over the entire length and breadth of Cemetery Ridge. So quiet was it, that we could distinctly hear the gunners barking orders to their crews as they charged their guns with powder and shell.

At one o'clock two single shots were fired, certainly a signal for the rest of the hundred to let loose upon us. As if all the lanyards were pulled by a single hand, the entire line spewed forth flame and smoke. Every man in blue stood no longer, but ducked low behind the stone wall, shielding his head and ears with his arms. Shells screamed over our heads and fell among the artillery batteries with dreadful results, blasting gun crews and draught horses and equipment alike.

The entire Federal artillery corps responded in kind and the shelling grew to such a continuous roar that it was impossible to tell one explosion from another. At times, the blast of exploding shell drowned out the roar of our own firing. How strange it was to be so near to a gun as it fired, yet not be able to distinguish its report from the general cacophony of the cannonade. The constant roar, like one long continuing blast, shook the ground; the concussions drove the earth up into my body as I cowered behind the stone wall. Waves of hot compressed air struck me like hammer blows from right and left and behind. Billows of thick, acrid smoke filled the air. Fearful, blinking, tearing eyes gazed back at me out of smoke-darkened faces whenever I looked around at any of my comrades.

The effects of the Rebel shelling were terrible and bloody. The men of the Rhode Island battery again worked their guns furiously and set up a rapid and steady fire. Several shells landed near them but did little damage—until one shot struck one of their limber chests, causing it to explode. Men near it were blown entirely apart and others were dealt grievous injuries. Helpers carried bloodied and mangled bodies over the ridge behind us, and the survivors set about working the guns again. I turned away from this grisly scene only to see three more chests in the artillery attached to Gibbon's Division explode in quick succession. The destruction there was even more ghastly, and the firing from that battery ceased altogether.

A general on horseback appeared out of the smoky haze. "Captain," he shouted above the clamor, attracting the attention of the commander of the Rhode Island battery. The general swung himself off his mount to the ground. "How is your command, Captain ..."

"Arnold, sir, Captain Arnold. General Hunt, sir, we've had four men killed and about a dozen wounded, but I believe all six guns are in working order."

"Fine, Captain Arnold, that's fine. You are to reduce your rate of fire and save your remaining ammunition. After the enemy has finished with their cannonade, there will certainly be an infantry charge. Save your ammunition for the infantry." With a crisp acknowledgement of Captain Arnold's salute, General Hunt mounted his steed and galloped off down the line.

At last there was confirmation of what I and every man on Cemetery Ridge both desired and feared. The Rebels were going to attack us; they will come. *Good, let them come; we are ready to receive them. We will give Fredericksburg back to them.*

The Rhode Island battery slowed its rate of fire gradually and then stopped altogether as did all of the Federal artillery. Across the way the line of Confederate guns also fell silent. I raised my head over the top of the wall. For a time, smoke enshrouded everything beyond the Emmitsburg Road, but after several minutes, the smoke drifted away and revealed a stunning sight. Drummers drummed a fine marching cadence while brigade after brigade of Rebel infantry emerged from the tree line across the way and moved out into the open fields. They formed in straight lines, perfectly dressed, over a mile from one end to the other, with their battle flags flying proudly in the afternoon sun. The field fell silent. I looked at my watch; it was about three o'clock. Mounted gray-clad officers rode among their men, issuing final orders and rallying the men for the battle to come. The hour of reckoning was at hand.

The long, distant wave of gray and butternut rippled as the men stepped off; a great shout reached my ears. The Confederates marched with precision and skill, as if on parade, weapons held at Shoulder Arms, and it was difficult not to admire the grand sight of this well-disciplined army going forward to battle. Their officers led them with obvious pride, brandishing sabers in one hand, waving hats high in the other.

This parade had not advanced more than a hundred paces when our artillery opened up on them. General Hunt had not been idle since ordering all of the Union artillery batteries to fall silent. Severely damaged batteries were sent to the rear to rest and rearm, and fresh batteries were sent forward from the artillery reserve. Now, guns from up and down the Federal line poured shot and shell into the lines of infantry. Fire was directed from the front and from either flank; our boys had the range zeroed in and they had saved plenty of ammunition. Shells exploding in the ranks threw men high in the air while solid shot ripped deadly holes several men wide. With determined discipline and precision the Rebels closed up the holes, centered their lines on their colors, and continued to come on.

It quickly became apparent that the Rebels were trying to concentrate the force of their attack at the center of the Federal line, including that portion of the stone wall held by a few determined men from Connecticut and the angle in the wall just to the left. Through several skillfully executed oblique moves, the Rebel lines that had stretched out over a mile began to contract toward the center. They overlapped each other in a way that at once reduced the width of their lines exposed to direct fire and increased the depth of the assault force in many places to three lines of infantry. On and on they came, ever closer, all the while enduring the most dreadful damage by our artillery. They approached the Emmitsburg Road and started to climb over, under, and around the fences. The artillery switched from shot and shell to grape and canister and started blasting even more of the oncoming minions to kingdom come.

"Fire at will!" cried Major Ellis, and our line of Springfields and Sharps erupted in a sheet of flame and lead.

I, however, held my fire for a few moments. There was no use firing at the faceless mass of gray and butternut. I wanted to pick my target with care. I wanted to watch the man fall, knowing it was my bullet that had felled him. I chose a tall, skinny man with a long beard and a black slouch hat. I triggered the round and the man was knocked over backward. "That's one," I muttered as I ducked behind the wall.

I pressed myself to load my rifle as fast as I could; how I wished that just this once I could load as fast as John. I bit at the cartridge savagely and rammed it home. I replaced the cap and rose up again, ready to fire. The Rebels were fewer now, closer by thirty yards, and on they came. The Rhode Island boys worked their guns furiously; each blast of canister blew a new gap in the advancing line. I drew a bead on a sergeant with a dusty gray jacket. Down he went. "That's two."

I dropped two more of them with two more shots before their advance was halted and they began to fall back in confusion. *A good start.*

Then the second line charged and the killing went on. Just

load, aim, fire, Sarge had said, and that is what I did. A ball seared a hot streak across the left side of my face; blood flowed freely down my cheek, staining my shirt and jacket. I cared not a whit and sent three more men tumbling, three more men who would never bother me again, three more dead men closer to home. This charge was shattered as well; those few who were still able drew back, then turned and fled. *Come back for more, you cowards.*

A third line now surged forward. Several North Carolina flags waved proudly in the breeze. The battery continued to blast away, and our musket fire took a terrible toll. Yet on those stubborn fiends came without wavering. I picked out a small, wiry man dressed in a filthy white shirt and dark jacket, with a gray kepi on his head and a red bandana around his neck. I shot the filthy man squarely, and he went down in a heap. Load, aim, fire—load, aim, fire. I loaded and capped another round and rose to fire. They were almost upon us, about twenty yards now, but they had stopped; they were bringing their weapons to bear upon us. I shot down another man just as one of the Rhode Island guns bucked with a blast of double canister. The North Carolina line was blown away; they were either dead or writhing grotesquely on the ground or crawling for the rear. "That's ten."

But the fight was not over. Just to our left, some of Gibbon's boys had been overwhelmed at the angle of the wall. Hundreds of Rebels had breached the wall and were trying to drive a hole through their line. Additional men were sent forward and desperate fighting ensued. Much of the fighting was hand to hand; men on both sides clubbed each other with the butts of their muskets.

The voice of Major Ellis rang out clearly. "Fourteenth, left oblique!" We stood and aimed our weapons into the mass of Rebels clawing their way toward our Pennsylvania and New York brothers.

"Fire!" cried Major Ellis. Our shots tore into the flank of the Rebel assault. The line wavered and then quickly broke apart. Gibbon's men surged forward and either killed or captured those few Rebels that did not immediately run for the rear. "That's eleven."

And then I was gone, vaulting over the wall and running after the fading Rebels, wanting more than anything else to finish this thing here and now on this hot July afternoon. Voices screamed after me to stop, to come back, but I paid them no mind. My duty was to kill the enemy and I was not yet done. I raced forward through the maelstrom, rifle at the ready. One hairy man just in front turned to face me; I stuck him in the gut with my bayonet, gave my Springfield a quick twist and pulled it free. One man raised a saber, an officer I think—stick, twist, pull. Another over here struggled to his feet—stick, twist, pull. How easy it all was. Yes, John, yes, I can kill a man. Something hit my right leg below the knee. I looked down. A pair of legs kicked and churned the air. Blood seeped through the clutching fingers of one hand while the other reached into a jacket pocket for something—a pistol or a blade maybe. I raised my rifle as high as I could and plunged it down with all my strength.

But my hand was stayed—stayed by a power clearly not my own, for all I wished was to add this man to my blood tally for the day. The point of my bayonet rested on the man's chest, but it would go no further. I raised my gaze past the red bandana and looked into the eyes of the filthy man I had shot shortly before, where I read the agony of a man about to die as clearly as one reads words on a page. My shot had struck the man in the abdomen. I stood motionless over the man as he slowly drew his hand out of his jacket and held a small book up to me.

"Please, sir, ... if you would ... read for me."

I didn't move. The filthy man's eyes pleaded once again.

249

Blood flowed from the gash on my face down to my chin, falling in great drops upon him, mingling with his own.

"Please, sir. I wish only to hear the words of my Lord as I pass from this life to the next."

I released my left hand from the Springfield and grabbed the book. It was a small testament, similar to the one that had been stolen from me two months before. The leather cover, probably once a rich brown, had faded to a pasty tan, but was now stained red and wet with blood. The pages were worn and tattered. I laid my rifle upon the ground and knelt down beside the man.

"Are you thirsty?" I asked him.

"Yes."

I reached for my canteen.

"No, sir, don't trouble with that. Read, sir, for my time is short. Where are the mountains, sir?"

"The mountains?"

"I would like to look to the mountains as you read. Where are they, sir?"

"Off there to the west." He turned his head as I pointed them out. "You can just make them out above the trees on the other side. What shall I read, Johnnie?"

"From the Psalms, sir. The twenty-fifth is one of my favorites."

My hands shook as I fumbled with the pages. I finally found the passage; a faint smile formed on the man's lips as I began to read:

Unto thee, O LORD, do I lift up my soul.
O my God, I trust in thee: let me not be ashamed, let not
    mine enemies triumph over me.
Yea, let none that wait on thee be ashamed: let them be
    ashamed which transgress without cause.

Shew me thy ways, O LORD; teach me thy paths.

Lead me in thy truth, and teach me: for thou art the God of my salvation; on thee do I wait all the day.

Remember, O LORD, thy tender mercies and thy lovingkindnesses; for they have been ever of old.

Remember not the sins of my youth, nor my transgressions: according to thy mercy remember thou me for thy goodness' sake, O LORD.

Good and upright is the LORD: therefore will he teach sinners in the way.

The meek will he guide in judgment: and the meek will he teach his way.

All the paths of the LORD are mercy and truth unto such as keep his covenant and his testimonies.

For thy name's sake, O LORD, pardon mine iniquity; for it is great.

What man is he that feareth the LORD? him shall he teach in the way that he shall choose.

His soul shall dwell at ease; and his seed shall inherit the earth.

The secret of the LORD is with them that fear him; and he will shew them his covenant.

I stopped reading because the man had died, his gaze still fixed upon the distant range, his lips still set in their joyful mien, the very likeness of tranquility now that his life was spent. He had been a feared enemy, fighting for a cause that I could neither understand nor find sympathy for, and I had been just in killing him. I was the instrument of God's justice upon this man and his sin.

I turned to the front of the Bible and read the inscription, written not in a softly feminine script like Jessie Anne's, but with a bolder, coarser hand:

May 17, 1861 —

To my dearest husband, may the Lord bless you and keep you.
  May His Word always be bread for your heart and soul.

                        Your loving and affectionate wife,

                        Constance

  Then at the bottom of the page, in another hand, presumably the man's own:

              Augustus J. Wyatt
              Jeff Davis Mountaineers
              26th No. Carolina Troops

  I turned to the next page and a small, well-worn, hand-painted image fell to the man's still chest. I picked it up and looked into the faces of what must surely have been the Wyatt family: Constance seated in the middle surrounded by a young girl and two small boys—Rebecca, William, and Alfred, according to the baptismal records in the Bible.
  I returned to the psalm and finished as I had begun, reading aloud as if the dead man could still hear:

  Mine eyes are ever toward the LORD; for he shall pluck my
    feet out of the net.
  Turn thee unto me, and have mercy upon me; for I am
    desolate and afflicted.
  The troubles of my heart are enlarged: O bring thou me out
    of my distresses.
  Look upon mine affliction and my pain; and forgive all my
    sins.
  Consider mine enemies; for they are many; and they hate me
    with cruel hatred.

O keep my soul, and deliver me: let me not be ashamed; for I
   put my trust in thee.
Let integrity and uprightness preserve me; for I wait on thee.
Redeem Israel, O God, out of all his troubles.

My voice and my hands trembled as I read these words, for I
could hear the voice of the dead Wyatt speaking them. The dead
man before me was a fellow believer, trusting the justness of his
cause and fighting for it as completely as I did mine. And yet I
had killed this man—but even more, I had despised him and I
had cursed him in my heart without knowing him. Here was a
simple man of the South, seeking his Father's will to do it until
death, but I had judged him to be a demon from hell, the source
of all my despair and misery. I had been his enemy and I had
hated him *with cruel hatred*.

"It's all over, Corporal Palmer." I sat motionless, knowing
the voice of Captain Carpenter before I looked up at him. "Dry
your tears, man. A great victory was won here today, Palmer, a
great victory in the greatest battle ever fought on this continent.
They'll not be back for more," he said as he watched the last
few straggling Rebels melt away into the western afternoon sun.
"You're a sight, Palmer. I hardly recognized you with your face
all bloody like that. You should have it tended to."

"I will, sir."

Captain Carpenter waved at Mr. Wyatt's lifeless form. "Did
you know this man? Was he a friend of yours, Palmer?"

"No, sir," I said, fighting against the quaver in my voice,
"not a friend, sir, . . . a brother. He was my brother."

Captain Carpenter shook his head slowly, then walked away.
The dead lay in a thick carpet before the wall of stone and the
silent guns; the wounded swelled a frightful chorus of moans
and wails most pitiful. How many of these myriad dead had

also named the name of Christ? Surely many—and I had hated them all.

The heart that had at once been hot with fury and cold in the killing both cooled and thawed. I sat next to Mr. Wyatt in that blood-soaked field for some time without moving, playing the dreadful scenes of the just-finished fight over and over in my mind, fixing them forever in my memory. Then I prayed. For the first time in many weeks—was it really since John had died?—I truly prayed, not for Mr. Wyatt, nor for comfort for his bereaved family, nor for my family far away, nor for my daily bread, nor for a hastened end to this terrible war, but for myself. In the dust and ashes before that stone wall this God-forsaking soldier had also been among the fallen. How great and numerous were my sins. Could His grace and His mercy possibly cover them all?

I finally stood up and walked slowly back to the stone wall, where I stacked my weapon. I had no wish to visit the hospital, for my wound seemed minor and I knew the scene at the hospital would be too distressingly gory. Jim Adams helped me clean and bandage my wound. Then I went back out on the field, along with hundreds of others, to help the wounded, both friend and foe, and to remove the dead for burial.

At twilight I returned to the wall. I gathered up some of the half-charred and splintered pieces of the blasted Rhode Island battery's limber chest and started a small fire for coffee. Nighttime showers washed away the grime and sweat and muted the cries of those wounded that remained unaided. For the first time in many weeks I slept peacefully; the cauldron boiled and spewed no more; my bedfellows had departed for parts unknown.

CHAPTER 25

New Recruits

If a wise man contendeth with a foolish man,
whether he rage or laugh, there is no rest.
PROVERBS 29:9

Sunday, July 22, 1863

Beloved Husband Michael,

The newspapers have been full of reports of the magnificent victory of our army at Gettysburg, Penna. Details of the exploits of the 14th Regiment have been particularly moving and distressing and I cannot but shudder when I think of your involvement. One account told of how the 14th made a "glorious charge" across the open field in the face of the enemy, how you quickly put them to flight with force of arms, and wrested a farm from their control. Another told of "tremendous cannonading" you were forced to endure. A third article reported how the men of the 14th "stood unwavering and unyielding against the onslaught of the finest soldiery of the Confederacy" during their terrible charge and how you turned them back. The writer exhausted many words in detailing the dreadful, bloody cost in dead and wounded in the 14th.

I can only thank God above that you were spared, as the receipt of your letter of July 8th at last confirmed. However, my

dearest Michael, I am somewhat perplexed that you made little
of the fighting, preferring rather to dwell upon a temporary lack
of rations and your weariness of marching southward once again.
If your desire is to spare me concern and anxiety over your well-
being — and were I in your place, perhaps I would do the same —
please know that I need you to tell me all, the best and the worst
of it, that we might bear one another's burdens. Allow me, *please*,
this privilege of being your wife.

Sarah, Edward and I walked over to the Robinson's house
yesterday. Our dear sister Abby continues to comport herself
bravely when in public, but her private sorrows are profound.
While the children played outside, she ushered me into her
bedroom. An empty chair now sits beside the hearth, a chair she
says no one will ever sit in again. John's dress coat is draped upon
the back of the chair, his forage cap and a pair of worn leather
gloves are laid in careful array upon the seat, along with John's
Bible and the letter from Captain Carpenter. The chair seems
to me a constant reminder of their loving, joyful life, of John's
faithful presence and the sweetness of family communion that is
forever past, all the more poignant and bittersweet now that it is
lacking.

Dear, dear Abby — I have no more words for her and wish only
to allow her some respite from grief. But what am I to do? In all
my dealings with her my constant guide is the knowledge that
I could easily be in her place, and then what care might I wish
from her? Perhaps, if in the coming weeks or months she seems
amenable to more social engagement, I might invite Abby and her
girls to dinner along with the widower George Allerton and his
boys. Perhaps.

Beloved Michael, I am ever mindful of your perils and pray for
you often each day. In some ways I miss you just as keenly as Abby
does John, but I have a confident hope that Our Heavenly Father

will yet be gracious and allow you to return to me in safety. *Even
so, Lord, may Your will be done.*

I am, as always, your loving
and devoted wife and friend,

Jessie Anne

❖

The three warring days at Gettysburg had taken a severe toll on
our army. Of the seven corps commanders of the Army of the
Potomac, General Reynolds of the First Corps was dead, our
beloved General Hancock had fallen with a bloody wound to his
upper leg, and General Warren was given temporary command
of the Second Corps. General Sickles of the Third Corps had
also been grievously wounded in the lower leg. General Gibbon,
commander of the Second Division of the Second Corps, had
been wounded as had Colonel Smyth, our brigade commander.

Regarding the Fourteenth, Major Ellis had fallen ill and
Captain Davis once more assumed temporary command of the
regiment. A sorry lot we were too. The pitying eye with which
we had regarded our brothers in the lowly Twenty-seventh Connecticut was now cast in our direction. The Fourteenth had
marched into Gettysburg on July 2nd with one hundred sixty-
six men of all ranks; it marched out just three days later with
fewer than eighty men fit for duty. Fourteen, nearly one in ten,
were killed or mortally wounded, dozens more had been seriously wounded, and several had been captured by the enemy. Of
those fit for duty, many bore evidence of minor wounds from the
fight. We proudly wore our blood-blackened wrappings as sure
evidence that we had remained steadfast and done our duty. As
for the bloody stripe on my own face, it was healing well with no
sign of festering, but it would leave an ugly purple scar.

Seven thousand men lost their lives at Gettysburg; an

additional 33,000 were wounded, many of them grievously. Thousands more were captured by the enemy and condemned to the starvation and pestilence of the prison stockade. Through this contest of arms of three days' duration, the course of the war was decided, and the future of the nation was established for generations yet unborn.

During the previous twelve months, the Army of the Potomac had passed through many a fiery trial. The soft of body and the soft of heart had been purged, either by death or sickness or desertion or through the expiration of short-term enlistments. The army had been reduced in number to about 80,000 men, but all had been weighed in the balance of war and had not been found lacking. Trials of every sort had brought out the best men and the best in them.

Now, as the victorious army of veteran warriors marched southward away from Gettysburg, all this was about to change.

Conscription was now the law of the land. As the war became longer and bloodier, it became apparent that the army could no longer maintain its strength solely through volunteer enlistments. Of those who were of a mind to volunteer, most had already done so during 1861 or 1862, so that during 1863, when the army sought to replenish its ranks once again, the well of volunteers had dried up, or nearly so. All men between twenty and forty-five years of age were liable for service in the army. If a certain fellow's name was chosen, he might try to escape the draft by claiming one of the hundreds of medical or other exemptions for himself, but if he failed in this, he might pay three hundred dollars to another man, either known or unknown to him, to serve as a substitute. The opportunities for fraud, favoritism, and other mischief abounded with this system in which little or no accountability existed.

From the beginning, the rich man could always afford the substitute and almost always chose to pay rather than serve. The working-class man could often conjure up an exemption because he was an only son, or because his occupation was vitally important to the war effort, or he could be exempted by a sympathetic physician. Thus the army supplemented its ranks from two distinct and divergent classes of men, the indigent poor man, who had no benefactor to spare him from his fate, and the paid substitute, who was often recruited not from the bustling establishment of commerce, nor from the pastoral dairy farm, nor from the hallowed college hall, but from the filthy streets of the city, where all manner of evil flourished unchecked. During the late summer of 1863, the first of this new breed of "soldier" began to appear in the ranks of the Army of the Potomac.

⊰⊱⊰⊱

The two armies sidled slowly and deliberately southward, much as they had the previous autumn. On Wednesday, July 15th, the Second Corps came upon the Hagerstown Pike and turned toward Sharpsburg and the Antietam battlefield. A sudden hush fell over the men at the northern end of the Miller cornfield. Not a man spoke as the column marched on; not a man averted his gaze from the scenes that were burned in his memory. Gone was the dreadful carpet of the dead; a new crop of lush green corn was reaching heavenward. The trees of the East and West Woods still bore their scars and ever would until they were felled by time and nature or by the woodsman's axe. To the right of the road, the simple whitewashed walls of the Dunker Chapel were now adorned with crude patches, silent testimonies to the ball and shot that had profaned this sanctuary of a peace-loving people. A little farther on, the land to the left dipped down into a swale and the sunken lane came into view. I hesitated to look at first, with the fleeting thought that the lane would still be filled with ghastly skeletal corpses, but it was not. The bodies were gone; the fences were mended; the crops were growing. It seemed that life along Antietam Creek had returned to its ante-bellum serenity.

The Second Corps passed by Harper's Ferry and crossed into Virginia. Thankfully, there would be no repetition of the sojourn at Bolivar. Once again we marched down the beautiful Loudon Valley while Lee's Army of Northern Virginia marched through the Shenandoah Valley to the west. At length, the byways of the Virginia hill country brought the Fourteenth Connecticut, along with the Twelfth New Jersey, eastward to a place called Cedar Run, a secluded, secure, and most pleasant place to rebuild and refit a pair of ailing infantry regiments. After a few peaceful weeks, the regiment moved to a new camp near the Orange and Alexandria Railroad at Bristow.

⋘⋙

Wednesday, September 2, 1863
Camp of the 14th Conn. Rgt. Vol. Inf.
Near Bristow, Virginia

Dearest Jessie Anne,

Please accept my deepest apology for not writing to you for almost a month — your letter of July 22 found its way to me August 19. Three weeks ago Captain Carpenter summoned me to his tent and promoted me to the rank of sergeant. Sergeant Morrison was promoted to second lieutenant and transferred to Company I to replace Lieutenant Seymour. Captain Carpenter said I'm the oldest man in the company, the fact of which I knew already, and therefore, at least to his thinking, the most mature and best suited to the job. The captain also told me he will be transferred to the Invalid Corps. He has not been well of late and in much pain, doubtless resulting from his wounding at Fredericksburg. Our new captain is likely to be Lieutenant Simpson from Company D.

New Recruits

Since my promotion I've been busily employed training about two dozen new recruits. These men know nothing, and we old soldiers know nothing of them until they prove their worth. We must always be on watch to prevent desertion. Hardly any of the new men hail from Connecticut; some are draftees, others substitutes. I can count a dozen nationalities in the regiment—Irish, French, Italian, German and such—and some speak hardly a word of English. These conscripts seem as chaff ready to be blown away by the ill winds of opportunism, self-preservation, and cowardice.

But there is one exception to this rule—a paid substitute named Otto Wehlmann, a lad of nineteen years. Otto is a giant next to me, a muscular and handsome fellow with straight blond hair and a closely clipped beard the color of fine straw. His voice is a soft tenor, colored with a slight German inflection. His first words to me were, "I hate the mules. Don't put me with the mules." Otto worked as a "hoggee," the mule driver for his father's passenger barge on the Erie Canal. Otto was forever following the hindquarters of the mule team, shouting endless curses at the beasts and flicking the whip without mercy in what seemed a fruitless effort to keep the mules pulling straight, and not veering off to the left or right in search of fresh clover.

This past June a pretty young lass aboard his father's boat caught Otto's eye, but a sense of his own lowliness and lack of prospects overwhelmed him. All during the seven days' journey to Albany, Otto could never summon the courage to speak with her and had, instead, stared with loathing at the hind ends of the mules as he drove them along in disgust.

Otto knew he could not make one more trip along that canal with the mules. With less than twenty dollars to his name, he left the family boat in Albany and boarded a river steamer bound for New York. Still without prospects, with no trade or skill that would be useful to an employer in the city, Otto entered a tavern on the waterfront, spent his last twenty cents on a flagon of ale, and sat down to glean whatever news he could of which merchant vessels might be taking on hands for an upcoming voyage.

A man sat down at the table with Otto and struck up a conversation. The man was an agent for some of Connecticut's wealthier citizens commissioned to search out substitutes for drafted relatives and friends. For Otto, who had never considered volunteering in the army and who had never heard of such a thing as conscription, the promise of three hundred dollars, regular food rations, and a monthly stipend more than outweighed any concerns he might have had for his personal safety, and he happily accompanied the man to the depot to board the next train bound for New Haven.

From the moment I met this young man, I liked him. Humble beginnings have produced a truly humble man of even temperament, trusting of others and trustworthy himself, genuine to the degree that I can name nothing false in him.

I cannot say the same of a draftee named Caesar Ferretti. He's an Italian bricklayer about thirty years of age from Bridgeport. He's short of stature and thickly built. He has a dark complexion with dark brown, almost black, wiry hair, a full, equally dark moustache, deep brown eyes, and a scruffy unkempt beard. His name came up in the draft, and he had neither the political contacts, nor the money, nor even the desire to avoid the army. Instead, he resignedly accepts his fate with a shrug of his shoulders. Although he speaks little English, Caesar made it clear he thought the army would be more enjoyable than masonry, but that was before he had been many days with us.

It is now my job to drill the men over and over until they are able to stand in line in the next fight and do their duty. I always recall the many lessons Sarge taught me and try to apply them to this new crop—I can hardly believe that in two short weeks he will have been gone a full year. When training the new men, I'm firm and demanding and I make sure each man knows what's expected of him. I've taught them how to load, fire, and care for their Springfield rifles. I've shown them how to march, and I've shown them so many things that will help them survive on the campaign, things I learned from Sarge. Jim Adams is a great help, for while I explain to the new men the steps of a new drill, Jim demonstrates each step, and this helps most of the men learn faster.

Otto Wehlmann has been a pleasant surprise, serious about the drill and quick to adapt to the disciplined life of the army. He does not chafe under the rules, and he never complains about the duties he is given, no matter how mean and low, as long as I keep him away from anything regarding the mules. He has learned the drills and the manual of arms faster than anyone in my memory. He has quickly become an excellent shot with his Springfield, and in time he should become a solid and reliable addition to our ranks.

It is not so with Caesar. I could excuse his lack of soldierly progress due to his difficulty with the language, but the repetitive nature of each drill, along with Jim's skillful demonstrations, make it abundantly clear what is required. Regular and repeated discipline has failed to produce any lasting positive effect—Caesar simply accepts his fate with a sheepish grin and a shrug of the shoulders. I can only conclude the cause is futile. I now think that even the supreme efforts of the noble Needham would have met with no better success. No, it has become sadly apparent that the cheerful Italian is not soldier material. Tomorrow we will march away from this place, no doubt in search of the enemy to give him battle once again. I can only hope when the fighting resumes, that Private Ferretti will cause no harm to himself or any others of the regiment who happen to be close by.

My dear Jessie Anne, you have asked me to tell all of what has happened to me. Please understand that limitations of time, paper and ink prevent this. There are also some happenings which no lady should ever have to envision, so I may never relate them. The reports you cited were largely correct; the 14th was in a desperately hard fight at Gettysburg. Jim Adams again survived unscathed, and I also, except for a small scratch. In the end there were many enemy dead before our position. I did my duty, and I sometimes shudder that I am forever changed because of it. I fear you will not know your husband should you see him again.

With my new duties as sergeant, I was required to remain here when others were selected to return home to escort bands of conscripts to the front, and although I will be among the first to be considered for furlough, all furloughs have been delayed until all campaigning has ended and the army has gone into winter quarters.

For now my needs are all supplied. I have no specific complaint except that I weary of remaining distant from you, my darling wife, and our beloved children. In about three weeks I think you should send me the three greatcoats, along with whatever other goodies you might choose. Pray that this all might end soon in final victory.

I remain your most affectionate husband,

Sgt. Michael G. Palmer

There was indeed much more I could have told Jessie Anne in my letters, but there was also much I could never tell her. How could I ever reveal all I had done at Gettysburg? How I had become no better than the murderous Cain? Did not Wyatt's blood cry out from the ground against me? Would I not be cursed from the earth? Had God forever turned His face away from me? What would she think of me? How could Jessie Anne still call this man her "beloved"?

CHAPTER 26

Dry Powder

And the LORD said unto Moses,
The man shall be surely put to death:
all the congregation shall stone him
with stones without the camp.
NUMBERS 15:35

THE NOTATION IN MY JOURNAL FOR SEPTEMBER 17, 1863, READS, "weather—fine and warm, mch by Cedar Mtn to Robinson's Run arr noon, execution 4pm," brief and accurate to be sure, but the events of that day were permanently etched upon my memory. I never spoke of this day with Jessie Anne, nor have I ever spoken with anyone else about it or written about what transpired near Robinson's Run on that day until now, yet I recall every grisly detail of the scene, and my part in it, as if it occurred only yesterday.

With over nine hundred names on its roster, and almost one-third of those listed as deserters, the Fourteenth Connecticut left Bristow on September 3rd and rejoined the army. Of those present and fit for duty, five of every six had been drafted or were paid substitutes. Liars, cheats, and thieves thickly populated our ranks, and until each of these new men had been proven under fire and found trustworthy in his dealings, each old soldier viewed each new recruit with a careful eye, keen and full of suspicion. From Bristow we marched southwestward to Culpeper. On the morning of September 17th, we marched a short distance beyond Cedar Mountain to the banks of Robinson's Run, a tributary of the Rapidan. We arrived there shortly before noon and began to set up camp.

At two o'clock I was ordered to Captain Coit's tent across the camp in Company G.

"Sergeant," he said, "I am about to give you orders that I want carried out to the letter. Listen carefully and don't interrupt me. When I'm finished, I'll ask if you have any questions. Do you understand?"

"Sir, yes, sir."

"About a month ago two of our new recruits deserted. They were arrested in New York City, tried by court-marshal and found guilty of desertion and dereliction of duty. They will be executed this afternoon at four o'clock. I've been ordered to raise two firing squads of twelve men each. Each of our ten company commanders has selected two or three men — all veteran men and able shots. You come highly recommended by Captain Carpenter, and since neither man is from your company, you will be my sergeant. First, we will drill the two squads in the proper military procedure for execution. Check each man's rifle, that it is in perfect working order and clean. Then you will draw fresh ammunition from the quartermaster. We just received a new issue when we passed through Culpeper, so make sure the cartridges and caps are from that lot. No old ammunition is to be used. We can't risk any chance of a misfire. From the time you leave the quartermaster until the completion of the execution, you will not let the ammunition out of your sight. Do you understand, Sergeant Palmer?"

"Sir, yes, sir."

"Any questions?"

"Just one, sir. Does the captain wish me to report back here after I secure the ammunition, sir?"

"Yes, Sergeant, the entire division will assemble to witness the execution, so an order of march has been drawn up. The provosts will direct us where to go and what to do."

With the Fourteenth in the lead, the division marched to a field near Robinson's Run where it formed a three-sided square with the open end toward the base of a hill. The men of the Fourteenth stood in the front ranks because the two men were of the regiment.

With the division so placed, a second procession entered the field. Two ambulances were drawn slowly in front of the division toward the base of the hill. Each ambulance carried an empty pine coffin, and sitting atop each coffin, struggling hard with hands and feet shackled to maintain his unsteady perch, was one of the condemned. A watchful troop of provost guards accompanied the ambulances, with bayoneted rifles at the ready. Then came Captain Coit, saber drawn and held stiffly at his breast, leading the two firing squads marching in perfect step, their rifles carried at the shoulder ready. I was the last man in the procession. I carried no weapon, only my cartridge box, full of new, fresh cartridges and my cap box.

"Prisoners, dismount!" ordered the provost officer. Both of the condemned men jumped down from the ambulances; both fell to their knees; no one offered a helping hand as the pair struggled to their feet. A squad of guards carried the two coffins a short distance up the slope of the hill and placed them next to two graves that had already been dug in the red earth. The lid of each coffin was removed and leaned against the side of the coffin. The two men would be executed at the gravesites, and each man in the division would have an unobstructed view of the deadly proceedings.

With an ever so slight nod of the head, Captain Coit ordered me to step forward. I went to each of the two dozen riflemen in turn. Each man took a cartridge from my box. When I reached the end of the line, I smartly about-faced. With a loud voice I called out the loading cadence. The twenty-four men moved as one man; each movement was sharp and crisp, just as we had drilled it. Once more I walked slowly down the line from one man to the next, this time giving each man a primer cap from my box. Once again I about-faced and shouted the order to prime muskets. Then I returned to my place next to Captain Coit.

The provost officer along with several guards marched the condemned men into the center of the open square. The provost officer read the official charges and the order for execution to each man in turn, Edward Eliott, a draftee, and George Laton, a paid substitute. Then the two men were marched slowly around the square formation of the assembled division, while Charlie Merrills led the band in the playing of "Adeste Fideles." Charlie chose a tempo perfectly suited to the solemnity of the occasion, and surely he had altered some of the harmonies from major to minor, thus achieving a more melancholy but not unpleasant orchestration exactly appropriate to the occasion.

Their doleful circuit completed, the two men were marched into the center of the open side of the square and up the slope of the hill. Each man was ordered to sit on the edge of his coffin and face the firing squads, Eliott to the left, Laton to the right. Chaplain Stevens stepped forward. He read from the Scriptures and bowed his head in prayer. The provost officer tied a black blindfold about the head of each man and ordered Captain Coit to proceed with the execution.

"At the ready!" Captain Coit barked. The squads raised and cocked their rifles.

"Aim!" Twelve rifles drew aim on the chest of Edward Eliott, twelve on the chest of George Laton.

"Fire!" Only a few of the two dozen rifles discharged. Eliott was struck once in the shoulder, knocking him over backward into his coffin. Laton was not hit at all.

"Reload," screamed Captain Coit. I ran down the line, giving each man a new cartridge and primer cap. The squad to the left furiously set about clearing and reloading their fouled rifles while Eliott struggled to free his hands and get to his feet. About half the squad was ready just as he started to rise.

"Fire!" cried Captain Coit again. Once again, only two or three of the weapons fired, but Eliott's chest erupted in red. He fell back into the coffin, obviously dead.

The squad to the right also cleared and reloaded their rifles. Laton managed to free his hands. He tore off the blindfold just in time to see twelve Springfields leveled at his chest.

"Fire!" Only the crack of the primer caps was heard.

In total disgust with the way the men of the Fourteenth were handling this episode of military justice, the provost officer ordered his guards to approach Laton. The first took careful aim at Laton's forehead and pulled the trigger. There was just the weak pop of the cap again—Laton shook visibly. With each of the six provost guards it was the same—the terror for Laton dragged on and on.

Finally, the provost officer himself stepped forward and put an end both to Laton's life and to this ghastly affair with a single shot from his revolver to the head of the trembling man. For a minute or two no one moved, no one spoke a word; there was utter silence.

"Sergeant." Captain Coit's voice was hushed, but furious nonetheless. "I gave you strict orders not to use old cartridges."

"Sir, yes, sir. I followed your orders—to the letter, sir. Those are the new cartridges—straight from the quartermaster—dry as a bone—I checked them, sir."

"I'll get to the bottom of this mess, Sergeant, and if I find you did anything wrong, I'll bring charges myself."

The Fourteenth was ordered to march slowly by the two dead men lying in their coffins. Then we stood aside as the rest of the division filed by. A dozen of our new recruits, those deemed by the officers to be less reliable and more likely to take flight, were chosen from the ranks to nail the lids on the coffins and serve as the burial party.

The men returned to their new camp. Dinner was cooked and coffee was boiled, but I suspect little eating and drinking was actually done that night. I sat before the small campfire and let the horror of that afternoon's events fall upon me. Once again it seemed that God's hand was against me, this time in a manner most dark and sinister.

I went to my tent and got Wyatt's Bible from my knapsack. I had been reading the book of Hebrews regularly of late, when duty allowed, and I thought to perhaps receive some solace from it that evening. As I opened the Bible to find my place, a verse in 1 John at the top of the page, just under the book and chapter reference, drew my gaze. *Whosoever hateth his brother is a murderer: and ye know that no murderer hath eternal life abiding in him.* A great chill came over me. Not only had I hated the man Wyatt, I had truly killed him. Of course I would be crushed under the wrathful hand of the Almighty. Surely I would know only more affliction and torment, and in the end receive due justice for my crimes, perhaps even justice like that visited upon Laton and Eliott.

Word of the execution at Robinson's Run and others spread quickly throughout the army. Thousands of deserters suddenly deemed it their patriotic duty to return to their units. Others who may have been considering how best to make their flight suddenly found the prospect of facing the lead of the Confederacy more appealing than facing that of the Union. Even so, many of these men were no better than Elliott and Laton, and with men such as these in its ranks, how could the Army of the Potomac fight even one more battle, let alone bring this terrible war to a successful conclusion?

But the men of the Second Corps, old soldiers and new alike, would fight and they would fight exceedingly well. The Rebels tried to move northward again during the first week of October. A lengthy, collective groan went up from the men of the Second Corps as we turned around and headed north once more. We marched into Bealeton on Saturday and stopped at the supply depot. In one of the great ironies of this man's war, the bungled executions of Eliott and Laton had uncovered a serious problem with the latest shipment of cartridges the army was distributing to the troops. Whether the crates had been left out in the rain or the powder was simply of poor quality from the factory, the plain fact of it was that most of those cartridges were worthless, and had we gone into battle with cartridge boxes full of defective ammunition, a great many of our boys would have been defenseless and needlessly laid low. The bad cartridges were destroyed and new, proven cartridges were issued. In this instance, the unnecessarily cruel deaths of two deserters served to spare the lives of many.

The armies came together once again near our old training camp at Bristow on Wednesday, October 14th. Colonel Smyth's brigade formed in line of battle along the railroad next to General Webb's men, and our boys, including our new recruits, did some good work. The enemy charged us twice and they were twice repulsed with heavy losses. Otto stood steadfast, as did most of the others in the company, diligently following my drill cadence as I called it out. One or two men of the Fourteenth were killed and some wounded, and Jim Adams had his arm creased by an enemy ball, his first scratch since I had known him. He visited the surgeon and returned to duty almost immediately sporting a very impressive bandage.

It was not so with Caesar Ferretti. I saw no sign of him

during the battle or for several days afterward. I feared he was lost during the long, hard marching on the way to Bristow. I did not think him a deserter because I did not think him to be one to consider it, nor was he one with sufficient mental acumen to devise a plan for escape. Rather, I suspected he fell back during the march or perhaps merely wandered off, only to be snatched up by the Rebels and sent to one of their dreadful prison stockades. I had no choice but to report him as missing.

CHAPTER 27

Back to the Enemy

O LORD, what shall I say,
when Israel turneth their backs before their enemies!
JOSHUA 7:8

O N NOVEMBER 7TH, FEDERAL TROOPS OF THE SIXTH AND
Third Corps defeated Confederate forces at Rappah-
annock Station and Kelly's Ford, allowing the Army of the
Potomac to once again advance toward Culpeper. The Second
Corps moved near the village of Stevensburg, where General
Warren ordered the corps to encamp and build winter quarters.
The granting of furloughs would soon begin again, and I was
very close to the top of the list.

Jim, Charlie, and I invited Otto Wehlmann to become the
fourth occupant of our winter hut, which very much pleased
the big German. The weather was cold and rainy most of the
time, but Otto worked tirelessly, even joyfully, as he felled trees,
axed notches in them and heaved the timbers into position. It
was with obvious satisfaction that Otto drove himself onward,
along with his other three companions, so that the hut was completed within seven days. It was Otto who finally fixed our half-
shelter tents in place for the roof and it was Otto who built and
lit the first fire in the mud-covered fireplace.

Thursday, November 26th was proclaimed by President Lincoln to be a national "day of Thanksgiving and Praise to our beneficent Father who dwelleth in the heavens." While most folks already celebrated a day of thanksgiving, this was the first time in many years that a national holiday had been declared. My friends and I began to think about what special foodstuffs we might be able to acquire to enhance our celebration. As at Falmouth the year before, the army built brick ovens, and we enjoyed a steady supply of fresh bread. With the entire army encamped, herds of cattle could now be slaughtered, making fresh beef a definite possibility for our special day. Slabs of real bacon were plentiful. In addition, Jim and I had received some goodies from home and, if we still lacked anything, the sutler had a variety of canned fruits and vegetables. It would be a real feast—a feast for which all would have to wait, a feast which many, even thousands, might never partake of.

In the early morning hours of Thanksgiving Day an order came down that the entire army was to prepare to march. Meager possessions went from hut to knapsack, half-shelters went from roof to blanket roll and we huddled together before the fireplace, drawing what scant warmth we could from the dying embers. Feasting was exchanged for marching and prayers of thanksgiving for grumbling as the army moved southward.

The Second Corps crossed the Rapidan River on a pontoon bridge at Germanna Ford. We were very close to the enemy now. Signs of his recent activity were everywhere—the carpet of fallen leaves disturbed and trampled, abandoned entrenchments, smoldering embers of dying campfires, camp refuse strewn about, the stench of human and animal excrement. And it was not lost on anyone that this forested country through which we marched lay just a few scant miles west of the scene of our greatest disgrace at Chancellorsville.

On Friday, the weather turned much colder. The brigade

deployed in line of battle in some woods near a small hamlet called Locust Grove. Furtive movements and rustling leaves told of enemy lookouts scurrying away at our approach. Breastworks were thrown up and we settled down warily for the night. Icy rain fell with the dawn on Saturday, but we still marched several more miles through dense forest and built more breastworks.

On Sunday it was more of the same. The cold rain was not constant but was sufficiently heavy and frequent to keep us damp and shivering all day long. We struggled for eleven miles over terrible roads—narrow, muddy, and deeply furrowed with ancient wagon ruts. Late in the afternoon, Colonel Smyth ordered the brigade to form in line of battle. The men of the Fourteenth Connecticut went forward as skirmishers.

Colonel Ellis's orders were crisp in the cold, damp air. "Fix bayonets! Arms at the ready! Forward, march!"

We advanced into yet another dense wood. We worked our way slowly forward, weapons at the ready. There were no colors in those woods, only shades of gray. I blinked my eyes again and again, trying to distinguish between the darker shades of the tree trunks and the lighter frosty voids, testing the several visible yards before me with all my senses—smelling, listening, feeling, watching—to learn if death waited for me within the gloom. Step by step, yard by yard, I advanced. Leaves rustled and jeering calls came from out of the shadows.

Another step and then another.

A tree several yards ahead and slightly to the right—two more steps and suddenly it seemed the tree had moved. A dark form stood motionless beside the tree trunk; a pair of arms raised a musket and leveled it squarely at my chest. I froze. *Jessie Anne, I'll not be coming home.*

"Bye, Yank," I heard the man say.

A soft click; his musket had misfired. Our eyes fixed on each other. The man's face twisted into a hideous, devilish sneer, and he spat a heavy wad of black spittle onto the ground between us. I brought my own rifle to bear and drew back the hammer, but in that short second or two, the man had vanished into the shadows. Damp powder had spared another life, but for how long and for what purpose?

"After them, men," cried Colonel Ellis. "Don't let them stop to reload."

We rushed over the crest of a low ridge and then down into a shallow valley, yelling and screaming all the way, until we came upon a small stream. We splashed across Mine Run, as it was known, without difficulty, but a few yards beyond the stream the woods ended and so did our pursuit. The main line of the enemy, toward which the pickets were fleeing, was only a few hundred yards away, atop yet another low ridge that had been cleared of trees. Artillery opened on us immediately, but did us no harm, though we were forced to spend the last hour of the day in extremely close contact with the cold, muddy earth.

The main body of the brigade advanced to our skirmish line, and we set about digging a shallow trench and building breastworks for protection against the shelling, our third such construction in three days. With nightfall the rain ended. A strong north wind arose and it grew much colder. Within a short time the mud-covered works had frozen solid.

Colonel Smyth came forward to address the brigade. Always an encouraging officer and usually in bright spirits, the somber tone of his voice caused all to pay close heed.

"The Second Corps is the left end of the Union Line. Our hard marching during the last two days was an attempt to get beyond the Rebels' right flank, but as you see, they have extended their works. General Warren is confident that the Second Corps can charge up that hill tomorrow and sweep the Rebels off it, so General Meade has ordered a grand assault all along the line."

A collective groan passed through the ranks.

"Tomorrow morning at eight o'clock, we will hear a signal shot from one of our guns in the center off to the right. There will then be a general bombardment of the enemy. We are to be ready to charge the hill as soon as the bombardment ceases. General Hays's division has been given the task of leading the assault along this part of the line, and this brigade will lead that division. We will be the front line. We will lead the assault for the entire corps."

Not a groan this time, but hushed, terse whisperings.

"I want you to know fully what we have been called upon to do tomorrow. We will fix bayonets and rush up that hill, not stopping, not firing a shot until we gain their works. The position of the Rebels is strong. Their works are formidable. I expect casualties will be high, perhaps extreme."

The colonel paused for a few moments to steady his voice before continuing.

"The army and the nation will be watching us tomorrow to see if we do our duty. Let it never be said of this brigade, of you men from New Jersey, Connecticut, New York, and Delaware, that we were found wanting in the time of trial. Let it only be said that we always did our duty to its fullest extent. We will fight together tomorrow as brothers, and as brothers we shall meet whatever the Almighty has in store for us. Let His will be done, and may He bless this army with success tomorrow."

❦

The night was bitterly cold. No fires were allowed because of the nearness of the enemy. Sleep was not possible or even desired, for if one was to fall asleep, he might never awaken; his frozen body would be found in the morning. And so it remained for each man to pass each long minute of that endless, frigid night in preparation for the coming battle. For some this meant gathering in twos or threes or fours to talk and joke of nothing in particular, laughing and stamping their feet and sometimes jumping up and down to keep their blood flowing. For others, and I include myself among this number, it was a time for solitude, perhaps for prayer and reflection, for death would call upon many tomorrow. I sat atop my folded half-shelter and leaned back against a large oak tree, wrapped in my woolen and rubber blankets, shivering against the cold.

The Rebels made no secret about what they were doing to prepare for the battle. Had we expected them to attack us, we would have done the same thing. We clearly heard the incessant chopping of the axe, the crashing of falling trees, the yells and grunts and curses of the men across the way as they worked through the night to strengthen their defenses. The metallic clanks of hundreds of shovels and spades spoke of a great volume of earth being dug out and thrown up. As we listened to them work, every one of us knew that for every chop of the axe, for every fallen tree, for every shovel filled with dirt, the cost in our blood grew dearer still.

Heavy footfalls approached; the massive form of Otto Wehlmann loomed over me. "Sit down, Otto," I said. I usually enjoyed Otto's company and conversation, and now we could help each other avoid the danger of falling asleep.

"Sergeant Palmer, is it going to be as bad as Colonel Smyth said?"

"I expect so," I said. "Colonel Smyth's always truthful with the men. The Rebs have been working all night up on that hill, so it will be very bad for us tomorrow. It could be worse than Fredericksburg, but General Warren thinks we can take that hill, so we'll have to try. It might be like Gettysburg, only in reverse. We could get all the way up to their works, only to be driven back. I guess it's in God's hands now."

"I'm not ready to die," said Otto, "I've seen so little of life. I could get married and have children like you, Sergeant, and work and ... there must be much more than I've seen so far. Maybe God should let me live so I—"

"Hey, Yank," a voice called from the darkness in the direction of the Rebel line, amid the incessant clanking and chopping. "Say your prayers tonight 'cause you're sure in for it tomorrow. Best be ready to meet your maker." The voice cackled a piercing, ghoulish laugh, and other cackling voices from the void added a chorus of hoots and hollers and taunts.

A shadowy figure approached. "Sergeant Palmer, is that you?" It was Chaplain Stevens. Otto and I started to rise. "No, no, don't get up. And who's that you're sharing this tree with? Ah, Mr. Wehlmann. I should have known, you're such a large fellow. Mind if I sit for a spell?"

"Please do, sir," I said.

"That man's right, you know. We must all say our prayers tonight. Unless the Lord is indeed most merciful, a big fight will occur here tomorrow and many men will die. 'Believe on the Lord Jesus Christ, and thou shalt be saved.' That's the best thing I can tell you tonight. If you trust in Him, even if you're killed tomorrow, you will live forever in glory with Him. You believe this, don't you, Sergeant?"

"I've always said so," I answered quickly.

"And now? When it appears your faith will be put to the test?"

I shifted uncomfortably against the tree. I recalled each of the men I had killed, until lastly, the anguish-stricken face of the man Wyatt seemed to appear before me. Had I not gone off to war to do the will of God? I had told Jessie Anne as much. How could I have been overcome by such malice and rage? I was a guilty man and I despised myself because of it.

"Well, sir," I said, "when I think of it ... it's just that my sin is so great ... so deep ... and dark. And when I think of my faith, sir, I'm afraid it's so small and weak compared to my sin."

"But Sergeant," Otto said, "you're a religious man. I've seen you reading the Bible and praying."

"Mr. Wehlmann, Sergeant Palmer has spoken from the heart," Chaplain Stevens said, "and you have raised an interesting question, Sergeant, so let me speak from the heart as well. The truth is that sometimes my own sin seems so great and my faith so small that I wonder where it has gone. It's a constant battle that rages inside me. But thanks be to God, He's not holding a balance, with my faith on one side and my sin on the other, waiting to see which way it will tip. Sergeant Palmer, Mr. Wehlmann—please understand that any faith I possess is not something for which I deserve credit. It's not because I'm a religious man or a minister of the gospel. No, the beauty of the Christian gospel is that my faith comes to me as a gift from the One in whom I trust, the Lord Jesus Christ, and I need only receive that gift and rest upon Him for salvation. This is my eternal and glorious hope."

"But what about tomorrow?" Otto asked.

"What of tomorrow when you go charging up that hill?" The chaplain paused for a moment before answering. "I can only say that He alone has power to strengthen me, even when I am weak and afraid. By myself, I would be worthless as a minister and as a man, but with Christ I can do what is required of me, and I know He will never leave my side. I will be by your side tomorrow on that hill, to minister to the fallen, and if He takes me, so be it."

"I should pray for faith such as yours," Otto said.

"Pray only that Christ might know you, Otto Wehlmann, and that you might know Christ. Trust that Christ alone can cleanse you of all sin, and then let Him carry your burdens. Your body may die just hours from now, but if you are truly in Christ, and if Christ is in you, then eternal glory is yours."

Chaplain Stevens offered a brief prayer. Then he shook our hands and took his leave to speak with others of the regiment.

Otto drew his blankets over his head and wrapped himself up tightly. I recognized the sighs and moans of a young man in distress, of a man wrestling with himself and with God. I likewise wrapped myself up as warmly as I could. On that cold, dark night, somewhere a few miles west of the Wilderness, my prayer was very simple. Certainly the time for reckoning was at hand. *Please, Lord in Heaven, watch over the widow Wyatt and her children and bless them most abundantly. Be gracious to this miserable sinner—may my end be swiftly and mercifully met.*

Indeed, how small was my faith.

⟨≶⟩⟩

With first light, a group of riders clattered across the stream behind us. I recognized Colonel Smyth and General Hays among the group. There was also another general officer, a thin, muscular man who sat perfectly erect in the saddle. Even in the dim light of that early morning, this general's eyes burned intently. He had a sharp, angular nose; the skin of his face was drawn tightly over high cheekbones. It could easily be said that this general's face resembled that of an eagle in that it possessed all the nobility and savagery of that bird of prey. This was General Warren, a true hero of the Battle of Gettysburg, now in command of the Second Corps while General Hancock was on convalescent leave.

The officers dismounted, clambered over the breastworks, and walked carefully to the very edge of the tree line where they could view the Rebel lines directly. The officers talked together for a few minutes and then returned. General Warren walked slowly with his head down, his lips forming words that only he could hear or understand. The grand visage of the mighty eagle had vanished. The general's countenance was now a specter of deepest gloom and despair. He had seen what every man in the line knew already, the slaughter at Mine Run would be greater by far than any that had gone before.

At eight o'clock sharp, the heavy thump of one of our thirty-two-pound howitzers echoed up and down the line. Within a minute or two, every Union gun joined in the bombardment. It was a wondrous thing to see our shells arc across that small valley and explode over the Rebel lines. Sometimes a shell would strike part of the Rebels' works and cause some damage, but as soon as the smoke cleared, dozens of hands quickly repaired the breach. Across the way a single Rebel soldier climbed atop the breastwork, defiantly daring our gunners to knock him off. He took his floppy hat in his hand and waved it in our direction, beckoning to us, yelling at the top of his voice words that were lost in the din of the shelling. But all who saw him knew exactly what he was saying. *Come on over here! Come on over and die, Yank!*

The bombardment abruptly ceased after thirty minutes. All that remained was the call of the bugle. We stood at the ready, muscles tense, breathing shallow and labored. A long, endless minute passed, then a second. We waited for two hours of terrifying eternity, counting every second of every minute of what remained of our lives, listening for the bugle call that would send us into that valley of near-certain death.

The call never sounded. When General Warren reported to General Meade that an assault upon the enemy's works would result in the destruction of the Second Corps, General Meade viewed the fortifications for himself and the grand assault was called off.

◆─◆

During the early morning hours of December 2nd, my footfalls echoed upon the decking of the pontoon bridge at Germanna

Ford. Once again, my back was to the enemy, and once again, I had been spared. Indeed I was truly thankful to God for His mercy, but *He was unto me as a bear lying in wait, and as a lion in secret places*. There would yet be an accounting.

CHAPTER 28

Winter Quarters

Husbands, love your wives,
even as Christ also loved the church,
and gave himself for it.
EPHESIANS 5:25

OUR LOG HUT NEAR STEVENSBURG MIGHT HAVE SERVED AS winter quarters for someone, but not for the men who built it. The men of the Fourteenth were ordered hither and yon to do this duty or that and did not receive orders to encamp until December 27th. Then we marched about two miles south of Stevensburg to a low, forested, rock-strewn hill known appropriately as Stony Mountain. Experienced builders now, we built our second hut in just a few days.

We had neither the opportunity nor the inclination to consider Christmas celebrations, but on the last day of 1863, Jim, Charlie, Otto, and I planned and enjoyed a hearty feast. As I had done the year before, I ordered each man a pair of Hickham's boots from home, although Otto's feet were so large that, even with my years of retailing, I could not determine the size. I simply traced both the outline and the profile of each of his huge feet on a sheet of paper and sent the sheets home to Jessie Anne.

Chaplain Stevens returned to Connecticut to take up his

pastoral duties once again. He had already extended his service with the regiment four months beyond the one-year leave granted by his congregation. He would be greatly missed by the men of the Fourteenth, and as it turned out, the chaplaincy would be vacant for some time to come. Chaplain Stevens was to me the last remaining voice of truth and wisdom in the regiment; I considered his loss but another manifestation of God's displeasure.

Charlie Merrills gathered the band members together and rehearsed them hour after hour. He invited me to sing again, but I politely declined. Perhaps General Hooker had been correct—it all seemed a frivolous waste of time and energy. Disappointed but undeterred, Charlie recruited several other men to form a small choir. The ensemble gave several concerts during the winter months, which reportedly were well received by both officers and enlisted men alike.

For my part, I preferred more solitary pursuits when in camp. Sunny afternoons, when it was not too cold or windy and no other duty called, I could often be found sitting on the log bench, once again hewn by Jim Adams. Sometimes Jim or Charlie would join me, but my most regular companion was Otto Wehlmann.

"Do your parents know where you are?" I asked the big German one January afternoon. "Have you written to them since you enlisted?"

"No, Sergeant." Otto studied the ground at his feet. "I just went away—never said good-bye. They don't know if I'm alive or dead."

I sagely puffed on my pipe. "The fifth commandment says, 'Honor thy father and thy mother.' You should write to them, Otto, just a short note."

"Maybe they should know I'm alive."

I went into the hut and returned a moment later with my

journal, quill pen, and ink bottle in hand. I offered them to Otto and received a blank stare in return.

"What's the problem, Otto?"

"I never learned."

"You never went to school?"

"No, Sergeant."

"But you speak well enough, and your accent is hardly noticeable. I'm surprised you were never taught to read and write."

"I think that's what I hold most against my parents. They never thought I would amount to much, so the only thing they taught me was canaling. But on the canal I met many people from many places, so I listened to them, and sometimes I would tell the mules long stories as I was driving them—just to hear myself talk, I guess. There wasn't time for school."

"Then tell me what you want me to write, and I'll teach you to read it."

We sat side by side for several minutes, Otto thinking of what he ought to put in the letter, and me puffing slowly away at my pipe, watching how the light blue-gray smoke from hundreds of hut hearth fires hung lazily just above the trees on Stony Mountain. Finally, Otto dictated the following note:

Dear Father and Mother,

I'm in Virginia with the Army of the Potomac. I'm well and I have enough to eat. Sergeant Palmer is looking after me and he's helping me write this letter. He's a good friend. I hope you will forgive me for leaving you, but I could not follow the mules anymore. I hope you had a happy Christmas and do not worry about me.

Your son,

Otto Wehlmann

As with my letters, I penned the date — *Tuesday, January 12th, 1864* — and the place — *Camp of the 14th Conn. Rgt. Vol. Inf.* — *near Stevensburg, Virginia.* I showed the finished letter to Otto and read it back to him, pointing to every word as I said it, as one would do with a small child. "What address shall I write on the envelope?" I asked.

"In winter we usually worked the eastern end of the canal, unless it was frozen. I think you should send it to Mr. Erich Wehlmann at the Office of the Erie Canal, Albany, New York."

"Done," I said, "and I wrote 'Please Forward' so that if anyone at the Albany office knows where your father is, they will send this letter on to him."

As we walked back from posting the letter, I said, "Otto, I'd like to teach you to read and write."

"You would do that?"

"Yes. We'll use the Bible. It'll occupy us during the long winter. We'll work at it every day we're in camp."

The bright happiness in Otto's eyes was all the thanks this soldier would ever need.

Indeed, my own eyes brightened later that same day when I received a dispatch from regimental headquarters. I had finally been granted a fourteen-day furlough. I would leave for home on January 25th.

⋙⋘

My head bobbed once, then jerked backward more severely as the locomotive *Alfred Bishop* started to pull out of the station at Seymour. I had counted down the hours; now I was counting down the minutes, just forty or so remained. In New York the previous evening I had gone to the Sanitary Commission lodge near the depot for a hot meal. At an establishment nearby I was able to take a hot, soapy bath for the cost of fifteen cents. Refreshed and enlivened, I had thoroughly enjoyed this morning's four-hour ride along the New Haven Line to Bridgeport at speeds sometimes in excess of forty miles per hour, according to Martin, the conductor.

But I was not home yet. There were so many things that might delay my arrival. We had yet to pass through the river gorge just south of Naugatuck, where rock falls were a common occurrence; at least one deadly derailment had occurred there. Seasonal floods could also be a problem, but January was not the time for flooding, and I had observed the depth of the river on the way northward just to be sure. At least the provosts could not block my way, for there had been none at Bridgeport and only a few local passengers occupied the car.

The train crawled two miles up the valley to Beacon Falls, the final stop before Naugatuck. I felt as if I could walk faster than the train, but of course this was not true. The maximum speed allowed on the line was twenty miles per hour because the rails were still of the brittle, wrought-iron sort, and with stops and starts, and embarking and debarking, and grades and curves to account for, one could expect to cover about ten to twelve miles in the span of one hour. The scheduled time to go from Bridgeport to Naugatuck, a distance of twenty-seven miles, was two hours and twenty-six minutes. Thankfully, our stop at Beacon Falls was a short one. It took just a few minutes to leave a few travelers on the platform and board a few more. Baggage and mail were handed down and more taken up into the car just behind the tender. With a blast of the whistle, the cars once again jerked forward.

It was a fine day for midwinter, chilly but not bitingly cold, with a clear, cloudless sky, and little wind. The fair weather foretold a frosty night to come, but I would be warming myself at my own hearth that evening. The bright sun warmed my face as the train headed into the gorge, but only for a few minutes as the craggy steeps soon cast deep shadows across the gorge. The engineer knew the hazards of this stretch far better than I, so I was content to close my eyes to rest. I felt the motion of the car gently tug at my body, first this way, then that, as the train followed the course of the meandering river. I listened to the changing squeal of wheel against rail as the friction waxed and waned.

I tried to imagine Jessie Anne's face as I had last seen it. During my many months away, I had often engaged in this exercise, but without much success, perhaps because I was fearful of the deepest longings that would surely accompany such a vision. But now her familiar warm, loving eyes and beautiful smile played across the inside of my eyelids. I smiled to myself and wondered how she had changed since last I saw her. Patience, I told myself, just a few more minutes, and the image will be sight.

I felt the train accelerate as the tracks straightened, and I now knew the gorge was passed. I stood, walked to the rear of the car, and opened the door. I would return in exactly the same manner I had departed. I stepped out on the landing, the same landing I had stood upon seventeen months before, waving good-bye as the tears flowed unashamedly. How the freed black man Noble Weston had warmed my heart that dark and stormy morning, when he stood at the very edge of the platform in the driving rain and executed the sharpest salute I have ever seen.

Minutes were now seconds, the station was now in view, and yes, as the train drew nearer, small figures could be seen waiting on the platform for our arrival — my arrival.

From the rear of the car, I saw her first, standing anxiously next to my father while he clasped Sarah and little Edward each by the hand. She was as lovely as ever, my Jessie Anne. I paused for a moment, taking her beauty in, laying up this vision of her in the deepest and most secret place of my mind, allowing the sight of her to renew my spirit. I stepped slowly down to the platform, never allowing my gaze to drift from her. Jessie Anne was looking toward the front of the car, and it was a moment or two before she turned and spotted me.

The bright and hopeful smile I had so expected and longed for darkened, just for a moment to be sure, but long enough for me to recognize a fleeting glimpse of shock and anguish, possibly of horror. No longer did she see the man she had known, the man she had given her life to. No, she saw me for the man I truly was, the man with blood on his hands. But in the next instant there was that smile again, glowing with happiness, and bright eyes shedding tears of unbridled joy. She rushed into my arms and we embraced for some time, each wrapped in the comfort of the other, oblivious to all else. Finally, we released each other and turned to the children.

"Sarah! Edward! Come greet your father," Jessie Anne told the children, who for their part seemed to prefer gaping at me with wild-eyed terror, while clinging desperately to their grandfather's strong hands. I approached my children slowly, speaking soft greetings as I knelt on the platform before them. I took first Sarah, then Edward into my arms, then both together, and suddenly I was home.

That evening after a splendid dinner of beef roast, mashed potatoes, and buttermilk biscuits, we read Scripture and prayed together as a family for the first time in seventeen months. Then Jessie Anne and I put the children to bed and retired for the evening. Jessie Anne was soon fast asleep, but I remained awake for some time. I lay on the soft bed thinking at once how luxuriously comfortable it was and also how uncomfortable it now felt to my ground-hardened body; it was simply too warm and too dry and too soft. I slipped quietly out of bed, turned up the lamp, and stood in front of the mirror that hung on the wall over the washstand.

It had also been seventeen months since I had viewed my own reflection, and now I saw what Jessie Anne had seen at the train station: a gaunt, haggard-looking fellow who, had I not known it was myself, I would have dismissed with disgust as a street derelict. My hair was long and unkempt, graying in places and thinning on top. My beard, also streaked with gray, did nothing to cover my hollow cheeks and protruding cheekbones; my eyes were sunken and dark; the soft flesh beneath them now sagged noticeably — how like those sketches of wanted criminals I had seen posted in the several depots I had passed through on the way home.

Soft arms encircled me from behind. I had not heard Jessie Anne stir, and I welcomed her touch, but was also discomfited by it, as if in her touching me, her goodness and beauty might somehow be corrupted. I unclasped her hands and guided her around to stand in front of me so that our positions were reversed, interposing her loveliness between me and the unsightliness of my own reflection.

"You are as beautiful as you were the day I married you."

"Oh, Michael, I am not, but I love you for saying so. See? I'm getting lines around my eyes and look here," she added, flicking a hand through her long tresses, "my hair's starting to turn gray."

"It is not," I protested.

Jessie Anne nodded sweetly. "Yes it is, but just a little." We stood gazing at each other for a few minutes. Indeed my eyes did notice the small lines and even a strand or two of gray, but my heart overruled my eyes. This marvelous woman was only growing lovelier with the passing years.

"Have I changed so much?" I asked.

"What do you mean, Michael?" Innocent eyes gazed at me in the mirror.

"You looked rather shocked when you saw me at the station."

"You are dreadfully thin, Michael. I can feel your ribs sticking out through your nightshirt even now." I made as if to relax my hold on her, but she would have none of it. "You will eat well while you're home, even if you aren't hungry."

"Yes, dear."

"And I've never seen you with a beard and your hair truly is turning gray, although you might look quite distinguished if your beard and mane are properly trimmed. You'll see Mr. Vincent tomorrow."

"All right." There was naught to do but agree.

Jessie Anne reached her soft fingers back over her shoulder and traced the line of the long scar on my cheek. "And what's this?"

I held her closer. "Gettysburg," I whispered in her ear. "I wrote about it in my letter."

"But you said it was just a scratch, and you didn't say it was on your face."

"I didn't want to worry you."

"But seeing that scar at the station was an instant reminder of the danger you constantly face. I hate the feeling of not knowing what's happening to you, if you're well or ill, or if you're wounded or a prisoner, or even if you're alive or dead. A week-old letter, though I dearly love them and what you say in them, still does little to quiet my aching heart."

Her hands increased their pressure on my encircling arms.

"I'll never get used to your absence or the thought that it might be permanent. I have so much desired to share my soul with you and for you to share yours with me; there is no one else under heaven. Tell me of your war, Michael."

Could I tell her all? Would she ever understand?

I stirred the fire and added a small log. Then we sat on the bed, side by side, hand in hand, gazing into the flames. I began to tell her many of the things I had seen and done in the war. I passed over the most gruesome details, for that is something no woman should think of. I spoke of Sergeant Needham and of

John and of singing with the band and of picket duty. I spoke of long marches, fierce fighting, and long days of doing nothing. I showed her the scar on my left thigh from the piece of shell at Fredericksburg, now a faded pink irregular star. I told her about Caesar and Otto. At times, tears of sadness streamed down her face and fell softly into her lap. At others, the tears were of joy as she laughed and laughed. Then I told her about the ball that bloodied my face at Gettysburg, and she winced at how close it had come to ending my life. But of the man Augustus Wyatt, and of the others who had fallen before me that hot July afternoon, I said nothing.

Jessie Anne squeezed my hand and turned to look directly at me. "I've invited Abby and her children to dinner Saturday evening—also George Allerton and his boys."

"Do you think that's wise?"

"Oh, yes," she said, nodding vigorously. "I've been watching them. I think both of them just need a little nudge."

"You still amaze me, Jessie Anne." I kissed her gently, then we crept back under the warm bed coverings.

"Will you still be here in the morning?" Jessie Anne asked as I turned the lamp down.

"I expect so, but if not, please look on the floor."

This last I said only half in jest, for I knew what I would do. A short time later Jessie Anne was sleeping soundly, her chest rising and falling gently with each breath. I turned onto my side to gaze at her. Her lovely face glowed in the firelight; fair, smooth skin was framed by long, silken tresses; her lips formed a slight smile. I saw the innocence and beauty of the girl I had loved so long ago—an innocence and beauty I no longer had warrant to.

I rose quietly, found an extra blanket in the chest at the foot of the bed, and laid the blanket on the floor before the fire.

CHAPTER 29

Eye to Eye

For we are saved by hope:
but hope that is seen is not hope:
for what a man seeth,
why doth he yet hope for?
ROMANS 8:24

JIM ADAMS SEEMED THE ONLY MAN IN HIGH SPIRITS WHEN I walked into camp.

"It's a Bowie fighting knife!" he exclaimed, proudly holding out the long-bladed weapon for my inspection. "I've seen some of the Rebs with them but never could find one for sale anywhere. The blade is almost a foot long."

"How did you get it?" I asked.

"Took it from a Reb."

"While you were out on picket?"

"No, Michael, we've been busy while you were on holiday. Saturday, the division was sent across the river—as brainless a move as there ever was—reconnaissance in force, they said. We could have told them the Rebs were still there without leaving camp. It was hard fighting until after dark—fourteen killed, but none from our company—about eighty wounded. Then they just told us to withdraw early yesterday morning."

"I should have been here," I said. "How did you get that knife?"

"Just after dark one of the Rebs stumbled right into me, must have lost his bearings or something. He reached for this knife to stick me with it, but I knocked him with the butt of my rifle. Broke his jaw as sure as I'm standing here—probably killed him. Anyhow, he wasn't in any shape to protest when I relieved him of this beauty, just look how it shines—took his sheath too."

Sunday, February 28, 1864

My Dearest Husband Michael,

Since your leaving three weeks ago yesterday, thoughts of you have been ever present with me. Indeed, more than thoughts, for I have concerns for you that grow all the more grave with each passing day. Perhaps I should have given voice to these concerns during your stay with us, but I wished not to cause a bother, or disturb your time of respite.

Please know that I make no complaint about how you comported yourself while here, for your tender compassion to Abby and her children was evident to all, and you were to Sarah and Edward every bit the loving and doting father. I understand and excuse your desire to bed down each night on the floor before the fire, for just as you said, it would indeed be most difficult to return to the conditions at the front if one became accustomed to a soft feather bed. As for me, you were most loving and tender, although we had no union—I did wish it, but did not press it. Of this too I make no complaint other than to express disappointment which has since passed. It may be, as you said, that another child should best wait until the war is ended, but at times I imagine you preferred me at a distance.

I confess that my concerns for you rose when I first saw you at the depot. "Have I changed so much?" you asked, whereupon I commented on changes in your physical appearance. But as I observed you during your ten days at home, and now even more so, as I have reflected upon them in your absence, I have concluded there is something else. Upon seeing you again I perceived something lacking in your gaze, a certain darkening of your eyes that I can only describe as a lack of luster or light, perhaps even a lack of life. Your eyes to me have always been bright beacons of hope and joy, true revealers of the man I came to know and love. With but a glance I knew if you were cheerful or sad, contented or perplexed. At first I attributed this darkening to fatigue and the rigors of war, which certainly must drain joy and vigor from any man, and I hoped that some days at home in the bosom of your family might kindle that old light and joy once again. But alas, it did not.

In your letter to me after John's death you wrote, "I fear I have become the man of Lamentations." At the time I attributed your dark disposition to your sorrow, a heart deeply aggrieved that would, in time, be whole once again. So it was not until your recent furlough that I fully comprehended your meaning, and now I, too, fear you have become that man.

My Dearest Michael, you are a man with a tender heart—this I have known for many years. But now I believe that heart is sorely bruised—how could it be untouched and untroubled, given the abundant horrors you have been forced to witness? Truly, that is more than any man can bear, unless God is his refuge and strength—how I pray you find Him so. And yet I fear that you see only darkness in your current circumstances, that you see only affliction, misery, and death, that you see nothing of God's light upon you. I fear that your heart, instead of being full of Godly love and thanksgiving for His bountiful mercies, has become a bottomless cistern full of sorrows.

Surely you must also know His promises to that man of

Lamentations, to *you*, my beloved, "It is of the LORD's mercies that we are not consumed, because His compassions fail not. They are new every morning: great is Thy faithfulness. The LORD is my portion, saith my soul; therefore will I hope in Him. The LORD is good unto them that wait for Him, to the soul that seeketh Him. It is good that a man should both hope and quietly wait for the salvation of the LORD."

This last is what you must do, Michael — hope and quietly wait for His salvation. It will surely come — in His time, not in ours. I believe this is what I saw lacking in you and I fear for you because of it. I plead with you, my dearest, do not let the troubles of this age outweigh the glory that awaits you.

I pray all the more earnestly that you may know anew the wondrous blessings of being a child of the Most High God. Draw near to Him and He will draw near to you.

> I am, as always, your loving and
> devoted wife and sister in Him,
>
> *Jessie Anne*

Jessie Anne was, of course, quite right. I read her words over and over, knowing the truth of them in my mind but failing to allow them to sink into my heart.

⋘⋙

The remainder of the winter encampment passed quickly and peacefully. Regular duties included marching and manual of arms drills along with regular rotations on picket duty along the river. The circumstances of daily life were so much improved that the drudgeries of the previous wintering at Falmouth — incessantly cold and wet weather, poor food, disease, mud, the tedium of basic existence — were infrequent and minor annoyances. The men were healthier and happier, storing up reserves of strength for the rigors of the spring campaign. Indeed my own health was as fine as it had been since my enlistment, but nothing seemed to lift the dark shroud that lay upon my soul.

❖～❖

One sunny and mild afternoon during the first week of April, Otto and I were again sitting on the log bench beside the door of our hut, engaged in a reading lesson from Wyatt's Bible. Captain Simpson approached, his pace quick and deliberate. We jumped to our feet and saluted.

"Sergeant Palmer." The captain's chest heaved with his exertions. "There will be riders in the camp ... general officers ... in ten minutes. Passing through. Grant, Meade, Hancock, and others. Order the men to turn out. Do something useful."

"Yes, sir," I replied. "Is there any particular duty the captain wishes the men to be engaged in?"

"Nothing particular. Just make it look good."

I called for Jim Adams, and we raced about to the fifteen or so huts belonging to the men of Company C, ordering them to assemble quickly. "Commanding generals will be passing by in a matter of minutes," I told the men. "Turn out in full uniform. Police the grounds near your huts. If the officers pass near you, hold your salutes until you see their backs."

And so it was that I was afforded my first and only glimpse of General Ulysses S. Grant. About twenty horsemen plodded slowly down the main avenue of our brigade's encampment. I immediately recognized General Meade, as I had seen him a few times before. On one side of Meade was General Hancock, now recovered from his wounding at Gettysburg and restored to command of the Second Corps. Both men sat tall in the saddle, well groomed, their uniforms crisp and clean, brass gleaming brightly in the afternoon sun.

On the other side of General Meade rode another man,

hunched over the pommel of the saddle, which he gripped with both hands, an almost nondescript man when seen alongside the other two generals. It was not that he was unkempt or unclean; he just didn't glitter like the others. This was General Grant who, during the first week of March, was given command of all of the armies of the United States by President Lincoln, and Grant was the man who would very shortly order us out of our camps and into battle.

I stood at attention at the side of the road and raised a crisp salute as the generals passed by. Meade and Hancock appeared to be engaged in a private conversation to the exclusion of Grant, who for his part seemed not to mind, preferring instead to ride close to the side of the road, close to the men in the ranks now under his command, perhaps taking private pleasure from the aromatic cigar clamped between his teeth.

He came abreast. I looked directly up at him, something I knew I should not have done, and he looked directly back at me. Was this really Grant? Was this the hero of Donelson, Vicksburg, and Chattanooga?

Our eyes held for but a few seconds, then with a slight nod he rode past. But in those few seconds I perceived something of the measure of the man. I saw a warmth and depth in his gaze, and perhaps a sense of somber purpose and steadfast dedication to the cause for which we would fight together as brothers in arms.

⋖≣⋗

"What do you think of General Grant, Sergeant?" Otto asked me later that evening, after our evening meal, as we sat before the fire.

"Everything I've read says he's a fighter. That's why President Lincoln wants him here. I think we're in for some heavy fighting, maybe worse than any we've seen yet."

"But what's changed in the past year?" Jim said. "We're

almost exactly where we were last April, just a couple of dozen miles west. We've had a long parade of generals who were either nerveless, skill-less, or witless. What makes you think Grant will be any better?"

"I saw the look in his eyes." I looked squarely first at Jim, then at Otto, then at Charlie. The heat in my own eyes forced each man in turn to drop his gaze to the flames. "Grant will fight us hard, and that's fine with me. I'm going to fight and fight and fight, as long as it takes, until we win."

"Or get killed," Jim said.

"Yes. Either way, the fighting ends."

CHAPTER 30

A Season in the Wilderness

For wickedness burneth as the fire:
it shall devour the briers and thorns,
and shall kindle in the thickets of the forest,
and they shall mount up like the lifting up of smoke.

ISAIAH 9:18

THE GHOSTS OF CHANCELLORSVILLE GREETED EVERY MAN OF the Second Corps as we marched through that dark place on the fourth day of May. The unburied skeletal remains of hundreds of Union dead lay scattered about, a stark reminder of the bleeding and dying that yet remained. The tragedy that had been visited upon this army the year previous was lost on no one, veteran and recruit alike, as the men encamped at the southern fringe of the battlefield for the night.

Now about 27,000 strong, the corps had seen several changes during the winter months. General Hancock had returned to command and seemed as hale and hearty as ever. General John Gibbon now commanded the Second Division, replacing General Hays. While the Fourteenth Connecticut remained in the Third Brigade, eight additional regiments filled its ranks, and a new brigade commander had been appointed, Colonel Samuel S. Carroll. This man would, I was confident, lead us well.

Thursday's dawn found us already marching toward the southwest on Catherine Furnace Road. Several hours later at the Brock Road, a great cheer arose from the ranks when we turned left. "On to Richmond!" was the cry, a cry soon stifled when the column first halted, then about-faced and marched back toward the dense thickets and entrapments of the Wilderness. At about half past four, echoes like that of distant thunder rolled over us. Every man knew without being told that, before the day was out, he would likely face the enemy in the forbidding depths of the Wilderness. All men of sound judgment knew no battle should ever be fought there, but battle there would be savage and bloody. The fighting and dying had commenced anew—our time was at hand, and this thought both thrilled and terrified me.

"Close up, men." I heard the urgency in my own voice. "Keep the pace. We're needed at the front. Stay in line!" Otto was marching beside me. "It's going to get hot," I said, "very hot and very soon, I think."

"I think you're right, Sergeant. I hope I do well."

"You will, Otto. You were steady at Bristow, and Corporal Adams said you did well at Morton's Ford. This will be a much bigger fight."

"Thank you for teaching me to write, Sarge. I wrote my 'pocket letter' to my parents, as you suggested. It's right here," he added patting his chest.

I smiled at Otto's use of the phrase *pocket letter*, which I identified with Needham.

The road through the heart of the Wilderness was soon crowded with men and the material of war, wounded men, resting men, waiting men, supply wagons, artillery pieces, limber chests, and caissons. We weaved around and between them and marched onward until we came upon the Plank Road, which ran

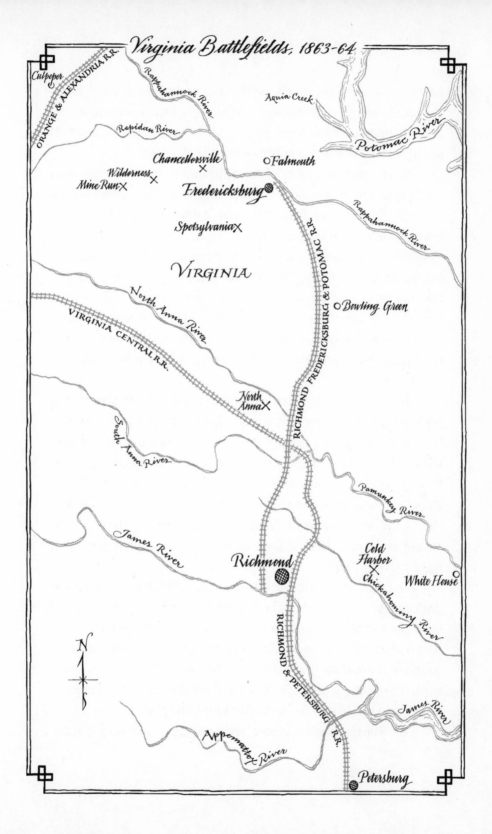

Virginia Battlefields, 1863-64

eastward toward Chancellorsville and westward toward Mine Run and Orange Courthouse. Hundreds of men were laboring to build breastworks along the left side of the road for hundreds of yards both north and south of the Plank Road.

"Fourteenth, left face!" The command came down just after we passed the crossroad. "Double line of battle, center on the Sharps." Companies A and B carried the rapid-firing breech-loading Sharps rifles, and their placement in the center of the line served as an anchor for the entire regiment. Four companies formed to the left of the Sharps men and four to the right. Under the supervision of Captain Simpson, I led the men of Company C to the far left of the line and deployed them in double ranks. At five o'clock a command was given. We vaulted over the rising breastworks and entered the densely wooded forests of the Wilderness.

The rattle of musketry came from somewhere ahead, but nothing could be seen. Close underbrush screened all but what was less than ten or twenty yards away. Onward we pressed. Musket balls cleaved the air above our heads and slapped into tree trunks. Yells and screams and, from time to time, the dreaded Rebel yell reached our ears. Bodies of Federal dead lay here and there; the walking wounded stumbled rearward through our strong and steady line. Volleys of musket fire erupted just out of sight in front of us.

We came up behind a line of men in blue firing into the darkness beyond. Muzzle flashes eerily silhouetted the forms of our men as they engaged in their deadly business. Some turned in panic at our approach, thinking perhaps the enemy had surrounded them, but "Friends! Friends!" we called out, and they turned back to the enemy. They fired off the last of their ammunition and made way for us to file into their places.

The Rebels saw us before we saw them and they fired a

volley at close range. A few of our men fell dead, several more were wounded.

"Steady, men, steady!" I called out. I raised my own rifle and took careful aim. "Fire!"

Many of our foes fell. The Rebels began to fall back, retreating slowly down a slope, turning to fire at us whenever they could. We pursued them, steadily driving them backward. After an advance of about two hundred yards, our officers called a halt. We lay down in the woods to avoid the Rebel sharpshooters and waited for night to fall.

After dark the men of Company C dug a shallow trench and piled branches and fallen logs atop the excavated earth. The position was as secure as the ground would allow. The men lay upon the low earthworks all night, muskets at the ready. Most fell quickly asleep, victims of fatigue. Not even the chilly night air or the occasional firing that flared from deep in the Wilderness disturbed their slumbers.

<figure>❦</figure>

"Brigade forward." Colonel Ellis ordered as soon as it was light enough to tell one tree from another. After a hundred paces we came upon a thin skirmish line. The Rebels fired a few shots hastily in our direction and disappeared into the forest. A few minutes later we came within sight of a line of enemy infantry behind a low barricade, much the same as the one we had built.

"Fire!" The crisp order of the Rebel officer carried clearly to my ears. Enemy muskets spewed bright flame; bullets struck home and more of our men fell.

"Forward," I cried, "Forward! Get them before they reload!" We ran ahead about ten paces to close the range and fired a tremendous volley into their ranks, striking many of them. The Rebel line wavered and began to fall back. They abandoned the barricade and retreated slowly, man by man, tree by tree, taking time to reload their muskets, taking deadly aim, and triggering off shot after shot at the advancing line of blue.

"I can't see them, Sergeant," Otto yelled. "There's no one to aim at."

"Fight Indian-style," I called out to anyone within earshot. Lessons from the previous year just a few miles distant had made me coldly proficient at the fine art of dealing with death within the thickets of the Wilderness. The time had come to take up the mantle of teacher.

"Stand behind a tree to load. Don't jump out to shoot. You won't see them if you look straight ahead. Look a little to the right or left and you'll see where they're hiding. Aim carefully— don't rush it. Make every shot count."

A minie ball zipped close by my head and slapped into a tree just behind me. "Otto! Look, over there to the right, thirty yards out, you can see about half of him leaning against that oak." Otto took careful aim at the half-hidden man and squeezed the trigger. The man slumped against the tree and did not move. Once again Otto had proven himself a quick study.

"Press on!" I cried. "Keep moving forward and drive them out of the forest. Press on!"

A line of Confederate reinforcements checked our advance. It was back and forth for about half an hour. Then an unseen battery of artillery opened up on us. Men began to fall all around. The men of the Fourteenth were forced to withdraw or risk being cut off. We fell back across a small clearing and took shelter among the trees just as the Rebels had done earlier.

"Stand with me!" Colonel Ellis cried above the din of battle. "Stand and do not yield, or the enemy will win the day! Rally on the Sharps, boys! Rally on the Sharps and give them all the lead you've got!"

The regiment reformed and started to pour a steady fire into the oncoming line of Rebels. One by one, other regiments in the brigade joined the fight and added the weight of their lead to the fight. Now it was the Rebels' line that wavered. They withdrew to the shelter of the trees on the other side of the clearing. Musket fire continued back and forth across that clearing for about another hour until nearly eight o'clock. When the men of General Birney's division came up to relieve us, the brigade returned to the Brock crossroad for a rest.

I had survived the Wilderness—no, more than survived. I had entered its depths in fear and emerged a victor. Its thick forests could be as much a friend as an enemy. We had met the Rebels on equal ground and driven them back.

"Well done," Colonel Ellis said as we sat beside the road drinking coffee. "You men followed orders under fire and fought well. But our work may not be done, so get some rest."

The colonel made his way over to the men of Company C. "Captain Simpson, your men were particularly steady this morning. You maintained your fire and did much damage to the enemy." I nodded slowly as I sipped my coffee. Yes, we had. It was about time.

The woods to the west from which we had just come suddenly erupted afresh with the din of battle. "Birney's boys are getting it now," Colonel Ellis said.

A rider clattered down the Plank Road. "Where's Hancock? Where's General Hancock?" he cried, his eyes wide with terror. Dozens of eager hands pointed to the general's headquarters near the crossroad.

An ammunition wagon drew up. Food and drink were cast aside as each man raced to fill his cap and cartridge boxes.

"Columns of four by company!" Colonel Ellis shouted a few minutes later. "We're going in again. Birney's men are being driven back. It's up to us to stop it. General Gibbon is counting on every man to do his duty today. We'll advance along the

309

road as far as possible, then move into the woods in support of Birney's division. Double-quick! Move out!"

The men of the Fourteenth ran up the Plank Road toward the fight, much as we had at Chancellorsville the year before. Once again the stream of walking wounded and slovenly shirkers parted before us and we ran until heavy musket and artillery fire from ahead forced us into the woods to the right of the road. Ten minutes of stumbling frantically through the underbrush brought us up behind Birney's men. I dripped with sweat; my head throbbed from the exertions. The Rebels had charged Birney's line and turned the left flank so that, when we arrived on the scene, the left end of the line was nearly surrounded. Birney's men were being fired upon from three sides.

"Charge!" ordered Colonel Ellis. We dashed forward and began firing into the flank of the Rebels. Our onslaught took them by surprise; our aim was true; many of the enemy fell. We fought fiercely, pushing the enemy back until the line was nearly restored to order. But we were only a single regiment and many of Birney's men, at least those who had remained in the fight, were nearly spent.

Our young color-bearer fell, seriously wounded. Lieutenant Colonel Moore picked up the fallen flag and waved it high. "Rally on the colors, boys! Rally on the colors!"

The Sharps companies maintained a rapid rate of fire and stood fast in the center of our line, causing the Rebels to veer right or left, thus increasing the pressure on either end of our line. At the left end, we were so hard-pressed that several times I had to order my men to fall back to avoid capture. Within twenty minutes, the line that had been nearly straight was bent in the shape of a horseshoe, the ends of which were being pressed ever more closely together. We were in great peril of being cut off from the rest of the army. The regiment was in a fight for its very existence. It was fight or die for every man.

"Surrender, Yanks!" yelled the Rebels. "We've got you! You're surrounded! There's no way out. Surrender or die!"

Was this to be the end of it? Was all I had endured and suffered for naught? Had God simply led me into this place and time to have me surrender? No, I had sworn to fight and fight I would—to the end, if need be, here and now—and it would be an honorable end. Sergeant Michael Palmer would not be sent off to die in some putrid prison camp.

"Steady, men!" Colonel Ellis called out above the clamor. "Steady! We're not whipped yet! Keep firing and make every shot count!" With a sharp, clear voice he gave order after order, withdrawing first one company, then another, pace by pace, keeping the regiment centered on the men with the Sharps rifles. We helped the wounded as well as we could, while facing the enemy and maintaining our rate of fire to keep them at bay. After retreating in this manner about three hundred yards, we were able to withdraw entirely from those dreadful woods back to the relative safety of the breastworks along the Brock Road. Once again, I had forayed into the Wilderness and emerged unscathed.

We could not have done more. Birney's men were relieved, the Rebel advance had been slowed, and the regiment had survived the desperate clutches of the enemy so it could fight another day. We were totally spent, exhausted, hungry, thirsty, and almost out of ammunition for the second time that day. But it was not yet noontime, and there was much of that day yet to be devoted to battle.

The fighting in the western woods raged for another hour or two. Panicked troops from other brigades and divisions flooded out of the woods and leaped over the works, happy to have survived their latest sojourn in the thickets. "They're coming," they cried. "Get ready. They're right behind us. Longstreet's Corps, and lots of them."

But Longstreet's horde did not come screaming from the woods. In fact, the fighting nearly ceased altogether, and an uneasy hush fell over the Union line along the Brock Road. Colonel Carroll reassembled his brigade and ordered all of the regimental commanders to send their men to the rear for rest and refitting. We marched a few hundred yards down the Plank Road in the direction of Chancellorsville to pass a peaceful afternoon, while the men still in place along the Brock Road set to work improving their fortifications.

It was about four o'clock in the afternoon that I first smelled the smoke, the not-at-all unpleasant scent of burning leaves and forest timber. I peered down the road toward the breastworks. Wisps of light gray smoke curled above the trees and drifted over the Federal line on a gentle, westerly breeze.

"Look there," I said, jumping to my feet. "The forest is on fire. Maybe it's only the underbrush, but there's a lot of dry timber."

Minute by minute the smoke increased, first in several steady plumes that roiled above the trees, then in a dense, heavy cloud that enshrouded that entire portion of the Wilderness. All stood and craned their necks to see what was happening. A low wall of flame, roughly parallel to the Brock Road, fanned and driven by the breeze, marched inexorably out of the tree line toward the stout works our men had so diligently built. The flames came to the base of the breastworks and rejoiced at the dry timbers they found to consume. Within a few minutes a long section of the barricade was engulfed, and our troops had no choice but to retreat in the face of such an assault.

"Look at those sly devils!" Jim Adams shouted. "They're jumping through the flames." Rebel infantry had used the fire as a screen, and as soon as the flames had captured our works, the Rebels secured the advantage. Hundreds of screaming, smoking figures vaulted over the barricade through the flames and set about shooting and bayoneting as many of our astonished men as they could. The shock of this unexpected attack sent our men reeling. The enemy had achieved a breakthrough; the Army of the Potomac was in great hazard of being split in two.

"On your feet, men. Load and prime! Fix bayonets!" Colonel Carroll himself screamed the order. "To the breach, men! We've got to close it. No rest for any man as long as any of those fiends remain alive within our works! Forward! Double-double-quick!"

We raced full tilt down the road toward the enemy and turned sharply to the left when we neared the crossroad. A thousand or more Rebels had packed themselves into a space about two hundred yards wide, with thousands of angry Federals both to the right and to the left. Heavy guns opened up on them at point-blank range. The yells of the Rebels died in their throats as they realized the full gravity of their situation. Colonel Carroll directed us across the opening in the Federal line, thus closing off our foe's only avenue of advance. It took only a few minutes to dress our lines.

Then the big guns fell silent.

"Fire!" screamed Colonel Carroll. Hundreds fell to the lead of our musket balls.

"Charge!" our leader screamed again. It was a brief but desperate and bloody fight. We ran forward, bayonets at the ready. Some threw down their weapons and started to raise their hands. We ran right through them, knocking them down with the butts of our rifles. Other Rebels who still had fight in them were run through with steel; some were bayoneted several times at once. Out of the corner of my eye, I saw Jim thrusting and parrying with both the bayonet and the Bowie as he slashed his way through any that stood before him.

A few survivors stumbled backward toward the barricade. A sergeant in gray planted a foot upon one of the timbers as if to clamber over it, but his foot slipped as he did so. With a great heave the sergeant threw his rifle over the works into the woods beyond. Then he tried to climb the works again. I lunged forward. My bayonet pierced him through between the shoulder blades, pinning him to the still hot and smoking timber. The man screamed in agony. I smelled the pungent odor of burning flesh. I twisted and pulled my rifle, trying to dislodge my bayonet, but I had driven it fast into the timber. I pulled again and again, each time causing the man further anguish, but it was no use. I could do nothing for the man but watch him scream and die.

Our third and final battle of the day was over in less than fifteen minutes. It was indeed a great victory, but I felt in no way the victor. Later in the evening, after darkness had fallen, we were sent to occupy a portion of the works along the Brock Road while those troops marched away to the south. Coffee and supper were fixed; then we lay our blankets out upon the ground.

I had fought well that day, very well. So had the others in the company. The colonel himself had commended us. We had given to the enemy as good as they had given to us. It was in every way what I had most desired: a fair fight, face-to-face, man-to-man. And yet I began to weep. I turned over and lay flat upon my stomach, using the crook of my arm as a pillow. I had killed several more men that day. Indeed, I had felt no malice toward any of them, nor any anger — I had just killed them. It was war. I was under orders. It's what I was supposed to do. But the tears came all the more readily as I thought about my latest victim. It had all been so effortless charging into that line of Rebels. Somehow, I knew exactly what to do, every blow of the rifle butt, every thrust of the bayonet, with no conscious thought, as if it was the most natural of acts. And this, I believe, I found most terrifying of all.

Lord God above, please hear this one prayer. Please take my life before I take another.

CHAPTER 31

The Mule Shoe

He brought me up also out of an horrible pit,
out of the miry clay.
PSALM 40:2

THE TWO ARMIES TRUDGED SEVERAL MILES DOWN THE BROCK Road to the southeast near Spotsylvania Courthouse, only to grind together again like two giant millstones with the men in blue and gray providing the grist for the mill. Tuesday afternoon, May 10th, the men of Carroll's brigade were called upon to assault a line of breastworks atop Laurel Hill. Colonel Ellis ordered Captain Simpson to scout the Rebel line.

"What do you think, Sergeant?" Captain Simpson called from his place behind a large red cedar about twenty feet to my left.

Similarly positioned, I surveyed the ground beyond the edge of the grove. "It looks like Mine Run all over again, except the slope is steeper and the distance is shorter, and there's abatis along the entire length."

"But can we succeed, Sergeant? Can we take the position as ordered?"

Always speak truth to officers, Sergeant Needham had counseled, *because your lives are in their hands.* "No, sir, we cannot. If we press it, sir, it will be another Fredericksburg."

"My thoughts exactly, Sergeant."

Captain Simpson's report made no difference and the assault began at four o'clock. It was much as I had predicted, and in some ways even worse. Rebel guns opened on the cedar grove as soon as the brigade entered it. Incendiary shells set fire to the carpet beneath our feet. Here and there one of the sap-filled trees burst into flames like a giant torch. I had seen the cedar grove as the last refuge before the terrors of the open land beyond, but it quickly became another source of peril. Hot flames licked at our feet, acrid smoke filled our lungs, and the cedar trees themselves seemed to have turned against us as their sharp branches tore at our clothing and stabbed at our skin, drawing first blood in this battle.

"Fourteenth! Double-quick!" Colonel Ellis ordered as we neared the tree line.

"Let's go, men," I cried. "Don't tarry even for a moment. There's nothing to fire at, so just stay low and don't stop." Through a storm of shots and bullet, the men of Carroll's brigade ducked and weaved farther and farther up the slope, all the way up to the row of abatis that guarded the approach to the Rebels' works. Hundreds more of our men were added to the ranks of the slain and grievously wounded who yet remained on that field from earlier assaults. Advancing beyond the abatis was impossible, and there we stayed, under heavy fire all the while, firing up at the enemy's fortifications until all of our ammunition was expended. Then it was every man for himself, as we bobbed and weaved and tumbled back down the slope to the shelter of the smoldering cedar grove.

I turned to gaze back up the hill. The carpet of dead and wounded was fuller now as far as I could see to the right and to the left. Fires started by the shelling spread quickly across dry, grassy fields. Here and there hideous screams arose as flames engulfed those unable to escape them. I turned away, eyes stinging from smoke and tears.

As calm as Jim Adams was in battle, he was just the opposite as we sat about our fire that night, waiting for the coffee to boil. "Nothing's changed, Michael, nothing at all."

"What do you mean?" asked Otto.

"Grant's in charge now and we're losing more men than ever. Battalions and whole regiments are being added to make up for our losses. This afternoon's charge was the same idiocy we've seen too much of."

"True," I said. "It was useless and nothing was gained. Only a week ago I had high hopes for Grant and this new campaign, but I heard he was watching us today. Our lives are meaningless. I've given up all hope of surviving this war. I've escaped too many times. And Grant won't stop. There will be no retreats, no withdrawals for rest and healing. We'll be back at it soon, maybe tomorrow, or maybe Thursday or Friday."

⋞⋗⋌⋗

I was proven correct. The brigade marched again in the dank and foggy blackness of Wednesday night. No man could say with any surety if he was marching north or south, east or west, toward the foe or away from him. It took all of our efforts, both mentally and physically, to follow the narrow road through the woods, treading in the footprints of the man in front, hoping that somewhere up ahead someone knew where we were going.

A faint glow penetrated the darkness; a watchman tended a signal fire at an intersection, posted there to steer the troops onto a lane that turned off to the right. An hour more brought us to what seemed to be a clearing around a farmstead. I could sense rather than see the presence of many men, perhaps thousands, gathered in the fields that surrounded the farmhouse.

"We're assembling for a dawn assault," Colonel Ellis said in a hushed voice. "The enemy line in this sector bulges outward in the shape of a mule shoe." Beside me, Otto muttered a low curse at the mere mention of the hated animal. "The entire Second Corps will attack the apex of the mule shoe works at dawn, and by God, we'll have them. They won't see us coming until it's too late, and not a shot will be fired until we're in their works. There will be three lines of assault with General Barlow's division first, then General Birney's division, and this division third. We'll drive in after the others to support them and hold their gains. It will be a tough and bloody fight, but this war could very well end today if every man of this corps does his duty."

Rain began to fall, lightly at first and then more heavily. The waiting thousands could do nothing but continue to stand and wait for the signal to advance, churning the ground under their stamping feet to mud. "Keep your powder dry," was passed up and down through the ranks several times, and "Don't load your muskets until we're about to move out."

The deep darkness brightened just a little, then a little more. Dawn was approaching, but it would not be one of those glorious, sun-streaked auroras that inspired the pens of many a bard. No, it would be a perfectly dismal day for killing and dying with low, gloomy clouds, heavy rains, and persistent fog.

No order was heard, but certainly one was given. Shadowy ranks of men to the front started forward into the trees at the edge of the farmland; the forms of individual men were indistinguishable given the gloom and distance.

"Third Brigade, march." The order was repeated in hoarse whispers down the line by regimental and company officers. We stepped off to follow the thousands who had marched a few minutes earlier. The only sounds were the tramp of thousands of feet upon the muddy earth, the muffled clanking that invariably accompanies even a small body of troops on the march, and the heavy patter of raindrops that continued to fall.

We were still moving through a thick stand of trees when the firing started. First there were only a few shots here and there, then hundreds, then a roar. The first line had surely reached the mule shoe and the fight was on. Several minutes later we marched out of the woods and onto the broad strip of cleared land that led up to the Rebel line.

Barlow's men had indeed surprised the enemy. With a rush and a yell they had vaulted onto and over the works. Startled from sleep, many Confederates tried to fire their weapons only to find their powder damp and useless while our boys poured hot lead into them. Rebels by the hundred fell before Barlow's charging troops; thousands more threw down their weapons and surrendered on the spot.

Birney's division jumped over the works and added their weight to the melee, forcing those Confederates still unwilling to yield backward yard by yard. Prisoners streamed back toward our line, and there was nothing to do except round them up and send them under guard back to the farmhouse we had just left.

The Second Corps continued to drive the Rebels, a hundred yards, then two hundred, then a quarter mile or more. It was magnificent. Perhaps the war *would* be won on this fine and dreary day. Orders were passed along for the brigades of Gibbon's division to spread out and occupy the reverse side of the works the Rebels had just abandoned. "Dig in and secure the line—just in case," Colonel Ellis told us.

"Dig, boys, dig!" I screamed. "Dig as though your very lives depend on it, because they do. Dig deep and dig hard! Make this side of the works every bit as stout as the other. If Barlow's and Birney's boys get turned around, they'll be needing a place to hide."

And they did get turned around. Thousands of fresh Confederates poured into the breach and checked the Federal advance. The fighting became hot and furious and our boys were gradually beaten back. Not more than an hour after pouring over the works in hot pursuit of the fleeing Rebels, Barlow's and Birney's men began vaulting and tumbling back over those same works, but now those breastworks protected us as much as they did the enemy and a deadly stalemate developed along that part of the battle line.

Crouched low on our side, we could see nothing of an enemy who lay crouched equally low only several feet away. If one of our men suddenly discovered a wellspring of courage lacking in the rest of us, he would rise up and fire his musket over the top of the barricade, but it was a risky undertaking, and he was more than likely to return to crouching with the rest, albeit now bleeding or even dying. On our side of the works, fresh troops trained loaded and cocked muskets at the top of the barricade.

"Show yourself, Johnnie!" we dared the Rebels.

"How 'bout showin' yourself, Yank?" the Johnnies taunted in return.

Many on both sides dared, perhaps thinking they could move faster than a bullet, but they were dead wrong. Men fell where they were struck, collapsing into the muddy trenches, and there was nothing for the living to do but crouch atop their departed brothers and fight on.

A trick the Rebels used was to stick their rifles over the top of the barricade while holding onto just the butt and the trigger so they could fire down at us. "Grab the barrel," I told my men. "Grab it, push it back at him and give it a quick yank." Several Rebel muskets were stolen in this way, yet they kept employing this tactic until one of the Rebs thrust his weapon over the works in Otto's vicinity. Otto gave the man's musket such a tremendous tug that the startled Reb came flopping over the works and into our trench directly beside Otto.

This bloody stalemate dragged on for the rest of the day. A few hundred yards out of sight to the right, an even more desperate struggle developed. Along a portion of the western side of the mule shoe breastworks, Union troops from the Fifth and Sixth Corps were locked in a bitter struggle with Confederates keen on throwing the invading Yankees out of the works they had so recently occupied. Each side threw more and more men into the fight and the numbers of dead and wounded mounted all day long. There were several times when the men in our sector on both sides simply sat awestruck at the din of the fighting, the constant roar of musketry and artillery, screams and shouts, and indistinguishable clamor. The fighting lasted far into the night, finally lapsing into restless silence at about three o'clock Friday morning.

⋘⋙

With the first gray streaks of dawn, our officers started to rouse the men. "It's too quiet over there," Captain Simpson said, gesturing toward the Rebel side of the works. "We need to find out what they're up to, Sergeant."

"I think they're gone, sir. I heard some voices and a bit of commotion about an hour ago."

"We need to know for sure, Sergeant. Take a squad and find out if they have indeed withdrawn."

"Sir, yes, sir."

I rounded up the remaining men from our dwindling Company C. I found Otto and five or six others, but Jim Adams was nowhere to be found. Perhaps he had been wounded and had gone to the rear for treatment. Perhaps like countless others he had become separated during the confusion of battle and the light of day would help him find his way back. No matter; it was a simple mission.

"No heroes now," I told the squad. "Just spread out about twenty yards apart. Creep up to the works and peer over. We only need to know if the Rebs are still there. Sing out if you see any."

It was just as I expected; the Rebels had left. Not a living soul could be seen on their side of the earthworks, but as I was turning rearward to report to Captain Simpson, something very strange caught my eye. About fifty yards to my right, at a point in the line where our works were nearly indistinguishable from those of the enemy, two men stood locked together in an embrace of death atop the works. The Confederate had raised his rifle high to thrust the bayonet downward into the chest of the Union man, while the Federal had struck lower, driving what appeared to be a large knife into his opponent just below the man's ribs.

I knew without further inspection who the dead Federal was, but I crept closer to the pair all the same. Each man leaned slightly into the other; frozen hands still clasped weapons. The head of the dead Rebel lay against his left shoulder; his face cast downward and away from me. The Federal faced his opponent directly, eyes open and fixed, his frozen, gaping face a vivid testimony to the surprise of his enemy's thrust, yet the man was familiar just the same. Had not Jim been with us last night? When had this happened? He must have remained alert, while others had slept, and spotted the Johnnie trying to sneak across to do us harm. Neither had cried out to raise the alarm; a silent struggle in the night had ended each man's war.

❖

Colonel Carroll rode up and down the line, ordering the brigade to form two lines of battle. "We must find out where the enemy has gone, if they have withdrawn in retreat or if they have fallen back to another line of works. We'll advance until we discover their present location, but we will not give them battle."

The colonel led the brigade southward through the interior

of the war-ravaged mule shoe. I wished not to look at the devastation, for I knew what I had already seen would remain with me for whatever days remained of my life. But it was impossible to shut my eyes to the heaps of dead men and animals. It was impossible to shut my ears to the groans of those who yet lived. It was impossible to seal my nose and mouth against the rising stench that enveloped the place.

Suddenly Colonel Carroll was knocked off his horse. He tried to stand; his right arm dangled uselessly at his side. Several men helped carry him to the rear. His war was done too and we would see him no more. Colonel Ellis and the other regimental commanders continued on and led us several hundred yards farther. The scenes of destruction passed, the ground beneath our feet became firmer and even grass covered in places — ahead was land green and verdant. Several Rebel guns opened on us; the shells either flew over our heads or fell short. A little farther and musket balls began to kick up the dirt in front of us. A drifting cloud of powder smoke hung above a dark line of breastworks atop a low ridge to the south.

"There they are, boys, sitting and waiting for us," Colonel Ellis shouted. "Our work is done. Fall back to our works."

We retraced our steps back to the mule shoe, back to the mud and gore, back to coming face-to-face with the horror of it. As we neared the corpse-filled trenches once again, my weary eyes focused on the most dismal and terrible sight of this man's war. About twenty feet away, rising out of the drying mud, was the bare forearm of a man, its fingers frozen half-clenched as if grasping for something, for a friend, for air, for life, or for heaven. I stared unmoving for some time, trying to determine whether the arm had been severed from its owner, or whether the rest of the man's corpse had been interred deep in the mud.

I could not go on. I was at my end. I took a few wavering steps over to the remains of a tree that had been shredded by an endless stream of musket balls and sat down heavily. I leaned against the shattered stump and stared at that arm.

"Sarge, are you all right?"

"I'm done, Otto, completely done."

I slept for about half an hour until Otto gently nudged me awake.

"Sarge? Sarge? Burial details have been by twice asking if you were dead."

"Not yet," I said, "but it may not be long."

"What do you mean, Sarge?"

"I've tried to see any sign of God's hand in this slaughter, but I don't. Perhaps He's finally abandoned us to reap the full harvest of what we have sown. How can anyone outlive this wicked war?"

Otto helped me to my feet and remained by my side as we walked back over that dreadful ground. Once or twice he reached out his hand to steady me when the footing seemed particularly treacherous.

"Sarge, I think I saw something move over there," Otto said, pointing off to the left. "There it is again. Do you see it?"

I bent my head in the direction Otto was pointing and strained to see what had caught his attention. I saw only a carnage-filled trench where corpses were piled several deep, a grisly testament to the fury of the battle, as the still living fought atop the bodies of the fallen, and who knew if there were others more deeply interred in the blood-red mud. "No, Otto, I don't see anything."

"Stay here, Sarge. I'll go have a look."

Otto went and peered down into the trench. He called out something I could not hear. A moment later he was beckoning wildly for me to join him.

"There's somebody down there, Sarge. I heard him groan and he moved a little. We have to help him."

It was the last thing I wished to do. It was brutal and nasty work, and Otto did most of it, given my weakened state. Bullet-riddled corpses filled the trench, Federal or Confederate we knew not which. There was no way to lift them except through close physical contact with each corpse and soon we were covered head to toe with mud and gore, indistinguishable from the dead except that we still moved and breathed. As Otto reached down to take hold of one body by the hand, the hand gripped Otto's in return.

"Thank you," said a faint, raspy voice.

It took a few minutes to free the man's arms and legs. He had been shot once in the side, but he did not so much as whimper when Otto grabbed him under the armpits and hoisted him out of the trench.

"Thanks, Yanks," the man said humbly. "Thought I'd be gone soon."

"What's your name? What's your unit?" I asked.

"Private Denny Allen, Tenth Louisiana, Stafford's Brigade, but I guess my war is done."

"It is," I said. "We'll take you back to the hospital."

"Might I have just a minute before we go?" the prisoner asked. I nodded grudgingly.

Private Allen fell to his knees beside the trench that had nearly been his grave, hands clasped tightly before him, head bowed low. For several minutes he moved not a muscle, save for his lips, which mumbled a penitent prayer heard only above.

Private Allen talked all the way back through our lines to the hospital. "Thought I was a Christian before, even been baptized, but I probably weren't till now. All my life I've heard many a sermon about the cross of Jesus and how I should look only to the cross. Well, I didn't pay much heed and pretty much thought I could do as I pleased. But last night, under that heap of dead men, when I couldn't so much as open one eye, let alone two,

I saw nothing but that cross before me, and I tell you, I was at peace, even when I figured I was about to breathe my last. Then one of you boys grabbed my hand. You boys saved my body from that pit, but the Lord saved the soul of this worm of a sinner. Praise be!"

I say unto you, that likewise joy shall be in heaven over one sinner that repenteth. Indeed, Otto seemed very pleased with our prisoner's confession. I remained silent.

CHAPTER 32

Assault at Cold Harbor

Eye hath not seen, nor ear heard,
neither have entered into the heart of man,
the things which God hath prepared
for them that love him.

1 CORINTHIANS 2:9

June 2nd, 1864
Camp of the 14th Conn. Vol. Rgt. Inf.
Cold Harbor, Virginia (near Richmond)

My Dearest Jessie Anne,

It has been four weeks since I last wrote to you. I am as well as can be expected, given the constant marching and fighting the army has been engaged in. I am not injured, nor am I ill, and I have sufficient food for my need. However, I am weary to the bone and wish for none other than to be done with this business one way or another. That I have more than fourteen months service remaining weighs all the more heavily upon me with each passing day. Pray with me that all of this might soon end.

In your last letter you wrote that Abby has agreed to allow Mr. Allerton to call on her. At first I thought this an inappropriate development, but I could find nothing reasonable to support my position and upon further reflection, I have come to see some merit in it. It may be that as I have always considered Abby to be John's wife, I shall need to revise my thinking and more kindly regard her happiness and the welfare of her children. Truly I would wish such happiness for you should I also depart this life.

Of the four men who left Naugatuck aboard that train so long ago, I alone still live. After a long, hard day of fighting near Spotsylvania Courthouse on May 12th that continued well into the night, Jim Adams was set upon by one of the enemy. In the fight Jim also killed his foe. Another good friend and soldier is in the ground. I wrote to Jim's parents a day or two after he was killed to express my sympathies, but if you meet them about town, please greet them and tell them personally how much I valued Jim. He was a soldier among soldiers and a trusted friend.

Charlie Merrills met with some trouble several weeks ago. He has not revealed the nature of it, but it possibly stems from an incident at a band concert back in April that aroused the ire of several officers. Although I know not the details, I am given to understand it was sufficiently serious for Charlie to be removed from his position as principal musician. He was reduced to the rank of private in my company, and now carries a rifle instead of a cornet, but he is not skilled as a soldier, and I try to place him in the rear ranks when possible.

No doubt the newspapers have followed our advances and have printed digests of the battles. The 14th has seen much fighting, and the men have given a good account of themselves. But our fighting strength has been reduced to less than two hundred again. Company C has only seventeen men fit for duty besides myself. In spite of this loss, everyone here believes the enemy has suffered even more severely. We have not retreated; our advances have not been reversed. We are at the doorstep of Richmond and I cannot believe the enemy can sustain this war much longer.

Indeed, I cannot sustain this effort much longer. Periods of rest do little good, and true sleep has been unknown to me for the last month. My strength is never renewed – every day it seems what strength I do possess is gone before I rise. Perhaps tomorrow it will all end, or the next day.

Until the end I remain ever faithfully
your affectionate and devoted husband,

Michael G. Palmer

A hand gently touched my shoulder. "Sergeant," Captain Simpson said in a low voice, "it's time to waken the men. You know the usual measures — no fires, no noise, no anything — and have them very quietly check and load their weapons and fix bayonets. Not a sound."

"Yes, sir, Captain," I said, getting to my feet, "not a sound. This means we're going in, then?"

"Yes, Sergeant, and it's going to get brutal in a hurry. The Rebs have been to this ball too many times not to know the steps to the dance. They know how fond General Grant has become of attacking at dawn, so they have to know we're coming."

"Captain?"

"Yes, Sergeant?"

"If I should fall ..."

"Say no more, Sergeant. I know. There are things of which old soldiers like us no longer need to speak. We know what's required. Say nothing of this to the men, but last night when our orders came down, Colonel Ellis said, 'The Fourteenth will do its duty as always, but there won't be any heroes made tomorrow.' I'm not sure what he meant by that and he wouldn't elaborate."

Rousing slumbering soldiers was a thankless duty at any time, but on this morning, with prospects only for battle with no coffee or breakfast, I knew the men would be particularly ill-tempered. Indeed the only "Good morning, Sergeant Palmer" I heard was from Otto. Under normal circumstances I would have ordered my corporal to do it, but in the three weeks since Jim's death, the regiment had been either on the march, in line of battle, or in an advanced picket position, so no corporal had yet been named for Company C.

It was Friday, June 3rd, and the armies were now pitted against each other about seven miles east of Richmond at a village called Cold Harbor. The predawn darkness was nearly total, but I guessed it to be about three o'clock. A light mist was falling. Up and down the line of the Second Corps, which ran from near the crossroad in the center of the village one and one-half miles to the south, the men arose and did as they were ordered, albeit with a fair amount of muted cursing and grumbling. At three-thirty a silent signal was given to fall into line. All was in readiness to once again step off into the leaden gale of death, and yet something was amiss.

⋘∽⋙

Sergeant Needham had been correct; the fear was always there, that anxiety of spirit and dread of the future when one could not say what the next few minutes or hours might have in store. It sometimes felt so close I could feel it lay hold of my shoulder, at times sharply, startling me with its swiftness, at other times gently, as a friend might do. Rather than panic, this fear was a building apprehension within me that often made itself manifest through restlessness deep in my soul, strain upon my emotions that caused both tears and giddy humor to be more frequent, and tension within the tendons and sinews of my body, so that no part of my being escaped its influence.

It seemed that fear would ever be my master, always tapping into the sap of my soul and draining it from me. We had

330

marched shoulder to shoulder away from the encampment at Stony Mountain only a month previous. Through the thickets of the Wilderness fear had gone with me, and it was there, and only there, and only for a few brief hours, that I thought him to be my servant. Indeed, there I seemed to feed upon his vitality, until the horrors of Spotsylvania finally revealed him to be the most traitorous of companions.

Thankfully, my fear would sometimes retreat a short distance into the shadows beside the roadside. Respite came when the Second Corps marched away from Spotsylvania after nightfall on May 20th. Three weeks of fighting had taken its toll— nearly one in three of the eager, confident men who had begun the campaign were now dead, wounded, or missing. Heavy artillery units from Washington's defenses exchanged their guns and limbers for rifles and cartridge boxes and were hurried to the front. With their uniforms bright and unsullied, these untried troops were easily spotted, and no one knew what to expect of them when the clamor of battle arose and hot metal filled the air.

My dreaded companion kept his distance for a few days as we marched south to Bowling Green, then southwest to the Telegraph Road at Carmel Church, but he closed ranks once again the morning of May 24th, when the brigade sprinted across a crude timber bridge over the North Anna River and once more found an imposing line of entrenchments blocking our way. Heavy skirmishing developed as we tested the enemy's strength and they tested ours, but no pitched battle developed.

The night of May 26th, as we withdrew north of the river, my anxiety abated once again. As before, we marched east and south, drawing ever nearer the coveted Confederate capital. Again the Rebels were waiting for us behind stout works as we approached Totopotomoy Creek from the north on May 30th. We drove their pickets across to the south side of the creek, pushed across ourselves, and then entrenched. Three days of artillery duels and deadly sharpshooting ensued. Other than picketing and digging, there was nothing to do in the hot, humid weather but to keep quiet and keep out of sight.

Nightfall on June 1st saw the Second Corps on the march again, again to the east and south to Cold Harbor. The distance traveled was not great, only about eight miles, but the night remained exceedingly warm and sticky, and the hot sun had baked the roads dry. Powdery clouds of dust covered me from head to toe, nearly choking the breath out of me, in spite of the kerchief over my face. It was impossible to see more than a few feet ahead. What should have been accomplished before sunrise lasted well into the next day. The Fourteenth filed into line about one-quarter mile south of the crossroad at about noon on June 2nd and waited to see what would happen next.

⋖⋗⋗⋖

I shifted my weight from one foot to the other, waiting for the signal to advance. Yes, something was definitely amiss. At first, I could not identify what precisely this strange sensation was, or its cause, but something was not as it should be. The men in the ranks were standing quietly, fidgeting as they always did. Because of the trees to our front I could not see our objective, but this was often the case, especially upon a damp and misty dawn. Otto was beside me in line as he always was, now that Jim was gone, and Charlie was in the second line a little to the left. Everything was as it should have been, yet something was still amiss. I contemplated this peculiar feeling for some time, examining several more possible causes, until it finally became clear to me.

The fear was gone. It was not among the dark shadows of the trees, nor was it taking coffee by the side of the road, ready to jump to my side when the killing began. It was really and truly gone. I was completely unafraid of what was about to transpire.

"Run away from that man as fast as you can," Sarge had said, and yet my body was limber and relaxed, my mind clear and alert, and my soul was perfectly at peace.

I had been spared too often while others close at hand had perished. I knew the perils I would shortly face, and I acknowledged the nearness of my own death, but there was no terror in this realization. What a gift from God, I thought. Oh, what comfort! Oh, what a blessed mercy it will be to go into battle fearless of the outcome.

At exactly half past four, a gun behind our lines fired a single shot. The long double line of blue soldiers stepped forward and the assault began. Our line advanced into a patch of dense forest. The branches of the trees seemed to envelop me. Were these the enfolding arms of Almighty God? Was He really so close at hand watching over me and guiding every step? My composure was absolute; my face was set for battle; my step was sure in the serene confidence that no harm could befall me that day.

I approached the edge of the woods. A few hundred yards ahead, atop a low ridge, I could now easily make out the dark earthen gash that marked the Rebels' works. Battle raged up and down the line as Confederate artillery and infantry mercilessly poured hot iron and lead into our troops advancing over open ground both north and south of the woods. As our brigade stepped from the protection of the trees, deadly missiles filled the air all around us.

"Step lively and stay low, boys," Captain Simpson shouted. "Move up toward those works and don't stop." When I echoed the order, the steadiness of my own voice surprised me.

We ran at a crouch up that slope, ten, twenty, thirty yards. Bullets whined past all around me, some plucked at my clothing, stinging my flesh. *In the shadow of Thy wings will I make my refuge, until these calamities be overpast.* Oh, the security of that Mighty Hand swatting every bullet aside and carrying me forward. On we ran, fifty yards, seventy-five, then a hundred. Men started to fall as we rushed up that hill.

"Fourteenth! Halt!" Colonel Ellis's strident voice carried clearly above the din. "Fourteenth, dig in!" he screamed. "Dig for your lives!"

I opened my mouth to repeat the order.

Something akin to a hammer blow knocked my right leg out from under me. I fell heavily to the ground, rolled, and pitched face down. Moist earth filled my mouth. I spat and gasped for air. Sharpest agony enshrouded me. I cried out and tried to stand; my leg would not obey my will; every effort only doubled my suffering. I clenched my teeth against the pain.

There, it is finished. Just a few moments more and the blood and pain and tears will be gone forever. The light dimmed, then brightened, then dimmed again.

How long or short a time I lay there, I know not. *Lord, be merciful to me, a wretched sinner ... upward, ever upward into glory ... only a moment's wait for bliss eternal ... dear Jessie Anne, until we meet again.* And then it happened, just as I had hoped and prayed. Strong, loving arms gently enfolded me, bearing me upward, lifting me ever so slowly from the earth. *Lord, I have shed innocent blood. Why sendest Thine angels to escort me heavenward? They shall mount up as on wings of eagles.* Surely, this must be preferred above even Elijah's transport. Just a few seconds longer ...

There was a heavy blow to my abdomen, and the last of my breath was crushed out of me. A terrible scream brought a sudden end to my idyllic illusions, perhaps a demon from hell shrieking at the sight of one more sinner escaping his clutches.

"I'm sorry, Sarge, but I need to get you to a surgeon." That wretched scream had been my own as Otto hoisted me over his shoulder. He set off at a heavy, loping trot; each of his weighty footfalls sending a shock of searing torment coursing throughout my body and eliciting groan after groan of deepest anguish.

334

"I'm sorry, Sarge ... I'm sorry, Sarge," Otto repeated every few yards as I watched large drops of dark red blood fall in a steady stream from the toe of my right boot.

"I'm sorry, Sarge," I heard Otto say one last time. We had reached the safety of the dark woods. Now, a much deeper, more ominous darkness overtook me, and the last thing I saw before I succumbed to its power was a huge pair of Hickham's boots plodding quickly but surely to the rear.

CHAPTER 33

Her Husband's Crown

Who can find a virtuous woman?
for her price is far above rubies.
PROVERBS 31:10

LAMES ONCE AGAIN LICKED AT MY FEET AS I WORKED MY WAY closer to the tree line at the base of Laurel Hill. Acrid smoke stung my eyes, drawing tears. A hail of bullets tore at the branches of the cedars on either side. Every musket was loaded and capped, bayonets gleamed in the sunlight that filtered through the trees. Officers screamed orders in anticipation of the charge everyone knew was coming. Confederates atop the hill watched intently for any sign of movement in the tree line below, their every gun trained on us.

Colonel Carroll raised his saber high.

"Charge!" rang the command up and down the line.

A thump on my shoulder. I flinched at the pain soon to follow, but it was a warm, gentle hand that had touched me. "Michael." A voice that did not belong—a woman's voice, a sweet voice. "Michael, where are you?"

The clamor abated, the flames and smoke receded. I turned away from the heat and flame. Jessie Anne stood beside me, leaning down to look into my face. "Michael, where were you? Which battle were you fighting this time?"

I turned back to gaze into the embers of the fireplace. My cold, unlit pipe drooped from my lips. As if of their own volition, rather than any conscious will, my shoulders shrugged.

"That's your response? A shrug of the shoulders? Is that all you'll allow me today?"

I did not, could not respond.

Jessie Anne drew up a chair and sat down beside me. Then she took my hand in hers.

"You know, Michael, I've asked myself that question hundreds of times; Where are you? I've never told you this, and perhaps I shouldn't tell you now, but I grieved for you every day you were gone. No, I didn't go about weeping into my kerchief all the time—I was too busy with the children and the store for that. But there was a vast empty place deep inside me, and I couldn't do a thing about it. It was very much as if you had died. You were just ... gone."

We spent the next few minutes in silence.

"Do you know what today is?" Jessie Anne asked.

"Saturday?"

"Yes, Saturday, and what sort of day is it?"

"What sort of day?"

"Is it cloudy or sunny or raining or snowing?"

"I think it's cloudy today, maybe snow later."

"No, the sun is shining and the day is mild. The snow has melted and the crocus and daffodils are peeking out. The beauty of springtime is appearing all around us." She paused for a moment before asking me the next question. "What's today's date?"

I stared blankly at the hearthstone.

"Today is the thirteenth of March," Jessie Anne said. "It's Sarah's birthday, Michael."

I lifted my head to look at her. "Yes, it is, the thirteenth of March."

"And do you know how old she is?"

"Nine, I think." Her fierce look told me I was wrong. "No, ten years old."

"She's thirteen! She's becoming a young woman, and you haven't seen it. Edward will be nine next month and little James is almost three." Jessie Anne looked directly into my eyes; her sorrow was evident, even to me. "Believe me when I tell you that I count it a small miracle that James was ever conceived. Do you understand what I'm saying, Michael?"

I nodded slowly. "But my leg ..."

"Yes, I know, Michael, your leg was buried in Virginia, but were you buried there as well? Where's the man who could always make me laugh? I can't remember the last time I heard you laugh. No, your leg healed long ago, years ago. You have been home four-and-a-half years." Every syllable of these last words was sharp and distinct. "Last fall you went to New York to see Doctor Hudson again. With this new leg you're getting about quite well. Your leg is as good as it's ever going to be, so stop blaming all your troubles on your leg."

"I'm sorry, dear, I'll try—"

"When you're at the store the work seems to occupy you, but if not for Otto, the store would go bankrupt and we would live in the street. It used to be that people at church would ask if there was anything amiss with you. Now they never ask, and you have declined Reverend Bainbridge's attempts to speak with you."

"He's very young. What does he know? I preferred Reverend Preston."

"Well, he's been dead two years, and Reverend Bainbridge preaches the Word. I know the war was terrible, Michael, but where is the man I married? Where is the wonderful, loving man

I knew before the war? You may have lost your right leg, but I lost my husband. Why have you not returned to me, Michael?"

I had never had a cogent answer to such complaints in the past, nor did I now. Several more silent minutes passed, but I knew she wasn't done.

"Michael, this morning I was doing some cleaning. I found something in the closet that I thought you should see." She placed a small bundle upon my lap. It was wrapped in a swatch of faded red cloth and tied with string. "You told me that Otto brought it to you at the hospital at Cold Harbor, and you carried it with you all during your convalescence at Annapolis, and you had it with you when you came home."

"I know." I tried to put the bundle aside.

"No, Michael, open it. It was important enough for you to keep, but it's been in the back of our closet ever since. Open it now, Michael." From her apron she produced a knife and deftly cut away the string.

I slowly peeled aside the layer of cloth, knowing what I would find and wishing not to see those things again. "My personal things, a journal, pen and ink, a letter to you I never posted."

"Let me see it." There was no denying her outstretched hand.

She read intently for a few minutes, in silence except for an occasional sniffle.

"You wrote this the day before you were wounded?"

I nodded slowly, once again staring into the firelight before me.

" 'Perhaps tomorrow it will all end,' you wrote. Did you sense that it would?"

"No, dear, my only hope was that the war would end quickly."

"And is this the way you feel now? 'Perhaps tomorrow it will all end?' Are you just sitting here waiting to die?"

Her questions stung me. "I don't think so." I fought to find more words but could not.

"And you closed with, 'Until the end I remain ever faithfully

340

your affectionate and devoted husband.' I think you still are this man, Michael, but I don't know if you do."

Once again I could not answer.

"And this journal. I read them all except this one. You write so well, yet you've written nothing since the war."

Jessie Anne reached for the last item. "And what's this?" I said nothing as she picked it up to look at it more closely. "Michael, this is not the Bible your father gave you."

I shook my head slowly.

"What's this dark stain?"

"Blood."

"Yours?" Her voice was a muted whisper.

I shook my head again.

She unfastened the clasp and opened the Bible. "What a darling portrait—a lovely family." She turned to the front plate. "Wyatt? It belongs to a man named Wyatt?"

"Belonged," I said. "He's dead."

"How did you come to have it, Michael?"

It was a story I had no wish to tell, for I knew that in so doing, I would reveal to my beloved exactly what sort of man she had married; yet tell it I did. In as measured and even a voice as I could muster, I told Jessie Anne every detail of my warring at Gettysburg, of every man I had killed there, and of my encounter with Mr. Augustus Wyatt of the 26th North Carolina. When I recounted how I had rejoiced when my bullet struck him, how I had wished only to finish him off with a thrust of my bayonet, and how I had knelt beside the man reading Scripture as he died, she sat with head bowed low to her lap, her tears staining her white apron. I went on to tell her of my killings in the Wilderness, and when I told her how my final victim died in agony upon the breastworks, she gasped and trembled beside me.

Jessie Anne remained silent and unmoving for some time. I

could tell she was deep in thought or prayer; I knew not which. Finally, she lifted her head and turned toward me. "No man should ever have to endure what you have, my dear." She took a white, lacy kerchief from the pocket of her apron to dry her eyes. "I think you should take it to her."

"What?" Perhaps I had not heard correctly.

"You should take it to her—the Bible. It was his. She gave it to him. It's their family in the portrait. If it was me, I would want it back, no matter how many years later. You must take it to her."

"We could send it by post."

"No, I think not. I think this is something *you* must do."

"I can't—"

"You must and you will."

"How could I ever . . . ?"

"Travel? To North Carolina?" Jessie Anne had set a straight course. There would be no turning to the right or to the left. "I think the stationmaster will help with the arrangements. We'll go to see Mr. Thomas first thing Monday morning."

⋘⊱⋙

Gordon Thomas turned from the large map on the wall. "The railroad will get you close," he said, puffing his pipe slowly. "You already know about half of the route, Michael. It'll be the Orange and Alexandria southwest to Gordonsville, then the Virginia Central into Lynchburg. The East Tennessee and Virginia line will take you through Roanoke and on down the west side of the Blue Ridge to Wytheville. Jefferson should be within two day's ride."

"I can't ride a horse, Gordon."

"I'll see what can be arranged." Gordon thought for several moments. He took a deep draught from his pipe, slowly letting the smoke escape as he traced his finger lightly over the map. "I'll need to send several telegrams to learn the precise nature of the rails and the schedules. Do you want me to inquire after lodging, Michael?"

"Yes, please, Mr. Thomas," Jessie Anne said before I could reply. "It will take several days to reach his destination, so please ensure the reputation of each establishment. Michael will be traveling through Rebel country, and his safety must be our chief concern."

"It will be, Mrs. Palmer."

"And no travel on the Sabbath, of course." Jessie Anne stood and went to look at the map more closely. "It's that last part over the mountains into North Carolina that worries me most. You said there's no railroad. Is there a coach route?"

"I'll need to inquire about that," Gordon said.

"Well, Michael can't make that journey alone," Jessie Anne said. "So if there are no coaches, he'll need someone trustworthy to take him, someone who won't take offense at going about with a Yankee soldier."

"I see you've given this some thought, Mrs. Palmer. It may take several weeks to make all these arrangements." Gordon turned to me. "When would you like to begin this journey?"

"May should be the best time," I said. "May was always the time for starting the spring campaign, so I think it fitting, and the roads should be firm."

"That should give us ample time. Do you mind if I ask you why you're taking such a long trip, Michael?"

"A private matter, Gordon." I glanced at Jessie Anne. "Something left over from the war that it seems I must do—someone I need to speak with, if I can."

"All right. I won't divulge your destination to anyone. Now, about the telegraphs, there will be costs."

"Here's twenty dollars." I retrieved a gold piece from my pocket and placed it in his hand. "I expect to pay all of the wire charges in both directions, so if you need more, please tell me. I will also pay you for your time."

"No, you won't," Gordon said. "You paid enough during the war, and besides, I am already paid by the railroad. Will your family be all right without you?"

"We'll manage well enough for two or three weeks," Jessie Anne said with a steady look at Gordon, "and Otto is more than able to manage the store."

"That's something about Otto and Dot getting married."

"Yes, it is," said Jessie Anne. "Perhaps something truly good did come from the war. I think John would have very much liked Otto as his son-in-law."

CHAPTER 34

Unto the Mountains

For I reckon that the sufferings of this present time
are not worthy to be compared with the glory
which shall be revealed in us.
ROMANS 8:18

ATURDAY, THE 15ᵀᴴ OF MAY, FOUND ME SITTING IN A ROCKER, smoking my pipe, on the veranda of the Wytheville Hotel, a narrow two-story brick structure directly across the street from the Wytheville railroad station. The smoke was particularly sweet and satisfying—I had procured some of Virginia's finest tobacco at the depot in Lynchburg. "Withful," the brutish stationmaster had sneered, "it's pronounced *Withful.*"

While not warm and welcoming, Mr. Waverly, the owner of the hotel, was at least cordial and efficient. A handwritten message awaited my arrival the previous evening. "Mr. Palmer," the message read, "Will meet you at hotel 10:00 a.m. Saturday. S. Jordan." I thanked the Lord for Gordon Thomas's diligence.

Early morning rains had ceased, but lowering clouds remained, obscuring all but the lowest slopes of the mountains to the south and east. At precisely ten o'clock, a young man walked out of the station and crossed the street.

"Mr. Palmer?" The man huffed and puffed as if trying to

catch his breath; droplets of sweat fell from his matted light brown hair.

"Yes, I'm Michael Palmer." I held out my hand.

"Sam Jordan." The man's huge sweaty hand crushed my smaller one. Samuel Jordan was a teamster by trade and he looked the part. About thirty years old, he stood about five feet six inches tall and was sturdily built, much like Jim Adams had been. Years of loading and unloading cargo and driving teams had developed the bulk of the man's chest, shoulders, and arms. He wore a simple gray cotton shirt, and his patched brown trousers were held up with a pair of blue suspenders. His black slouch hat had a white sweat stain all around the headband. At first,

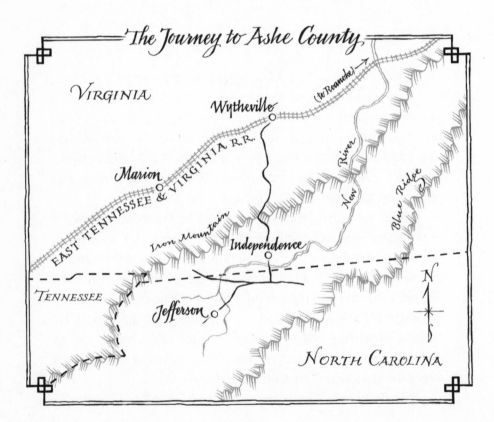

The Journey to Ashe County

he seemed rather gruff, but his deep blue eyes were warm and sincere.

"I've been loading the wagon for Monday morning because tomorrow's the Sabbath. I hear you want to go to Ashe County, Mr. Palmer."

"Yes, I do. How long will it take?"

"It'll take two days if the weather holds. Jefferson's the county seat. Is that where you want to go?"

"That will do for a start, but I'm searching for someone in particular, a Mrs. Wyatt."

"It's a personal thing then?" Sam asked, his eyebrows arched.

"Yes. Something left over from the war."

Sam's disposition darkened. "You're not looking to kill anybody, are you? I'll have no part in that."

"Nothing like that. You might say it's like the last page of a book that needs to be written."

"Fair enough. I won't pry further. We leave at dawn on Monday, spend the night in Independence just north of the state line, should be in Jefferson dinnertime on Tuesday. I start back at dawn on Thursday. Will one day be enough time for your business?"

"I hope so."

"You're a long way from home, Mr. Palmer, and there's not a lot of call to take someone into Ashe County. Most people in these parts are good, honest folk, but there's others who would just as soon slit your throat—as much for being a Yankee as for the dollars in your pocket or the shirt off your back." I shifted a bit uneasily in the rocker. "But you've nothing to fear from me. I'll be glad of the company."

"Speaking of dollars, I understand your fee is to be twenty dollars, half at the start, half when we return?"

"Yes, ten each way," Sam said, accepting the payment with

a nod and a smile. "By the way, Mr. Palmer, are you a church-going man?"

"I am."

"My family attends the Wytheville Presbyterian Church. It's just down to Church Street, then left a short way, just a five-minute walk. Service is at eleven. Afterward, you'll take dinner at our home."

⋘⋙

I was at the depot at dawn on Monday, tired and stiff in spite of two days rest, but ready for the journey nonetheless. Sam already had the team of four horses hitched to the large wagon. The cargo was covered with a large piece of canvas tied down securely with rope. As Sam helped me onto the wide driver's seat, I noticed a new repeating rifle and a scattergun under the seat. He was also wearing a holstered pistol on either hip.

"Expecting trouble?" I asked. Sam flicked the whip softly, hardly touching the flank of the lead horse, and the heavy wagon rumbled out of the depot.

" 'It happens to us,' " Sam said, " 'as it happeneth to wayfaring men; sometimes our way is clean, sometimes foul; sometimes up hill, sometimes down hill; we are seldom at a certainty: the wind is not always at our backs, nor is every one a friend that we meet with in the way.' "

"That's an interesting way to put it," I said.

"It's not Jordan. It's Bunyan, from *The Pilgrim's Progress, Part the Second*. I always pray for protection, but I also prepare for whatever may happen so I can get safely home at week's end."

That day the way was clean but mostly uphill as we traveled the thirty miles to Independence. Tuesday's route was easier, with fewer long climbs, but it would be longer—almost forty miles.

"Do you make this trip very week?" I asked Sam Tuesday morning.

"Not every week," he said. "I drive my team wherever there's a load to be had, but it's this run to Ashe County that puts food on my table.

"Is someone meeting you at Jefferson?" he asked a few minutes later. We were crossing the New River on a wooden plank bridge that groaned under the weight of the loaded wagon, and while Sam seemed perfectly at ease, my white-knuckled hands gripped the wagon seat, thinking the next moment would see us plunging into the swiftly moving water below. Once safely across, I reached into the breast pocket of my coat and took out the priceless sheet of paper that Gordon Thomas had given me.

"I'm to meet a man by the name of J. Crane at the Jeffersonian Hotel."

"That's Jubal Crane, Old Jube, most of the local folk call him, a bit of an odd fellow and a Unionist, I think. Lots of mountain folk were against secession, but when secession passed, there was no shortage of volunteers. Many heroes came from this area."

"I met one of them."

Sam looked at me sideways. "The last page of that book again?"

"Yes."

We arrived in front of the Jeffersonian about six o'clock that evening. Sam helped me descend safely from the high seat of the wagon and handed me my travel bag. "Until Thursday at dawn," he said, and with a strong handshake he was off to unload his cargo.

<figure>❦</figure>

"Jubal Crane? Sure, everybody knows Old Jube," said the proprietor. "Has a room over at the widow Barclay's boarding house.

I'll send a boy over to fetch him while you're taking dinner." I thanked the man, picked up my bag, and slowly ascended the stairs to the second floor. I unpacked my travel case, washed the road grime from my face, and went downstairs to the dining room.

The fare at the Jeffersonian was not elaborate but it was tasty, a hearty beef-and-turnip stew with bread and butter. Afterward I sat sipping a cup of hot black coffee when a shrunken but energetic old man shuffled into the dining room.

"You Palmer?" he asked in a high, raspy voice as he approached my table.

"Yes, I am. Are you Mr. Crane?" My extended hand went unnoticed.

"Yep. None other. Mind if I ...?"

"Please sit down. Would you like a cup of coffee?"

"Don't mind if I do, sure enough." Jubal Crane was completely bald except for several stringy shoulder-length silver strands that sprang out from over his ears and from the back of his head. White, bushy eyebrows framed the tops of his small spectacles, behind which gleamed a pair of small brown eyes. A full white moustache covered his upper lip and partially hid his mouth. He had on a well-worn white shirt, a faded green tweed jacket patched in several places, and he held a large straw hat in his bony left hand, a long striated pheasant feather stuck gaily into the hatband.

"I was given your name as a man who knows just about everyone in Ashe County."

"Pretty near, but there's been some new folks comin' in since the war that I ain't never met. Foreigners, I call 'em. You that sort?"

"No, Mr. Crane. I was hoping you might be able to help me find Mrs. Constance Wyatt. Do you know the Wyatt family?

I have a portrait." I passed over the old, worn likeness of the woman and the three children. The old man sat sipping his coffee for several minutes. His small eyes narrowed to thin slits as they darted between the faces in the portrait and my face.

"What do you want with her?" he asked.

"To return the portrait, and also her husband's Bible."

The old man shifted uncomfortably in his chair several times as if weighing a difficult decision. When he spoke, his words were soft and somber. "He was my grandnephew. My daughter's the one that done the paintin'. Last time I saw Wyatt was about eight years ago when the Jeff Davis Mountaineers went off to join up with the Twenty-sixth. Wyatt was killed up north. How come you have his paintin' and his Bible?"

"He was shot in front of my regiment at Gettysburg. I was with him when he died."

"Then I'm guessin' you'd like to talk to Constance?"

"If possible."

"She got married in sixty-five to Elmer Ennis. They have a sheep farm about six miles west of here, out by Claybank Creek. Take about two hours to get there. I suppose I should go with you—haven't seen that family for some months, before the winter, I guess. I can't say yea or nay if she'll see you, but I expect you've nothin' else to do."

"Thank you, Mr. Crane. But there may be one small difficulty."

"What's that?"

I rapped the tip of my cane on my false leg. "I lost it at Cold Harbor and can't mount a horse. Do you have a small carriage? I'll hire it for the day."

"I use Mrs. Barclay's runabout whenever I need it, and there's no need for money to change hands, long as we're goin' to see family. I'll be by in the mornin', Mr. Palmer, about eight."

⊰⊱

The Ennis place lay atop a knoll just across the lane from Claybank Creek. Split-rail fences lined the lane, just like those I had used as firewood during the war. Chickens scurried about as we drew up to the house; laundry flapped in the breeze from a rope stretched between two trees; a large well-tilled vegetable patch appeared to have already been planted.

"Wait here," Jubal said, "I'll ask if she'll see you."

The door of the house opened and a woman with a straw broom in hand stepped out onto the porch before Jubal had mounted the first of its three steps. On sight, I knew her to be the woman in the painting, save that she appeared much older now. The two hugged and the woman kissed Jubal lightly on the cheek.

"Uncle Jubal, how nice to see you," I heard her say. "It's been so long. What brung you way out here?"

The two spoke privately for a minute or two, occasionally throwing glances in my direction. Then Jubal turned and headed back to the carriage.

"She'll see you, Mr. Palmer. Let's get you down so you can meet Constance. Then I'll just go on up the road a piece to see Elmer. He's workin' in the north pasture."

Constance Ennis could not have been over thirty-five years of age, but she appeared years older than me. Her long, light-brown hair was streaked with gray, leathery creases in the skin of her face and neck told of years of hard mountain farming and childrearing. When I offered my hand in greeting, her grip was the strongest I had ever known from a woman; her hand was thickly calloused and cracked.

"Uncle Jube says you're someone I should talk to—a Yankee down from the north with news of Wyatt. Come into the kitchen and set a spell." She offered me a simple wooden chair at the kitchen table. A large pot of something that smelled heavenly simmered atop a soot-covered wood stove in the middle of the kitchen. "Becca and the boys are down to the school. Elmer's drawin' water off the creek for the sheep, and little Stevie's asleep in his crib. Like some tea? Always keep a pot on the stove when I'm cookin'."

"Yes, ma'am, thank you."

Constance filled two heavy pottery mugs and set them on the table. "Tell me, Mr. Palmer," she said as she sat down, "how is it that a Yankee comes a-knockin' at my door this fine day?"

"Just call me Michael, please."

"I never use a man's Christian name till I know what sort he is. Where you from?"

"From Connecticut, Mrs. Ennis."

"Where's that?"

"Up north between New York and Boston."

"Sounds like a long way, and a hard go of it to get here." She paused for a moment, deep in thought. "I figure the Lord brung you."

"You may be right, Mrs. Ennis, because I've had much help along the way."

"So why'd He bring you?"

"Mrs. Ennis, I met Augustus Wyatt during the war. I believe he was your husband."

"Yes, but he was known as Wyatt, just Wyatt—never liked Augustus." A faint smile passed across her lips. "Said it ain't Christian, but he never took another name for fear of shamin' the memory of his dear mother. Got a letter from his captain, I did." Her gaze fell to her hands embracing the hot mug in front of her. "It said Wyatt was killed up north at Gettysburg, but they never found him. You know about that?"

"Yes, Mrs. Ennis, I do." She lifted her eyes to mine expectantly. I reached into my breast pocket and took out the Bible that had been in my keeping for almost six years. She gasped and snatched the Bible from my hands. Then she rose quickly from

353

the table and went over to the stove, where she stood, quiet and still, with her back to me and the Bible pressed to her lips.

A few minutes later, Constance took a kerchief from the pocket of her apron and dabbed her eyes several times. " 'Although the fig tree shall not blossom, neither shall fruit be in the vines; the labour of the olive shall fail, and the fields shall yield no meat; the flock shall be cut off from the fold, and there shall be no herd in the stalls: yet I will rejoice in the Lord, I will joy in the God of my salvation.' "

"Mrs. Ennis?"

Constance turned to face me. "Wyatt said them words whenever there was trouble, from Habakkuk, I think." She sat down at the table again. "Thank you, Mr. Palmer," she whispered. "I gave him that Bible last time I saw him, the day he left. Thank you."

"And the portrait is inside," I said.

Tears welled afresh as Constance gazed at the image that had become so familiar to me. She clasped it to her breast and seemed transported to another place.

"But how ...?" I knew the question she couldn't finish.

"Wyatt was shot before our line. He was still alive when I came upon him. He asked me to read a psalm to him as he died. My own Bible was lost so I kept his for the rest of the war, and then I was wounded and sent home. I made some inquiries and learned that Wyatt must have lived here in Ashe County."

"I'm such a silly woman for grievin' so much over a man long dead." She held the kerchief to her eyes once again.

"No, ma'am, I still grieve over lost friends."

"But I'm so, so happy you brung it to me. But to come all this way? With a bad leg? Mayhap you should've posted it."

"Yes, but my wife insisted that I come."

Constance drank some tea. Then she closed her eyes, apparently pondering what had transpired since I had come to her door. When her eyes reopened she looked at me directly. "But the post would have brung it, if that's the only reason you come such a far way."

"Mrs. Ennis, I've never forgotten your husband, and I thought I should tell you the circumstances of his death in person."

"Please do, Michael. I'm done with my cry." She had used my Christian name.

I paused for a moment or two to make sure of my words. Then, to this woman of the backwoods I recounted every detail of how I had come to be at Wyatt's side at the moment of his death. I spoke of the debacle at Chancellorsville and of being sent back to the front when I was so close to home. I told her of the long, torturous march northward to Pennsylvania and of our activities at the stone wall before Pickett's tragic, final charge. I withheld nothing of how I had with fierce hatred gunned down perhaps a dozen men, taking special delight as each bullet struck home, and of how I had rushed forward to finish off several of the defeated Confederates as the last wave of their assault broke under our fire. And I told Constance how my hand had been suddenly stayed when I came to Wyatt.

"He held out this Bible with his own blood on it and asked me to read. He asked me to turn him so he could see the mountains as I read. I read the Twenty-fifth Psalm. He died as I read to him, still looking at the mountains."

"That's beautiful." Her voice was the barest whisper.

"Beautiful, Mrs. Ennis?" I was not sure I had heard correctly.

"Yes. Wyatt wouldn't have had it any other way—Holy Scripture in his ears and lookin' up to heaven." She looked across the table at me. "Are you the one?"

"The one, ma'am?"

"Was it you that killed him?" It was a question that I had prepared for weeks to answer.

"Yes, Mrs. Ennis, I killed him. I'm so very sorry, and I beg your forgiveness."

"That's what brung you to my door?"

"Yes, ma'am."

"Now I see why you're so gray."

"Gray, ma'am?"

"Oh, yes, gray, you're very gray. When first I saw you stumblin' up to my door, your head was down, lookin' close at every step I guess, and I thought, *Here comes a gray man.* Not real dark, storm-cloudy gray, mind you, just sort of low and dreary gray, like when the mists come down the valley here."

"I don't understand, Mrs. Ennis."

"Just a silly game I play. Some folk make me think of colors. Uncle Jube—he's always so light and cheery, so he's yellow. Not scaredy-cat yellow—sunshiny yellow. Now Wyatt was green— had a gift for growin' things, he did, and he always said he was a-growin' to be like Jesus. And Elmer's blue, true blue's what they call it, 'cause there be nothin' false in that man."

"But gray, ma'am?"

"You asked me to forgive you. Your bullet put my Wyatt in the ground, sure enough, but his soul went home to glory. Wyatt never held this world close. He was always lookin' forward to glory, like no man I ever did know. Sure my heart was broke, but the Lord Jesus healed it. Elmer's a good Christian man too, and we been blessed with little Stevie. God gave Wyatt what he wanted, and now I count God's blessin's every day. Tell me what I need to forgive you for."

I had no answer for this woman of the backwoods. I had come to her door expecting all of the anger, hostility, and bitterness that could possess a person after a great loss. Instead, I found in this woman a vibrant love for the Lord that so affected every part of her being that she, in spite of her coarse appearance, was the very expression of that most Godly of attributes—grace.

"How old are you, Michael?"

"Forty years old, ma'am."

"You a Godly man?"

"Yes, ma'am."

"Have you been saved by His grace?"

"I've always believed so, ma'am."

"Have your sins been washed away by the blood of the Lamb?"

"I believe so."

"You say you hated Wyatt and the others?"

"Yes, ma'am, I did. But not anymore."

"And you killed men without regret?"

"Yes, ma'am."

"Mayhap God sent you off to war just to show you somethin' about you and somethin' about Him. Before the war, you didn't know the hate and the killin' was in you, did you?"

"No, Mrs. Ennis. I did not."

"Mayhap God was just gettin' it out of you."

"But I think God's turned His back on me because of it," I said. "It's been a long, long time—"

"Ain't God that done the turnin'. You done it. Sounds like you're sayin', 'Oh, woe is me, 'cause I'm a sinner.' But you also said your sin been washed away. Well, then, your guilt's been washed away too. Best be rid of it, or you'll carry it around till the day you die and be no good to anybody. So where's the glory, Michael Palmer?"

"The glory, ma'am?"

"If you been saved, you best *look* like you been saved. When the Lord Jesus takes sin away, He don't leave us empty. He puts His glory in—the Holy Ghost, that's what it is. So where's that glory, Mr. Palmer?"

I sat in silence and stared at the mug before me.

"Mayhap that awful war made you stop seein' the Lord

357

doin' what He does," Constance said. "Mayhap you just quit listenin' to the Holy Ghost. I think you best stop hangin' your head and look up. Open your eyes and let His light in so you can see what He's tryin' to show you and get out of His way so he can do His work on you. And, Michael, He's given you a life to live, so you best get busy and live it, and mayhap you won't be gray anymore."

Constance rose and went to the stove. She busied herself with the stewpot while I sat quietly, sipping the now-cold tea.

Cane in hand, I pushed back from the table and stood. "Mrs. Ennis, I would like to thank you—"

"No thanks needed," she said, turning toward me once again. She went to the door and opened it. "Now go outside and set for a spell, Michael, while I set the table. You and Uncle Jube be stayin' for some lamb burgoo before headin' back to town. Maybe go down by the creek." She pointed a thin cracked finger toward the pastureland across the lane. "That's where I always do my reckonin'. I'll ring the bell when the men come back."

I hobbled down the three steps and walked across the dusty earthen yard toward the lane as clucking chickens chased every faltering step. At the lane I paused, studying its deeply rutted contours and protruding stones for the path across least dangerous, least likely to cause me to trip and fall. Indeed, I almost turned back, thinking the risk too great, but something akin to a gentle hand in the small of my back nudged me forward, compelling me to cross over. I paid careful heed to each step.

I lifted my gaze and was greeted with a remarkable sight. Brilliant sunshine bathed a strip of fertile pasture perhaps fifty yards wide that sloped gently downward toward the creek just out of sight below its tree-lined bank. Mingled grasses and clovers composed a patchwork of every imaginable shade of green, dotted all over with multihued blooms of the season's wildflowers—clover florets of white and violet, daisies of yellow and white, black-eyed Susans, red and white poppies, phlox of brilliant pink around which flitted dozens of colorful butterflies, and hundreds of small flowers with deep blue petals and yellow centers I had never seen before.

The pristine nature of the land before me attested that no flock had yet grazed upon this land this springtime. I took a few steps into the pasture; the ground was fairly smooth, my footing secure. A few more steps caused a startled bird to take wing several yards ahead, a meadowlark by its bold yellow and black markings. Swallows darted busily back and forth, sometimes soaring high above, sometimes diving low and fast until just inches from the earth.

Perhaps above or below the Ennis farm Claybank Creek was a typical mountain stream, raging downward from the heights, tumbling over rocks and fallen timber in its haste to merge with other waters and rush onward to the New River, but on that day, as I came upon the bank of that stream at the edge of that verdant pasture, its flow was placid and unhurried, as if the water itself had come upon the glories of that land and had quieted itself so as not to disturb the tranquility. A pair of wood ducks paddled slowly against the almost-still water, the gentle current evidenced by only the faintest of meandering, shimmering ripples.

I found a sunny place near the creek and eased myself down to sit amid the tall grasses and wildflowers, enveloped in that glorious festival of light and color and sound. A gentle breeze stirred the leaves of the trees along the creek. I turned my face upward toward the sun and closed my eyes against its beaming brilliance. Trilling notes of birdsongs filled my ears, from cardinal and chickadee, warbler and wren. Every leisurely breath brought with it the sweet aroma of honeysuckle in full bloom. I could not help but lift my eyes and thoughts heavenward.

How far have I gone from You? How often have I cut myself off from

You? Yet You did not forsake me. I thank You for the simple words of Mrs. Ennis, words filled with Your grace and truth. I know You brought me here for this. Now give me the grace I need every day to put the evils I have seen and done away, so that others may see Christ living in me and give You all the glory because of it.

I took my pipe from the right pocket of my jacket and the tobacco pouch from the left. Child, mother, father, I thought as I pressed the shreds into the bowl. I felt a smile crease my face as I thought again of John, and the smile remained as I regarded the toes of my shoes before me, the right one now two sizes larger than the left. For a time I just sat and smoked with the glories of the created realm all around me. Then I lay back among the pasture grasses and clasped my hands behind my head.

Be still, and know that I am God, the psalmist wrote, and indeed, my storm-tossed heart was stilled, as surely as the Lord Jesus calmed the waters of Galilee. No longer did shades of death darken my sight. Terrible images of killing and dying, of flame and destruction, passed from my mind and I beheld, if even through a broken mirror, a glimpse of the glory to come, glory for all of eternity to be sure, but also glory for the here and now, as God's transforming power did its work upon this miserable wretch. My soul was renewed within me, and for the first time in all my days, I possessed the most precious jewel any man can have — blessed, complete, and unclouded contentment.

I slept then, but only for a short while, I think, as the sun was still near its zenith when the loud clanging of a large cow-bell summoned me to return to the austere mountain cabin that had once been Wyatt's earthly home, to sit at his table with his widow's husband and old Uncle Jube, and to partake of a hearty midday meal of lamb burgoo prepared by that leather-skinned saint of the backwoods, his widow Constance. I smiled at the marvelous harmony of it all.

I tottered a little on the irregular ground as I rose. Turning away from the stream, I set my gaze upon the upward slope toward the cabin and heard Jessie Anne's stinging words once again— *Why have you not returned to me, Michael?*

I took one tenuous, uneven step, then another, and another up through the verdant pasture. *It has been a long time, my dearest, but my war is done. I am finally coming home. May it be so, Lord, may it be so.*

❖

May 14, 1902
Mr. Henry Mills Alden
Harper Brothers Publishing Company
331 Pearl Street
New York, New York

Dear Sir,

The manuscript before you is entirely the work of my father, Michael Gabriel Palmer. Shortly before his death almost one year past, when he knew his time was near, he entrusted the work to my care. "Do with it what you will, dear," he said. "Perhaps others will learn of God's everlasting faithfulness to me, for I certainly was not faithful to Him." Then, in spite of obvious physical pain, he raised himself to lean against the headboard, and with his hazel eyes lively and gleaming, he said, "And perhaps a printer will find some redeeming quality in it and you may reap a small profit."

Throughout the last three decades of my father's life, his business flourished and he became one of the wealthiest men in town, yet to the hundreds who attended his memorial and filled the church to overflowing, his standing in the community was not what drew them. First and foremost he was known as a man of sincerity, humility, generosity, and integrity, a servant to his church, his country, and his fellow man, always ready to forgive any slight, for as he often said, "I have been forgiven much and am a debtor to Divine mercy." He was buried beside his beloved Jessie Anne in Hillside Cemetery. We wept tears of sadness then but now view eternity all the more fondly because both Mama and Papa are there.

My father's original handwritten manuscript was passed from family to family and read over and over by his children and grandchildren. Many pages became frayed and torn. At my own expense I contracted a local clerk to typewrite four copies of the original, one for each of my two brothers, one for myself, and the fourth which you see before you. As you may surmise from this brief letter, my motive in forwarding my father's story to you is not to reap financial reward, but to make it available throughout the length and breadth of this great land, that others may learn and profit from it, as we, his grateful children, have.

The favor of a response is requested. Correspondence may be addressed to: Palmer & Wehlmann Co., Naugatuck, Conn. If in the negative, please return the manuscript at your convenience.

With warmest wishes and regards,

Sarah Anne (Palmer) Allerton

Share Your Thoughts

With the Author: Your comments will be forwarded to
the author when you send them to *zauthor@zondervan.com*.

With Zondervan: Submit your review of this book
by writing to *zreview@zondervan.com*.

Free Online Resources at

www.zondervan.com

Zondervan AuthorTracker: Be notified whenever your favorite
authors publish new books, go on tour, or post an update
about what's happening in their lives at www.zondervan.com/
authortracker.

Daily Bible Verses and Devotions: Enrich your life with daily
Bible verses or devotions that help you start every morning
focused on God. Visit www.zondervan.com/newsletters.

Free Email Publications: Sign up for newsletters on Christian
living, academic resources, church ministry, fiction, children's
resources, and more. Visit www.zondervan.com/newsletters.

Zondervan Bible Search: Find and compare Bible passages in
a variety of translations at www.zondervanbiblesearch.com.

Other Benefits: Register yourself to receive online benefits
like coupons and special offers, or to participate in research.